Fate & Fried Chicken
A Sapphic Romantic Comedy
Cheryl Terra

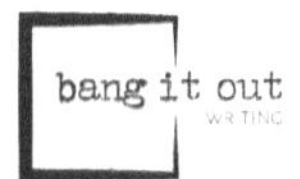

Bang It Out Writing

Author's Note

PLEASE NOTE THAT THIS book is written in Canadian English, which differs from both UK and US English; we use rules and spellings from both.

Full content/trigger warnings can be found on my website at cherylterra.com/trigger-warnings, however some of the main things I'd like to highlight include mild transphobia (on page, but immediately addressed, and out of ignorance versus maliciousness), parental death (off page, past event, but discussed), medically-assisted death, adoption/prejudices against adopted children, ADHD/neurodiversity representation, and a whole lot of chaos.

Chapter One

Thirteen Point Whiz

Isla

ONE OF THE MANY things my mother never said was this:

"Isla, people who make plans do not end up trying to decide between renting a shabby second-floor apartment and living on the streets of the most populous northern city while watching a man piss off his third-floor balcony of the aforementioned apartment building."

That was because my mother never willingly made a plan in her life, so most of the things she said were like this:

"Isla, people who make plans don't find their soul mates on a gravel back road in the mountains while running from the cops."

Or "Isla, people who make plans never get a first-hand look at the intricacies of the subway system in a city they mistakenly ended up in because they don't speak the language and ended up on a train going the wrong direction."

Or "Isla, people who make plans end up sitting in their miserable cubicle at their miserable job at a miserable call center being yelled at by miserable people in between bouts of wondering what to do about the miserable thing they found out their miserable boyfriend has been miserably thinking for the last two miserable fucking years."

Well, she may not have said that last one specifically. But it was *like* something she'd say.

The point is, my mother didn't make plans. And if you asked her or anyone else, they would have said that I, Isla Monroe, was a *planner*.

Yet between the two of us, I was the one sitting there, watching with a morbidly dejected sense of fascination as urine splashed into a wilted flower bed ten feet from the hood of my car.

My mother would have been so proud.

She would have called it an adventure. She'd tell and retell the tale over glasses of wine and cups of coffee and campfires in the woods. Each time, it would get both more and less embellished, and the people listening would laugh hard enough to cry or spill their drinks or pee themselves.

Then, with liquids everywhere, Mom would purse her lips into a cheeky smirk and say, "See? This is why I never bother with a plan."

And my father—

Well, he wouldn't be there. But if he was, he'd be shaking his head, trying not to laugh as he told me I should've known better than to quit my job, dump my boyfriend, and head west with nothing but a couple of suitcases and half a tank of gas until I found myself drawn somewhere, which is how I'd ended up in Aurora Flats, Alberta.

I mean, it sounded perfect. Aurora Flats? The name that inspired romance. Whimsy. Quaintness. A closeness with nature and a place with endless night skies full of colours and stars to remind you that even though we're specks of dust in a vast nothingness, the universe is still *there*, taking care of us.

It was supposed to be the place where I'd find my grand romantic adventure.

I left thinking I'd drive wherever the winds and the roads took me. When I arrived at wherever my heart was leading me, I'd simply know I was there. Passing by the sign welcoming me to the city—because *obviously* it would be a city—I would smile, turn the radio up, and bring myself to the trendiest part of downtown. There, I'd spot an eclectic-looking apartment building full of character and style. I'd pull my car over and get out, hands on my hips as I looked up at the building.

"I guess this'll do," I would say, and the ratty old canvas backpack I had in the passenger seat would magically transform into a wicked cute weekend bag I'd sling over my shoulder. And the building, of course, would have a trendy studio apartment available for rent right away. An apartment manager would trip over himself to help me unpack the rest of my belongings from the car as a peppy, upbeat soundtrack played while I strutted up to my new home.

That was what I'd expected when my heart drew me to Aurora Flats. But this place?

Not cute.

Not quaint.

Not romantic.

It wasn't a city at all, but a town around an hour from Edmonton. But I'd imagined getting there would be a calming drive on a secondary highway lined with trees in the throes of autumn bliss Instead, I'd spent most of the drive on a highway surrounded by greyish-brown farmer's fields abandoned for the season. Once I'd turned off the highway, I crossed a set of train tracks before driving through an industrial area full of blocky buildings with names like Jenkins Machinery and Bola-Flo Manufacturing.

And then there was the reason I was here in the first place: this building, one of the only apartment buildings in Aurora Flats, and one of the few places in the whole area both in my budget and owned by a landlord who would look past my lack of current employment and fixed address.

It had white siding, once upon a time. Now it was grey, like everything else. Back home, we wouldn't have even called this an apartment building. I mean, it only had three floors. My apartment in Burnaby had eighteen floors and I had lived on the sixteenth. It wasn't cheap—nothing in the Vancouver area was—but with two of us, it was affordable.

And it was cozy.

It was safe.

It was part of the plan.

Not, like, a five-year plan or anything. I didn't have a checklist of accomplishments to hit before I turned twenty-five next year or something.

But just... the plan.

The life plan.

The plan I'd had for as long as I could remember. Long, long before everything changed. Finish high school, go to university and get a finance degree like Dad had. Work in business, maybe as a financial analyst and eventually a finance manager like he was. Or maybe something else. That part of the plan had never been super specific, mainly because there was never any guarantee that the job market would be the same after graduation as when one started. But whatever it was, I was going to get the degree, find a career, and build a good life for myself.

Oh, and find my soulmate.

Obviously.

I'd never told Dad about that part of the plan. Mom was a huge believer in destiny and universal energies and magic rocks doused in essential oils, but Dad was a lot more... practical. And my mom said I'd always taken after my dad, though she never said it like it was a bad thing.

"I knew you'd be like your father," Mom would say. "You were so polite when you were in utero. Didn't move much while I was sleeping and your kicks were tiny little knocks, like you were a sweet little bluebird tapping on the walls to say hello. That's why he got to name you."

I was thankful for that, since he'd picked the name Isla. That was far better than what my mom picked for my younger sister, who she deemed was herself reincarnated.

"You can't be reincarnated if you aren't dead," Dad would remind her, but she'd shush him.

"This one is the embodiment of passion," she would say, groaning as my sister pummelled her insides with tiny feet. "I'm naming her for the goddess of love."

"Aphrodite?" my dad had asked skeptically.

"Oh, God no. I don't want her to be made fun of," she said, then named my sister Venus.

But Venus turned out to be as romantic as my dad's reasoning for picking my name, which was that he'd opened a book of baby names to a random page and picked the first name he'd never met someone with that only had four letters because he figured four letters were easier to spell and that would give me an edge when I started kindergarten.

Between me and my sister, I was the romantic one. I was the one who believed in soulmates. Who wanted nothing more than the improbable romanticism that proved the world was more than a coincidence.

I wanted a sign that was brighter than neon on a dark, snow-filled night.

A single spontaneous moment where the universe aligned for *me* and my soulmate before we were back to being specks of dust floating around in the sunbeam that was existence.

I'd left Burnaby because I was tired of my miserable, dead-end call center job. I was tired of settling for a boyfriend who settled for me. I was tired of my comfortable routine, of never fitting in but never standing out. Of being a square peg surrounded by other pegs and holes of every shape and colour and style *except* square.

More than anything, I was tired of that.

Of not being alone, but not belonging anymore.

I wanted something other than "Oh, we both swiped right or left or whatever direction it was to say 'Yes, I'd consider boning this person.'"

I wanted more.

I wanted someone to be proud of me again.

But something told me a dirty second-floor apartment beneath a man and his friends cackling as he whizzed over the side of his balcony wasn't where I'd find that.

So...

So maybe the spontaneity thing wasn't meant for me.

Maybe the grand romantic adventure wasn't designed for me.

Maybe the meet cute story of a lifetime wasn't destined for me.

So maybe they'd all been right.

It would only take me a day to get home. A long day—twelve or thirteen hours of driving, plus stops for gas and bathroom breaks—but I could be back in time to go to work tomorrow.

Except I'd quit.

But I was good at my job. I could say I'd made a mistake. They'd probably take me back. And so would Nick, if I asked nicely or maybe begged. He'd been upset when I broke things off and asked me to think about it first. I could pretend I'd changed my mind.

Even if he didn't forgive me, it didn't matter. Without a doubt, I already knew I had absolutely no plans whatsoever to stay here.

Fate, however, had a different plan.

My phone automatically switched to Do Not Disturb while I was driving, but I'd been sitting there long enough for it to decide I wasn't driving anymore. Which meant it vibrated to tell me about the messages I'd received, ending any chance for me to stop my little experiment in impulsiveness while still maintaining a hold on my old life.

Because after being gone for three whole *days*, someone finally noticed I'd left.

Venus

> *Nick just said you broke up? What's going on, Isla??*

> *What the fuck? YOU LEFT TOWN?????????????*

> *Guess I'm going to pick up the stuff you left at Nick's now…*

There was a new message from Nick, too:

Nick

funny how you said you were gonna stay with your mom and yet your sister just called and said neither of them know where you are

you didn't even give it a second thought, did you? ghost me after two years and won't even tell me why?

thought you were better than that, isla

"Ten points!"

A muffled shout stole my attention. The man who had been pissing off the balcony had put his dick away and was now watching as *another* man finished peeing into the flower bed.

"Just ten?!" shouted the pisser. "This is at *least* a thirteen-point whizz!"

"You aren't even close to the middle!"

"My piss-pressure is *way* higher than yours, you Chicken McFuck. Are you blind? You can see—"

My phone vibrated before I could even wonder what a Chicken McFuck was. Chin trembling, I looked at the screen to see a message from my mom, who had never quite figured out how to turn capslock on and off.

Mom

THAT'S MY GIRL. DAD WOULD BE SO PROUD. OK MAYBE NOT BECAUSE HE WAS A WET BLANKET BUT I'M PROUD OF YOU AND THAT MEANS HE WOULD BE TOO.

I looked up at the building, where the guys on the balcony were now arguing about what constituted a thirteen-point whiz.

"I guess this'll do," I whispered, then grabbed my backpack off the front seat, took a deep breath, and opened my car door.

Chapter Two

Chaos Gremlin

Ellie

"Alright, you crazy son of a bitch," I said. "We're doing it."

"*Yeah,* we are!" Tyler hooted, clapping his hands together.

"No, she isn't," Jayce said, clamping a hand on my shoulder.

I rolled my eyes, trying to shrug off their hand. "You're not my parental unit. You can't tell me what to do."

They tightened their fingers like they were expecting me to run for it. Which was fair, because I *was* going to try.

"I'm not telling you what to do," they said. "I'm telling you what's going to happen. You're not going with him."

"Aww, come on, dude," Tyler said. "Stop speaking for her and let her do what she wants."

"Not a dude," Jayce replied. "And this has nothing to do with me speaking for her. She hasn't realized it yet, but she *truly* doesn't want to go."

"Why not?" I asked, offended that they seemed to know something about my thoughts that I didn't.

Jayce set exasperated eyes on me. "Ellie."

"Jaycie."

"Don't call me that."

"Don't look at me like that."

Their lips twitched with the hint of a laugh. "You don't want to go, Ellie-Bean. For one, you don't have the money. For two, you despise flying. For three, your passport is expired."

"It is not expired!" I said.

"When did I take you to Disneyland?" they asked.

"Like, last year," I said.

"It was six years ago," they answered. "And have you renewed your passport since then?"

I twisted my mouth to the side. Their lips twitched again.

"So it's expired," they said. "And for four, he'll probably sell you for drugs in Amsterdam."

I rolled my eyes. "Why would he need to sell me for drugs? You can get weed all over Amsterdam."

They raised their eyebrows. "You think he'd sell you for *weed*?"

I thought for a moment, then conceded. "Good point. Sorry, Ty. Sounds like I'm out. Have fun in Europe."

"No worries, my gal," Tyler said. "But for the record, I definitely wouldn't have sold you for drugs."

"Sounds like something someone who'd sell her for drugs would say," Jayce said. "Now get out."

Tyler scoffed in offense. "What?! Why?"

Jayce's lips tightened into an annoyed line. "Because this all started when I was so kindly interrupted by Ellie trying to 'help' me kick you out of my bar for doing a line of coke in my bathroom."

"Oh," Tyler said. "Right. That's fair. I'm never gonna be allowed back in here, am I?"

"It's looking less and less likely," Jayce said.

Tyler sighed. "Damn. Okay. Well, thanks, bud."

"You gonna let him back in next weekend?" I asked Jayce as Tyler started towards the exit, pausing to shout at his friends that he was heading home because he got caught doing drugs in the bathroom again.

"Of course." They sighed. "Tyler may have approximately twelve brain cells left and while eight of them are dedicated to making sure he doesn't forget how to breathe, he means well. I can't exactly afford to lose regulars."

"It'll be fine," I said, picking up my camera. "We'll take a few more of these shots and this time next week, you'll be rolling in the dough. Then we can take pictures of *that* and tell everyone we're selling pizza made from dough personally rolled in by Jayce Wheeler, Aurora Flats' hottest bar manager."

Jayce's lips tightened into what looked like an unimpressed line, but I knew them well enough to know it was their version of a smile. "You seem to have a lot of faith in both my attractiveness and your abilities as a photographer."

I rolled my eyes. "Fold your arms and turn your head towards me a bit so I can see your scar."

They gave me an unimpressed look. "Why would I do that?"

"It looks badass in this lighting. Come on." I shook my camera a bit. "The grizzly bartender with the eyebrow scar is basically a movie trope. And tropes are great for advertising."

They sighed, then did what I said. The moment they were facing my camera, I "accidentally" flicked the flash on, pointed the camera at them, and hit the shutter. Jayce recoiled as light burst in the dimly-lit bar, their eyes slamming shut.

"For fuck's sake, Ellie," they grumbled as I snorted between cackles. "Did you *have* to flash me?"

"I figured that kind of flashing would be more welcome," I said. "Otherwise I would've gladly shown you my boobs."

"Hmmph." They blinked a few times, probably trying to get the ghost of white light out of their eyes. "You're right. I'll take the light storm over that."

"Ouch. How dare you insult my boobs like that?"

"They're decent, as far as boobs go." They turned, moving behind the bar and grabbing a bar towel. "But as we both know, not my flavour."

"Trust me, I know," I said. "So I was thinking we can take some candids of you mixing cocktails—"

"Red light," Jayce said. "Back it up."

I sighed. "Why? There's nothing—"

"Why did that upset you?" they asked.

"It didn't."

"I insult you and your boobs all the time. You didn't even mutter something half-baked about my scraggly facial hair or overpriced skin care routine." They folded their arms across their chest. "Talk to me."

The worst thing about my friendship with Jayce was that we'd been friends for coming on two decades. If we hadn't been friends for so long, I could've just rolled my eyes and scoffed and told them they clearly didn't know me that well because I was obviously fine.

But half the time, Jayce knew what I was thinking before I did. They knew how I was feeling before I could even name what the feeling was. They remembered the things I forgot before I forgot them, returned things I'd lost before I realized they were gone, and I was pretty sure they knew when my next period was starting at least three days before I did.

I mean, shit. The local pharmacist let Jayce refill my ADHD meds on my behalf even though we weren't related in any way, and we'd made it *very* clear that we were friends.

Not "just" friends. Friendship wasn't a consolation prize for not wanting to be in a relationship. Jayce liked men and masc-presenting people, and I was a chaos gremlin of a bisexual disaster with tomboy tendencies, whimsical romantic fantasies, and a lack of any meaningful talent, skills, or motivation.

And also a woman, I guess.

A very obviously *single* woman.

"Bethany got engaged," I said.

"Your cousin?" Jayce asked.

"She announced it at Thanksgiving last weekend."

Jayce nodded slowly. "So that means…"

"I'm the last unmarried grandchild." I forced a laugh. "Because I *really* needed one more last place ribbon. You know, to just"—I mimed jabbing a dagger forward, which had almost nothing to do with my metaphor except in an allegorical way—"make it clear I'm not one of them."

"Marriage isn't a marker of success."

"It is when you're my grandmother," I muttered.

"And you're not your grandmother," they said. "Ergo, it matters not."

I knew they were keeping their voice light and lofty to make it seem like it was a light and lofty sort of thing, but it wasn't. Still, I made myself smile. "I guess so."

"Elle—"

"Let's just do these photos," I said.

"No." They folded their arms. "My failing bar can wait. This is more important."

"Your bar isn't failing," I said, annoyed. "You got sucked into modernizing a family business that hasn't been modernized since they invented the word while stuck in a small town that, while more progressive than most, is still a small town in Alberta. You're a pioneer."

"I'm a perpetually exhausted magpie, actually, but I appreciate the sentiment," they said. "But to get back on topic—"

"Oh my God, look over there!" I shouted, pointing behind them.

They stared at me in unmoving, judgmental silence.

"Now that your distraction attempt has failed," they continued after a moment, "tell me the rest."

I sighed, setting my camera on the bar. "It's the same old shit, different obligatory family holiday. One of my high-achieving cousins does something impressive. My grandmother subtly reminds me I'm a college dropout loser who doesn't deserve to have her family name. It'll happen again at Christmas when Paige's kid gets a Nobel Peace Prize at the ripe old age of six-and-a-half while

I pretend I'm happy with my illustrious career in schedule coordination at a discount HVAC company."

"I'm fairly certain you exist in a level of chaos that wouldn't allow you to qualify for the Nobel Peace Prize, but you don't have to be miserable at your job, you know."

"Oh, what a grand idea!" I clasped my hands in front of me, looking up at them. "Why didn't I think of that?!"

They didn't lift their energy to match my cynicism, instead gesturing to my camera. "You've loved photography for as long as I've known you."

"We've been over this."

"Just because you have to do some business stuff—"

"Ninety percent of it is boring business stuff!" I almost threw my hands up in aggravation. "Ten percent of it is the fun stuff. The rest dealing with asshole customers who I can't tell to fuck off because they'd be paying me and, like, fucking *math*. Why would I take something I love and fuck it up like that?"

"Because I'm tired of seeing you unhappy," they said.

"And it's all about you, of course."

"Some of us are born with main-character energy." They nudged my camera towards me. "Look, you're like a sister to me, Elle. Which is why I'm going to tell you things you don't want to hear." They put their palms on the bar top, setting their hazel-green eyes on me with a deep, meaningful stare. "You're almost thirty."

I clutched at my chest. "How dare you say the 'th' word?!"

"I know this shit isn't easy for you," they continued, ignoring me. "I know school was not your friend. I've been next to you the whole time. So that means *you* know I know what I'm talking about. So I'm going to tell you that to find your happiness, you have to stop coasting."

"There's something to be said for coasting."

"Is there?"

"Jayce, what do I do if I fail?" I asked bluntly. "*If* I started a business, *when* I inevitably mess something up and lose it all, I wouldn't be able to pay my rent. I know myself well enough to know I'd get into trouble and then have to go crawling to my parents for help *again*. And I don't want to do that."

"Ellie—"

"Yo, barkeep!" shouted a regular named Bruce as he waved a hand in the air. "Whose ambiguous genitals do I have to suck to get a refill around here?"

"Get the fuck out," I snapped.

Bruce snorted. "'Scuse me?"

"Don't talk to them like that," I said, turning to glare at him.

"I was bein' inclusive!" he insisted.

"It was inappropriate," I said.

"I don't hear *them* telling me it was a problem."

"Well, I didn't exactly enjoy it and would prefer you not do it again," Jayce said. "So perhaps you could apologize and refrain from talking about my genitals in the future, and in return we can get you that refill."

Bruce's lips had twisted into a look of sheepish understanding as Jayce spoke. "A'right. Here's the thing. If you were a dude, I woulda asked whose dick I had to suck to get a refill, you know? So I thought making the same kind of joke but not about dicks would be okay."

As much as I hated the fact that Jayce dealt with this often enough to have a level-headed and reasonable response at the ready, I had to admit they were startlingly good at dealing with people like Bruce. The man was the very picture of a typical small-town Albertan: loud, blunt, and confident his opinions were facts. He came across as conservative as his father had been before him, with the kind of raspy voice that could've been the result of decades of cigarettes or just the fumes of whatever job he had that kept dirt under his fingernails.

But even though they had the outward demeanor of a slightly-less-attractive and significantly-less-Muppety Oscar the Grouch, Jayce was inwardly one of the most patient, optimistic, and giving people I'd ever met, especially when dealing with people who weren't exactly *hateful*, but more ignorant.

Like Bruce. He might be crude, but he was a regular at the Flat Tire instead of one of the other bars in town because he'd found out a guy on his crew was trans. And that guy never joined them for beers after work because the bar they used to go to was owned by people who were *very* insistent on having what they called "gender-exclusive bathrooms."

So his whole crew started coming to Jayce's bar instead, and between the six-to-ten of them that showed up a few times a week, were probably responsible for keeping the lights on most months.

"Thank you," Jayce said, nodding at Bruce. "Apology accepted."

"You know I'm not doin' it to be mean," Bruce said. "But if someone doesn't razz you a bit, how d'you even know if they like ya?"

"You don't," Jayce said. "And have I mentioned lately that you're a jackass?"

Bruce burst out laughing, along with the others at his table.

"Got me there, kid," he chuckled.

"Yeah," said one of the others. "You're pretty cool, man."

"I'm not a man," Jayce said, but their voice was drowned out by Bruce smacking his friend on the back of the head.

"They're not a man, dude!" he exclaimed.

The other man grimaced. "Fuck. Sorry!"

Jayce's mouth tightened into their smile-that-wasn't-a-smile and they shook their head, then looked at me as the regulars went back to their conversation.

"Are we good?" they asked.

"Yeah," I said. "Of course. Always."

They nodded brusquely. "Fine. Then stop slacking and start making me look good in photos so I can get more business into this godforsaken place."

"I'm a photographer, not a miracle worker," I said, then immediately snapped a photo of Jayce flipping me off.

Chapter Three

The Chick Magnet

Ellie

"Right, uh-huh," I said, staring at the computer screen in front of me. "But I don't see how that's *our* fault, Mr. Kotyk."

"I don't give a seagull's left tit whose fault it is!" Peter Kotyk's words crackled through my headset as he huffed into the speaker like someone who wasn't responsible for the situation he'd created. "I don't care who you have to pay, who you have to bribe, who you have to *fuck* to get this done; just fucking *do* it!"

"Mmm, right," I said in a flat tone. "Unfortunately, while it is legal for me to offer my 'services' in exchange for goods or money, it *is* illegal for you to solicit it."

"I'm not paying you to give a racoon's saggy nipple about what's legal and what isn't!"

"I understand, Mr. Kotyk," I said. "But regardless, I don't see how selling my body would help me go back in time and make you order your client's air conditioner a week earlier. Here at Air-U-Need Budget Air Conditioning and HVAC, we now obey all laws, including those of time, space, and prostitution."

His indecipherable sputters were so loud, I could almost feel the fine spray of saliva misting from his mouth through the phone.

"Supervisor," he finally growled. "*Now.*"

"My supervisor isn't currently available," I said. "Could I take a—"

"*I'LL FUCKING HOLD THEN!*"

"It may take a while, though, she's at lun—"

He cut me off with another unintelligible blast of words.

"Alrighty then. Hold please." I tapped the hold button on my phone, then yawned and turned towards my boss's office. "Hey Paulette? I'm gonna go on lunch."

"Why do you think I care?" came the gruff response. "And stop yelling across the office, you fucking disgrace. This is a workplace, not a brothel."

"You're welcome for that," I said. "And there's no one else here."

"I'm here," said a meek voice from one of the cubicles a few rows away.

"You don't count, Ivan," I said.

"Why not?" he asked.

"Accountants are barely human." I took my purse out of my desk drawer. "At best, I'd qualify you as some kind of lizard hybrid."

"That's fair," he said.

"I know." I shrugged my jacket on and pulled out my phone to text Jayce to see where they were.

Jayce

Already in line. He's parked in the usual place.

Fuck yes.

The Chick Magnet had the best fried chicken in the entire province—possibly the world, even, but I hadn't tried fried chicken everywhere. During the summer, the owner usually opened by eight-thirty in the morning every Monday and Friday to hit the chicken-and-waffles crowd. Now that it was September, though, he was winding down for the season, and by next month, it'd be hit-or-miss if he'd be there on any given day. And as soon as the snow stuck to the ground, he'd be gone until spring.

"You're going to trip," Jayce said as I reached the lineup of people waiting outside the white food truck. They were dressed up more than usual that day, wearing a pair of tight-fitting jeans with leather boots and a corset-style vest. They'd also filled their scraggly goatee in with eyebrow pencil and had highlighted the slit caused by the scar on their eyebrow with concealer.

"Trip on what?"

They scooted their leather boot forward and pinned my untied shoelace to the ground. "Your shoe is untied."

I rolled my eyes. "They're always untied. It'll be fine."

"You say that, right up until the day you're drinking your iced coffee from an eco-conscious tumbler and fall eye-first onto the metal straw after your shoelace gets caught in an escalator," they said.

"That has literally never happened."

"I read about it online."

"Yeah, and I read a crossover fan fiction of Jean-Luc Picard and Professor Xavier simultaneously developing both cloning machines and the ability to cross parallel universes so they can fuck each other, but that doesn't mean it's true."

They lifted an eyebrow at me. "Since when do you read? And since when do you read *Star Trek fan fiction*?"

"It was less about the franchise and more about the unhinged-ness of the concept."

They let out an unimpressed hum. "Is that why it took you forever to get here?"

"No, that's because I was being asked to sell my body to fund time travel."

"As one does," they said, not taking the bait. "I got your email with the photos, by the way."

"Yeah? What'd you think?"

"Aside from the one where you Photoshopped a dildo onto my forehead—"

"Ah, yes," I said, grinning. "I call that one the Jaynicorn."

"—they were decent," they finished. "So now what?"

"What do you mean, now what?"

They sighed impatiently. "You said I needed to take new photos for branding and stuff. Now what do I *do* with them?"

"I'm your photographer, not your marketing assistant. You figure it out."

They let out a huff of annoyance. "So we took those photos for nothing, then."

"No, we—what's wrong?" I asked, frowning. "You're upset about something."

"I'm not *upset*," they said, clearly upset. "I'm frustrated that we wasted a bunch of product and time posing for photos that I'm finding out are useless."

"They're not useless," I said. "What's this really about?"

"I told you, it—"

"Jayce." I folded my arms and gave them my best "I'm not mad, I'm disappointed" look. Which worked, somehow, because Jayce took a deep breath and let it out slowly.

"I had a meeting with my uncles this morning," they said.

That was all they needed to say to explain everything.

Jayce's grandparents had owned the Flat Tire for years. Their grandpa was the kind of person who planned to work to the day he died, putting the same amount of devotion and energy into building his business from the ground up as he had put into raising his four kids. He was also the kind of person who loved his wife with every ounce of his being, deeply and unconditionally and beautifully.

So when the doctors gave her a year to live, he decided to spend every second of that year by her side.

He'd asked his kids to help with the bar so he had something to go back to after the day he lost everything. Not one of the four was able or willing. Jayce stepped up to help, but under the guise of "just wanting what's best for Dad," two of their uncles had volunteered to supervise their management of the bar, mainly so they could show Jayce's grandpa it would be better to sell the place and retire.

"Is that why you're so dressed up?" I asked.

They let out an indignant scoff, which meant I was right. "I always look this good. My sales report from last month, however, did not, since sales are dismal, as my uncles have so kindly pointed out yet again."

"Well, we need more customers," I said.

"Your intellect knows no bounds."

"Things like the new photos are supposed to help with that," I said. "You can use them for your social media or on your website."

"And say what? 'Hey, come drink at this bar in the middle of buttfuck nowhere'?"

"I think we're more on the outskirts of buttfuck nowhere," I said. "There's a heck of a lot of nowhere north of us."

They folded their arms across their chest, saying nothing and not looking at me.

"Let's start with the basics," I said. "Who are you trying to attract as a customer?"

"People with money who want to drink alcohol," they answered flatly.

"Okay, but how are we going to set you apart from all the other places they can do that?"

"We're not," they said. "It's not like I can go make huge changes to the bar. I'm not the permanent owner. My grandpa—"

"—isn't here," I interrupted. "You are."

"He'll come back."

"You don't know when that will be," I pointed out. "Your uncles are using everything they can to show him that he should shut the bar down. We need to improve sales otherwise he might not have something to come back *to*."

It was a little harsh. I knew that the moment it came out of my mouth. But one of the many great things about Jayce was that despite acting like everything annoyed them, they weren't that easily offended. So while they didn't meet my eyes, they nodded slowly.

"Jayce, you've wanted to run a bar for as long as I've known you," I said. "And that's a disgustingly long time."

"It is pretty disgusting," they agreed. "But *this* isn't the kind of bar I wanted."

"So let's make it that kind of bar," I said.

They rolled their eyes. "Right. Because a nightclub would do *so* well in a town this size."

"You might not have your dream club right away, but that doesn't mean you can't have some of it," I said. "Think of Bruce."

"Fine, but I'm not doing it in a sexual capacity."

"He started coming because he knew you're the 'inclusive' bar in the area. So lean into that. Host drag shows. Put on events. Hire a DJ and have a club night with a dance floor."

Jayce's lips twisted to the side, which was a good thing because it meant they weren't talking. And *that* was a good thing because it meant they *were* considering what I said. But before they could respond, the people in front of us stepped out of the way and it was our turn to order at The Chick Magnet's window. And by order, I mean the owner peered out the window, saw me and Jayce, and let out a dramatic sigh.

"You want more goddamn chicken?" he asked as he started tapping our order into the register. "Again?"

"What are you complaining about?" Jayce asked as they took their card out to pay. "I'm fairly certain the two of us have nearly financed your entire winter trip on our own."

He snorted and passed Jayce the credit card reader. "Not enough for two first-class tickets to Mexico City. My poor wife has to sit in economy."

"Sounds like a her problem," Jayce said.

The owner snorted. "Right up until we land and she tells her family. Then it's all 'Carlos, why didn't you just buy two economy tickets so you could sit together?' and I have to tell them it was my reward for dealing with you two fuckin' weirdos all summer."

It didn't take long to get our chicken, which was good because Jayce had to get back to the bar and bad because it meant I had no excuse not to go back to work. Once I was at my desk, I took my time unwrapping my meal—two spicy drumsticks and the extra cornbread Carlos's wife always snuck in for me—and took a bite before putting my headset back on and clicking the phone line that was flashing.

"Good afternoon, this is customer retention supervisor Roxanne," I said in a nasally voice muffled by the best fried chicken I'd ever eaten in my life. "I understand you have a problem with your order timeline, Peter?"

"I've been on hold for over an *hour*!" came the aggrieved shout.

I rolled my eyes. It had barely been forty-five minutes. "I apologize for the inconvenience, sir. I was handling another call my employee Ellie had difficulty with, and I've only just sorted it out."

"Ellie?" he repeated. "That's who I was talking to! What kind of business are you running over where that bimbo still has a job?"

I sighed heavily. "Honestly, sir, between you and me, I wish I had control over that. But I just get stuck cleaning up all her messes. What seems to be the problem?"

Between trying to explain the situation with his client's air conditioner not being ready paired with various interludes complaining about that customer service girl Ellie and her lack of willingness to prostitute herself for HVAC-related bribes, it took until after I'd finished my entire meal and was staring up at the ceiling tiles for Peter to stop yelling.

"Oh, that's just awful," I said in my fake nasally voice when he finally asked what the hell I was gonna do about all this. "I'm so sorry for your experience, sir. Let me see what I can do here, but I thi-*ink*—" I reached for my keyboard and let my fingers fly across the keys, clacking them as loudly as I could while I typed nonsense. "Mmm, just as I suspected."

"What?" demanded Peter. "Don't tell me that bimbo was lying about my furnace being there."

"No, no, not at all." I let out an unhappy hum. "It's those damn government regulations."

"The what?"

"You know," I said. "The regulations. Complete waste of our tax dollars and all it's doing is, uh... pandering. To the... environmentalists? I'm sure you've heard of them. All over the news right now."

"Of course I've heard of them," he said about the fake regulations I'd invented. "Those bastards at the legislature will do anything to keep their pockets lined. Why couldn't that other nitwit tell me this when I first called?"

"Oh, she has no idea how to look these things up," I said. "But at least she's pretty. Best-looking girl in the office, my sales guys say."

"Must be how she gets away with keeping her job," he grumbled.

I agreed, then promised him I'd review the new fake government regulations I'd invented with Ellie. After hanging up, I took my headset off and turned to my computer to do my actual job, which was coordinating our project schedules and trying not to die of boredom. An hour later, Paulette stormed up to my desk, her leathery white skin flushed with anger and her wild grey hair sticking up more than usual.

"You're fired," she snapped.

"No I'm not," I replied.

"You lied to a customer."

"No I didn't."

Wrinkles appeared along her forehead and around the edges of her pursed lips. "No? So Peter What's-His-Face just emailed me to compliment my helpful supervisor Ruth-Anne who made up for my useless tit of a customer service agent Ellie because he thought it might be funny?"

"Typical. He didn't even remember my fake name was Roxanne."

"You're fired," she repeated. "I don't tolerate liars. You can't just make up new employee names when you decide to be terrible at your job."

"I'm not terrible at my job," I said.

"Your customer service skills are shit."

"Good thing you hired me to be the scheduling coordinator," I said. "I'm not even *supposed* to be answering the phones after the Monarch Construction incident. But you haven't replaced the customer service team yet, and there's no one else willing to get screamed at by angry men who can't admit to their own mistakes."

We both knew I was right. Paulette sputtered for a moment, then glared at me. "Fine. You're unfired. For now. But count your fuckin' days, Burns. Once I have a new customer service team, you're going to be on thin ice."

"Got it," I said as she turned on a heel and stormed away. "Let me know when you get around to hiring that new team so I can prepare myself for my inevitable unemployment."

"Immediately," she spat over her shoulder, then caught her thigh on a desk and nearly stumbled. "Tomorrow. I'm going to hire the next goddamn person I find, and once you've trained your replacement, your ass is gone."

Thankfully she was still going the other direction, so she didn't see me roll my eyes. Considering I'd been doubling as customer service and scheduling coordinator for months, I'd believe that when I saw it.

Chapter Four

Improbability Drive

Isla

MY SISTER LIKED TO make things harder than they needed to be.

"Why doesn't she call me herself?" I asked my mom the third time she'd called to tell me Venus had a question about something I'd left at my old apartment. "It would be a lot easier."

"Oh, probably," Mom said. "But you know how Venus is."

I sighed. "What's she asking about this time?"

"Well, she said there's a whole bookcase here that Nick says is yours."

"Bookcase?" I repeated. "But I emptied them all. What—*oh.*"

My heart dropped as I realized what she meant. Nick and I had kept most of our hobby-related things in our spare room. His snowboarding equipment, some old weights, and the two bookcases that I'd cleared out so he didn't have to deal with it after I moved out. I'd dropped off most of the books at my favourite used bookstore, though I'd packed a choice selection that were now displayed on the sparse shelf in my new apartment.

But we'd had three bookcases, the third one being in our bedroom.

And that being the one I kept all my favourites on.

"I can't believe I forgot them," I mumbled.

"It's fine, bluebird," Mom said. "I can tell her to get rid of them, if you—"

"No!" It came out as a yelp and I cleared my throat. "No, please. Not those ones. Or—" I swallowed hard. "At least, not all of them. If it's too much trouble to store them or whatever.

25

"It's not," my mom replied. "Venus just said they'll be too heavy to carry, but she's there with... oh, what's his name?" She clicked her tongue. "Nick's brother."

"Marcus?"

"That's the one. Venus said he's spent most of the day yapping about CrossFit. Show me a guy like that who *doesn't* trip over himself to carry things for a poor, weak damsel and I'll show you a fucking liar."

I almost laughed. "You really think so?"

"Of course. He's probably itching to bench press something as we speak."

"I meant the whole thing about getting a man to do things for a perfectly capable and independent woman is decidedly unfeminist of you."

"His unfeminist actions are not my unfeminist thoughts," she said. "Though, there's something to be said for playing on the fact that you can jump into nearly any man's car and convince him to help you run from the cops by looking at him with teary eyes and tugging your shirt down a bit."

Once upon a time, that would've made me laugh. It was another one of her twisted stories, the kind that changed a little with each retelling to serve the context of whatever she was talking about. Except it was one I'd heard so many times that I knew that wasn't *quite* what happened.

The thing she'd said about running from the cops was true. She'd been at a protest trying to block a pipeline being built across some protected piece of land and had, in her words, been a *little* less pacifist than she usually was because they'd started loading up the only outhouse in the area.

"They were trying to do whatever the bathroom equivalent of starving us out is," she'd say. "I was just trying to be responsible and use the designated facilities. And when I couldn't access them, I went as close to them as I could."

Which had been on the roof of the truck loading up the outhouse.

As it turns out, people don't like it when you shit on the roof of their car. So my mom had booked it into the nearby forest to lose the cops that were chasing her.

Meanwhile, my dad was lost.

He'd taken a wrong turn about two hours earlier in the day. He was on his way to a work retreat somewhere in the mountains and only noticed he was lost when he'd ended up on a gravel logging road instead of the highway he should have been on. That ended up being lucky because it meant he wasn't going very fast when a sunburnt woman with wild blonde hair burst out of the trees and he ran over her with his very sensible Ford sedan.

"I almost shat myself," he used to say. "I thought I'd killed her."

"I was fine," Mom would reply, rolling her eyes. "I rolled over the hood. It's not like I'd never been hit by a car before."

Dad had slammed on the brakes and was about to get out of the car when Mom popped up and dusted herself off. She looked up, eyes wide, then wrenched the passenger door open and dove in.

"Drive!" she shrieked.

So my dad did, unaware that he was now an accomplice instead of a standard-issue nerd. A few hours later, she navigated him to his work retreat, followed him into his hotel room and, in Dad's words, "just never left."

It was why I couldn't understand how my dad didn't believe in fate. It had been unquestionably improbable for him to not only fall in love with Mom, but to have crossed her path in the first place. How could someone live through that and not believe in destiny? In love that lasted forever?

But he didn't, and it was why that story didn't make me laugh quite so much anymore.

Mom and I talked for a few more minutes, but because it was the third time that day she'd called, there wasn't much else to say. Once we hung up, I fidgeted with my phone, hesitating before I tapped on the screen and lifted it back to my ear.

"Hello?" came the bored-sounding answer.

"Hey," I said. "It's me."

"I know. I have caller ID," said Venus.

I bit back my natural instinct to be offended by Venus's tone. My sister looked exactly how people expected when they heard she was named for the goddess of love. She had golden-blonde hair—though *nobody* was to know it was the same flat, medium brown as our dad's—and fair white skin that was impossibly blemish-free. She didn't leave the house unless she was meticulously contoured, bursts of rosy blush on the round cheeks of her heart-shaped face and pink gloss coating her lips.

Paired with her abrasive opinions, blunt statements, and chronically bored tone of voice, people thought she was beautiful in a mean way. Which was unfortunate. I didn't always get along with my sister—I rarely got along with her, actually—but she wasn't a mean girl. She just looked like one.

"Yeah," I said. "I thought this might be easier than going through Mom."

"I guess. I didn't want to bother you."

"I know. But I thought I'd try to help since you're doing me a favour."

She made another nonchalant sound. "Fine. What do you need to tell me?"

"If it's too much to pack all those books, I was hoping you could just grab a couple for me. The really important ones."

She sighed heavily. "Which ones?"

I closed my eyes, picturing the shelves, and listed a few. She let out a grunt of affirmation each time she found one, right up until we got to the most important one of all.

"*The Hitchhiker's Guide to the Galaxy*," I said. "It's on the top shelf. Somewhere in the middle."

"It's not," she said.

"Uh... okay." I frowned. "Maybe the second shelf?"

"No, I mean it's not on this bookcase at all," she said.

My heart sank. "It... it has to be."

"I don't know what you want me to say. There's nothing here with that name."

"It *has* to be," I repeated. "Please don't fuck with me, Venus."

"Why would I be fucking with you?" she asked. "If you're so sure I'm lying, why don't you come here and find it yourself?"

That stung. "I'm not saying you're lying. I just... it has to be there."

"Isla, I may not have a single fucking clue about why you up and quit your entire life, but I'm not lying about your book," she said. "It's not here. And while we're on the topic, you know no one knows what happened, right? Marcus said Nick has no idea. Mom has no idea. You left like you didn't have a good, steady thing going here with him."

My mouth was dry, my eyes burning with an anxious sting. "Maybe I don't want steady."

"Says the person who's the definition of wanting things to be steady," she said.

"Yeah, and maybe I don't want that anymore," I said. "Maybe I want to work somewhere more interesting. Maybe I want to experience more things, you know? I want to meet new people and eat new foods and... and... I don't know. Wear fun hats. Have a meet cute. That kind of thing."

"Wear... fun... hats?" she said slowly.

My face burned. "You know. Like... because it's... quirky."

"You don't have the face for hats. It would make your hair all puffy."

I touched the end of one of my locks of curls. "I can wear hats if I want to."

"Well, no one's stopping you, technically" she said. "But seriously, Isla. I can't believe I have to be the one to say this, but you're not being logical."

I couldn't believe she was the one saying it, either. "What?"

"You broke up with your boyfriend because you didn't have a good enough meet cute and you don't think you can wear hats? That doesn't make any sense. You're not that kind of person. Like, okay, sure, we all wish we could have a meet cute, but you can't just *plan* to have that happen. Which we both know means it's not going to happen because if you can't plan it, you don't do it."

I didn't say anything. Venus waited for a moment, then sighed.

"Is there anything else you need? I have stuff I want to get done today."

I did have something I needed, which was to know where the fuck my copy of *The Hitchhiker's Guide to the Galaxy* was. I asked her to double check the books she'd packed up one more time, but if it wasn't there, she could donate the rest to the used bookstore. She grunted her agreement and a few minutes after we hung up, texted me a photo of the box she'd packed up to prove it wasn't there.

And if it wasn't there, and it wasn't here, that meant it was gone.

Which was devastating.

My dad and I had always had different taste in books. He was a non-fiction guy. Biographies, accounts of different historical events, scientific theories, psychological studies… pretty much the only category he'd avoided was self-help.

"The entire genre is based on a lie," he'd told me once. "Unless they wrote the book, it's not *self*-help."

I loved fiction. Fantasy was my go-to, though I loved everything from thrillers to love stories to sci-fi. So even though we both loved to read, my dad and I didn't often talk about books, since there wasn't a lot of overlap.

That book, though?

That was one that we'd always agreed was one of the best books of all time.

His copy of *The Hitchhiker's Guide to the Galaxy* had rarely been on the bookshelf in his office because if he wasn't in the process of re-reading it, I usually was. We'd read the whole series together countless times and I could recite huge chunks of it from memory.

But I wasn't upset just because it was my favourite book. It was that *copy* of the book. That book, with a page near the back taped together from when I accidentally ripped it out one of the first times I read it. The corners had curled edges. The inside cover had my dad's name in his meticulous handwriting.

That copy was irreplaceable.

I cried about it for a while because of course I did. Then I took a deep breath and decided to comfort myself the best way I could, which was to find a bookstore.

I probably shouldn't have. I mean, I'd quit my job with no notice. It wasn't like I could collect employment insurance. And I didn't have anything lined up. I'd been applying for jobs every day since I got here, but I'd been rejected from half the jobs already, and it had been radio silence on the other half. I didn't have the money for an impulsive trip to the bookstore.

Which was why I decided to go.

Second Avenue—the beginning and the end of Aurora Flats' version of downtown—wasn't quite the main street dotted with quirky boutiques and punny cafes that I'd conjured up in my fate-goaded fantasies. It had a few local businesses and a Starbucks, and the buildings were made of brick and siding that lent an old-timey sort of feel to the area without leaning too heavily on a cartoony Western aesthetic, but it wasn't the kind of place that would have a hat store.

Which meant it had to be fate.

What else could it be? What were the chances that I'd have this conversation with my sister, find out my favourite book was missing, decide to go to the book store, and end up parking in front of an odd little convenience-store-slash-gift-shop that had a black pork-pie hat displayed in the front window?

And what were the chances that when I walked into the only bookstore in Aurora Flats, a used bookstore creatively named Books that sat at the end of Second Avenue, the owner would be putting out a box of new-to-them books?

What were the chances that she was putting out *that* book, at *that* moment? If I hadn't chosen to call my sister, if I hadn't chosen to ask about the book, if I hadn't decided I needed a trip to the book store and hadn't parked where I did and hadn't stopped to buy the pork-pie hat now sitting on top of my curls, I wouldn't have seen it.

It didn't have the same cover as my dad's copy. But the title was there, bold blue text standing out from a black background. I barely processed that I'd moved; the first indication I had that I'd lifted my arm to reach for it was when the sensation of warm fingers grazed the back of my hand.

Oh, I thought, the word soft as it rolled around my mind.

Oh.

How could this be anything *but* fate? How could it be anything but a sign I was on the right track?

The man looking back at me was about my age. He was an average height with brown hair and large blue eyes hidden behind wire-framed glasses. He held a stack of three books in one pale white hand, and the other?

The other was soft.

And smooth.

And practically caressing my skin.

My heart stuttered, my breath catching in that place at the base of my throat, just next to where my pulse was.

I could be moments away from him smiling and chuckling softly before taking his hand back from mine.

"So sorry," he might say. "I've just been wanting to read that for ages, but you were clearly here first."

And I'd laugh too as I dropped my hand.

"Oh, that's okay," I'd say. "I mean, I've read it before."

Then maybe he'd smile and take the book from the shelf.

"Tell you what," he'd say as he held it. "What if I take it, but you give me your number, and once I'm done, it's all yours? I'll sell it to you for the cost of a coffee date."

When it came right down to it, improbability and fate were intrinsically entwined. Fate itself was so improbable that it became probable; one might not be able to count on any specific improbabilities, but the existence of those improbabilities? I mean, the book itself posed the question. What was the probability that a set of missiles could morph into a sperm whale and a bowl of petunias?

What was the probability that this man was The One?

The touching of our hands at that precise moment, in that precise store, reaching for that precise book without so much as an awareness of each other before our skin met... it was improbable. But it happened, and if an Infinite Improbability Drive could make a spaceship cross the universe, it could make fate do its work between two people who just—

"Not a fucking chance," the man said, his voice unexpectedly nasally.

Before I was even half-dragged out of the scenario I'd conjured up in my mind, he slapped my hand out of the way and lunged forward, snatching *The Hitchhiker's Guide to the Galaxy* from the shelf. With a self-satisfied smirk, he looked at me and pushed his glasses up his nose. "You snooze, you lose."

"Ow," I said, cradling my hand. "Rude."

He glared at me. "Don't even try the sympathy card. I've been looking for this forever. And I saw it first."

And then he stormed off to the register.

That settled that, I guess. Not fate.

Just a nerd who wanted a book more than my number.

Which was fine. I mean, the whole thing was ridiculous. Something or someone wasn't trying to communicate with me via books on shelves; that wasn't how fate worked, no matter how much I might have wanted it to. Clearly I was just projecting, hoping that there was a sign *somewhere* telling me I was in the right place at the right time. That Aurora Flats was supposed to be my new home. That I would find love, and friends, and the sense of belonging I'd been missing for years.

But considering I couldn't even find a job...

Well.

Maybe the reason there wasn't a sign was because I was wrong.

God, that was depressing. I swallowed my disappointment and started browsing, doing whatever I could to lose myself among the books.

And honestly, it helped.

The best bookstores are places that feel both infinitely large and inconceivably cramped, partially from stack after shelf after table full of books but mostly due to it being full of the welcoming sort of magic that wraps itself around you as easily as an old, cozy sweater. That magic is what tells time itself to go ahead, take a break, let this person search the worlds contained here with no regard to the limitations of the clock in their own world.

For a while, nothing existed but the scent of old books and the ironically comforting glow of the fluorescent lights above. Lost in a world all my own, I meandered, floating along aimlessly as I searched for something that I couldn't name, plucking interesting looking covers off the shelves and stacking them in my arms.

"That's quite the selection," the store owner said when I came up to the register with ten more books than I'd planned to buy. "These are some great choices."

"Thanks," I said. "You don't happen to be hiring so I can buy more, do you?"

She laughed. "Not right now, but you can leave your resume on file if you want."

"That's okay," I said. "I don't have a copy with me. But I *am* looking for a job. Do you know of anywhere else that might be hiring?"

She grimaced. "Not many places are, unfortunately."

"Did you just say you need a job?"

I blinked, turning to my right to see a short woman with wild grey hair giving me a hard look.

"Uh... yeah," I said.

"You got customer service experience? On the phone?"

"Yeah," I said.

"You know anything about air conditioning?"

I grimaced and shook my head. "No. Sorry."

"That's fine. You can learn." The woman opened her purse, rifling through it for a moment before she pulled out a scuffed-up business card. "Here. We need a customer service person."

I took the card, which was for a place with the redundantly long name Air-U-Need Budget Air Conditioning and HVAC. According to the address, it was just a couple of blocks away from Books.

"Thanks," I said as the woman started looking through her purse again. "Do I just call to set up an interview?"

"What's your name?" she interrupted.

I blinked a few times. "Isla Monroe."

She took a scrap of paper and a pen from her purse. "Eye-lah Mon-row," she muttered, dragging out each syllable. "Alright. You can come in Monday?"

"Yeah," I said, trying not to sound shocked or excited, even though I was definitely both. "Absolutely. What time?"

"Nine a.m.," she said, capping the pen and shoving it back in her purse.

"And who should I—"

"Enough questions. Don't be late."

And then she turned and walked away.

Chapter Five

It's An Oat Latte, Honey

Isla

I WAS GOING TO be late.

The *one* thing the mysterious lady who probably worked for some kind of money laundering scheme or worse had said was to be on time.

And I was going to be late.

"Come on, come on, come *on*," I whispered as the ancient dryer in the building's laundry room made clunking noises that were according to the grammatically incorrect sign taped to it, were totally normal. The single pair of grey dress pants I owned spun listlessly and I chewed on my lip, glancing at the old-style flip clock on the shelf by the window. With my heart hammering desperate hope into my ribcage, I wrenched the dryer door open. Air that had all the heat of a gentle sigh brushed my bare forearms as I reached in and grabbed—

"*Fuck,*" I whispered. The wetness across the thighs of my pants was still blatantly obvious and the few spots that had managed to dry out were tinted brown and scented with coffee, even though I'd rinsed them as thoroughly as I could.

Great.

Fucking *great.*

My one pair of dress pants were soaked and stained, my curly hair was a half-styled mess, and I was going to be fucking *late* to the interview for the only prospective job I'd been able to find.

Late and *coffeeless.*

Fuck, fuck, fuck.

I twisted the pants in my hands as I returned to my apartment, fretting and trying to figure out what I could get away with wearing. The call center I'd worked at before had a casual dress code and I'd almost exclusively worn jeans or leggings with tops long enough to pretend they were a dress, so my business-casual style clothes were few and far between. And there had only been one day between meeting the mysterious woman and my interview at Air-U-Need Budget Air-Conditioning and HVAC, so I hadn't had a chance to go shopping.

Or the money to go shopping.

Or the knowledge of where in Aurora Flats carried plus size clothes. And yeah, I could've driven into Edmonton to go shopping, but plus size clothes weren't cheap, and I had a pair of dress pants anyway so why would I have bothered?

So like the planner I was, I put my outfit out on the dresser the night before so I didn't have to rush in the morning after I showered.

Except then I'd decided to have a big mug of coffee while I got ready, set it on the dresser beside my clothes, and after diffusing half of my hair, caught the handle with the cord of my blow dryer and knocked it all over my dress pants.

Safe to say none of this was going according to plan.

Throwing my closet open, I rifled through my clothes. Jeans, leggings, more jeans, more leggings, a few cocktail dresses, a couple of skirts—

"Skirt," I said out loud, spreading the hangers and looking at my options.

Which were a black miniskirt—far too short for work, even with tights—a denim skirt, and a tight blue-and-green plaid designer pencil skirt that wasn't my style at *all*, but I'd let Venus talk me into buying it years ago and couldn't bring myself to throw away because I'd paid way too much money for it.

Seriously. I was pretty sure it was the most expensive thing in my closet, and the most I'd worn it was when I tried it on every so often to see if it still fit.

Which it did, as I verified again as I pulled it on and looked in the mirror.

It was a little less demure than I wanted to wear to work, let alone to a job interview. A little tighter than I preferred and short enough to be called alluring, which was only a step before sexy.

"But I guess this'll do," I whispered.

Because it had to.

As for the hair situation...

Well.

I was just going to leave it. The woman at the bookstore had puffy grey hair, so I figured I could bank on some level of empathy for the disaster that having curly hair could be. But just before I left my apartment, I paused as fate stepped in again.

Because hanging there on the hook next to my door was the black pork-pie hat.

It wasn't job-interview appropriate. But it *was* a piece of my reinvention into an independent, quirky, spontaneous person.

And me stopping to buy it had made it so I was in the book store at the same time as the lady from Air-U-Need.

Sure, maybe it was silly to think the hat had gotten me the interview in the first place. But also, it didn't *not* get me the interview.

Before I could over think everything, I grabbed the hat and jammed it on my head, then bolted out the door, fumbling with my keys as I thundered down the stairs and out the front door. Jumping into my car, I booked it down the street towards the address on Third Avenue.

And here's the thing.

I used to live in Burnaby.

Burnaby wasn't Vancouver. It was next to Vancouver. But the cities were *really* close together, and both had the same ridiculous amount of traffic. So when I'd planned what time I should leave for my interview, I left what I thought was a reasonable amount of time to account for rush hour traffic.

You know, so I would still get me there a few minutes early and make a good impression.

Except Aurora Flats wasn't Burnaby. Its version of rush hour was not only on a much, *much* smaller scale, but it was a hell of a lot earlier in the day since most people commuted to the city or the industrial areas nearby for work.

So instead of being five or ten minutes early for my nine a.m. interview like I'd planned, I got there at, uh… eight-twenty-six.

Thirty-four minutes early.

There weren't even any other cars in the parking lot.

But, I told myself, that was okay. Because while my plan for the morning had gone to shit, it had gone to shit for a *reason*. If it had gone the way I thought it would, I would've been even earlier than I was. And while it seemed like a dick move for the universe to sacrifice my cup of coffee to delay me the way it did, it also made sure I'd still be taken care of.

That is, by getting to work early enough for me to hit up the Starbucks on Second Avenue.

Hopefully.

The line wasn't insignificant when I walked in, but I figured it would move quickly enough. I mean, I still had almost half an hour before I needed to be there. It would be silly of me to worry about being late when I had so much time *and* when I was trying to believe that not making the plan myself didn't mean there wasn't one. It just meant the universe was making it for me.

However, my mother hadn't called me her silly little bluebird for nothing. So I fidgeted as subtly as I could while I waited, trying not to tap my foot impatiently or let the tight anxiety in my chest make me lightheaded before I finally made it up to the counter to order.

"Good-morning-welcome-to-Starbucks-what-can-I-get-you," said the barista dully.

"A grande honey oat latte, please," I said. "Oh, and can you add whip on top?"

She tapped on the screen, then frowned. "Whip has dairy in it."

"I know."

"The honey oat latte has oat milk."

"I know," I said. "I can have dairy. I just like that latte."

She frowned. "But it's made with oat milk."

"I... I know. I want the honey oat latte and to add whip on it."

"I can't make the whip dairy-free just because it's an oat milk latte, *honey*."

I gritted my teeth, trying not to let her condescension get to me. "That's fine."

She stared at me, then half-shrugged. "Okay, but we aren't remaking it if it's wrong."

"That's also fine. I understand."

"Hmph. And your name?"

"Isla."

She scrawled something onto a paper cup as I paid, then stepped to the side to wait.

And wait.

And *wait*.

Glancing around the coffee shop to distract myself from the building anxiety in my chest, I took in the mish-mash of people clad in everything from suits and skirts to coveralls and jeans. Most were idly looking at their phones as they waited, or tapping their feet impatiently in line while they watched one barista rushing around making drink after drink, or staring blankly into space as they waited for their turn with the cranky barista at the register until she finally started helping the other one.

A few steps away from me was a man about my age. He was leaning against the wall, head tilted down and absorbed in the book he was reading. The front cover was facing me, but the way it was tilted, I couldn't see the title or the author.

And he was… well, he was relatively good-looking. Like, conventionally speaking. I'm sure he could've been called attractive, but I didn't really think of people that way.

Like Nick, for example. Venus had always talked about how gorgeous he was. And objectively, I knew he was, but it just didn't seem to matter as much to me. It wasn't why I liked him. If anyone had asked me, I would've said the most attractive thing about him was his compassion. His sense of humour. His understanding.

So it didn't bother me that I wasn't, like, breathless at the sight of the man beside me. What mattered more was that he was reading—something I loved to do—and waiting for a coffee—something I loved to drink.

Maybe it was him.

I had the perfect opening. I could ask him what he was reading. We could talk books and I could mention that I was new to town and he could offer to show me around.

Except I was on a set time limit before I had my job interview. And it wasn't exactly the something spectacular I'd hoped for.

But, I thought slowly, what if I set *myself* up for something spectacular?

Like, maybe I could run into him. I'd have to be careful to not spill on myself. I'd have to spill on him. But then I could get his number so I could pay to clean his shirt and—

"Venti vanilla iced latte for Amos!" yelled one of the baristas.

The man beside me snapped his book shut loudly and huffed, glancing at me like he was looking for commiseration.

"I keep telling them it's Thomas," he said, sounding annoyed, but before I could even chuckle or agree or say anything, he worked his way up to the counter, grabbed his drink, and left.

So there went that idea.

"Grande latte for Ella!" called the cranky barista, looking in my direction.

I swallowed hard, distracted by unreasonable disappointment as I turned back to the counter just as someone else started reaching for my drink.

"Hey, wait!" I said. "That's mine!"

She was tall, thin, and had the kind of effortless quirky coolness that I wanted for myself. Deep chestnut brown hair was tied into a careless bun on the top of her head and beneath a well-worn canvas jacket was what appeared to be a vintage concert t-shirt, but upon closer look, was actually a bunch of cats playing guitars. Her face was friendly, with pinkish-white skin, sparkling brown eyes, and a thin upper lip that spread into an apologetic smile.

"Sorry," she said, a hint of a lisp hanging onto the word. "I thought they said 'Ella.'"

"They... did," I said, frowning. "But I thought they meant me."

"Your name is Ella?" she asked.

"No, but it's Starbucks. They never get the name right so I thought they mispronounced 'Isla.' If you're Ella, it must be yours."

She pressed her lips together. "Well, no, but what are the chances? I'm Ellie, but it's Starbucks. They never get the name right."

"What... really? Your name is Ellie?"

"Ellie and Isla," she said. "It has a nice ring. Our couple name could be Ella."

We stared at each other for a moment, then both started laughing at the same time.

"So, how do we know if it's yours or mine?" she asked.

"I'll ask," I said, still smiling as I tried to flag down the barista. "Excuse... excuse me? What drink is this?"

The barista who had made the drink didn't hear me, but the one who had taken my order did. "Ma'am, I *told* you we wouldn't remake it if you ordered it wrong."

"No, it's not that. We're just not sure who—"

"You ordered a dairy-free latte and added dairy," she interrupted, folding her arms. "That is exactly what you wanted. A honey oat latte with whipped cream. *Cream*. It's dairy."

Ellie started giggling again. "Wait, you ordered—"

"I just want to know if that's *this* drink," I said exasperatedly, ignoring her. "The name is wrong."

The barista rolled her eyes. "We don't remake a drink if just the name is wrong."

"I'm not asking for it to be remade," I said, my voice pitching up with panic. "I don't have time for that. I'm going to be late for a job interview. We just want to know if this is a—"

"Honey oat with whip for Ella!" called the other barista, placing another drink on the counter without acknowledging any of us, and that's when Ellie *really* lost it.

"Here," she said, holding out the first drink. "I ordered the same thing."

I gaped at the drink, then at her. "Wait, what?"

She shoved the drink into my hands. "We both have amazing first names and excellent taste in mixing dairy-free beverages with dairy-full toppings. Now hurry, before you miss your interview."

Then, before I could say anything else, she tilted her drink at me and strode out of the coffee shop.

Chapter Six
Acute Bisexual Panic

Ellie

That skirt.

My God, that *skirt*.

I wasn't going to stop by The Chick Magnet before work, but I needed to collect myself.

"Where's your friend?" the owner grumbled when I reached the window.

"Asleep," I said. "We'll be back for lunch later."

He snorted as he typed my order in. "Ridiculous."

"Yeah."

He hit a few more buttons, but the permanent frown lines on his head deepened even more before he looked up.

"What's wrong with you?" he demanded.

"Huh?"

He pulled the order ticket from the machine but didn't turn to put it on the line right away. "I said, what's *wrong* with you today?"

"Nothing's wrong," I said, too distracted to be offended. "I want my chicken, old man."

"Ah, there it is." His frown relaxed. "Don't act weird. I don't like it."

"I'm not paying you to like things," I said.

Another gruff snort. "Shut up and wait for your order."

It probably worried him that I stepped aside without saying anything else, but whatever. I was currently contemplating if I was any better than some horndog teenage boy who'd just seen his first pair of tits.

Like yeah, the girl—Isla—was probably nice. She was probably funny. She probably had plenty of qualities about her that meant far more than her looks.

But the acute bisexual panic currently in control of my body wasn't thinking about any of those things.

It didn't happen to me very often, but once in a while, I'd see a woman—yes, I was attracted to men, too, but women triggered a different type of bisexual panic than men did, which was different than the type of bisexual panic that non-binary people triggered, and no I could not elaborate on why any of that was except to say that hot people in general forced me to live in a constant state of panic—who made my brain short circuit. It was always sudden, some out-of-nowhere interaction that took all the logic in my brain and turned it into static.

Like Isla.

Isla and her legs in that goddamn skirt.

She was everything I liked. Roundness and curves, with the kind of softness I wanted to dig my fingers into, all shown off by a fitted plaid skirt that didn't try to hide her shape. Big blue eyes that made her look innocent and irresistible all once. Blondish-brown hair that would be a *dream* to hold in my hands, her curls puffing out from an adorable black hat that made her seem approachable and friendly and fun. Faint freckles dotting the warm pinkish-beige white of the skin on her cheeks. And a sweetly anxious smile that made me want to curl myself around her body so I could protect her.

And then I'd gone and *walked out of the fucking Starbucks.*

Without getting her number.

Like an *idiot.*

I didn't know everyone in Aurora Flats—it wasn't *that* small of a town—but I knew the usual faces around this area of town. Second Avenue was the main retail area in Aurora Flats, but also the main business area. Almost everyone who wasn't working in the trades or industrial shops or whatever worked nearby.

Her, though... she was new.

Which, in hindsight, I should have figured out from her saying she was going to be late for her job interview.

But in fairness, she'd turned my brain to mush.

I had to fix that before I went to work for the day, and everyone knew the best remedy for a mushy brain was fried chicken. So after stupidly leaving the coffee shop, I'd caught sight of the white food truck and jaywalked across Second Avenue to The Chick Magnet, which had no lineup because it wasn't even nine a.m. yet.

By the time my breakfast was ready a little after nine, I'd started to think of things other than the creases under the swell of Isla's belly in that skirt. I figured it was because the Chick Magnet's fried chicken was so good that even the scent of it was enough to treat brain mush. The alternative was that the crisp September air had helped lower my body temperature until I could think again, but I didn't want to credit fresh air for anything I didn't have to.

Tucking the fried chicken into my bag, I sauntered back to the office. Once I was there, I popped my head into the sales office.

"Morning," I said. "How was the Home Show?"

"Pointless," said Kyle, one of the newer sales people. "People who want sketchy budget air conditioning aren't usually going to the Home Show."

"Maybe it has something to do with the fact that you keep calling it sketchy instead of using words like 'value' or 'discounted,'" said Shawna, the senior sales manager. "*Some* of us came away with a ton of leads instead of flirting with the girl at the hot tub booth all weekend."

"And *some* of us got the number of the girl at the hot tub booth," Tony replied.

Shawna glared at him. "Three different people at that booth told you she has a boyfriend."

"Yeah, and her boyfriend told me they're in an open relationship when he picked her up last night he gave me her number." Kyle leaned back in his chair. "So who really came out on top here?"

"The girl at the hot tub booth," I said, lifting my cup and draining the last of my latte before tossing it into the garbage can. "She was getting laid no matter what."

Shawna rolled her eyes, then frowned. "Wait, *he* gave you her number? Her boyfriend?"

"Yeah," Kyle said. "Her hands were otherwise occupied at the time. As was her mouth. And she didn't stop sucking when he knocked on my car window, so—"

I snorted as Shawna let out a disgusted groan.

"You're awful. *Awful*, Kyle."

"Hey, neither of them left until I repaid the favour. I'm not that bad."

"I swear to God, I'm going to HR about you," Shawna muttered.

"Paulette would need to hire an HR team for that," I said. "So you're safe indefinitely, considering she won't even replace the customer service team."

"Wouldn't."

I jumped at the sound of Ivan's voice as he came up behind me, shooting a glare in his direction as some of my latte sloshed out of the lid. "What?"

"She *wouldn't* replace the customer service team," he repeated.

"Thanks for the non-consensual grammar lesson, nerd," I said. "You're such an *accountant*."

"It's not a grammar lesson. She hired someone."

I stared at him. "Seriously?"

"Mm-hmm. Started this morning. Though, I'm not holding my breath on how long she'll last, considering she thought she was coming in for a job interview. But you're supposed to be training her."

It was a rare occasion that I rushed to work, even when I was late.

Don't get your hopes up, part of me was screaming as I bolted towards my cubicle. It's a coincidence. Plenty of people are starting new jobs today, probably. Just because Paulette finally hired someone doesn't mean—

"—when she drags her ass in here, she'll show you how to get the phones back up each month," Paulette said as I moved towards my desk. "Once you know how to do that, I can finally get her—"

"—promoted to the head of the support team too, since I'm also the only person who knows how to fix the BTX-C line of air conditioners?" I interrupted loudly.

Paulette's head swivelled towards mine at the same time as the person sitting in the cubicle directly across from mine.

A person with a familiar head of curly blonde hair capped with a pork-pie hat, her round eyes even wider than they'd been that morning, and her lips parted in surprise.

Coincidence? Maybe.

But maybe Isla sitting there was fate.

Chapter Seven

Fried Chicken Cleanse

Isla

THIS WAS ONE OF the weirdest days in memory.

And considering I'd recently rented an apartment beneath a guy who pissed off the balcony after running away from everything I knew, that was saying something.

It was weird enough that I'd walked into Air-U-Need's office expecting to be taken into an office or maybe a boardroom and interviewed, only to be informed I was now head of the customer service team.

But now she was here.

The girl from the coffee shop.

Ellie.

"About time," the grey-haired woman said, her voice dripping with unimpressed vitriol. "Add this as another reason to the list."

"What list, Paulette?" Ellie asked, setting her purse on her chair and shrugging off her canvas jacket. "The list of reasons I'm Employee of the Month?"

"You think I'm joking, huh?" Paulette—thank God someone had finally said her name, because she'd definitely never introduced herself and it had already been too late for me to ask—straightened up, glaring at Ellie with an icy look that would have had me trembling, but Ellie met her eyes confidently. "You think you're indispensable? You think it's okay to be disrespectful and... and a thief?"

"A thief?" Ellie repeated. "What did I steal?"

"Time!" Paulette slapped my desk, making me jump. "You expect to get paid for being late, you expect to get paid for the time this conversation is taking, you expect I won't kick your ass to the curb? It's been years of this, Burns. I've had enough."

"What are you saying?" she asked.

"I'm saying I've had enough. Just because you're one of the most senior employees doesn't mean you get special treatment." She drew herself up to her full height, which barely reached Ellie's shoulders. "You're fired."

Silence.

Painful, sickening, stomach-turning silence.

"I am?" Ellie asked, her voice small. "But I got stuck in traffic. There was an accident."

"An accident," she repeated. "That caused you to be twenty minutes late for work."

Ellie nodded. "On Rosa Way. The tire popped off one of the cars, so it couldn't even be moved, and it was blocking Jeffords Court. Which is a cul-de-sac and, as you know from my employee file, where I live."

"Is that so?" Paulette asked.

I wasn't sure why she was so skeptical. The lie flowed from Ellie's lips so smoothly that I was convinced she was telling the truth, and I *knew* she was making it all up.

"I was already on my way to work because I wanted to get here bright and early," Ellie continued. "But I witnessed it, which meant I had to stay there and the RCMP wanted me to sign a bunch of things. It was horrible and I'm having such a bad day already. Can't you just fire me tomorrow instead?"

"You expect me to believe there was an accident?" Paulette said.

"Actually, I heard about that, too."

The words came out without thinking. I almost didn't realize I'd spoken until Paulette and Ellie both looked at me. For a moment, I froze, as though by not moving I would disappear and escape from Paulette's harsh, accusatory eyes, but... well. That doesn't happen in real life.

Instead, I glanced from one to the other, then cleared my throat. "My friend lives near there and she, um, texted me. This morning."

She looked at me for a long, harrowing moment, then at Ellie.

"Come on, Paulette," Ellie said, her voice gentle. "At least let me stay long enough to show Isla how to fix the phones. Then, if you *really* think I deserve to be fired for stopping to help someone who got into a car accident, I'll go."

Paulette's whole demeanor changed. She folded her arms, but instead of repeating that Ellie was fired, a self-satisfied smirk twisted across her lips.

"Alright," she said. "I'll tell you what, Ellie. If you can answer *one* question truthfully, I'll unfire you. And if you can't, I'll fire you tomorrow."

"Go for it," Ellie said.

"How did you know her name?"

Shit.

I didn't even dare to blink, but before I could start trying to figure out how I was going to find another job when finding this one had already been unlikely enough to consider it fate, Ellie smiled and motioned at my desk.

"You hired me because I'm detail-oriented, Paulette," she said. "It's written right there on Ella's coffee cup."

Paulette glanced at my cup, which read "Ella" in big block letters.

"You didn't say Ella," she said. "You said Isla."

Ellie looked at her skeptically. "I'm pretty sure I said Ella. But they sound pretty similar, don't they?"

Paulette pressed her lips together. "Fine. You're not fired. For now. But you're on probation again."

"Got it," Ellie said. "I won't let you down."

"Too late for that," Paulette muttered, then looked at me. "Ellie will show you anything else you need to know. If you have any questions she can't answer, figure it out yourself."

With that, she turned on a heel and stalked away. Ellie and I watched, silent until she reached the hallway and was out of sight.

"Well, congratulations on your successful job interview," Ellie said, sliding into her desk chair and digging into her purse. "And for putting your ass on the line for me on your very first day."

"I didn't know it was going to be my first day," I said.

"Either way." She grinned at me. "I appreciate it. That's the fifth time this month she's fired me. I thought she might mean it this time."

"Really?"

"Mm-hmm." She started pulling random things out and placing them on her desk. "I was late twice. And then last week she caught me sleeping under my desk. She fired me three times for that. Wait." She stopped digging through my purse and frowned. "Hmm. I guess that was the sixth time she's fired me this month."

"How many times has she fired you before?"

She started looking through her purse again. "Oh God, like five hundred. Usually for something stupid, though I'd say I deserve it maybe sixty percent of the time. Some of them were totally worth it, though. Did she tell you the fish thing?"

"Fish thing?"

"No fish in the office?"

I shook my head. "She didn't say anything about fish."

"Oh. Well, don't bring fish to the office. I got bored one day and made fish bombs. It involved tuna, marshmallows, Saran wrap, and the microwave in the break room." She grinned up at me. "Got all of us the afternoon off, though. But most of the time, she fires me for being late."

"How were you even late?" I asked. "You got your coffee right after me."

"I needed breakfast. Speaking of which—" She withdrew a foil bag from her purse that, when opened, revealed two crispy fried chicken drumsticks and two pieces of cornbread. "I'm starving."

"You're having... fried chicken," I said. "For breakfast."

Ellie's uninhibited grin showed off all her teeth. "You know how when you're a kid, you think the best part of being an adult is that no one can tell you that you can't eat just the marshmallows out of the Lucky Charms for breakfast?"

"Uh, sure."

"Totally not true." She took a bite of the drumstick in her hand. The skin was so crispy, I heard the crunch from where I sat and my mouth watered. "When you're an adult, no one can tell you that you can't have fried chicken for breakfast. You don't have to have breakfast foods at all, if you don't want to. We get so caught up in rules that we don't even realize we're still following the rules, even when we think we're rebelling."

"That's deep," I said, fascinated by watching her.

She swallowed her chicken and grinned again. "Right? Also, the fried chicken truck's gonna be done for the season soon, so I have to take every opportunity I can to have it. Especially since he only stays in Aurora Flats on Mondays and Fridays."

"It's that good?" I asked.

Instead of answering, she held out the half-eaten drumstick. I stared at it until she snorted. "Go on. I don't have cooties."

I tried to tell myself not to take it. Like, that was gross, wasn't it? There was a sane part of me that knew Ellie may, in fact, have cooties, and I wouldn't know because I'd known her for a collective total of ten minutes.

However, that part of me was easily won over by the fact she was offering me a bite of fried fucking chicken, which I loved. So without a word or another moment's hesitation, I took the drumstick from her.

Just like when she bit into it, the skin crunched as soon as it met my teeth. Flavour burst into my mouth: juicy, rich dark meat beneath crispy, herby, fried goodness, followed up by a searing punch of spice that heated my taste buds and made my lips tingle before I'd even chewed it twice.

"Holy shit," I said through the mouthful of chicken.

"Amazing, right?"

"This is the best fried chicken I've ever had in my life. And I've had a lot of fried chicken."

"And just think, you're a grown-ass adult. You could have that for breakfast every Monday and Friday, if you wanted to." She held her hand out. "Except today. Give me my chicken back."

Almost begrudgingly, I handed it back to her. She took another bite immediately.

"Maybe not every day," I said. "Not if I want to be on time for work."

Ellie's mouth turned down thoughtfully. "Fair point. I guess I'd better smarten up if you got hired to replace me. Or not. I wouldn't say no to a few months of that sweet, sweet employment insurance money."

A twinge of something blue played in my chest. "You're on the customer service team, too?"

She shook her head. "God no. I'm the scheduling coordinator. And sometimes the customer retention team. And I occasionally moonlight on the support team because when Jin—the old support team—finally had a breakdown, I had to take over and learned to fix a bunch of stuff. But then we hired Samantha to be the new support team, so I trained her how to do everything. Except how to fix the BTX-C line. Gotta have *some* job security, you know. Even if this is the worst job in the world."

My mind was swirling trying to keep up with her. "The... why do you keep calling one person a 'team'?"

"Paulette says it's more impressive if it sounds like we have a team for everything," she said, still chewing. "Other than the sales team, which actually does have more than one person. S'where the money is, right? But if we say all the departments are a 'team,' then people won't suspect we're less effective than a bunch of circus monkeys doing tricks for peanuts. 'Specially since we can't have peanuts because of an allergy on the support team."

"Oh. So I'm—"

"The customer service team, yep." She swallowed, then took a bite of her cornbread. "And you should probably get your team started for the day. I've been doing what I can, but no one's checked that voicemail since Amyra quit. There's probably about nine thousand for you to go through."

"Right," I said faintly. "Okay. That's not unreasonable. I mean, if each voicemail takes one minute then that'll only take like... what, a month to get through?"

"Only a month? You might be the most efficient person we've ever had on the customer service team. Don't let Paulette get wind of that. She'll realize how badly the rest of us are slacking and might actually expect us to do some work around here."

I twisted my mouth to the side. "Hmm. Seems like I'm doing a lot of covering for you already."

My deadpan tone might have been too convincing. For a moment, Ellie looked uncertain, but when I glanced up and met her eye, she realized I was joking.

"Ah, come on, newbie," she said. "Be cool."

"I'll have you know I am the opposite of cool."

She smirked. "I mean, yeah, you're pretty hot, but what does that have to do with the conversation?"

Surprised, I burst out laughing. "I dunno if I'd describe myself as *hot*, really, but thank you."

Rolling her eyes, she ate more of her cornbread. "Come on. Look at you, in that hat? Gorgeous. You better not be the kind of coworker who's gonna talk to me about Botox or doing celery cleanses or something. I might have to put fish bombs in the microwave again if you do."

"I don't think I've ever talked about celery before."

"Thank God. So you're cool? You'll lie to our boss for me and put the bare amount of effort in so the rest of us look good?"

"Maybe my coolness can be bought. For a price."

Ellie raised her eyebrows, intrigue sparkling in her eyes. "What's that?"

I tilted my head towards the empty foil packet on her desk. "Fried chicken for breakfast. I like it extra crispy."

"A steep price, but a worthy one. Cornbread, too?"

"No thanks. I'm doing a fried chicken cleanse."

She burst out laughing, shaking her head as she ate the last of her cornbread. "You know, Isla, I think we're about to become best friends."

Chapter Eight
That Never Stopped You Before

Ellie

"This was a terrible idea," Jayce muttered.

"Shut up, it was not," I said.

A sigh so annoyed that it blew a few strands of hair back from my forehead puffed out of their mouth. "*Why* did I let you talk me into doing it this weekend?"

"*Why* do you have to breathe in my face like that after eating garlic bread?"

"To ensure you're still not a vampire." They purposefully blew their next breath at me. "And as payback for convincing me Halloween weekend was the perfect time to have the very first club night at this godforsaken bar."

"Convincing you? I literally said, 'Hey, you'd make a shit-ton of money doing it this weekend because everyone loves getting drunk on Halloween,' and you said, 'I know, Ellie-phant, that's why I've decided to have an anti-costume party,' which I said was kind of weird but you were very insistent that people would love the kitsch of it all."

"You're misremembering."

"An Ellie-phant never forgets," I shot back.

The pained groan they let out was almost worth being on the receiving end of a third blast of garlic breath. "Look, it doesn't matter who said what. We're cancelling the event."

"We are *not* cancelling the event."

"No one is going to come, Ellie!" Their voice raised, but they pulled it back after a quick glance to the tables of patrons to make sure no one had heard them.

"How could you possibly know that?" I asked.

"I just have a feeling."

I lifted my eyebrows at them. "You sure that's not gas? You have been stress-eating more cheese than usual."

They flicked a look of annoyance at me. "This is going to be a disaster."

I sighed inwardly. Outwardly, I also sighed, because I was tired of the circles we'd been talking in. Drumming my hands on the table, I ventured into a slightly different circle, hoping some common sense would convince Jayce's anxiety to back the fuck off.

"If you cancel now, you'll be out the deposit you paid to the DJ," I said. "Not to mention the drag queen you'd be cancelling on, and you *know* how stoked Lady of the Lake is. She bought a whole new wig and everything."

"But if no one shows up—"

"And speaking of money you'll be out, there's the money you're going to earn from the people who show up expecting the day-after-Halloween party you've advertised." I gave them a pointed look. "Even if less people show up than you expect, they're still paying customers. What's the point in earning zero dollars when you can at least earn some dollars?"

Jayce sucked on their teeth, not looking at me.

"Is it 'cause you're scared?" I pressed.

"Of course not," they scoffed, like their attitude would cover the fact that it was a giant lie. "I'm being practical."

"Practically terrified."

They glanced towards the bar, where one of their staff members was chatting with Bruce and his crew, then sighed. "What if I end up pushing away my regulars over a one-night event? A club night with drag shows and a dance floor isn't their scene. This has been a small-town dive bar for years, and I'm upending that for something completely different."

"Bruce took a stack of flyers to hand out on his job site," I said. "Tyler has shared every single social media post you made to his own page *and* promised he wouldn't even bring any cocaine to do in the bathroom. I don't think one night is going to make a difference to your actual loyal regulars. If people want a small-town dive bar, they can go to any of the others here."

Their lips pressed into a silent line, which was more confirmation that I was right.

"Look, you *know* that people will show up. I can guarantee at least ten people are coming," I said. "I will go to every single one of our friends' houses and drag them here myself if I have to. But I *won't* because they're all fucking thrilled about the party."

Jayce finally looked up at me, one of their eyebrows arching gracefully. "Ten?"

"Kevin said he's bringing some guy from his flag football team."

They let out an unimpressed hum. "I thought you were going to say you're finally bringing your new work bestie to meet me."

If they were trying to annoy me enough to take the focus off them and their fear of success, they picked the perfect thing.

"I *will*," I said, not bothering to hide my exasperation. "Once I figure out if we're friend-friends or just work-friends."

"Does it matter? You're already in love with her either way."

"Oh my God, Jayce." I rolled my eyes hard enough to hurt. "I am not."

"You said you knew instantly that you were going to be best friends."

"Yeah? And?"

"You've never had a best friend you didn't fall in love with."

"Untrue. I never fell in love with you."

"Because we're menaces, not best friends." They sat back in their chair, clearly pleased with themself for changing the topic. "But work besties, on the other hand..."

"I am ninety-eight percent sure she's not interested," I said.

"So there's a chance."

"I am a hundred and twelve percent sure this is a bad idea."

"You've always been terrible at math," they countered.

"At no point has she ever given me *any* indication that she's even interested in women."

"That never stopped you before."

Jayce was usually very purposeful in the way they spoke. They always had been. They chose words carefully and phrased things in a way that was distinct to them. But at the end of the day, Jayce was as human as the rest of us, and sometimes things slipped past whatever section of their brain was responsible for curating their sentences.

Things like that.

As soon as they realized what they'd said, Jayce grimaced. "That didn't come out right."

"It's fine," I said. "I know you're a stickler for grammar and there should have been a 'has' in there or at the very least, an apostrophe-*s*, but I could figure out what you meant from the context."

"That's not what I meant and you know it."

"It's fine. Just drop it."

"It isn't, and I absolutely will not." Their frown deepened. "I'm sorry."

"Apology accepted. Now to get back to planning the event—"

"No."

I let out a groan loud enough that a few of the bar's customers looked our way, but Jayce didn't flinch with embarrassment the way I'd hoped.

"One of my favourite things about you is how easily you love," they said.

"Why? All it does is ruin friendships and break my heart," I said, not quite intending to sound so darkly dramatic, but not *not* intending it, either.

"It's why it's also one of my least favourite things about you," they continued. "It may have been out of line for me to remind you about Nico—"

"Nico?" I said. "I thought you were talking about Jessica."

"Of course I'm talking about our mutual childhood friend and not some random girl you went to NAIT with for two months. Why would I even remember her?"

"I don't know. Why did you?"

They ignored me. "Look, I know you don't want to think about him, but we both lost a friend over this."

I glared at the table, my eyes beginning to sting without my consent. "Thank you for reminding me it was all my fault."

"Stop hogging the credit. I was at least fifty percent at fault."

That wasn't exactly true. I mean, Jayce *did* have a surprising amount of fault in the whole situation considering it was between me and the third person in the musketeer trio we'd fallen into growing up, but there was no way it was fifty percent.

Unless they were saying Nico wasn't at least fifty percent at fault, which also might be the case.

"He was the other fifty percent," they said, as if they'd known what I was thinking. "You couldn't help your feelings."

"I could have not said anything."

Jayce reached across the table to touch my arm. "I don't regret taking the side I did. And I don't ever want to see someone hurt you like that again."

"Stop being so heartfelt about shit. It's creeping me out," I muttered, batting their hand away.

"I will. Right after I tell you that this is why I'm going to at least ensure this new best friend is worth your attention. Especially when she might stop me from poaching you as my next employee."

I stared at them. "What?"

They shrugged nonchalantly, looking at their fingernails. "I was doing some thinking."

"Hell must have frozen over for that to happen."

Their lips tightened into a smile. "You're not too bad at this whole business thing."

"This again? I don't want to start my own photography business. I told you, if it fails—"

"What if it was part-time?"

"What?"

"You do good work with marketing. And event planning." They shrugged. "I could start paying you to help me with this shit. Which would give you time to start your business."

"I don't need a handout from you."

"I'm not saying a handout. I'm saying if you're that miserable at Air-U-Need and the bar starts doing a bit better in the new year, I could justify hiring an additional person to help me with these things."

"So I'd trade one dead-end job for another?" I asked flatly.

"At least at this one you'd be able to tell your boss to fuck off without the risk of being fired." They grimaced. "The pay is comparatively shit, though."

"You almost had me there. Telling you to fuck off is a passion of mine."

"And your new bestie wouldn't work here. Which might be enough to keep you at Air-U-Need."

I sighed. "Honestly, I barely know her."

"You've worked together for over a month," Jayce said. "Considering you find out everyone's deepest, darkest secrets within hours of knowing them *and* declared you thought you'd be best friends the day you met her, I find that hard to believe."

"Well, believe it." I shrugged. "Maybe I thought wrong. Like yeah, we're friendly, I guess."

"Your boss writing you up because she thought you were playing hooky when you were really hanging out in Isla's cubicle all day hints at something more than *friendly*," they said.

"That doesn't mean I *know* her." I fidgeted with the paper in front of me. "It's like she's hiding something. Every time I think she's about to tell me more about herself, she changes the subject. And that's why I'm definitely not going to fall in love with her. You know I need *way* more communication than that."

Jayce pursed their lips as they tilted their head to the side. "True. You do get squirrely when people don't tell you things."

"Squirrely?" I repeated. "What's that supposed to mean?"

"You know." They waved their hand vaguely. "Squirrely."

"I terrorize bird feeders and shove a bunch of nuts in my mouth?"

"Exactly." They started laughing and I couldn't help the giggle that slipped out. Once I did, their grin widened. "Look, I still want to meet her. You should bring her to the event. At least invite her. Maybe she'll bring some of her other friends along."

"Yeah, maybe," I said, then looked up. "Wait, does that mean you're going to stop trying to cancel it?"

"As you said." They sighed. "I'll lose my deposits. And Lady of the Lake *will* be devastated if she bought a brand-new wig for nothing."

Chapter Nine
Ella Two

Isla

I DIDN'T KNOW HOW to make friends.

It should have been easy. Making friends was something children who don't even have a full grasp of their native language could figure out how to do. And I spent forty hours a week—though only thirty-seven-point-five of them were paid—sitting beside someone who *clearly* wanted to be my friend.

Yet over a month had rolled by without me being able to figure out how to go from "What did you get up to last night?" to "Hey, wanna hang out after work?"

It would have sucked if I was lonely and friendless because I hadn't met any potential friends in Aurora Flats, but it sucked even more because I *had*. I wanted to be Ellie's friend. I wanted to ask if she'd meet up with me at Starbucks on the weekend or go swimming with me at the rec center or only laugh at me a little before helping me learn to skate because I'd somehow made it to the age of twenty-four without ever having learned, and that was practically anti-Canadian.

But something inside wouldn't let me. And Ellie...

Well.

She had lots of other friends. She told me about them all the time. While I was pretty sure she'd agree to hang out with me outside of work if I'd asked, it wasn't like she had a reason to ask *me* to hang out with *her*. Which she didn't.

So instead, I fell into a routine about as satisfying as low-fat, low-carb, sugar-free, gluten-free, dairy-free, egg-free, flavour-free ice "cream."

I'd go to work.

I'd spend the day chatting and laughing with Ellie, occasionally answering the phone, and trying not to let my anxiety take over each time Paulette "fired" Ellie for something.

Some days after work, I'd walk down the street to Books to exchange whatever paperbacks I'd finished in the last day or two. When I brought them up to the till, I'd chuckle good-naturedly as the owner commented on how fast of a reader I was instead of telling her I was devouring a book a night because I had no friends, no hobbies, and no life outside the ones brought to me in paper and ink.

And sometimes when I got home, the guy who lived upstairs was on his balcony smoking weed and he'd shout down a hello.

But a lot of days, wishing Ellie a good night before leaving was the last time I spoke to anyone until I saw her again the next morning.

Or, if it was Friday, until I ordered breakfast at The Chick Magnet, since that was my day to pick up fried chicken for me and Ellie. She'd tried to say that she should get it on both Mondays and Fridays since she was supposed to be bribing me to cover for her at work, but I'd refused.

I'd been joking. And I didn't want her to think I was *actually* only being cool because she bought me things. And I also figured it was one less day a week she'd be late for work, which meant she was less likely to get fired, and I was less likely to lose access to the only sort-of-friend I'd made so far.

So that was why Ellie was already on the phone when I walked into the office a few minutes late that Friday morning.

"Right, uh-huh," Ellie was saying as I reached my desk. She looked up at me and rolled her eyes. "But as with the last time this happened, I don't see how that's *our* fault, Peter."

Ellie waited, staring at the computer screen in front of her as I dug out the two bags of fried chicken.

"Mmm, right," she finally said. "Unfortunately, I still cannot provide those kinds of services in exchange for your—" She paused as he said something else. "My willingness to do so matters less when you consider that whatever controls the flow of time itself probably isn't open to sex as a form of payment."

I raised my eyebrows as I slid the foil bag of fried chicken onto her desk.

"Mm-hmm, yeah," Ellie said. "Well, frankly, if I could make that kind of thing happen by selling my body, I'd be using it for far more important things than getting you an air conditioner on time." She paused. "Yeah, sure. But it's going to be a bit of a wait, so... mm-hmm, right, but she's on lunch... I know, but she was hungry... Alright, sure thing. Hold, please."

She tapped the hold button on her phone and took her headset off. Unfolding her legs from beneath her, she tilted back in her chair and stretched, her shoulders and neck releasing a soft symphony of pops and cracks before she reached forward and started opening her foil bag of chicken.

"Thanks, Ella Two," she said.

"Ella Two?" I repeated. "Why am I Ella Two?"

"Because I was here first. I'm Ella Prime. The OG Ella."

"My coffee came first, though," I said. "So doesn't that make me Ella Prime?"

"Yeah, well, I'm older than you." She stuck her tongue out at me.

"Okay," I said. "But also, I have a quick question for you."

"What's up?"

I gestured at her phone. "What the fuck was that about?"

She burst out laughing. "Which part?"

"The whole 'selling my body to whatever controls the flow of time' thing is probably what I'm most confused about."

She picked up a drumstick. "Peter keeps telling me he doesn't care who I have to fuck to get his order to him three days before he placed it. Personally, I'm kind of flattered he thinks I'm good enough in bed to make physics cease to exist."

"Oh, God."

"I know." She sighed heavily. "Ask me something else. Anything to distract me from him."

I glanced at the phone on her desk, where the red hold light was still flashing, but decided not to ask. "Uh, okay. What'd you do last night?"

"Last night was what, Thursday? Thursdays are wedding nights."

"They're what?"

Her eyes sparkled as she sat up. "Wedding shows. *Bridal Shower Makeover* first and then *World's Worst Flower Girls* and then if I'm not bawling by the end of that, I usually catch the last half of *Rodeo Brides*."

"Oh," I said. "Like, reality TV?"

"Absolutely. Wedding Thursdays aren't as good as Paranormal Wednesdays, though. Did you see the last *Haunted Hot Air Balloons*? I was so pissed about that cliffhanger."

"Uh... no," I said. "I don't watch much reality TV."

Ellie stared. "What?"

I shrugged. "It's not my thing."

"Not at all?"

I shook my head.

"Nothing? You don't even watch *Secret Rednecks*?"

"No."

"*Junkyard Boss*? *Beverly Hills Ghost Whisperers*?" She looked despondent as I kept shaking my head. "*Literal Cougars*?!"

"That's a real show?"

"I can't believe this." She flopped her head back against her chair. "None at all? Not even, like, *Doomsday Hermits* or *Dragalicious Diva Smackdown* or something?"

"Oh, I do like that one," I said. "The drag one."

Ellie heaved a huge, dramatic sigh. "Thank God. I thought I was going to have to tell you we couldn't be friends anymore."

And obviously that was a joke. I smiled like it was a joke. I pretended like I hadn't just been thinking about how I was horrible at making friends.

But Ellie didn't seem to buy my forced smile.

"What's wrong?" she asked.

"Nothing."

"I don't believe you."

I felt my cheeks turning red. "I'm just a little tired."

She nodded knowingly. "Out too late partying last night?"

"On a Thursday?"

"It was Halloween."

I gestured vaguely around us. "Yeah, but you know. Work. And I wouldn't even know where to go."

"It's a small town in Alberta," she said. "We have like, ten bars and sixteen liquor stores."

"I haven't been to any of them."

"Really?" Ellie raised her eyebrows. "Where did your friends take you out?"

"What?"

"To celebrate your new job? Everyone knows your friends take you out when you get a new job. Wait." She paused, then let out a knowing sound. "They took you into Edmonton, didn't they?"

I shook my head. Ellie looked taken aback.

"They didn't take you out at all? But that's what your entire first paycheck should go to. You know, because you're supposed to treat them since you got the job and all?" She scoffed. "Jeez, what were your friends thinking?"

"What friends?" I mumbled.

"What?"

I shook my head again and turned towards my computer. "Nothing. We should get to work."

Ellie lunged forward and grabbed my arm rest, jerking me back to face her. "Hope. Nuh-uh. No way. I *just* told you about my shameless reality TV addiction. Real reality drama is a close second. I've gotta know about this."

I couldn't bring myself to look at her. "There isn't much to know. I don't know anyone here."

"*Eehh*," she said, making a loud buzzer noise. "Wrong. You told me you're from Vancouver. How did you end up in Aurora Flats if you have no friends here?"

"I'm from Burnaby," I clarified. "And I ended up here because the rent was cheaper than in Edmonton."

"Yeah, but that raises more questions. Like how did you end up in Edmonton?" She folded her arms and gave me a significant look. "No one just comes to Edmonton. It's not like... I dunno. Like Toronto or New York or something. The weather sucks and the first thing people ask you when you move here is 'why the fuck did you move to Edmonton?'"

"I don't know," I said. "I just started driving."

"From Vancouver?"

"Burnaby."

She stretched one long leg out and nudged me with her toe. "Come on. We've been work besties for weeks and I barely know anything about you. Tell me your story, Ella Two."

My heart thudded in my chest, powerful and weak all at once. "I... I don't think I can."

Sympathy pooled in her eyes. "Why not?"

"Because I... it's..." I sighed, resigned. "I'm a bad person."

She let out a low *oooo*ing noise. "Like a murderer?"

That tore my gaze up to hers. "What?!"

Ellie grinned. "Or a hitman—hitwoman, sorry. And you're on the run from the law?"

I gaped at her for a moment. "If I was, would I even tell you?"

She snorted. "Look, you can't be all secretive and mysterious and dramatic saying you're a bad person without me thinking we're gonna have to bury a body or something."

"Oh my God." I let out a resigned sigh. "I didn't kill anyone. I just kind of... ghosted them."

"Now we're getting somewhere." She leaned forward. "Who?"

"Everyone."

"What?"

I shrugged. "Like, everyone. My mom. My sister. My job. And my boyfriend. Ex-boyfriend. I came here because it seemed like a good place to start over after we broke up."

I caught a glimpse of something flashing across Ellie's face, but not enough of it to know what it was. "You must've had a good reason."

I stared down at my hands. "Not really."

"Were you in love with his dad?"

My head shot up. "What? No!"

Ellie was grinning. "Oh, I see. His *mom*."

"Of course not. I'm not in love with any of his family. Or anyone else." I sighed. "It started when I got off work early one day and decided to surprise him with ice cream."

"Oh, *no*," she groaned, but in a breathless, sympathetic sort of way.

"Not like that!" I said, feeling my cheeks burn pink as I got more flustered. "I didn't walk in and catch him balls-deep in some other girl or something. He's a good guy."

"A good guy that you broke up with."

"I... I mean, he did nothing wrong."

"A good guy who did nothing wrong that you broke up with."

"He was... he said things I didn't want to hear."

"What was it?" Ellie pressed. "Come on, Ella Two. Just spit out the plot twist."

And I didn't know what made me do it. After all that time, I didn't know what finally made me say the words out loud to someone. It wasn't like no one had asked me why I'd done it. Nick had asked. My mom. Venus. The few friends who had reached out on social media when they found out what happened under the guise of concern, only to fade away from the conversation when I gave them the same answer I was giving everyone.

Or maybe it was just the fact that Ellie was the one asking.

Whatever it was, I finally *said* it.

"He wanted my sister."

Chapter Ten
You Can't Set A Clock By Fate

Ellie

Finally.

Finally.

It was bittersweet. Obviously I was ecstatic that I was finally getting to *know* Isla, that she finally trusted me enough to share something like that with me. Because we were meant to be friends. I could *feel* it.

But hearing the hitch in Isla's voice when she told me why she'd left Burnaby made my chest ache. The way her eyes shot down, the wrinkle that appeared on her forehead, the pain set in the tightness of her lips and the tensing of her cheeks and the squinting of her eyes...

It was bitter that earning her friendship hurt her so much.

"He wanted my sister," she blurted, and suddenly it was like every thought in her head spilled out at once. "He wanted me to be more like her. He wanted someone who wasn't boring and couldn't understand how I was even related to her or my mom because both of them do whatever they want whenever they want and I have to plan everything. And so I decided to show him just how spontaneous and adventurous I could be and left without saying anything so I could reinvent myself as some kind of quirky-cool-fun version of myself who wears hats and has meet cutes, except all that's happened is I've learned that maybe Nick was right."

Her voice broke and she put her elbows on her desk, almost slamming her face into her hands for a moment.

"Sorry," she said after a moment. "I didn't mean to vent."

"Luckily you did, since it was needed." I scooted my chair closer to her. "So, first of all, your ex is a piece of shit."

"What?"

"He said all those things to you? That's not okay."

"What? Oh, no. I overheard it."

"...while he was saying it to you?"

She shook her head before she started rambling again. "He was venting, I think. He and Marcus—his brother—were at his parents' place. Nick's a carpenter and Marcus—well, he does some kind of coordinating thing with a church or something because his family is really religious, but Nick not as much. But he's pretty handy and like, strong and stuff, so while his parents were on a weekend trip, they surprised his mom by making these built-in bookshelves for her and—"

She stopped and took a deep breath, like the air would help her scattered thoughts blow into place, and let it out once they were arranged.

"They were working at his parents' house," she said. "I thought it would be nice to surprise them with ice cream. They had some kind of saw going and music playing, so they didn't hear me come in. And I didn't go into the room right away because, like, I didn't want to distract someone if they were using a saw."

"Makes sense. I feel like the ice cream wouldn't make up for an unexpected amputation."

That got a hint of a smile from her. "Except they must've been mid-conversation because Marcus started talking right as the saw turned off. Which wouldn't usually make me stop, except he said, 'Mom thinks you're not proposing to Isla because you know it bothers her that you're living together already.' And Nick said, 'Mom needs to get it in her head that her feelings have nothing to do with me proposing to Isla.'"

That wasn't what I'd expected, which must've been clear on my face, because Isla let out a sad sort of chuckle.

"Right? So I'm standing there thinking he's getting ready to propose. And I felt sick. Like, my heart was in my stomach. I thought it was because I'd ruined the surprise for myself." She bit her lip. "But it was more that deep down I didn't want to marry him. Which was good because the next thing he said was, 'I'm not proposing to Isla because I don't know if I'm ready to be bored for the rest of my life.'"

Fuck. Those words would have hit her like a sucker punch in the gut, right where her heart had ended up. They hit me like that, and they weren't even *about* me. "Oh my God."

"Mm-hmm." Her cheeks rounded like she was smiling, but it seemed more like she was trying not to cry. "Marcus sounded shocked. He was like, 'What do you mean, bored?' And Nick said it was all the same, all the time. We'd work, eat dinner, fuck, watch HGTV. He said I made him feel like furniture."

"Because you sat on his face on the regular?"

The sadness in her voice tried to strangle her laugh as it came out, but it escaped all the same. "No. I mean, yes, but… no." She coughed. "That was another part of the problem, apparently."

"That you didn't sit on his face?"

"That he felt like I was settling for him." Her face was turning pink. "He said he felt like I didn't want him. Like, sexually. Which I still don't understand. We had sex all the time. And I… I mean, I liked it. Obviously."

"I mean, you can have sex with someone you're not attracted to and still enjoy it."

The pink on her cheeks deepened into an even darker rose. "I know, but he *is* attractive. But I guess it didn't seem like I thought so and he didn't feel, you know. *Wanted*." She sighed again. "Marcus asked him why he didn't just break up with me. Nick admitted he was being, like, a little dramatic about it all. But that part of him was also hoping I'd become more like my sister."

I frowned. "What?"

"He couldn't understand how I was related to her or my mom. Like, apparently the most exciting part of his week was visiting my mom on the weekends because she was always getting up to some kind of crazy shit. And a couple of weeks earlier we'd been visiting my mom when Venus showed up and was like"—she lowered her voice into a husky sort of monotone—"'I booked a flight to San Francisco because some friends and I want to go to this club,' and my mom was like, 'Oh that sounds fun,' and Venus was like, 'Yeah, so I'll see you tomorrow if I can get a return flight.' And then she just fucking went to San Francisco for the night."

That sounded like something I would do if I ever managed to save up the kind of money that would let me do it, but I didn't think that would be helpful to mention. "Wow."

"He said he couldn't stop thinking about that. That she just up and took off because she felt like it." She sighed again. "Nick said he was just stuck. Like, he wanted to be with me. He liked our relationship. He just wanted me to be more like Venus. Marcus did ask if he was, like, interested in her and just couldn't admit it and he said no. Even though both of them agreed she's hot."

"You're not doing much to convince me that Nick isn't a piece of shit."

"Okay, but my sister *is* objectively gorgeous," she said. "Even I can admit that."

Another point towards Isla being straight. "That doesn't mean he should say it."

"He didn't know I was listening."

"That *still* doesn't mean he should say it!"

"Fine. But he's not a bad person."

"Why are you so insistent that he's not?"

"I just… because he's not." She paused, like she was trying to sort her thoughts out again. "He was a good boyfriend ninety percent of the time. And I was a good girlfriend until I decided to do exactly what he wanted me to do and be spontaneous, except it was more out of pettiness because I realized I didn't really love him anyway."

"Wait, what?" I gaped at her. "You just said you were attracted to him."

She smiled sadly. "Love isn't necessarily about attraction. You can be with someone you're not attracted to and still love them."

"Throwing my own words back at me with a twist. I like it." I folded my arms. "So what made you realize you didn't love him?"

"You're going to laugh."

"That means nothing. I also laughed when I broke my arm as a kid because it hurt so bad. Doesn't mean I thought it was funny."

She frowned, but accepted the explanation. "Because I didn't feel like us being together was, like"—she waved a hand vaguely—"fate or whatever."

I lifted an eyebrow. "Fate?"

The pink on her face had faded, but it started rising up her neck again and she wouldn't look at me. "I know it's stupid. Venus has made that clear. But I… I like the idea of it. Of there being a person out there that I'm meant to be with, and I'll just stumble into them one day."

"What do you mean?"

She pressed her lips together. "Like, okay. When I first came here, I went to Books. And there was this book—"

"A book at Books?" I said before I could stop myself. "Revolutionary."

She took it as intended, which meant she giggled before continuing. "I saw this book at the same time this other guy did. And we kind of bumped into each other."

"*Ohhhh*," I said, drawing the word out. "And then you did the whole 'You take it, you saw it first, no I insist you take it, okay how about I take it but I get your number—'"

"'—so I can call you when I finish reading it and we can go for a coffee date—'"

"'—that lasts six hours because we clicked so hard we lost track of time and talked about everything under the sun,'" I finished, and she was smiling as she nodded. "So you want a meet cute."

"I guess, yeah. Except instead of any of that, he shoved my hand out of the way, took the book, and told me, 'You snooze, you lose.'"

I laughed. Not at her or because it was funny; it was part unintentional, part disbelief, part not knowing how to react.

Okay, and a little bit because it was funny.

But I wasn't laughing at *her*.

Luckily for me, Isla joined in again. "And there was this other guy at the Starbucks on my first day of work. I thought, like, maybe he's supposed to bump into me or something. Or our orders were supposed to get mixed up."

"Or the barista wrote a name on the cup that could be either yours or the tall and attractive dark-haired stranger who also enjoys oat milk and whipped cream?" I said.

"Yeah, exactly! If you were a guy, that would've been perfect." She grinned. "That never happened with Nick. We just met online. And I…" Her eyes flicked down. "I don't think it'll ever happen."

I scoffed, despite the explicit confirmation of Isla's straightness prickling in my chest. "Yes, it will."

"How? I'm a planner." Her voice was almost bitter. "Like Venus said, you can't plan a meet cute."

"Why not?"

She gave me an incredulous look. "Because that's not how it works."

I shrugged, tilting my head to the side to look up at the fluorescent lights above us as if regarding them would make me sound smarter. "But maybe it is. Maybe it's planned spontaneity."

"Planned spontaneity," Isla repeated. "So a total oxymoron."

"Or a mix of both." I looked back at her, blinking to get the lingering blotches that resulted from staring directly into a light source out of my eyes. "Maybe fate takes responsibility for part of it. Like, it gets you there at the right time, and finding the right place is up to you."

She stared at me in skeptical silence.

"Okay, for example." I leaned forward. "The guy at the coffee shop. Maybe you were supposed to run into him."

Her lips parted, but she still didn't say anything, so I kept talking.

"Like, maybe you *were* supposed to take a few steps to the right or something. Help fate out a little by making sure you're in the right place, which was obviously directly in the path between him and the door. He runs into you, you do the whole 'Oh no, you've ruined my sexy little skirt and I'm going to be late for work!' and he offers to wash it for you back at his house just down the street even though there aren't really any houses near the Starbucks. And since you're standing there all pantsless..." I grinned, spreading my hands out like they would finish the sentence for me. "*Voila.* A spontaneously planned meet cute."

Isla stared at my hands for a moment before looking back at me.

"Ellie," she said slowly, like the realization I was brilliant was blossoming in her mind.

"Yeah?"

"That's the stupidest thing I've ever heard."

I laughed loud enough that Paulette shouted something unintelligible from her office.

"It is not!" I said, lowering my voice so Paulette wouldn't come out and yell at us. Not that I cared, but Isla did. "Planned spontaneity describes you perfectly."

"It does not," she said. "Planning, sure. Sometimes. But Nick wasn't wrong. Yes, it sucked to hear that he thought I was boring and wished I was the opposite of myself in every way. But I'm *not* spontaneous."

"I call bullshit." I folded my arms. "What brought you to Aurora Flats?"

"I was trying to be spontaneous," she said. "But—"

"And what are you gonna do next?" I interrupted.

She blinked at me. "Um... I don't... know?"

"Exactly. You have no plan."

"It's not just about not having a plan," she said. "You can not have a plan and still live the same day over and over again. That's what I've been doing for years now. And even when I tried to change it, it was just to prove someone wrong and all I managed to do was trade one sad routine for another. I uprooted everything and what do I have to show for it? I don't even have friends here. I don't know what to *do*."

"And that's why you're here." She jumped as I suddenly rolled my chair back towards my cubicle. "Come on. Let's go."

She gaped at me. "What? Where?"

I stood up and grabbed my purse. "We're taking lunch."

"It's first thing in the morning. We can't just take lunch now."

"Says who?" I asked.

"Our boss." She looked in the general direction of Paulette's office. "Who pays us."

I rolled my eyes. "She pays us either way. Trust me. Fate brought you here for two reasons. First things first: a lesson in spontaneity. Let's go get fried chicken."

"We just had fried chicken."

"Exactly, and now it's all gone, so we need more."

She motioned at the phone on my desk. "You have someone on hold."

"So?"

She stared for a moment, but somehow, that convinced her to grab her purse and follow me, though the stricken look of shock didn't leave her face.

"What do you think is the other reason fate brought me here?" she finally asked as we walked towards the exit.

"For us to be best friends," I replied.

A reluctant laugh slipped from her lips. "How can we be best friends? We've known each other for a month. There are still voicemails on the phone older than our friendship."

I looped my arm through hers, which was harder than expected because she was shorter than I'd thought, but I kept it there anyway.

"You can't set a clock by fate, Isla," I said. "I told you on day one that we were meant to be best friends. And as your best friend, I completely dropped the ball on taking you out to celebrate your new job. So we're going out tonight, and we're gonna force fate to give you a meet cute."

Chapter Eleven

Magic Hat

Isla

"STOP PLAYING WITH IT!" Ellie said as I adjusted my skirt. "Isla I-Don't-Know-Your-Middle-Name Monroe—"

"It's Athena," I said.

"Athena?" she repeated.

"Yeah. It's my mom's name."

"And your sister is Venus? Is your dad Zeus or something?"

I laughed. "No. David. He picked my name and Mom picked Venus's."

"Well, Isla Athena Monroe, stop messing with that outfit. It's perfect as it is."

I glanced at myself, feeling exposed. Probably because I'd just hung my coat up in the pseudo-coat-check and was now standing there in the outfit Ellie had picked for me: my pork-pie hat, my short plaid skirt, and a black bra.

Just a black bra.

Granted, it was longer than an average bra. Not quite a bustier, but it covered my ribcage and had boning sewn into the satin fabric. And while it plunged to the absolute base of my cleavage, a stretch of sheer lace between the cups offered some semblance of coverage.

How I'd let Ellie talk me into wearing this, I didn't know.

Well, no. That was a lie. I knew how it had happened; I'd given her my address so she could pick me up after she insisted on taking me out to belatedly celebrate my new job and she'd realized I lived within what she called stumbling distance of the place she wanted to take me to. So she went home after work, grabbed some things, then come to my place so we could get ready together. And when

I'd asked her what kind of outfit I should wear, she'd answered by flinging my closet open and rifling through my wardrobe.

So I knew how it had happened. What I didn't know was *why* I let her talk me into it.

Actually, that was a lie, too. She'd talked me into it because, plain and simple and with no real justification, Ellie was the gag to my voice of reason.

Ellie was the metaphorical ski-mask-clad captor of that voice. Ellie had taken my voice of reason, bound it to a chair with handcuffs fashioned out of the scrunchies she'd found in my bedroom, and infected it with a case of Stockholm Syndrome strong enough to convince me to venture out in public wearing a bra as a shirt.

In November.

In *Alberta*.

"My tits are going to fall out by the end of the night," I said as Ellie hung up her coat.

"Like I said, it's perfect." She grinned. "You're almost making it too easy for fate."

"You seem confident this whole 'forced meet cutes' thing is gonna work," I said.

"Of course I am. Look at us." She slung her arm around my shoulder. "A drop-dead-gorgeous and dangerously curvy lady in a magic hat and a chaos gremlin using a low-cut top and a push-up bra to hide the fact that she's a bisexual disaster ready to hack the soulmate system? Fate won't know what hit it. So it had *better* be here tonight."

And glancing around, I had to admit that given how packed it was, it seemed like our chances were good.

The Flat Tire was bigger than I'd thought it would be based on Ellie's description. She'd described it almost like a dive bar, the kind with a lot of after-work regulars who came in still wearing their workboots and coveralls. And maybe it was most of the time, but that night, it was...

Well…

I didn't quite know what it was.

It wasn't a nightclub, but it was trying to be. The music thundered in my chest and colourful flashing lights illuminated a dance floor, though no one was on it yet. Tables and chairs were set up around the dance floor like it was a stage. And of course, parts of it still seemed like a typical small-town bar; barstools surrounded a worn but gleaming counter and there were booths with high backs and overstuffed benches.

"Good evening, asshole," someone said from behind us.

Shocked, I looked at Ellie, but she was already laughing. I turned to see a person about the same height she was, though they weren't quite as slim and had warm olive-toned skin. Beneath thick eyebrows were dark brown eyes highlighted by shimmery gold eyeshadow and long, curled lashes. At first glance, they appeared to have a slit cut into their left eyebrow, but a closer look revealed it was actually a deep scar that cut across their brow bone. Their hair was thick and dark, shaved on the sides with longer curls left on top. I didn't know much about designer clothes—the plaid skirt I wore was probably the only designer piece I'd ever own because being plus-size, it wasn't a space especially inclusive to me—but the black dress shirt they wore and the dress pants they were tucked into both looked expensive.

"Is that how you talk to your customers?" Ellie asked, chuckling.

"Not the ones who pay to be here," the person replied.

"I paid for my ticket," Ellie said, insulted.

"Well, you're also an asshole." The person turned to me. "I'm Jayce, by the way, since Ellie-Bean doesn't seem to have a polite bone in her body."

"I'm Isla," I said, extending my hand to shake theirs.

"The infamous work bestie," they said.

"The one and only," Ellie said cheerfully.

"I've heard so much about you," Jayce said.

"You have?" I asked, surprised.

"Of course," they said. "Ellie's been yammering about you for weeks and keeps ditching me for our usual lunchtime excursions to the Chick Magnet."

"You've been invited every time," Ellie said, rolling her eyes.

"Yes, well, you keep taking lunch during your actual lunch hour, which is one of the few busy times at this illustrious establishment you find yourself in now," Jayce said. "But it's no matter. Between you and me, I'm glad there's someone else out there who's willing to put up with you."

"You're such a jackass," Ellie said, laughing. "Here I am, bringing you brand new customers to your very first big event, and you're insulting me?"

"Of course," they said, looking at me with a gleam of laughter in their eye. "She's going to make people think this is where all the pretty girls hang out, and I'll have to send them away disappointed next time when they realize you're the only one here." Ellie cackled even as they patted her on the shoulder. "I have to go check on the queens. Lady forgot half her makeup kit at home and is in a panic. Try not to agree to any international trips with people who would definitely sell you to fund their cocaine habit like you usually do, would you?"

"Does that happen often?" I asked, concerned, but Jayce had already started walking away.

"Just once, and I don't think Tyler would've *actually* sold me for drugs," Ellie said. "Anyway, that's Jayce. Be prepared for them to hype you up and insult the very fiber of your being in the same breath."

"Fair. How do you know them?"

"They're my childhood best friend."

"They're not your best friend now?"

She snorted, looping her arm through mine. "We're more like siblings. I think. Neither of us have any actual siblings so we're kind of making it all up."

"Everything's just made up if you think about it," I said.

"That was deep. And you haven't even had a drink yet." She hooked her arm through mine. "Which we should change immediately."

She took me over to the bar and we ordered a couple of cocktails. Once they were in hand, Ellie led me to a large table in the corner of the bar with two empty seats at it. She went around the table, shouting introductions one-by-one.

"—and this is Maximillian von Schnouttraupe," Ellie finally said, gesturing at the final person, a man with a black trilby hat and an oddly familiar face. "He's a professional online dating profile ghostwriter and boasts an incredible eighty-six percent success rate in helping people find the closest thing to a soulmate their dating app of choice has to offer. He also has the only permit in Alberta to keep a quokka as an exotic pet."

Before I could respond, the guy sitting beside "Maximillian" laughed and slapped him on the back. "Sorry. I should've warned you about Ellie."

Ellie cackled. "Yeah, I've never seen him before in my life."

"This is Corbin," the other man said. "He's a friend of mine from flag football."

"Nice to meet you!" Ellie hollered over the music, then gestured at me. "This is Isla. Like 'eyelash' without the 'sh'."

"Nice hat," I said, gesturing at the black trilby perched on his head.

"Thanks," he said.

There was an awkward pause, then the guy who'd introduced him elbowed him and said something I couldn't hear. Corbin glanced up at me. "Oh. I mean, uh. Yours too."

"Thanks." I smiled. "Maybe I can sit with you so us newbies can get to know each other?"

"Uh... sure," he said.

Ellie looked from him to me, then groaned. "Already?! It's gotta be the hat, Isla."

"What's the hat?" Corbin asked.

"It's a magic hat," Ellie said, then reached over and yoinked it off my head. "Let me try it."

"What is she *talking* about?" Corbin asked, turning to me with bewilderment on his face.

"I know it sounds silly, but it's my lucky hat," I explained. "I just, like, randomly got a job while I was wearing it."

"Yeah? How'd that happen?" he asked.

"I was at Books the other day—"

"You like to read?" he interrupted.

"Yeah. You?"

He nodded. "What's your favourite book?"

I laughed. "Funnily enough, it makes an appearance in the lucky hat story, too."

"Yeah?" He sounded mildly interested. "How so?"

"I saw a copy while I was at Books. Except some asshole saw it at the same time as me." I rolled my eyes. "And instead of being, like, nice about it or whatever, he goes"—I twisted my voice into a nasally, mocking voice—"'You snooze, you lose, lady' and grabbed it away from me."

Corbin didn't say anything.

"But it kind of worked out," I continued. "When I asked the owner if they were hiring, there was this other woman in the store who heard me and offered me a job. Who knows if she would've been there if he'd let me take the book."

"Mmm," he said. "Well, I didn't think *The Hitchhiker's Guide to the Galaxy* was that good. Definitely not good enough to call someone an asshole."

I stared at him, my stomach filling with the dreadful sensation of hoping there was *some* other explanation. "How did you know what book it was?"

Corbin looked at me incredulously. "Really? I didn't think you'd be too stupid to put two and two together."

"Hey!" Ellie said from across the table, her voice dark. "Fuck you."

"Fuck you," Corbin spat back.

"Whoa," one of the other people at the table said. "Dude, what the fuck?"

"He called Isla stupid when she was *clearly* just hoping he wasn't the same asshole from the bookstore," Ellie said.

"I didn't call her stupid for that," Corbin said. "I called her stupid because she is."

"Man, stop it," the guy who'd brought Corbin said, looking at him with a disgusted sort of bewilderment. "I didn't bring you here so you could be a dick to my friends."

"She called me an asshole," Corbin whined.

"Probably because you were an asshole to her," Ellie said. "Maybe try being nicer to strangers."

"Maybe she should try being less of a bitch," Corbin said.

"Dude, what the *fuck*?!" said one of the other guys at the table, but it didn't matter. Ellie was on her feet and behind Corbin's chair before he'd even finished speaking. She yanked the back of it, pulling him away from the table, and I felt all the blood drain out of my face.

"Ellie, don't!" It came out like a squeak.

"It's time for him to leave," Ellie said. "I'm just being helpful."

"Please tell me you're not the one starting shit, Ellie."

Everyone stopped as Jayce appeared, almost out of nowhere. Their arms were crossed across their chest.

"She absolutely did," Corbin said, his voice taking on the distinct nasal tone I remembered from the bookstore. "She grabbed my chair!"

"He called Isla a bitch," Ellie said.

Jayce didn't so much as hesitate. "Get out."

Corbin snickered.

"That was directed at you, if that wasn't clear," Jayce said, glaring at Corbin.

"You're kicking me out when *she's* the one who grabbed me?" Corbin said.

"You have five seconds to stand on your own before Anthony does it for you," Jayce said. "Get out of my bar. Now."

Corbin scoffed. "Who's Anthony?"

"That would be me."

A shadow fell over the table. Literally. The figure that came up behind Jayce was nearly a foot taller than them, standing about six-foot-eight in heels. And that was before the towering blonde wig was added in.

"Although, I usually go by Lady of the Lake when I look like this," the drag queen continued. "Fun facts about me: I'm a Libra, my favourite colour is Pedro Pascal's nipples, and I go to the gym five days a week." She nearly knocked Ellie over as she walked up to Corbin. "You know, I bet I could carry this whole chair out, just like this."

Corbin grumbled and whined and complained, but I had no idea what he said since he was facing the other direction and storming away while he did it. I wasn't sure if everyone at the table was staring at him as he left, but I was, hoping that no one could see how red I was.

"Well, Jayce, dear," Lady of the Lake said, breaking the silence. "I hope you know I don't usually moonlight as both entertainment *and* security. I should be charging you double."

"You should be." Jayce pursed their lips. "I didn't think I'd need to hire a bouncer, but I guess I know for next time. Send me an updated invoice after tonight."

Lady of the Lake put a thick arm around Jayce's comparatively delicate shoulders. "I'll let it slide this time. You're lucky you're cute. And that you pay well. And that I personally find it hilarious to threaten emasculation upon sad little men who are mean to gorgeous glammed up girlies." She turned to me, raising her eyebrows. "You okay, by the way?"

"I'm fine," I said quickly, but it didn't stop my face from burning even more. "Thank you."

"There's no need to thank me," Lady said. "You can just tip me double whatever you originally planned."

It made me laugh, which was good because Ellie laughed, too, and some of the awkwardness disappeared from around the table.

"I appreciate you backing me up as well," Jayce said. "Are you ready for your set now or do you want a bit more time to get ready?"

"This is as good as it's getting, honey," Lady said. "Usually I add more glitter when I'm doing the bar thing, but I'm so used to doing looks for classes that I forgot half my kit. I didn't even bring anything to collect tips."

"You can use my hat," I said.

Both of them looked at me.

"It's a lucky hat," I added nervously, and suddenly my mouth wouldn't stop. "So maybe it'll get you even more tips than usual. It's not like it's doing me any good tonight. But it has before, like I was saying about the whole thing where it got me a job. Except you weren't here for that. But maybe it's, like, a job-getting lucky hat or something. Or it doesn't work on other people who have hats. But whatever it is, if it's not working for me, someone else might as well try to get lucky."

"Isla, hon," Lady said. "You're rambling. But more concerningly, you're not wearing a hat."

Ellie burst out laughing and motioned at herself. "It's *this* hat."

Lady's painted lips twitched. "Well, you've got me figured out. I can't say no to a silly little prop for my silly little set." Lady reached forward—well, *down* and forward—and plucked my hat from Ellie's head, setting it on her own and tilting the brim over her face. "And this way, you can't tell I forgot my eyeshadow palette and made do with a blush-and-contour pallette."

I didn't know if the hat was really lucky. And if it was, I didn't know if it made her perform better than usual or if people were just especially generous that night.

But when Lady pulled me out of my chair during her set with a request to run around and pick up the cash she'd collected from various patrons over the course of the night, I returned to her with a pork pie hat almost overflowing with the fives and tens and even a few twenties stuffed in it.

Chapter Twelve

Spoonin' Time

Ellie

I**T WAS A GOOD** thing I didn't have a penis.

There were a multitude of reasons for that. One was the ADHD side of me. I had a hard enough time focusing on things without having to divide my attention span between two heads. I mean, it was bad enough getting distracted by my own boobs—which happened a lot, and anyone with boobs who said otherwise had to be lying because come *on*, they were great—and those were just *there* most of the time. I couldn't imagine a world where I was constantly distracted by a dangling protrusion hard-wired to be a sort of hot-people-radar-stick.

There were various other reasons I was happy with the current state of my genitals, but the most relevant of them currently was that if I did have a penis, I would have woken up with it jabbing into my best friend's unfairly perfect butt, and *that* would have been awkward.

Especially considering how good waking up that morning felt. In the mornings, I wasn't so much of a person as I was a loose conglomerate of fogginess, yawns, and pre-caffeinated aggravation. Even on my best days, I rarely rolled out of bed feeling anything less than irritated at the existence of the world in general.

But that morning, my slow wakeup was accompanied by a tingling feeling that started in my core, gently insisting that I pay attention to the soft and cozy and enticing thing my body was curled around. A smile started to spread on my lips before my eyes had even opened, and I felt my nipples hardening against the warm weight of what I was holding onto.

That smile froze when I remembered I was in Isla's bed and realized that the thing—well, *person*, obviously—turning me on was the best friend I was spooning.

So if I did have a penis, it would have been nestled right up against her ass crack. Which would have been a disaster, considering I'd told Jayce I wasn't going to fall for my best friend and also, Isla was straight.

I had no idea when we ended up like this. Not because I was so drunk that I blacked out or something. I remembered stumbling back to Isla's place at the end of the night, and I remembered her drunkenly attempting to pick me up by putting me over her shoulder—which she failed at because she was laughing too hard—when I tried to say goodnight.

"You can't drive!" she'd almost screamed.

"Of course not," I'd said. "I'm just gonna walk home."

"It's too far. You drove over here and we got ready here 'cause it's too far from your house."

"It's not *too* far. I'll be fine."

"No!" She'd stomped her foot, nearly losing her balance as her heel clacked against the sidewalk. "You can't walk home by yourself in the dark. 'S too dangerous."

"It's Aurora Flats. The biggest danger here is me tripping on a scooter some kid leaves on the sidewalk and falling face first into a still-lit cigarette butt some asshole tossed out the window of his four-by-four pickup. Or getting eaten by a coyote."

"Neither of those are good options!" She grabbed my hand and dragged me towards the door. "You're staying here. You can stay in the guest room."

"Okay, fine," I'd said, following her inside. It wasn't until we were halfway up the stairs that I frowned. "Wait. You don't have a guest room."

"Yeah I do. We just use it to store Nick's snowboarding stuff most of the—" She'd stopped suddenly, her eyes going round. "Oh my God. I forgot where I live. I don't have a guest room. I don't even have a Nick!"

Then she started laughing so hard she had to grab the railing and crouch down so she didn't tumble back down the stairs, and I started laughing because she was laughing, and we had to stop for a few minutes before we could resume stumbling up the stairs.

"Don't worry," I'd said. "You're being nice and letting me invite myself to stay over. I'll make do with wherever I can sleep. Even if that means sleeping by myself in your bed while you insist on taking the couch because that's what good hosts do."

"I hope you're prepared to be disappointed by my hosting abilities."

"Are we sharing a bed, then?"

We'd reached her apartment door and she'd started digging her keys out, but couldn't seem to find them in her purse. "Yeah. Why wouldn't we?"

Part of me cringed and I couldn't look at her. "I mean, you know I like women a little, I assume."

"Oh," she'd said, her voice unnaturally slow. "Well, okay."

My stomach had knotted. "Is that a problem?"

"There they are." She'd pulled her keys out of her purse. "Uh, what problem?"

"I can sleep on your couch, but also, if it *is* something you have a problem with, that's a little bigger than figuring out where to sleep."

"Why would you sleep on my couch?" she'd asked, fumbling with her keys.

"If you don't want to share a bed with me."

She managed to get the door unlocked and opened it. "I mean, if you can't sleep without it, I don't mind doing it for you. What are friends for, right?"

I'd gaped at her.

Like, full on, jaw-to-the-floor-but-not-really-because-I-wasn't-that-short *gaped* at her. She hadn't noticed until we were both inside her apartment and she'd closed the door behind me.

"What?" she'd asked, looking confused.

"Do you—Why would—Did I... did..." I'd taken a deep breath. "Not that I don't appreciate the offer, but you see why it's kind of, uh... *shocking*, right?"

"Well, I don't think any of my other friends asked me before, but it doesn't bother me," she'd said. "Do you have a preference or is it sort of an 'it-depends' thing? I don't mind either, but I do like a turn as little spoon once in a while."

I'd stared at her, then blinked. "What do you think I said?"

"What?"

"What do you think I said after I asked if we were sharing a bed?"

She'd stared back. "Uh... 'If it changes your decision, I'm little spoon'?"

"Um, no. I said, 'You know I like women a little, I assume?'"

"Oh. Well, yeah, I obviously know that." She'd tilted her head to the side. "But that does make more sense than what I thought I heard. So you *don't* want to spoon?"

I couldn't quite explain the intense feeling that washed over me in that moment. Relief, maybe, but also something like gratitude that Isla thought I asked her to spoon with me and just fucking went with it. "Whoa now. Don't put those words in my mouth. I'm not a psychopath. But I also don't need you to spoon me to go to sleep."

"Okay," she'd said. "We can take turns."

Then she'd half-skipped off to her bedroom. When I got there, she'd tossed one of her t-shirts at me to sleep in, apologized for not having pyjama pants that I wouldn't be swimming in, and crawled into bed with her makeup still on. I'd brought her a wipe from the bathroom and made her wipe her face off before crawling in next to her.

"Alright," she'd mumbled. "Spoonin' time."

She'd curled up behind me, arms going around my waist. I'd frozen in surprise for a moment, then relaxed, then fell asleep to the steady rhythm of her breathing.

And that was the last thing I remembered. So *how*, exactly, I woke up the next morning on my other side with my arms around Isla and my nose buried in her soft, curly hair, and my panties starting to get uncomfortably and unwelcomingly damp, I had no fucking idea.

It was ridiculous. Ridiculous, and embarrassing, and I was insanely grateful Isla would never have to know about it. Like, this wasn't who I was. I could control myself around people I was attracted to. It wasn't like I couldn't go to the beach or the locker room at the gym without making it all sexual or something. I'd shared beds with tons of friends and never woken up craving them the way I was craving Isla.

I had to get out of there.

Slowly, I started to unravel myself from Isla. Taking my arms back was easy enough, but both of us had our legs curled up and her feet were resting against my shins. So of course, as I tried to scoot back so I could straighten my legs, I woke her up.

"Wha' time is it?" she mumbled.

"Sorry," I whispered, even though it was stupid because no one was asleep. "Didn't mean to wake you up."

"That's not a time."

A laugh slipped out. "No idea. I don't know where my phone is. But given my usual sleeping patterns, I'll say around eleven?"

"Eleven?" She shot up so suddenly that I almost tumbled backwards out of bed. "In the *morning*?!"

"Well, considering we got back here at, like, two... yeah." I sat up. "Do you have plans?"

"No. That's just…" She trailed off, shaking her head. "I haven't slept that long or that well in… well, years, I think. I was expecting to be insanely hungover, but I feel great, actually."

"The magic of spooning," I said. Either that or she was still drunk, but I didn't actually think that was the case.

"Must have been." She yawned and stretched. I didn't let myself look at her while she did.

Since she'd already told me she didn't have plans that day and I didn't have plans in general because of who I was as a person, I decided I was going to make us breakfast as a thank you for letting me stay over while Isla took a shower. Then I'd let her get on with whatever she actually wanted to do that day. I borrowed one of her hoodies, which was a terrible idea because it was soft and smelled good and reminded me of being held by her when all I wanted to do was forget it so I could stop leering after my best friend, and went to the kitchen.

By the time she got out of the shower, I'd managed to remind my body that we weren't looking at Isla like that and calmed myself down, burned half a batch of pancakes because she had barely any counter space in her kitchen, and changed my mind about not spending the day with her.

"Does the backseat of your car flip down?" I asked as she wandered into the kitchen, her skin glowing.

"Those look great," she said, eyeing the pancakes I was flipping. "And yes. Why?"

"Because mine doesn't and you need an island."

"Okay," she said. "Private? Tropical?"

"Kitchen." I patted the back of the pancake with the spatula like it was a good little pancake. "We're going to IKEA."

I thought she'd protest because Isla was the kind of person who liked to plan and research and plan some more before doing or purchasing anything, but she agreed to it far more eagerly than I'd expected. After we ate our pancakes—the unburned ones being not too terrible, if I did say so myself—I drove home with Isla tailing me in her car so I could change, then hopped into the passenger seat.

"Also, the Chick Magnet is at a farmer's market near there," Isla said like we'd been mid-conversation as I sat down. "So we can stop for fried chicken. And, like, vegetables, I guess, if we want to be adults about it."

"How'd you find that out?"

She held up her phone. "Google."

"I adore you."

She grinned, her cheeks rounded and pink. "I adore you, too."

God, I thought as she slung her arm around the back of my seat so she could back down the driveway, whoever we eventually forced a meet cute with for her better treat her right.

Chapter Thirteen

Chicken?

Isla

I DIDN'T NEED AN island for my kitchen.

Between the counters and my table, there was more than enough space for me to cook for myself. There *wasn't* space for an entire piece of furniture I had nowhere to store.

But I'd spent most of my time in the shower trying to think of ways to ask Ellie if we could keep hanging out without sounding desperate and needy. So when she was the one who suggested going to IKEA, I jumped on it.

Plus, despite living fairly close to the city—relatively speaking, of course, since it was still about an hour away—I hadn't spent much time in Edmonton. I wasn't a big shopper, but the IKEA was around a *ton* of stores that Aurora Flats definitely wasn't big enough to justify. My plan was to "notice" another place I wanted to stop once we got there and ask Ellie if that was okay.

I mean, I could have asked her ahead of time. She would've said yes, probably. But I was pretty sure it was the "probably" part of the whole thing that was sending a surge of nervous butterflies fluttering through my stomach.

I wasn't used to feeling so insecure. It was a side effect of being a planner. Before I left Burnaby, I'd been confident in everything I did because there was never any variation, which was how I liked it. If Nick and I were going shopping together, I would tell him exactly what stores I wanted to visit and how long I expected each stop to take, and he'd tell me where he wanted to go and I'd fit it into the internal schedule I was making for us. I'd know when we needed to have lunch so we'd be hungry again around dinner and if we would need to stop for snacks and where we could get a mid-afternoon energy drink because Nick usually got grumpy around three-thirty if we were going to be out all day.

If I was shopping with Venus or my mom, I knew to block off the whole day because there was always one more store they wanted to visit, and suddenly we were at the McArthurGlen Outlets near the airport when we'd only planned to go to the Metropolis at Metrotown. And I made sure I had a granola bar in my purse for when Venus would get hangry because she probably didn't eat enough at breakfast and an extra lip balm that I didn't mind potentially losing because my mom would inevitably forget hers and there was a fifty-fifty chance she'd forget to give mine back after borrowing it.

I had no idea where Ellie and I were going to end up that day or how long it would take. There were no granola bars in my purse. I didn't even know where we could stop for coffee.

And for one of the first times in my life, I liked that.

I liked it right up until we were wandering around the IKEA showroom and Ellie came to a sudden stop in the mattress area.

"Isla," she said. "Do you feel it?"

"Feel what?" I asked.

Her eyes sparkled as her lips curled up into a tight, excited smile. "It's here."

"*What's* here?"

Her voice lowered dramatically. "Fate."

I blinked at her a couple of times, which was apparently not the reaction she was looking for.

"*Fate*," she said again, drawing the word out with a mystical-sounding breath. "We have a meet cute opportunity."

"We're still doing that?" I asked skeptically.

She looked offended. "Why wouldn't we?"

"The spectacular failure that was last night's attempt."

Ellie scoffed. "That doesn't count at *all*! What were you gonna tell your grandkids? 'Oh, it was a meet cute for the ages. We met at a bar, but we were both wearing *hats*!'"

I laughed in spite of myself. "You were pretty damn certain last night that it was a meet cute caused by my so-called lucky hat."

"And I was wrong. But *this* could be the moment."

"What could?"

She motioned as subtly as she could, which was not very subtly because she'd stolen the hoodie I'd loaned her and the significantly oversized sleeve flapped as she gestured at a curly-haired man wandering amongst the mattresses. He was completely oblivious to us, probably because he was on the other side of the store and had no reason to suspect we were staring at him. Reaching down, he pressed on the mattress next to him, then sat on it and bounced a few times before swinging his legs up onto the bed and flopping onto his back.

"He's *cute*," she whispered loudly. "And he's buying a bed, so you know what that means."

"That he probably lives on his own and is fiscally responsible?"

She looked at me like I'd grown a third boob: like she thought I was weird, but she was also slightly intrigued. "No. That he needs to break it in." She closed her hands into fists and swung her arms back as she pumped her hips forward. "And if you meet-cute him fast enough, you could probably sway his opinion towards whatever bed you think is most comfortable."

I stifled another laugh. "Funny, but no way."

"Why not?!"

"Because I—" I stopped, not sure what to say.

"See? No good reason." She put a hand around my back and lightly shoved me forward. "Come on. All you need to do is flop down on the bed next to him and pretend you thought he was the friend you were with. Go test fate."

I hesitated. Thankfully, Ellie didn't shove me again.

"What's wrong?" she asked.

"I just... I think we were being silly about all this," I said. "All that's gonna happen is me getting into awkward positions I wouldn't be in otherwise."

"That's kind of the point."

I twisted my mouth to the side. Ellie frowned.

"You can't lose faith already. We've barely started trying. And you've got your lucky hat with you again."

I lifted a hand without thinking, adjusting the brim of my pork pie hat absentmindedly.

"It's not going to work every single time, Ella Two," Ellie continued. "It only needs to work once. Well, twice, technically. Once for each of us."

"True." I pressed my lips together. "So why don't you do it?"

"What?"

I flicked my eyes towards the guy on the bed. "If you feel like fate is here and this is meant to be a meet cute, you go get in the bed with him."

She straightened her shoulders and lifted her chin. "Fine. I will. On one condition."

"What's that?"

"When it works, I get your hat."

The offended gasp and hand I pressed to my chest to convey my shock were mostly for dramatic purposes, but not entirely. "Excuse me?"

A sly grin widened on her face. "Let's make this project more interesting. Let's make a bet."

"A bet for what?"

"For your hat." She flicked the brim of it. "If I win the bet and you find your soulmate, you get to keep it. And if you're right and you *don't* have a successful meet cute, I get your hat."

"Wait, so if I *win* the bet, I lose my hat?!"

"Yeah, because you get a soulmate. Why would you need a magic hat anymore?"

My heart was pounding hard enough that I was worried Ellie could see my pulse in the base of my throat.

"Come on, Ella Two," she said, grinning when I didn't say anything. "You're not chicken, are you? Because the only type of chicken I like is fried."

I knew she was joking. Ellie would still like me if I didn't take a bet. But something inside of me, something deep-seated and anxious and willing to do anything to keep my one and only friend, took control of my mouth.

"Of course not," I said. "But it still doesn't make sense. Technically by those rules, you'd be able to have my hat right now, since I haven't had a meet cute yet. And it doesn't seem fair. What about if *you* don't meet-cute someone?"

"Good points." She twisted her mouth to the side in consideration. "Okay, we have until Valentine's Day. I think fate would like that little tie in. And if I meet-cute someone, I get to forever and irrevocably be known as Ella Prime. If I don't, I bestow the title of Ella Prime to you, and will begrudgingly accept my demotion to Ella Two."

"Fine," I said, my voice pitching up as I thrust out my hand. "You're on."

Ellie grinned and grabbed my hand, shaking it hard. "Excellent. Then excuse me while I go win my part of the bet immediately."

Before I could say anything, Ellie turned on her heel and beelined across the room. After hesitating for a moment, I followed, lingering far enough back that I could pretend we were two friends who'd gotten separated at some point, but close enough that I could hear what was going on.

"Oh my God, are you *still* trying to decide on a mattress?" Ellie said, then flopped dramatically onto the mattress next to the curly-haired man. "Do you want me to pretend to be your partner so you can see how it holds up to vigorous fu—oh, *shit*!"

Her startled gasp sounded almost real. Maybe it was. Both she and the man beside her shot up to seated positions wearing twin expressions of surprise. But where Ellie's surprise stayed, the man's expression dissolved into one of panic and his face went pale.

"Oh, shit," he echoed, but his voice wavered. "Not again."

"I'm so sorry," Ellie said. "I thought you were my friend. My ba—"

"Robbie! Who the hell is that?"

The loud screech came from behind me and made me jump. An older woman with wide hips and bleach-blonde hair pulled up into the tightest, most painful looking ponytail I'd ever seen stormed past me, her face as red as the lingonberry sauce they served with the meatballs in the restaurant.

"It's not what it looks like!" Robbie said urgently. "She thought I was her friend and—"

"Who is this?" the woman demanded.

Ellie, who had clambered off the bed, took a few steps backwards. "It was a mistake. I thought—"

"There are no mistakes, young lady. Everything happens for a reason."

The woman extended her arms and I bolted forward, ready to tackle her out of the way so she didn't hurt Ellie, but I wasn't fast enough. Which was probably a good thing, because instead of wrapping her hands around Ellie's throat and throttling her for suspected infidelity or something, the woman clasped both of Ellie's hands in hers.

"He *never* introduces me to his girlfriends!" the woman said. "Always with the sneaking around because he doesn't want to let them meet me. I hope he treats you better than he treats his mama. How long have you been together? Are you ready to move in together? You can take him whenever you want, no questions asked, sweetie. I can't give you anything for the wedding because his deadbeat asshole of a sperm donor hasn't paid a lick of child support since this one turned eighteen because he's insisting the younger four aren't his kids. So it's been five years of living on a fixed income because of this big ol' growth—did he tell you about this? Hey, are you a nurse or something? He's always liked nurses and if you are, you can take a look at this and—"

"Mommy, for fuck's sake, put your shirt down," Robbie mumbled, taking the opportunity of her letting go of Ellie's hands to rush around the bed and squeeze between them so she couldn't grab Ellie again. "I've never seen her before in my life. She's probably not a nurse."

"I am definitely not a nurse," Ellie said.

The woman smacked Robbie's arm away from the hem of her shirt and stepped around him, lurching towards Ellie again. "He lies, you know, you'll have to watch out for that. That's a man thing. All of 'em are born that way, with lying streaks longer than their pee-pees so they can lie to you about that, too."

"*Mommy,*" Robbie said, and I swore he was about to cry. "Stop. I don't *know* her. You're making a scene."

That seemed to trigger something in the woman. She finally took her attention off Ellie and whirled towards him. Robbie made eye contact with Ellie and jerked his head to the side.

"*Go!*" he mouthed. "*Hide!*"

"I'm sorry!" Ellie whispered, but Robbie just repeated the action with more urgency. She scurried towards me and grabbed my arm, which led to an offended shout from the woman, but she wasn't fast enough to turn. Ellie and I half-ran the wrong way through the showroom until we reached a model room with a patio that we could duck into. I nearly lost my hat as we dove beneath a fake window that faced the store, slamming it back on my head as we crouched to watch for anyone approaching.

"Oh my God," Ellie said, her voice low and her eyes wide. "That was…"

"Terrifying?" I finished.

"What the fuck?" She glanced at me. "Do you think he's okay? Should we call someone? That's not normal, right?"

"Not even a little bit." I chewed on my bottom lip, watching the parts of the showroom I could see. "We should probably tell *someone*, but what are we supposed to say?"

She made a soft humming noise. "I don't know."

"Me neither." I adjusted slightly, sticking my neck out a bit further to see if the insanity that was Robbie's mom was coming. "But I think this is proof we shouldn't be forcing meet cutes. It's not working."

"It didn't work *twice*. That doesn't mean it'll never work." She stifled a giggle. "And at least we got a story out of it."

"A story that ends with us stuck in an IKEA model room instead of falling in love," I said. "What a great story. How long do you think we have to hide here?"

"Depends. What are we hiding from?" a deep voice asked from between us.

Both Ellie and I screeched. I fell backwards on my ass. She leapt to her feet. I almost puked as my eyes fell on the man who'd crouched down behind us and was now laughing his ass off while simultaneously laughing on his ass, since he'd fallen over, too. Something about him was vaguely familiar, but I couldn't say I recognized him. Ellie seemed to, though, because she slapped him on the arm even as she grabbed her chest.

"Goddamnit, Anthony!" she exclaimed, laughing.

It still took me a moment before I connected Anthony with the drag queen I'd met the previous night. Even when he wasn't in drag, he looked almost as meticulously put together as he did when he was Lady of the Lake. His bright yellow shirt and employee vest were neatly pressed and his long black hair was pulled back in a single braid.

"Oh, damn, that was funny," Anthony said, wiping a hand across his cheek. His light tannish brown skin was significantly less smooth than it had been the previous night, but I was pretty sure he was still wearing foundation and blush. "Jesus. That went better than I expected."

"What are you doing here?" Ellie asked.

He tilted his head to look up at her with raised eyebrows. "Clearly I'm a fan of stylish eco-friendly furniture and look stunning in yellow."

"I didn't know you worked here," I said, which was kind of stupid because why would I know that?

"Yep. When I'm not shaking my hip pads to Cher or Tina Turner or The Weather Girls, I moonlight as an IKEA associate." Anthony stood with a groan, then reached down with an extended hand to help me to my feet. "I saw that fabulous hat-and-curls combo rushing through the store and thought I'd come say hello. Although, I'm still curious about what we were hiding from."

"This lady," Ellie said. "I think we need to do something but I don't know what. I sat on a bed next to this guy—"

"Oh, fuck," Anthony said, cutting her off. "Young guy? Curly hair? And the woman is blonde and absolutely insane?"

"Uh, yeah," Ellie said. "We're worried about him."

Anthony sighed and grabbed a radio from his belt. "Hey, Markie? You-Know-Who is back... yeah, in Mattresses. They got an unwitting participant... Fine, I actually know them... A couple of minutes ago, I think?" He looked at Ellie for confirmation and she nodded. "Yeah. You'll wanna get someone there... No way, it's Steve's turn. Tell him to get 'em before she gets her pants off or we'll have to call the cops again and I don't wanna deal with those assholes today... Nope, management said it's for nudity too, not just when they start fucking." He put the radio back on his belt and sighed again. "What a day. And I barely got any sleep after the show last night."

"That sucks," I said. "Also, quick question. What the fuck was that about?"

He burst out laughing. "I wish I could explain it, but all I know is it's some weird sex thing. Once in a while people'll talk to them and they turn it into a game, but most of the time we just catch him nailing her in one of the roomsets."

"Nailing his *mom*?!" Ellie asked.

Anthony wrinkled his nose. "Oh, God. Is that the one they were playing today? Yikes. Anyways, no, they're not related." He frowned. "Or maybe—no." He shook his head. "I refuse to believe it's any more fucked up than it already is. Regardless, it's just some weird sex thing. They're technically banned from this store and every other IKEA in existence, but apparently the allure of having sex in a fake bedroom is too strong for them. How'd you get roped into it, anyway?"

I grimaced, not quite sure I wanted to tell Anthony about our forced meet cute plan, but Ellie didn't hesitate.

"We're trying to find our soulmates," she said.

"As one does," Anthony replied. "And that involves IKEA and weird sex things?"

"Yes and no," Ellie said.

"*Mostly* no," I interjected.

"We're just helping fate help us by making some meet cutes happen," Ellie said. "Like accidentally flopping on a bed that someone else is already testing or maybe tripping on a curb in the hopes an attractive stranger will catch us."

Anthony looked at her, then slowly turned his head to look at me. "That is—"

"—really stupid, I know," I said.

"—absolutely brilliant," he finished, his face lighting up.

Ellie slapped my arm. "See?! We can't quit after failing *once*."

"Okay, but we failed *badly*," I said. "That was kind of scary."

"Valid," Anthony said. "But that doesn't mean it won't work. Maybe you need somewhere with more of a controlled environment, but that's a little out of the ordinary."

"Like what?"

Anthony's eyes sparkled. "Like at the Aquasize class I teach at the rec center."

"You teach Aquasize?" I asked.

"Yeah, on Tuesdays and sometimes on Sundays if I'm not doing brewery tours," he said.

"Brewery tours? How many jobs do you have?"

"All of them," he said. "Come to Aquasize. It would be so perfect for you to find your soulmate there."

I hesitated, trying to figure out the best way to ask how I was going to find a soulmate among a pool full of old ladies in floral swimsuits. Luckily for me, Ellie and I were on the same page.

"Look, if my soulmate is a seventy-year-old grandma, that's cool, I'll make it work," she said. "But Isla's not into women."

"Oh, there are a ton of single guys," Anthony said.

"Really?" I said skeptically. "At *Aquasize*?"

"At Aquasize the way I teach it." He grinned. "I'll see you next Tuesday. Which is also what you'll be serving, so make sure you wear your cutest swimsuit."

Chapter Fourteen
See You Next Tuesday

Ellie

"THIS SWIMSUIT WAS A damn waste of money," Isla grumbled as we exited the locker room the following Tuesday night.

"It absolutely was not," I said.

"I should've never let you talk me into this."

"If I had it my way, I'd talk you out of it."

Isla rolled her eyes. "Ha, ha. I already had a swimsuit."

"And now you have another one." Only one, to my dismay. After Anthony invited us to Aquasize, Isla had mentioned she didn't think she had a swimsuit that was meet-your-soulmate-worthy. Which was great, because I'd been desperately trying to come up with an excuse for us to keep hanging out once we were done at IKEA.

So we'd gone shopping. And despite looking like an absolute snack in everything she tried on, she'd settled on this: a black pin-up-esque suit that fit her perfectly, the sweetheart neckline showing off an enticing amount of cleavage and a perfect bow tied between her generous breasts.

If fate decided her soulmate was going to be in the rec center pool that night, she'd win our bet immediately.

"Where am I gonna wear this?" Isla argued. "It's almost winter. I can't go to the beach."

"That's not true," I said. She raised her eyebrows at me. "You can't go to the beach because we live in Alberta and we have no fucking beaches here. But you're wearing it perfectly fine in the rec center. Are you saying you don't want to go swimming ever again?"

"No, I do. But..."

"But what?"

She glanced towards the pool, then back at me. "Do you *really* think we're gonna find soulmates here?"

"Why not? It's like Anthony said. Okay, so maybe his definition of 'a lot' of single men and ours is a little different, but there's at least five."

"Ellie," Isla said, looking exasperated.

"*What*?" I tried not to laugh. "There are!"

"I'm pretty sure they're all more interested in *each other* than they are in women."

"You don't know that *all* of them are gay."

Her exasperation turned into an unimpressed frown, and I couldn't hold back my laughter anymore.

She wasn't wrong. About the class demographics, at least. Of course we couldn't say that every single guy in the pool right now was gay without submitting to stereotypes and assumptions, but one of them was talking loudly about going to the gay bar in Edmonton—the one Jayce happened to be banned from, incidentally—and two of the others couldn't seem to keep their hands off each other.

Which I guess meant the pool of potential single men who may have been interested in women was three.

"Even if they are, maybe some of them have straight brothers," I said as we reached the steps to enter the pool. "And I'd bet money that some of these grandmas will fight over introducing you to their very nice, very handsome grandsons."

"I don't think there are as many grandmas here as you think," Isla said.

"Yeah, but there are *some*," I said. "And the rest of them probably have sons our age, so you know. Same argument."

"I still don't think they're as old as you think they are," she said. "And my point stands that the swimsuit was a waste of money."

I rolled my eyes and shivered. The eye-rolling was because of her claim it was a waste of money and the shivering because I'd followed her into the surprisingly chilly water. I definitely wasn't rolling my eyes to keep them off the shimmering water lapping at Isla's belly or the outline of her nipples that had suddenly peaked the fabric of her suit. Which also wasn't why I was shivering.

"Isla, you look like an about-to-be-soaking-wet dream," I said, hoping it sounded like something I'd say as her best friend and not as a lecherous creep who was completely thankful the water made it a lot harder to check out her best friend's ass. "If fate doesn't hand you a soulmate on a platter, it's missing a perfect opportunity."

"I don't think fate has anything to do with this," Isla said.

"Don't say that." I slogged forward and bumped her with my hip. "Fate definitely had something to do with this. Otherwise, how do you explain me getting the last two drop-in passes for tonight?"

"Typical amounts of luck?" she said.

I pssh'ed at her. "Anthony said this class is *popular*."

"Surprisingly so," she admitted. "But we're still at a rec center in Aurora Flats." She glanced around, a wrinkle between her eyebrows. "Are we supposed to line up or...?"

It was a fair question. Everyone in the pool was intermingling and chatting, some clustered into circles and others treading water as they shouted across the vague hint of lines that had formed. It must have been clear that neither Isla nor I knew what we were doing because a moment later, a plump older woman in an orange-and-pink floral one-piece whose thick salt-and-pepper hair was cut in the exact style one pictures when they think of a plump older woman with short hair waved at us.

"Come on over, newcomers," she called. "There's lots of room near the wall here. We don't bite."

"I might bite," I said as Isla turned to them.

"Well then, we don't bite unless you like it," said the younger woman beside her. She was wearing a completely inappropriate bright red bikini. Not because she was too old to wear a bikini—I wouldn't have guessed she was a day over thirty—but considering it was Aquasize, her boobs had a good chance of popping out of that thing and hitting someone in the face.

"Looks like you might have a chance at finding a soulmate still," Isla said, failing to fight back a giggle as the women all laughed.

And I mean, I wasn't picky. If fate said my soulmate was an old lady, preferably one with a padded bank account from the mysterious passing of her first, second, fourth, and sixth husbands, I'd take it. Even if just to stop thinking about the way Isla's swimsuit was clinging to the perfect crease of her waist and—

"First time?" the short-haired woman asked, though she had to raise her voice because loud music had started to play.

"Yep," I said, jumping on the chance to turn my thoughts off. "You?"

"Oh, no." She laughed. "My granddaughter and I come to the ladies' class every week. You're gonna have a blast."

"Just remember, no one knows what they're doing and it's all for fun," said the woman in the red bikini. "I'm Alison, by the way. This is my grandma, Betty."

"I think you mean your *sister*, Betty," I said.

"Oh, *stop*, young lady," Betty said, waving a hand at me even as she grinned. "I'm married."

"The good ones always are," I said with a resigned sigh.

"Not always," Betty said, shooting me a sly wink. "You know, I have a grandson. He's a sweetheart. Takes good care of his grandma. Smart as a whip and needs a sassy young lady to keep him on his toes."

It took everything in me not to whirl towards Isla and shout that I'd told her so. "Is that so?"

"I'm sure Ellie would *love* to meet him," Isla said. "Does your grandson ever come to the co-ed class?"

"We've yet to talk him into it," Betty said. "He keeps saying it's a class for old women."

"To be honest, we thought it would be like that, too," Isla said.

Betty grinned. "A lot of people think that. But look around—you both fit right in."

"I think we might be a *little* younger," I said, laughing.

"Well, I suppose you might be a little on the young side," Alison said, tilting her head at Isla. "You're what, twenty-five?"

"Twenty-four," Isla said.

"Ugh." Alison pretended to gag. "Jealous. But as for us"—she motioned between herself and me—"there are a solid amount that are in their thirties."

"Thirty?!" I said, pretending I was offended to cover up the fact that I was a little offended. "How dare you? I'm only twenty... nine."

The last word came out slowly. So slowly that Alison and Betty hooted with laughter because they thought I was joking. Which was good, because that made me look a lot less stupid than someone who just remembered she *was* almost thirty.

Isla, on the other hand, tilted her head and frowned. "You're twenty-nine?"

"Apparently," I said, trying to laugh.

"Since when?!"

"Uh... since my birthday."

Isla's frown deepened. "I thought you were younger than me."

I snorted. "Nope. I'm just not very good at being an adult."

"I meant that you look younger than me," she said. "But for the record, I've wondered more than once how you seem to have so much more figured out than I do."

God damnit.

God fucking damnit.

First she had to go look like my greatest fantasy come to life, and then she had to go and make me feel *good* about myself?

I'd told Jayce I wasn't going to fall for Isla, but she was obliviously doing her best to make me break that promise.

"Well, regardless, the ladies' class is so unique that they did a whole story about it in the paper," Betty said. "Not the Aurora Flats one. The *Edmonton* one. We were all so proud."

"It sounds like it would be a fun class to check out," I said, trying to distract myself again. "When is the ladies' class?"

Alison gave me a strange look. "Uh... that's what you're here for. It's right now."

Isla looked towards the group of men. "Okay, but there's a bunch of guys—"

Then it hit me.

And by it, I mean the water.

And by hit, I mean "was poured on."

And by me, I mean me and Isla, who let out a surprised yelp and nearly fell over.

Luckily, at the same time it hit me, I also had the realization that they weren't saying "the *ladies*."

They were saying "the *Lady's*."

As in "the Lady of the Lake."

And by Lake, I mean the bucket of pool water she'd dumped on our heads.

"Welcome, *friends*!" came a loud, deep voice rolling over the laughter and my sputters as I wiped water off my face.

I turned and looked up at the same time as Isla, who'd just finished pushing her wet curls off her forehead. Standing at the edge of the pool wasn't Anthony, like we'd expected, but Anthony in almost-full Lady of the Lake drag. She was wearing a red one-piece swimsuit, a mini-skirt-length sarong tied around her waist. From this close, I could tell she was wearing nylons, probably so she had something to hold her hip pads in place as well as prevent anything from popping out of the high-cut leg holes of her swimsuit, but instead of the six-inch heels she usually wore, her feet were stuffed into giant purple Crocs. She wore a long blonde wig pulled up into a bouncy ponytail, and her face was done up in the most no-makeup-makeup look a drag queen could possibly do. Which was still pretty glam, but not overly glittery. Probably so the glitter didn't get in the water or something.

Grinning, she crouched and set the bucket down.

"Sorry," she whispered, putting her hand over her microphone headset. "But I had to."

Isla's face was either still wet or she was laughing so hard she was crying. "It's fine."

"Asshole," I said, sticking out my tongue so she knew I wasn't serious.

Lady laughed as she stood back up and spoke into her microphone. "Don't take it *personally*, dears. The Lady of the Lake has one big rule, which is...?"

"You're here to get *wet*!" the class answered.

"Exactly." She strode confidently to her place in front of the class. "Welcome, everyone, to the Lady of the Lake's Drag Queen Aquasize. This is a one-of-a-kind Aurora Flats Recreational Facility experience. Today, we're going to what?"

"Work our tushies off!" the class answered.

"Literally," Lady said. "It would not be the first time my ass pads fall out of the back of my swimsuit."

Isla was still laughing so hard I thought she might actually drown.

Having never been to any other aqua-related exercise class before, I had no idea how it compared to a typical one. Something told me most classes didn't focus so much on doing water-assisted death drops, which was sort of just like flopping on your back with your leg tucked under you, and I was pretty sure describing jumping jacks as "Snatch that wig, now throw it down, now snatch that wig, now throw it down..." was a Lady of the Lake thing.

But for the most part, it was kind of what I'd expected, which was an aerobics class but with water. Which meant I remembered about halfway through why I hated going to exercise classes.

"Come on, my pretty little fitness floozies," Lady shouted. "Keep sashaying those arms."

"They're gonna fall off," I gasped, desperately holding myself back from calling her a see you next Tuesday for getting me into this situation.

"They are not," Isla said, barely out of breath.

I groaned, nearly falling over as my biceps trembled. "This is *hard*. When can we stop?"

"When you start doing it right," Lady answered, her voice booming through the microphone. "Let's go, Ellie. You've got this." She started clapping her hands to a beat that did not match the song playing in any way. "And one-two-sashay-sashay, one-two-sashay-sashay—that's right, Isla, you got it! Great form. You keep that up and soon you'll be able to shantay away with hips like these."

"But this is an arm exercise," Isla replied as Lady ran her hands up and down her body.

"Well, *duhhh*," she said, rolling her eyes at me. "It takes a good amount of upper body strength to cut out foam this smoothly, smarty pants."

"I have a better idea," I said, huffing as I flailed my arms through the water. "What if you just ate a whole bunch of ice cream while watching TV?"

"That gets you hips like *these*," Betty said, water sloshing around her as she clapped her hands to her hips beneath the surface of the water. "And thighs, and belly, and butt..."

"You're supposed to be talking her *out* of sitting around eating ice cream, not *into* it, you glimmering gorgeous fox of the sea!" Lady said. "Yeesh, Betty. It's like you don't even know I get paid per attendee for these classes."

"Does that mean I can pay you so I *don't* have to show up?" I gasped.

"You don't want to come back?" Isla said, a puppy-dog look crossing her face. "I thought we could make this, like, a Tuesday night thing."

"You'll need"—huff—"more swimsuits"—puff—"for that," I said.

"We could go shopping again this weekend. And maybe Betty will talk her grandson into coming."

I pretended to groan, but I already knew I'd be back the following week.

Time seemed to stand still as everyone sashayed and jumped and splashed, but eventually, Lady turned the music down and waved a hand towards us as if she could bat the noise of the pool out of the air.

"Alright, *alright*," she said into the microphone. "It's time."

The class cheered.

"Time for what?" Isla asked Betty, who was pumping her hands in the air.

"Lip sync battle!" she exclaimed.

"Oh God. What does that mean?" I asked.

"Just do your best," Lady said from the front of the class. "You're on a team but also, you're on your own. The winner of the battle gets the joy of not being the loser of the battle. Clear?"

"Not at all," I said, then took a deep breath and girded myself for whatever the hell was about to happen. "Let's go."

"Perfect." Lady pressed a button on the wall, took her headset off, and struck a pose as *It's Raining Men* started blasting through the pool.

And *that* was when I figured out why this was fun.

I had no idea if we won. I had no idea if we lost. I had no idea what anyone else was doing anywhere. It was the exact opposite of synchronized swimming: nothing was in sync, and it couldn't be called swimming. There was so much splashing and shouting and flopping that I couldn't have even said which direction I faced half the time.

It was the most fun I'd had in any exercise class ever. The chaos of movement, the thundering music, the old ladies—excuse me, the ladies of my far-more-advanced-than-I'd-thought age—dolphining back and forth through the pool... it almost made it worth going through the torture of the previous workout.

Almost, because not all of us were having fun.

"This is fucking insane," Isla said, sputtering as water sloshed in her face.

I laughed, but only for a moment before I realized she didn't mean insane as in "This is an enjoyable amount of chaos," but insane as in "I am surprisingly short and we're in the deeper side of the pool which was fine when we were just floating around doing weird water crunches but now I'm about to be swept in a way in a wave of floral one-pieces." The smile that had been almost permanently fixed to her face the entire class was gone, replaced by a forced one that made it clear she was holding in an immense amount of panic.

So I did what any good best friend would do.

"*HALLELUJAH!*" I scream-sang directly into Isla's face as I grabbed her arm and tugged. She stumbled towards me, seemingly startled as I pulled her in closer even as I turned away.

"What are you—"

"Get on my back," I shouted over the music. "So the Lady can see you lip syncing."

"I'll drown you!" she protested, but it didn't stop her from clamping her arms around my shoulders and lifting her legs so I could hook my arms around her thighs and ferry us both to the shallow end of the pool. By the time we spotted Betty and Alison, who were sending cascades of water out as they twirled and danced, Isla was singing loudly and cackling, one arm extended in the air dramatically.

And that... specifically *that*, was why I immediately decided this part was definitely worth going through the torture of an exercise class.

Her having a blast, I mean. It had nothing to do with the feel of her thighs clenched around my hips.

Okay, maybe a little.

But like, a little-little. Little enough that I'd joke about it later in that flirting-with-your-friends sort of way.

"I think we're winning, girls!" Betty shouted as we reached them.

"What do we win?" Isla asked.

Betty didn't have time to reply. Half a second later, Lady of the Lake pointed towards a group seemingly at random, screamed out the word "Losers," and took a running leap before cannonballing into the pool.

Bright purple Crocs, bouncy blonde wig, and all.

Chapter Fifteen
Completely

Isla

"THERE AREN'T ACTUALLY ANY winners or losers," Anthony said as he pulled off his wig. "I just pick the spot in the pool I'm least likely to land on someone near the end of the song."

"That's considerate of you," I said.

"Well, this class is already an insurance nightmare for the rec center. That's why I have to wear the Crocs now." He rolled his eyes. "Their lack of faith in my ability to teach Aquasize while wearing an itty-bitty four-inch heel is frankly insulting." He started wringing the wig out carefully. "But you do make a good point about the lip sync battle being hard for you shorties."

"What kind of setting spray do you use?" Ellie asked, ignoring both of us. "Your makeup still looks perfect."

"Right?" Anthony smirked. "I may go through wigs at an alarming rate on account of the constant chlorine damage, but doing this class has taught me makeup skills like you wouldn't believe. I could probably be waterboarded under Niagara Falls and the battered remains of my corpse would still have a flawless contour. I'll send you a pic of the bottle." He turned back to me. "I have an idea that might help. Are you coming back next week?"

"I'm not sure—" I started.

"Yep," Ellie said.

I looked at her. "Really? I thought you hated it."

"Yeah, a little," Ellie said.

Anthony huffed. "Rude."

"What?" Ellie asked plainly. "First of all, you can call them wig-snatchies all you want, but it's just putting lipstick on a jumping jack. And second of all, you promised us a bunch of potential soulmates."

"There were a ton of guys here!"

"There were five of them," Ellie said.

"Okay, but normally there are a couple more."

"And are any of those ones the type of guys who swing in our particular direction?" Ellie asked.

Anthony started to answer, then twisted his mouth to the side. "Oh. Right. Now that you mention it, just because I found a boyfriend here that one time doesn't mean it's a great place for straight girls to find a soulmate."

"I'm bi," Ellie corrected immediately. "But even though I hate exercising and there were no soulmates for us to force into a meet cute, the last bit?" She brought her fingers together and made an exaggerated kissing sound as she touched them to her lips. "Chaotic screaming in the pool while my super-hot best friend wraps her legs around me? That's my second-favourite type of cardio. The first also involving legs being wrapped around me, but you can't do that in a public pool."

"Ellie!" I said, laughing as my face heated up.

She snickered. "So yes, Anthony, even though you were a dirty liar and also tried to kill me with those weird lunge-y kick things, we will, in fact, see you next Tuesday."

Which Anthony was delighted about, of course. Enough so that he promised he'd block off two spots in the class for us because he had an idea for using the floatie belt things that might make the lip sync battle a little less waterboard-y for those of us who couldn't touch the bottom at the far end of the pool without water covering both their noses and mouths.

"And I know I can trust you to be honest about if it works," he added. "Seeing as you have no problem admitting you hated my class to my face."

"That was Ellie," I said. "Maybe I wouldn't say anything."

"Doesn't matter," Ellie said. "I would, and since I know everything you think or feel because we're best friends, he'll still get the honest feedback."

The whole "thinking/feeling" thing might have been an exaggeration, but not by much. I still couldn't quite figure out how Ellie had known I was struggling during the lip sync battle. I'd thought I was putting on a smile and pushing my way through the panic that sloshed through every splashing wave, that the stinging sensation in my eyes could clearly be passed off as a reaction to the chlorinated water battering me in the face.

But she'd known. Almost immediately, she'd known. And she'd made helping me a part of the game rather than pulling me aside, drawing attention to the fact that I was struggling. Not that I would have been mad if she did that, of course. I would've been more than grateful for the help.

But I appreciated that she already knew me well enough to know I wouldn't want to be the center of attention in that moment.

After saying goodbye to Anthony, Ellie and I went to the change room. We both showered, but even though it was chilly that night, I didn't bother drying my hair.

"You have time," Ellie said as she untwisted the towel on her head. "I'm drying mine. It's fucking cold out."

"Not cold enough to freeze yet," I said. "And I've got a toque. I'll dry it properly when I get home and have all my creams and stuff. And yours won't take anywhere near as long as mine does to dry."

"You sure about that?" she asked, her mouth twitching into a smile.

I rolled my eyes. "Your hair is as straight as the Saskatchewan border. There's no... way..."

My words trailed off as Ellie's hair tumbled, and tumbled, and *tumbled* out of the towel.

I'd never seen her with her hair down.

It was one of those things you don't realize until you do. Her hair was always in a bun. Sometimes messy, sometimes neat, but always on the top of her head.

Sure, it was full of volume, but my sister's hair had always looked like that even though she had flat, straight hair. She'd tease it and comb it and sometimes even wrap things into it so it looked fuller when she pinned it into a bun, but her hair was only ever just past her shoulders at its longest.

Ellie's hair was nearly to the small of her back. And even though it was wet, even though pieces of it were clumped together in not-quite-tangles, even though she was snickering as I gaped at this part of her that I'd seen every time I saw her but had never *known* about, I thought her hair was one of the prettiest things I'd ever seen.

"You were saying?" she asked, her lisp slightly more pronounced as she struggled to hold in a laugh.

"Holy hell, Rapunzel," I blurted.

She lost the battle with her laughter, grinning as she grabbed the hair dryer and flipped her hair over her head so she was nearly folded in half.

I tried not to stare as she dried it, but I couldn't help watching. Washing and drying my hair was an entire production, so of course I was curious about how someone who didn't have hair that felt like a ball of yarn used as a soccer ball by kindergarten kids would dry theirs.

And since my hair was the darkest shade of blonde before it could be considered brown, of course I was mesmerized by the way Ellie's dark hair was only imperceptibly darker when soaking wet.

Of course I wanted to see the difference between the shine of her hair when wet and the shine of her hair when natural.

And of course I wanted to touch it. Who wouldn't? It looked soft. And smooth. Like it would glide between my fingers while I played with it, arranging the strands into a neat pattern.

Because I wanted to… you know. Braid it.

Which made complete and total sense. And completely explained the completely foreign feeling in my chest as I watched her fingers slide through her hair while it danced beneath the hot air.

I wanted to braid it.

Or something.

Despite its length, I was right that Ellie's hair wouldn't take anywhere near as long to dry as mine would have. It didn't take long at all, actually; barely long enough for me to stop being mesmerized by it.

"I guess it feels longer to me," she admitted when I pointed out it had only taken a few minutes. "All this kind of tedious crap feels like it takes forever when you don't get a dopamine hit at the end."

By the time we'd finished packing our things up and were ready to leave, I'd forgotten about the whole reason we'd come to Aquasize in the first place. It wasn't until we'd walked out of the warmth of the rec center into the chilly darkness of almost-winter that fate popped its head out to remind us why we were there.

"—so chores tend to feel like they take way more energy and time than someone whose attention doesn't have a deficit," Ellie was saying as I dug out my car keys. "Luckily my parents realized it wasn't just typical 'kids-being-kids' and trying to get out of doing stuff, so they got me tested and sure as shit, the doctor was like 'Oh yeah, this child's brain is fucked' and—"

"They didn't actually say that, did they?" I asked.

"Oh, of course not. What's a good story if not slightly exaggerated?" Ellie said. "The doctor was just like 'Bing boom bam, here's some Adderall.' Bye, Alison! Good night, Betty! It was nice to meet you!"

I'd spent enough time around Ellie so far that the sudden switch in conversation didn't jar me. Or maybe it was the fact that I'd also started waving at the three women crowded around a black sedan parked in the fire lane. Whatever it was, Betty and Alison turned at the sound of Ellie's voice, along with another woman who'd been in the class.

"Oh!" Betty said, and her face brightened from beneath a bulky purple knit toque. "Perfect timing. Ellie, dear, do you need a ride home?"

"Well, I actually carpooled with Isla, so—" Ellie started.

Betty cut her off with a squeal of delight as she smacked Alison on the arm. "I told you! It's meant to be, chickpea."

Ellie's head tilted to the side. "What is?"

Alison sighed, a reluctant laugh on her lips. "You know that grandson my grandma said you should meet?"

"I do remember that," Ellie said.

"Well, I forgot to tell this sweet handsome gentleman of a young man that Alison and I had plans with the girls after Aquasize, so he showed up to drive me home anyway," Betty said. "So I thought perhaps you could use a ride home so he didn't waste his time on his old forgetful grandma."

And of course I was thrilled.

Completely thrilled.

Yes, Ellie's face was smug as she glanced at me with an "*I told you this would work*" hidden in her smirk, but it was all good-natured. Of course I was ecstatic that this convoluted meet-cute thing had worked. Even if it meant I was technically losing the bet. That's why there was a sinking feeling in my stomach, obviously. No one likes losing a bet, even if it's a silly one they didn't think would work. And it wasn't like it was for anything serious. I mean, what was letting Ellie have the Ella Prime nickname when it also meant she'd met the love of her life?

So this was good. I wasn't upset. The sinking feeling in my stomach was just because no one likes losing a bet, even if it's a silly one that they didn't think would work. It wasn't jealousy.

Not at all.

Or, well...

Not... completely.

But somehow, also not of Ellie.

It was of the situation. That had to be it. I was sort of sad and sort of jealous that Ellie got to meet her soulmate first. Because I'd been trying, you know? And I'd been worried. I'd been wondering if I made the wrong decision when

I left Burnaby. So it would've just been nice to have that sign that I was doing something right.

And none of that was Ellie's fault. The blame lay entirely on fate. And I couldn't even fully be angry about that, you know? Because it was still a sign that we were on the right track. And frankly, I should be grateful. Like, how freakin' lucky could one person be, to feel like she had a hand in her best friend meeting her soulmate *and* getting to witness that moment?

Probably super lucky.

Unfortunately, the only luck I seemed to have was bad.

Because this wasn't a sign. It was more like a message. A little note from fate as it held up both metaphorical middle fingers while walking backwards away from me.

And both of those middle fingers were wearing black trilby hats.

"Ellie, dear, this is my grandson, Co—"

"You've got to be fucking kidding me," Corbin interrupted, staring at me like I was some kind of mutant. "You, *again*?!"

Chapter Sixteen

Sparkling Fish Eggs

Isla

"Maybe he *is* your soulmate," Jayce said.

Ellie reacted with the same amount of horror and disgust as if they'd taken a freshly hatched baby bird, gently laid it on a bed of soft hay beneath a warm lamp, then smushed it.

"How *dare* you?!" she gasped over the half-finished bottle of beer clutched in her left hand. "You absolutely sick child of a bit—"

"Hear me out, drama queen." Jayce flipped the bar cloth they'd been using to wipe the gleaming wood in front of us over their shoulder with a practiced, professional ease. "Your whole concept here relies on cliches to work. You didn't consider that the tropiest trope of them all might worm its way into your soulmate storyline?"

"What do you mean?" Ellie asked.

Jayce rolled their eyes. "The enemies-to-lovers arc, obviously, Ellie-Bean."

"That's the stupidest thing I've ever heard."

"How? It's the single most popular romance trope. Billions of dollars have been made on the concept."

"It's problematic as *fuck*. Those dollars are made trying to convince women that 'he's mean to you because he likes you' is a valid way for a man to romance you without having to buy flowers or respect you."

"Even if that was always the case—which hit's not—it's not like they never change their ways. Mr. Darcy—"

"Don't you fucking start with me on the *Pride and Prejudice* bullshit again. It's a terrible movie—"

"It's a book, you heathen."

"And it's terrible. I—"

"I will *not* stand for Jane Austen slander in my own bar. If you don't think I'll kick you out—"

I stayed out of it. Ellie was stubborn and I didn't know Jayce well enough to insert myself between two people who'd known each other long enough that they'd had this argument more than once.

Especially when Ellie was in the wrong.

Not just about *Pride and Prejudice*. I mean, she was obviously insane for that take, but I didn't think taking Jayce's side would be great for our friendship given the way Ellie was glaring at them.

But the enemies-to-lovers thing...

I took a slow sip of my wine, then another. Then a third, and when it was clear neither Ellie nor Jayce were paying attention to me, I knocked back the rest of the glass.

Unfortunately, that meant my glass was now empty. Fortunately, Jayce had only agreed to sell me a bottle of the half-priced wine they had on special that night if Ellie had a glass, since legally they couldn't sell an entire bottle of wine to only one person. And since Ellie hated wine, that glass was still sitting in front of her, untouched, while she drank beer.

"—it's a goddamn classic, you uneducated taint-licker," Ellie said as I slowly inched my hand towards her wine.

"On what *planet*?" Jayce snapped back.

"This one!"

Jayce jabbed a finger towards the exit. "Get out."

"You get out!"

"It's my bar!"

"And you—oh, shit!"

My fingers had just reached the stem of the wine glass when Ellie gestured wildly towards the door and knocked into my arm. I jolted and the glass tipped over, sloshing wine across the freshly-cleaned bar top.

"Sorry," I said, grimacing as Jayce righted the glass before grabbing another bar towel.

"Don't be. Ellie's the clumsy oaf with foul taste," they said, efficiently cleaning up the spilled wine. "I'm more impressed that you've already finished that entire bottle of wine. Though, I say that as your friend. As a purveyor of alcohol, I am of the very strong opinion that your next beverage should be a glass of water. And perhaps accompanied by some mozza sticks."

"At least you have some correct opinions," Ellie muttered. "I figured you'd be anti-mozza stick since you obviously hate *joy*."

Jayce rolled their eyes as they tapped something into the register beside us. "You're gonna come into my bar and in the same argument tell me that *Pride and Prejudice* is 'dull horseshit' but *Secret Rednecks: The Cinematic Extravaganza* was a classic? And then question the quality of *my* opinions?"

"You're the one who brought up the stupid enemies-to-lovers thing and tried to argue that some fictional Regency himbo is the ideal romantic partner," Ellie said.

"Maybe they have a point," I said.

The surrounding noise of the Flat Tire filled the space around us like it had burst through a dam as both of them went completely silent. It roared into my ears, chatter and music and clinking glass, meaningless sounds that did nothing but highlight the expression of absolute betrayal on Ellie's face and the one of dry glee on Jayce's.

"Well, I should have guessed you'd say that," Ellie finally said. "All you book nerds think *Pride and Prejudice* is literary caviar when it's really just fish eggs."

"Caviar—That's not what—What I mean is—" I took a deep breath to steady my thoughts. "I wasn't talking about *Pride and Prejudice*. I was talking about the enemies-to-lovers thing. Meet cutes and enemies-to-lovers go hand-in-hand.

It's the single most popular romance trope. So if this whole fate thing is actually real, chances are one of us would end up with an enemies-to-lovers arc. Also for the record, caviar *is* fish eggs."

"You can't be serious," Ellie said.

"I am. It's the roe from certain types of sturgeon. You can get roe from other fish, too, but it's one of those 'if it's not from the Champagne region of France, it's just sparkling fish eggs' situations."

"You know I mean the enemies-to-lovers thing," she said. "If you're seriously implying that you think Nasally Hat Boy is actually your soulmate because he keeps popping up everywhere you go, I'm reporting Jayce to the liquor board for over serving a patron."

"It's more like I'm popping up and ruining his life wherever *he* goes," I said. "I called him an asshole. And got him kicked out of a bar after making his friends mad at him. And made him look like a dick in front of his grandma—"

"I may have only been present for one of those incidents, but I can firmly state that it's his fault he got kicked out of the bar. Same with his friends being mad at him," Jayce said. "Nasally Hat Boy acted like an asshole. You didn't make him do that. By my understanding, you were being extremely nice to him."

"And you didn't make him tell his grandma that he'd never in this lifetime or any other consider dating you and if you were the last woman on Earth, he'd make do with his hand," Ellie said.

"Whoa," Jayce said. "Wait a second. He *said*—"

"Mm-hmm," Ellie said. "So how my gorgeous goddess of a bestie could even *entertain* the idea that he's her soulmate is beyond me."

"I'm not," I said. "I'm just saying maybe the enemies-to-lovers thing is possible."

"Good," Ellie said. "Because if Corbin was the last man on Earth, I'd help you move to Mars."

I burst out laughing. Ellie grinned and even Jayce smiled, though there was a wryness to it as they glanced from me to Ellie.

"Are you two certain you need to continue this meet cute experiment to find your potential soulmates?" they asked.

"What do you mean?" I asked.

Jayce shrugged. "I was simply curious. Perhaps the reason these meet cutes aren't working is because you're missing something that would render the experiment meaningless."

"Or because it's been a week," Ellie said, sounding annoyed. "We've tried, like, three things. Maybe instead of pointing out that it's not working, you could do something useful like help us think of new things to try."

Jayce tilted their head to the side. "Well, you could go back into the city and take the LRT so you can tumble into someone's lap when the train stops."

"I think we'd be more likely to get stabbed than find a soulmate that way," I said.

"True." A plate of not just mozza sticks, but mini spring rolls and potato wedges and fried chicken wings appeared. Jayce slid it between me and Ellie. "You've already discussed the various ways of tripping on curbs and spilling coffees on men in well-fitted designer business suits who are rushing to very important meetings?"

"Why does everyone forget I'm bi?" Ellie mumbled as I helped myself to a mozza stick. "It could be a woman rushing to a very important meeting."

"I don't forget that, Ellie-Bean," Jayce said patiently. "I simply assume that ruining a man's designer outfit is far less likely to earn you a mortal enemy, and clearly you're anti-enemies-to-lovers."

She tilted her bottle towards them in concession. "Fine. That's fair. But yes, we've already thought of that."

"And pretty much every other way that we could meet a soulmate but also die," I said. "Like assuming someone'll catch us if we fall down the stairs or yank us out of the way if we end up in the path of an oncoming bus."

"I'm sure there are less life-threatening ways to meet people," Jayce said.

"Like what?" I asked as I reached for a chicken wing at the same time Ellie did. "Oh, sorry. I—"

"Yes, that," Jayce said. "Exactly. You both reach for the same piece of chicken at the same time." Their voice lowered, taking on a misty, almost seductive tone. "Your hands meet. A gentle touch. Lingering fingers as you look up at each other."

I glanced up at Ellie, who was fighting not to laugh.

"You both laugh a little and one of you chivalrously gestures to the other to go first, and the other giggles and says for them to go ahead. And you barely even notice that your hands are still touching because you feel... *something*."

"I think it's the chicken grease on my fingers," I said solemnly.

Ellie snorted, then batted my hand out of the way so she could take the chicken wing. "I mean, it's a little unoriginal."

"And I already tried it," I said.

Jayce raised their eyebrows. "Have you?"

I helped myself to another one of the chicken wings. "At the bookstore. Corbin and I were reaching for the same book."

"Okay, but books are for nerds," Ellie said.

"Thanks."

"No problem, nerd." She popped most of the chicken wing in her mouth, stripping most of the chicken off and setting the bone down on the edge of the plate. "I think food is where it's at for this one. Anything shareable. Pizza. Nachos."

"A well-stocked veggie tray?" I suggested.

She shuddered and stuck her tongue out. "Sure, if you want to meet some boring dude who gets off on eating celery and ranch dressing."

"You know my feelings on celery."

"Exactly, so no veggie trays."

"What about if you borrowed someone's dog?" Jayce asked. "You could take it to the dog park. And then when there's a steaming pile of poop somewhere, your plastic-bag-clad hands could brush together. 'Oh, let me get this, I think it's my little Fido's pile.'"

Ellie lowered the tone of her voice. "Oh, I couldn't possibly let you do that, beautiful. I'm certain it's from my Rover here. I feed him a special diet and you can see some of the undigested corn poking out—"

I retched and Ellie snickered.

"More of a cat person, Isla?" she asked.

"Not really," I said. "I've never wanted a cat."

Jayce inhaled sharply. "Now you've done it."

I looked up at them. "Done what?"

"You've triggered the cat distribution system," Ellie said.

"What's that?"

"It's the idea that the universe will give you a cat," Jayce said.

I stared at them, not quite sure if they were fucking with me or what. "That's... stupid?"

"Is it? Or do you know countless people who have been living their lives until one day, a cat appears in their garbage can, and suddenly they own a cat?"

I rolled my eyes. "No one says they have to keep the cat."

Ellie gasped and pressed a hand to her chest. "You'd let a poor innocent cat be without a home?"

"No, I'd call the animal shelter or look for a lost-pet poster or something," I said. "You don't have to keep a cat just because you find one."

"Keep talking," Ellie teased. "It's getting more and more likely. I wonder what kind of cat you'll end up with."

"I can picture you with an orange cat," Jayce said. "One of the really stupid ones."

"Oh my God. No," I said. "I'm not getting an orange cat."

"Aw, you're right!" Ellie said. "I can totally see her with an orange cat. What are you gonna name it?"

"You should name it something really stupid," Jayce said. "Like Potato. Or Dump Truck."

"I'm not naming it anything!" I said. "I'm *not* getting a cat!"

"Pretty sure the great Mr. Darcy once said that the moreth one dost protest, the more tempted does fate becometh," Ellie said.

"The same 'fate' that's being tempted to give us soulmates?" I asked. "Because if so, I think I'll be okay. It's either completely resistant to temptation or a total scam."

There was a quiet pause before Jayce huffed and turned to Ellie. "Mr. Darcy absolutely did *not* say that."

Ellie heaved a huge sigh. "Oh my God, Jayce. It was a joke. I know you haven't heard of them before because all your dusty old books are about metaphors and shit, but—"

I sighed a quiet breath of relief and ate another mozza stick, glad they'd gotten distracted and changed topics. It wasn't until after Ellie and I had stumbled back to my apartment and crawled into my bed that it came up again.

"I think we should alternate weeks," I said.

"For what?" Ellie asked.

"For little spoon. You got to be little spoon first last week. So now I get to be little spoon."

"I little-spooned you at some point during the night."

"Yeah, but not to fall asleep." I rolled away from her and pulled the covers up to my chin. "C'mon. Spoon me."

She didn't say anything. A moment later, she curled up behind me, arms around my waist and blankets around our bodies as the darkness of my bedroom surrounded us.

"I thought you'd argue more," I murmured.

"Yeah," Ellie said, her voice distracted. "Can I ask you something?"

"Hmm?"

"Do you believe in fate?"

I frowned. "Huh?"

"Tonight. You said something about 'if' fate was real. And when we talked about the cat distribution system, you called it a scam."

I swallowed hard. "I... don't... not believe that it is or isn't real."

"I had too much beer to figure out if those negatives cancelled each other out. So yes or no?"

I sighed. "I mean... maybe Jayce had a point."

"I'm gonna kick Jayce's bony little ass for this enemies-to-lovers thing."

"It's not that. Not *just* that," I corrected. "They said that maybe the meet cutes are meaningless. And maybe that's because fate isn't real."

"I don't think that's what they meant," she said.

I didn't say anything.

"I think you're questioning what you do or don't believe because of this whole thing with Corbin," she continued. "And I don't think you should give him that kind of power. He doesn't deserve it. And for the record, I *refuse* to believe fate would give you an enemies-to-lovers arc, especially not with him. You're the nicest person I know."

There was something warm in my chest, though it was achy, too. "What if—"

"No. He's not your soulmate, Isla."

"But maybe it's not me."

"What?"

I swallowed hard. "Betty wanted him to give you a ride home, not me. Maybe I kept running into him so he could meet you."

Ellie paused, but even in the silence, her shock was obvious. "You can't believe I'd want to be with him."

I licked my lips. "I wouldn't be mad if you did. I'd understand."

More silence.

More shock.

"Isla," Ellie said.

The sadness in her voice roused a lump in my throat. I swallowed again, not quite able to say anything, and after a moment, Ellie snuggled in even closer.

"Isla," she said again, so close I could feel her breath on my neck. "I would literally rather die alone."

I struggled to force out a watery laugh. "No, you wouldn't. Don't say that."

"I don't want him," she said. "I don't want to spend my life with someone who acts like that towards my best friend. I deserve better than that, too."

"But what if that's the person fate picked for you?" I asked.

"Then fate can go fuck itself. Because I pick you, Ella Two."

I laughed.

I had to. If I didn't, the lump in my throat would've released tears, and this was a stupid thing to cry over. "Okay, but if he pops up again, I'm pretty sure that's fate trying to tell us something."

"He won't."

"He might." I frowned. "Unless this is your way of confessing you're secretly a serial killer, in which case, I think we have a bigger problem."

She snorted. "Are you kidding? You've seen my bedroom. And my desk. And my car. There's no way I could clean a crime scene up enough to not get caught."

"That's valid."

She chuckled. Once the sound faded away, we were quiet for a few moments.

"We're not giving up, right?" she asked. "We're still going to find our soulmates?"

"Yeah," I said. "Yeah, of course. I have a bet to win, you know."

Behind me, Ellie shifted, and for some reason I knew she was smiling. "Okay. Good."

I closed my eyes, listening to Ellie's breath deepen and grow steady, her arms wrapped tight around me. It wasn't until I was on the cusp of sleep that I realized the reason I knew Ellie had been smiling was because I'd felt her lips pressed to my shoulder.

Chapter Seventeen

You Know What They Say About Assuming

Ellie

"And Isla looks at me and, right in the middle of Jayce's bar, yells, 'Have you seen my pussy?'" I said.

"She does not!" my mom said, gasping.

"I'm serious. The Flat Tire goes silent and both Jayce and I are like, girl, what the fuck? And then from behind us we hear Lady go, 'No, but if you've lost it, I can search the last place you saw it.'"

"Who's Lady?" Mom asked.

"Lady of the Lake. It's Anthony's drag name. Her show was so popular at Jayce's Not A Halloween Party they asked her if she'd do a set regularly. But Anthony has like eight jobs, so he can only perform every other Friday or Saturday, depending on which one is an even number."

"What—"

"I dunno, something about garbage collector schedules. Anyway, Lady cracks this joke, but Isla's so worked up she doesn't laugh at all. Like, she's totally oblivious to the table of trades guys gaping at her, and just stamps her little foot on the ground and jabs her finger at the bulletin board." I stifled a laugh. "And then she yells it again."

"Oh, good God," Mom said, laughing.

"So Jayce's like, 'Isla, my dear, I think we have established that no one here has seen your pussy and as I would kindly ask you not whip it out in the middle of my bar, perhaps you could elaborate on why you're asking.'"

"I can almost hear them saying that," Mom said.

"It's because I do a perfect impression of Jayce," I said. "So Isla huffs and stomps across the bar, still *completely* ignoring all these guys who are completely confused about this girl yelling about her pussy—"

"Sidebar, did any of them make nasty jokes?" Mom interrupted. "Other than Lady, but I'm guessing because you and Isla know her—"

"—she didn't mind, yeah," I said. "Anthony checked in with her after. He's really good about that, at least with Isla. He's got a soft spot for her. But no, no one else did. Which is a total testament to Jayce, honestly. They've really made it clear there's zero tolerance for gross behaviour without being preachy about it."

"That's impressive," Mom said. "I'm so proud of them. They've come so far."

"Don't tell Jayce I said this, but me too."

"Are their uncles still causing issues?"

"No more than usual. Not since the last time. Jayce is doing everything they can to make it so there's nothing for them to criticize and honestly, they're doing pretty good. But anyway, Isla stomps over to the bulletin board and starts flipping through all the community posters Jayce is too nice to take down even though they definitely don't still need to be up, and grabs this missing cat poster."

"Oh my God." Mom started cackling.

"Right? Huge block letters, right at the top: *HAVE YOU SEEN MY PUSSY?* It was like, two layers deep. I have no idea how she remembered seeing it, but sure enough, it's Tony—"

"The cat's name is Tony?" Mom asked.

"Tony Baloney, actually. So she didn't get to keep it. But I'm sure the cat distribution system will bite her in the ass eventually."

She laughed. "Well, Isla sounds like a peach, Ellie-Bellie, and she's clearly been good for you. When do I get to officially meet her?"

I frowned. "What do you mean, officially?"

"That was my attempt to segue into a question about when you'll be coming home for Christmas," she said.

"Oh," I said. "I figured I'd drive down on Christmas Eve. But what does that have to do with Isla?"

"Are you not bringing her?"

"I'm pretty sure she has her own family Christmas to go to," I said.

"Oh, darn." She sounded put out. "I was looking forward to meeting her. I even argued extra hard for you to have a room instead of an air mattress on the floor in the basement."

None of this made any sense. "What are you talking about?"

"At the cabin," she said. "Paige was insisting her kids get the bed but I told her they're absolutely not getting a private room before you and your girlfriend. I mean, they're children, they can use the air mattress. They'll bounce back a lot faster than an almost-thirty-year-old."

"Please stop reminding me I'm almost thirty," I said. "But also, what... and the cabin... what girl... Isla isn't my girlfriend, Mom."

"She's not?" Mom said.

"No. We're just friends."

"Oh," she said knowingly. "That's fair. My coworker Sloane said lesbian relationships move faster—something about U-hauls? I didn't really understand the joke—when I told her you've only known each other for a couple of months—"

"Whoa, whoa, whoa," I said. "First, even if we were together, it wouldn't be a lesbian relationship because I'm not a lesbian. I'm bisexual. That doesn't change if I'm dating a woman, just like I don't become straight if I'm dating a man. Second, *why* were you talking to your coworker about Isla?"

"Because I didn't know she wasn't your girlfriend yet," she said apologetically. "We were just chatting about life and such, you know, and I mentioned it. And you talk about Isla more like how you've talked about your girlfriends and boyfriends, not your friend-friends. With that and you mentioned trying to find your soulmate... I shouldn't have assumed you were there yet. Sorry, hon."

"There's no 'yet' about it. She's straight." Something twisted in my stomach. "And the soulmate stuff is something we're both doing. We're trying to trigger meet cutes."

"Meet cutes?" she repeated.

My face burned. "Yeah. Like, when we found Tony Baloney, I went with Isla to bring him back to his owner because I was trying to convince her that maybe the cat distribution system was working with the soulmate system and the way she was gonna get a cat was by hooking up with the cat's dad. But the owner wasn't single. Which is fine, because even though Isla was feeling a little bummed about everything that happened with Nasally Hat Boy, she's having fun with it again now that we seem to have shaken him."

"Who's Nasally Hat Boy?"

"This guy we kept running into every time we tried one of our meet cute ideas." I rolled my eyes. "He was an asshole, though. But he hasn't shown up since his grandma yelled at him for telling her he'd rather jerk off than date Isla, and she hasn't gotten all angsty about not believing in fate again. And she told me, like, four more times that she's definitely not getting a cat, so even though it didn't work out with Tony Baloney she should be chosen for one any day now." I cleared my throat. "But can we also circle back to that whole air mattress thing? What... why would I sleep on an air mattress instead of my bedroom? I thought we were just going to Gran's for Christmas dinner."

"Oh, *right*," Mom said. "That's why I called. Since there's so many of us coming to Christmas now, your grandparents decided it made far more sense for us to get together at the cabin instead of their house!"

Whatever was in my stomach did another sharp twist. "Oh."

"Right?!" Mom said excitedly. "It's been *years* since we all went out to the cabin! And Canmore at Christmas will be so festive and beautiful and—"

"Right," I said. "But if there's not enough beds for everyone, I can do a daytrip instead of staying overnight. It's not that far from Cochrane."

"Not a chance," Mom said. "Just because the others have partners and families doesn't mean you should get shafted. You're as important as everyone else there."

"That doesn't mean I want to stay there."

She sighed, which triggered the immediate and visceral guilt response that any mom can conjure up with a sigh like that. "Ellie-Bellie—"

"Mom—"

"Hon, I know you don't love spending time with family." There was sadness in her voice. "I understand. But they're still your family."

I bit back what I wanted to say, which was that they were *her* family, because all that would do was cause a fight. "What if, instead of a Christmas present, you let me sit this one out?"

"Of course not," she said. "I already have your presents ready and wrapped. But if that's what you want, it's... it's okay."

Inwardly, I sighed, resting my forehead in my hand. "It's fine. I'll come."

"If you don't want to—"

"Don't try to talk me out of it," I said. "Otherwise I'll change my mind."

"I appreciate you, sweetie."

"Thanks, Mom."

She switched subjects so we didn't have to end the conversation on the topic of spending yet another holiday in the cabin of my nightmares, but after discussing the latest episode of *Secret Rednecks*, I told her I had to go and hung up. Once my mom's voice was gone, I put my head down on the break room table with a quiet groan.

"Do you hate money, Ellie?" asked a raspy, unpleasant voice almost as soon as my forehead hit the wood.

Fuck. This. Day.

"No, Paulette," I said monotonously. "I'm a normal human who likes money."

"Hmph. Then maybe the best way to get you to stop wasting my time is to cut your paycheck to make up for all the money you cost this company," my boss snapped.

"You can't do that," I said.

"Not to mention the clients we're losing because you're not at your desk scheduling them—"

"I have nothing to do. No one's scheduling any HVAC on the last workday before Christmas. We're not even here next week."

"There's always something to do. Which is why you should be back at your desk."

"I'm entitled to a break."

"Funny. I thought you took your break first thing this morning when you were half an hour late."

"I was three minutes late," I said. "Because of the snowstorm. And even though I was the second person here, somehow no one else got told they have to stay here for lunch despite being later than me."

"Because somehow, everyone else is here on time every other day."

"Sounds like this is something you should have addressed on those days instead," I said. "Especially since I did what you said. I stayed here."

"To make up for the time you keep stealing from me," she snapped. "You were late, which means your lunch break—"

"—is something she's still entitled to as per employment standards and company policy."

The voice of an angel and the scent of chili interrupted Paulette as Isla walked into the room. She was carrying a paper bag from the grocery store deli down the street, snowflakes clinging to the curls framing her face.

Paulette's untamed grey eyebrows pinched together even tighter. "Excuse me?"

Isla set the paper bag on the table beside me. "Alberta employees are required to take a minimum thirty-minute break after the first five hours of work. Ellie's shift starts at eight-thirty. She was here at eight thirty-three. So she was legally required to take a break by one-thirty-three and it's now"—she looked up at the clock on the wall—"one forty-five."

"So I'm supposed to take the loss on the time she didn't work," Paulette said in a flat voice.

"No, you could've told her to take three minutes less on her break," Isla said, sitting down. "But you told her she had to stay at the office, which means you have to pay her for it."

"It does *not*—"

"If you put restrictions on an employee's break, it must be paid," Isla said, barely even flinching beneath Paulette's cold gaze. "It's in the Employment Standards Code. And technically part of your company policy, too. I think it was on page three of the handbook."

Something was going on.

Don't get me wrong. I loved watching Isla school Paulette like that. But even though Isla was a rule follower, she was also a people-pleaser. I knew she was trying to break out of her comfort zone and yeah, she was doing a good job of it, but mouthing off to her boss was definitely a few kilometers too far from the zone.

"Well, Miss Spends-Too-Much-Time-Reading-Labour-Laws," Paulette said, her glower deepening. "Maybe you can remind me what the company policy on employee fraternization is."

The aura of flinching surrounded Isla, though she remained still as she frowned uncertainly. "Uh... I'm assuming it's not allowed?"

"I see. And you know what they say about assuming, right?" Paulette said.

"It makes an 'ass' out of 'u' and 'me'?" I guessed.

"What?" Paulette said, looking at me. "That's the stupidest thing I've ever heard. No. They say assuming makes you a brainless fucknugget because facts are more important."

"That's very catchy," I said.

"I haven't read the fraternization policy," Isla said. "It wasn't applicable to me, so—"

"Oh, it *wasn't*?" Paulette said, turning her attention back to Isla. "That's excellent to know. It was a pain in the ass to fill the customer service role after having to get rid of the last floozy who couldn't keep it in her pants." She shot a pointed look at me. "There is a *zero*-tolerance policy for you little shits getting into relationships with each other."

Jesus. Why did everyone think Isla and I were dating?!

"I guess it's a good thing Isla and I aren't involved with anyone," I said.

"I guess so," Paulette sneered, then turned on a heel. "Finish lunch and get back to work, you fucking slackers."

"Merry Christmas to you too, Scrooge," Isla muttered as Paulette left the room.

"Wow, you're grumpy," I said.

Isla apparently didn't catch the admiring tone in my words because hurt settled into the crease of her eyebrows as she sat next to me. "You're welcome for standing up for you, I guess."

"I didn't mean that as a bad thing," I said.

"Okay."

I watched as she pulled fresh-baked buns from the bag, followed by two bowls of chili. She slid one to me, then dug out two spoons.

"Are you?" I asked.

"Am I what?" she replied.

"Okay?"

"Yeah. Of course. Are you okay?"

I took the spoon she handed me. "Yeah. Of course."

"I don't believe you."

"Well, I'm sick of Paulette's shit and half-considering not coming back after Christmas," I said. "It'd serve her right."

"It would."

"Like, yes, I'm late sometimes. A lot." I fidgeted with the spoon, staring at my still-sealed lunch. "But I don't drop the ball. I get my work done. I do it *well*. I stay late when I have to. And somehow that means I shouldn't get to eat lunch?"

"It's definitely unfair."

"But what the hell else would I do?" I pressed my thumb to the back of my spoon. "Jayce says I should be a photographer. But I would hate running my own business. Especially because it's all the stuff I'm *not* good at and I don't want to do stuff I don't like."

The spoon snapped. I grumbled in frustration, but Isla handed me her spoon, then reached into the bag and grabbed another one.

"And the fallout of failing would be awful. I can't afford for it to not work, you know?" I said. "So unless fate decides to get off its ass and set up the meet cute with the sexy rich billionaire who's destined to be my soulmate, I'm shit out of luck."

"That sucks."

I frowned at her. "Are you sure you're okay?"

"Yep."

"I don't believe you, either. Is it because it's our last day working together before the Christmas holidays?" I asked. "Because I'm not leaving for my parents' until Sunday. You've still got a whole day of access to my lovable shenanigans."

"I'm fine, Ellie."

I popped the plastic lid off the chili, the scent of tomato and meat and spice rising from the bowl along with a healthy amount of steam and reminding me of the other odd thing I'd noticed. "Did you find any meet cute candidates while you were out?"

"No."

"Oh. Is that why you're grumpy?"

"I'm not *grumpy*," she said, setting her spoon down in exasperation. "I'm just... annoyed. Because I've spent months trying to let fate guide me to where I'm supposed to be, and instead of helping me find my soulmate or giving me even the slightest hint of a sign that I'm on the right path, it decided to help Venus instead."

"Venus? Your sister?"

"Mm-hmm." She let out a dry laugh. "Because fate decided it would be funny to sell me out or something. She's found *her* soulmate. And now they're getting married."

Chapter Eighteen
I Should've Stayed In Bed

Isla

I should have stayed in bed.

Each time I thought it that day, it became a little more true.

Opening the curtains in my living room to see eight inches of snow had fallen overnight?

I should have stayed in bed.

Pushing the foyer door open and watching it scrape a foot-and-a-half of snow away because the biting wind had blown it into drifts against the buildings?

Should've stayed in bed.

My puffy winter jacket soaking through as I tried to brush off my car?

Bed would've been warm and dry and cozy.

Feeling my car sway from side to side as I navigated the unplowed streets, slipping on unseen ice buried beneath the tire tracks that now defined the lanes because God knows where the actual lines were?

Bed would have been better.

Getting snow in my boots because they weren't tall enough?

Bed.

Ellie realizing she'd forgotten to pack her lunch after Paulette gave her shit for being less late than everyone else and offering to go to the grocery store at lunch to get us the delicious hot chili and fresh buns from the deli?

Believe it or not, should have stayed in bed.

The grocery store deli made the kind of food you'd expect to find in a down-home diner, lovingly cooked by a grandmotherly type who'd perfected

146

the recipe years before I'd even been born. The chili they made on Fridays was almost as good as the fried chicken from The Chick Magnet.

Almost. Nothing could overtake fried chicken as my favourite food. But that chili was a close second.

Plus it was our last day of work for a while, since Air-U-Need Budget HVAC and Air Conditioning closed the office over the Christmas holidays as one of their few-and-far-between perks. So I figured I could pick up some groceries and stuff so I didn't have to go out much while spending the holidays alone for the first time in my life.

The point was, I had to go to the grocery store. And I was looking forward to it. So one would think I shouldn't have needed to wish I'd stayed in bed.

And then as I waited for my chili to be scooped into takeout bowls, Venus called.

"What's wrong?" I answered, since out-of-nowhere calls from my sister were rarely a good thing.

"Hello to you, too," she said.

And then she burst into tears.

I was stunned for a moment. Venus wasn't the type of person who never cried, but she didn't cry often. And I couldn't remember the last time I'd heard her sob like—

No.

No, actually, I could remember.

"Is Mom okay?" I asked immediately, my heart in my throat.

"Y-Yes," she sniffled. "Mom's fine."

I swallowed hard, not because of my heart being in my throat but because I had a sudden flash of guilt for asking about my mom first. "Are you okay?"

"Mm-hmm."

I tried to think. "Grandma or Grandpa Monroe? Gam? Pops?"

"They're fine. Everyone's fine. No one's hurt or dead o-or anything and it's... it's fine."

"Okay," I said slowly. "So what happened?"

"Don't be mad," she said.

My stomach sank. Nothing good ever started with those words. "About what?"

"I know how this is going to sound," she sniffled. "But now that you and Nick have been broken up for a while, I need to come clean."

My stomach had sunk too early; now that it was gone, a hollow vacuum of dread weighed on me heavier than gravity. "About what, Venus?"

Her voice shook. "I know it's selfish, okay? I know. We were sneaking around for months because we didn't want to make it weird."

The world around me stopped. All I could hear was the sound of Venus crying and my heart still pounding in my throat, echoing in the hollowness of the rest of me.

"Are you serious?" I asked.

She sobbed harder. "Y-Yes. I'm s-so s-s-sorry."

"You've been sneaking around with Nick for months?"

"Wait, *what*?!" The sobs were shocked out of her voice and it pitched up so high I checked to make sure the display case in the deli hadn't cracked. "Of course not. Oh my God, Isla, how could you think that I'd do something like that?!"

"Um, because of what you said?" I replied.

"Oh, no. *God* no," she said. "I would never. I mean Nick's brother. Marcus. We've been secretly dating for a year."

Marcus.

Marcus?

I mean, yeah, it was a relief to know my ex-boyfriend *hadn't* been cheating on me with my sister after everything, but I couldn't even remember Venus and Marcus meeting before, aside from my mom telling me they'd both helped Nick get the rest of my stuff from our apartment. And Marcus was Nick's older brother. Venus was two years younger than me, so there had to be five or six years between them. Not that twenty-two and twenty-seven seemed like that bad of an age gap, but it meant they didn't run the same social circles.

"It just happened," Venus said when I didn't say anything. "And I didn't want to tell you right after you'd broken up with Nick, especially if you and him got back together or something because Marcus said Nick might've wanted you to come back. But you didn't and we can finally be together without hiding it."

"You could've been together before, too," I said.

"You don't think it would've been weird? If you and Nick had gotten married or something, we would've been like, family."

"We're already family," I said. "You're my sister. And Nick and I didn't get married. Neither have you and Marcus, so—"

"Not yet," she said.

I blinked. "What do you mean, not yet?"

She mumbled something.

"I can't hear you, Venus."

"—Marcus"—another mumble—"...him."

"Marcus did what?"

She let out a loud grumble. "He asked me to marry him!"

My instinct was to congratulate her, because of course it was. That was what you *did* when people got engaged. Even if it was weird because your sister was marrying your ex-boyfriend's older brother she'd secretly been dating for a year.

But nothing came out. Not because I *wasn't* happy for her. But...

"Why are you crying, Venus?" I asked gently.

She didn't answer. Not right away, unless you counted the watery sniffles and muffled sobs that filtered through the phone. But eventually, she took a deep breath and blew it out, though she was kind enough to move the phone away so it didn't blow static into my ear.

"Because I'm supposed to be happy," she said.

Because that made so much sense. "And you're not happy."

"No, I am." She sniffled again. "But this whole thing is such a mess. I didn't want to do it over the phone but Mom said since you're not coming home for the holidays, I had to tell you because family is supposed to know these things first, and we want to tell Marcus' family at Christmas but now you're gonna be mad and—"

"Wait, wait," I said, my head spinning. "You think I'm mad?"

"Aren't you?"

"Why would I be?"

"Because..." She trailed off into silence. "You're not?"

"I'm not," I said. "I'm confused and a little overwhelmed, but I'm not mad."

"I thought..." She took another big breath and let it out, though that time some of it caught the speaker. "Marcus wants to have an engagement party. He said you might be upset about that. Because he's asking Nick to be his best man."

"That makes sense. They're pretty close."

"Yeah. And Marcus asked me if you are, um, going to be... like... my, uh..."

Oh, fuck.

I should have stayed in bed.

"...because he might feel weird about it," she said. "And I... like, you're my sister, but I wasn't... I mean, you know I love you, but..."

Oh, thank God.

"Venus," I interrupted, trying not to sound relieved. "I'm not going to be offended if you don't ask me to be your maid of honour. I won't be offended if you don't ask me to be in your wedding at all."

She paused. "Really?"

"Really."

"Oh." She cleared her throat. "Okay. So, um, I guess... that's... taken care of."

"I would if you wanted me to," I said uncertainly. "It has nothing to do with Nick or any of that stuff. But you have a lot of friends and I know that's important to you."

"Yeah," she said softly. "Yeah, I do."

"So you have nothing to worry about if Nick's the best man. It won't be a problem at all."

"For you."

"What do you mean?"

She sighed. "I mean, I just said to Marcus that I didn't even know if you'd come to the engagement party. Like if you couldn't get time off work. Since you have to travel now. And if you felt like things were awkward with Nick..."

I frowned, trying to figure out what she was and wasn't saying.

"Is Nick going to be uncomfortable if I'm there?" I finally asked.

"I don't know," Venus said.

I nodded, even though she couldn't see me. "Okay. Well, all I can tell you is you have to do what's best for you. But I wouldn't let what happened with me and Nick stop me from being there for you. I'm okay with, like, seeing him and stuff. And being civil or whatever."

"I was just trying to be thoughtful." There was an unexpected snideness to Venus's voice that stung. "But I would really, really like you to be there."

It took me another moment to process what she'd said, and another after that to realize part of not talking to my sister in a while meant I'd forgotten that she just sounded like a mean girl. Her tone was flat and her words were blunt, but they were always honest.

So I knew, without a doubt, she wanted me to come.

"Then I'll be there," I said. "When is it?"

"We haven't decided yet." She laughed shakily. "I suggested over Christmas since everyone's in town anyway—well, except you, but I thought you might... But it doesn't matter. Marcus shot that down. I guess he wants it to be kinda big and formal and catered and stuff. So... sometime in the new year."

We weren't on the phone for much longer. I congratulated her and assured her I was happy for her again, then hung up so I could go up to the deli counter to get my and Ellie's lunches.

And I *was* happy for her. I was. It was just the same kind of happiness that was making Venus cry.

The kind of happiness that hurts.

"Why does it hurt?" Ellie asked.

I blinked a few times, bringing myself back into the break room, my half-eaten bowl of chili in front of me. I couldn't have said what I'd specifically talked about, just that I'd told Ellie what had happened, and that there was no longer steam coming from my chili.

"Because I... I want that." I sighed, setting my spoon down. "I want to find my person. I'm happy she has, but it makes me sad I haven't."

"That's not it, though."

I looked up at Ellie, whose bowl was empty and whose bun was nothing but crumbs on the paper wrapper. "Are you calling me a liar?"

"No," she said. "But you are lying."

"I'm not lying to you."

"Not to me," she said, leaning back in her chair. "You're lying about something to yourself. Is it because it's Marcus?"

"No." I thought for a moment, frowning before I realized the thing that was keeping my chest hollow had nothing to do with Venus getting engaged at all. "It's... Christmas."

Ellie's eyebrows flicked up, but she nodded like she believed me. "That does make sense. I thought you were going home for Christmas. I'm sorry you're missing all your family celebrations and stuff."

"Oh, we don't really celebrate," I said.

She gaped at me. "What do you mean, you don't celebrate Christmas?"

Christmas was one of the few things my parents argued about.

Well, not *argued*, per se, but there wasn't a better word for it. Before Venus and I came along, it hadn't even been a conversation. The first year they were together, Dad bought Mom a Christmas gift. She'd refused to open and told him to save it for her birthday because Christmas was a mix of her two least favourite things: organized religion and capitalism. Dad, who already loved Mom in the of way where he'd do anything she asked, obliged.

When her birthday rolled around the following summer, she opened the package still wrapped in brown kraft paper. It contained a toque and mitten set Dad had made after teaching himself to knit. The wool was sheared, spun, dyed, and wound into balls by a pagan vendor at a night market they went to once in a while, who'd agreed to give him the wool in exchange for helping them repair a fence on their farm, and the knitting needles had been borrowed from his grandmother.

"It had to be thirty degrees that day, I swear," Dad would say whenever he told the story, a quiet laugh on his lips. "But Athena put that toque on her head, and I spent the rest of the day with my palms sweating from holding her hand because she refused to take her mittens off."

When my parents went from being David and Athena to Mom and Dad, though, my mom's unwillingness to celebrate Christmas became one of the few things where my dad didn't let her have her way.

"I like Christmas," he would say. "It was an important thing to me growing up. I want our children to have that, too."

Mom would roll her eyes. "Neither of us are Christian, David."

"Lots of non-Christians celebrate Christmas. It's not about religion."

"Right, it's about materialism and capitalism," she said.

"It's about family. And love. And togetherness."

"And corporate greed."

He would sigh. "And corporate greed, sure. But also about creating memories with our children."

They eventually compromised. Venus and I got some of the typical Christmas traditions: a tree and decorations, but only on the tree. There were never any glittering lights on the outside of our house, since the extra energy use was bad for the environment. Presents, but only from family; when we were little, we asked Santa to bring his presents for us early so we could take them to the Santa's Anonymous boxes at the mall so kids got gifts, too. And we always had Christmas dinner, though Mom refused to cook a turkey, so instead we would make homemade pizzas and have ice cream for dessert.

But then Dad died.

And even though I knew he didn't want the few traditions we had to die with him, they did.

"I'm sorry," Ellie said. "I didn't know. About your dad, I mean."

The level of chili in my bowl hadn't changed this time when I blinked out of my memories. My spoon was still on the table. I'd been staring at it. Maybe.

"It's okay," I said. "He planned it. Not like... like he didn't..." I sighed. "He had cancer, which was obviously unplanned, but he planned the whole dying part. Mom used to—well, she still does, actually—she laughed about it. Not in a mean way. It was just how she and Dad coped with it. Like he was so structured and organized that death was on his schedule, not the other way around. When they told him the cancer was terminal, he just..." I stopped, swallowing hard. "No one wants to be in pain. He talked with Mom and the doctor and then with me and Venus and he decided medically assisted dying was the best option."

"I can't even imagine," she said softly. "I'm sorry."

"It's okay. I mean, it sucks, obviously. But we got to say goodbye. And I'm glad he wasn't in pain for longer than he had to be. I just miss him a lot. Talking about it changes nothing." I cleared my throat, forcing out a slight laugh. "But that's probably why it hurts. Just being reminded that I'm... I'm not going home. My mom asked me and Venus what we wanted to do about Christmas the year my dad died and Venus started crying and said she couldn't do anything Christmas related because it made her too sad."

"That makes sense, I guess. Sucks, but I get it."

"Yeah. Except she still wanted presents and cried when I didn't get her anything, even though she didn't get anything for anyone either."

Ellie snorted. "Your sister is something else."

"I know. She's matured a lot since then."

"Oh. Sorry. I might not be the biggest fan of children—"

"No, really?" I said. "The person who has literally referred to kids as 'fuck trophies' isn't the biggest fan of them?"

Ellie grinned. "Well, not to their *faces* or something. I don't begrudge kids for being kids. I just didn't realize your sister was a kid when she said that."

"Oh," I said. "No. It was three years ago. But she'd just graduated high school, so technically..."

Ellie's mouth dropped open. "Three years?"

"Yep. It's Christmas Number Four." I let out a shaky laugh. "It's fine. I can't force my mom or my sister to want what I want. I just kinda wish it was different. Dad loved Christmas. It might not have been the same as how other people celebrated, but that didn't matter. It was never about that for him. It was about making memories and traditions so that when one of us was g-gone—"

My voice cracked.

My eyes started to sting.

I should have seen it coming. The lump in my throat, the tightness in my chest... and yet I still sat there, talking and talking and *talking*. Mortified, I lurched forward and grabbed my spoon, digging it into the bowl of chili and shovelling a long-cold spoonful into my mouth. I don't know why that was my instinct; all it did was make it more obvious that my throat had closed and my heart had broken and suddenly my hand was in Ellie's as she pulled me out of my chair.

In silence, she ushered me out of the break room. I kept my mouth closed, holding it together until we got into the single-stall bathroom at the end of the hall.

If I'd learned anything since my dad had died, it was that there often wasn't any particular logic behind when or why or how the fact someone was *gone* would hit you. I hadn't cried during any of the three Christmases that had passed since he'd died. And sure, I guess it could be connected. I'd been talking about

Christmas with Ellie, and about my dad, and about feeling happy but hurt and things were emotional and *yes*, okay? The reasoning was there.

It just felt like it didn't make sense.

Ellie, being Ellie and being incapable of doing anything without lending her own strange quirkiness to it, locked the door behind us and sat on the toilet, pulling me onto her lap. I half-laughed and half-sobbed as she hugged me fiercely.

"Why are you sitting on the toilet?" I croaked.

"I dunno," she replied. "Why does it matter? I kept my pants up."

Another strange sob-laugh escaped my throat before I dedicated myself to crying on Ellie's shoulder.

"Come with me to my parents' for Christmas," she said a while later, when the sobs had faded to choked hiccups.

I chuckled, the sound wet as I dried my cheeks with a piece of cheap toilet paper. "It's okay. I don't want to impose."

"It's not. You'd be doing me a favour, actually. We're going to my grandparents' cabin and I hate it there, so you tagging along would be way more fun. I know it won't be exactly how your dad did Christmas, but wouldn't he rather you have a big Christmas dinner with your best friend instead of sitting by yourself and reading?"

And yeah, Ellie had never met my dad, but it was like she knew him.

Chapter Nineteen

The Burns Family Christmas

Isla

I INSISTED ON DRIVING since I was the one imposing on Ellie's family's Christmas. Ellie refused until I agreed to take back the part about imposing on her family's Christmas, then happily agreed to let me drive because she didn't enjoy driving that much.

It was barely past noon when we got to the Burnses' house. I hadn't even taken my seatbelt off when a tall man with a bushy mustache, thick brown hair, and cowboy boots bounded out the front door, jacketless even though our breaths were hanging in the biting air. He was so tall that Ellie, who was tall herself, looked tiny as he pulled her into a tight hug; I couldn't even imagine how odd it looked when he moved to the driver's side of the car and hugged me, too.

Especially because I wasn't expecting it and froze for a moment before hugging him back.

"It's a real pleasure to meet you, Isla," he boomed, the corners of his sparkling blue eyes crinkling. "I'm Garth. Welcome to the Burns Family Christmas. It's as legendary as you're imagining."

Garth insisted on collecting the bags Ellie and I brought, even though I could have easily carried my backpack. Pristine snow buried the yard and tall plastic candy cane decorations lined the walkway to the house, which was framed in every colour of light possible. A huge green wreath with a festive red ribbon tied at the bottom hung in the entryway and the moment Garth flung the door open, the spicy scent of cinnamon and pine floated out on a wave of warm, welcoming air.

"Beloved!" he called. "Ellie-Bellie is home!"

"Oh, thank God." Moments later, a petite woman with thick red hair, plump pink lips, and wide blue eyes rounded the corner. She yanked Ellie down into a tight hug. "I missed you, baby girl."

"I missed you too, Mom," Ellie said.

Ellie's mom let go of her and looked at me, clapping her hands together. "And you brought *Isla*!"

She said it like my presence was a surprise, which it wasn't. I'd been there when Ellie called her mom to tell her I'd be joining them. Not to mention that I'd never met Ellie's mom before, so the fact that she knew my name made it clear she'd known I was coming.

But damn if that look of delight didn't make me feel like I belonged.

"It's nice to meet you, Mrs. Bur—"

"Ah, ah, ah," she said, cutting me off with a flap of her hand before pulling me in for a hug that literally cracked my spine. "It's Karina, dear."

"Okay," I half-gasped. "Nice to meet you, Karina."

"And you, gorgeous girl." She flicked her eyes at Ellie in a way I didn't understand.

"Great," Ellie said. "Now that you've both met my best friend, can we have a sec to bring our stuff to my bedroom?"

"You have until the milk is ready for the hot chocolate," Karina said. "Then you get your butts back up here so I know how much Bailey's to add to each of them."

The Burnses didn't have two guest rooms, but that was fine. It wasn't like Ellie and I were strangers to sharing a bed. I mean, we spent almost every Friday night not just sharing a bed, but full-on spooning each other. So I grabbed my backpack and followed Ellie down the stairs to her childhood bedroom.

It was a surprisingly massive room compared to my childhood bedroom, which had barely fit the double bed my parents got me when I turned thirteen, even when it was pushed against the wall. Ellie's room was big enough for there to be a nightstand on both sides of her neatly-made queen-size bed and also hold a desk I couldn't picture her studying at, plus a dresser she'd decorated with a variety of colourful stickers. On one wall was a large painting of a mountain landscape, and on the other, a collage frame containing school pictures of Ellie. I bit back a smile as I looked at them; each one showed the same wide smile and sparkling dark brown eyes, her brown hair getting longer each year until she started wearing it in a bun on top of her head.

"Wow," I said. "I didn't think people actually left their kids' room set up after they moved out."

"They didn't really," Ellie said. "I mean, this *is* how it was set up, but it was more that they left it set up as a guest room. And I boomeranged home for a while after dropping out of college before moving to Aurora Flats with Jayce, so... you know." She shrugged and put her bag on the desk chair. "Trust me, it didn't look like this when I was growing up. I didn't have pictures of myself on the walls. My mom put those there when I moved out the second time. And I always had clothes *everywhere*. But—oh my God." She burst out laughing.

"What?" I asked.

She gestured at the nightstands. Each one had an identical basket full of what looked like travel-sized toiletries. "I told you my mom is a little extra, right? Enjoy your welcome basket."

Extra was one word for it.

At first, I thought it was full of bottles of shampoo and stuff that you steal from hotels. I'd packed everything I needed, of course, but it was still more than thoughtful of Karina to set that all out for everyone.

But as Ellie started to unpack, I realized I was wrong.

There were small bottles of shampoo and body wash, of course. And a toothbrush and toothpaste, makeup wipes, and small packs of Advil and Tylenol and Tums.

But there were also socks.

Fluffy Christmas socks, to be exact.

And a red mug with snowflakes etched onto it.

A fancy lip balm and a small tube of hand lotion.

A face cloth, exfoliating mitt, and a candle.

And...

"Wow," I said, pulling out the four-pack of Crunchies. "What are the chances of your mom picking my favourite chocolate bar?"

"Pretty high," Ellie said, crossing the room to look through her basket. "Seeing as she asked me what it was."

"Wait, what?"

"I thought she was just going to make sure she had some in the house," she said. "But I guess I should've warned you. She *loves* to dote. Like, if you're full at dinner, don't bother putting a napkin or something on your plate. She'll just get you a new plate and fill it up again. Your best bet is to leave something on your plate and push it around with your fork every once in a while so it looks like you're still eating."

"How do you know when a meal ends if she keeps getting people new plates?" I asked.

"The food's gone," she said. "Or if she goes to get stuff from the kitchen or something, I start clearing the table. But also, don't worry about offending her if you don't actually eat every single bite. I think she just gets uncomfortable if someone doesn't have food in front of them. And she likes to spoil people. Do I need a stocking as a grown-ass woman? No. Would she have a minor heart attack if I suggested she didn't have to do one for me? Absolutely. And—ah, yep." She pulled the fluffy socks out of hers, revealing the coffee mug. "This is why we're having hot chocolate. She always buys us special mugs for Christmas Eve."

I stared at her as she sat on the edge of the bed, tugging her socks off and replacing them with the Christmas ones. Beautiful confusion rippled through my chest as I processed the fact that this woman, my friend's mom who I had never met, had put this together for me after being informed less than two days earlier that I'd be crashing her family's Christmas.

"Oh, and I guess while I'm warning you about things, don't get my dad started on politics," Ellie continued.

I glanced up, alarmed. "Because we'll disagree?"

"Oh, no, not at all," she said, then tilted her head. "Well, maybe. He loves politics but hates politicians, so if you like any political figures, you'll probably disagree a little. But overall values, no. He's always been that guy who's like 'Well of *course* we should use our taxes to invest in social programs, that's how you save money long-term' and 'Why should the government care if two dudes want a wedding? You don't like gay marriage, don't get gay married.' It's just that once he starts, that's it. That'll be the conversation for the rest of the night. But if you *do* accidentally get him started, start talking about cars. He loves cars, too."

It was the first ripple of many made by Ellie and her family, actions they saw as no more than a pebble but that sent waves of emotions out from my very core. After going upstairs and thanking her profusely for the basket as Ellie chuckled in the background, we sat in the Burnses living room to enjoy our spiked hot chocolate. I'd finished one cup and was working on the refill Karina had poured in without asking when the next pebble dropped.

"I should have enough gas to drive us to Canmore if we want to drive ourselves," I said when Ellie mentioned taking separate vehicles to her grandparents' cabin the next day.

"I would hope so," Garth said, frowning as he sipped his hot chocolate. "If you filled up in Red Deer, you should be good for a while."

"Well, yeah," I said. "I just like to top it off whenever I can. I'm overdue for an oil change."

He nodded knowingly. "Yeah, that'll getcha. But how overdue is it if you're worrying about the mileage?"

"Um... a bit," I said reluctantly.

Garth raised his eyebrows. "What's 'a bit' in this context?"

"Like four... thousand kilometers," I said.

"Four thou—!" Thankfully his mug was empty as he set it down on the table with a loud thud. "Are you serious, Isla—wait." He pointed a finger at me. "What's your middle name, young lady?"

I couldn't help it. I burst out laughing, glancing at Ellie. "You can tell you two are related, eh?"

"Yep. And it's Athena." Ellie stuck her tongue out at me before looking at her dad. "Isla Athena Monroe."

Garth set his stern look on me again, though it was lessened by the laughter in his eyes. "Well, Isla Athena Monroe. You *absolutely* need an oil change done. Where are your car keys?"

I frowned. "Why?"

He held his hand out and raised his eyebrows. "I need to move your car into the garage so I can change your oil."

My mouth fell open and I looked at Ellie, who simply shrugged. "He's not gonna let it go until you do it, so you might as well give him your keys now. If you're lucky, he'll take it to the car wash, too."

"That's not—"

Garth cut me off by opening and closing his hand, clapping the tips of his fingers against the base of his palm. "Keys, Isla. I'm not letting you drive anywhere until that car has fresh oil in it. Should check your brakes, too."

"But it's Christmas Eve," I said.

"Oh, that's right," he said, then clapped his fingers to his palm again. "I'll definitely take 'er to the car wash! There'll hardly be anyone there!"

"But—"

"Her keys are in the right pocket of her jacket hanging in the front closet," Ellie said.

"Excellent." Garth rose from the table and strode across the kitchen. "I'll see you girls in a few hours."

My look of utter betrayal didn't go missed by Ellie, who smiled sweetly at me.

"Consider it an early Christmas gift," she said.

"I don't need a Christmas gift from your parents!" I said.

"Oh, it's not a gift for you," Karina said. "It's for him. He loves working on cars."

I nodded slowly, not sure how to communicate what I was feeling. Her family was doing so much for me; so many things, big and little, that made me feel... something.

Like yes, I was an adult. No, I didn't *need* someone to mother me like this.

But damn if it wasn't... well...

Nice.

Sort of.

Because my instinct was to pitch in. To go to the kitchen and see if Karina wanted help preparing dinner. To set the table, or chop veggies, or pour glasses of wine and keep her company as she puttered away at whatever she was making.

But Karina refused to even let me in the kitchen.

"I *want* to help," I insisted as she urged me onto the couch next to Ellie. "I'm the one crashing your Christmas."

"That's a weird way to pronounce 'You're our guest,'" Karina said, setting a warm blanket she'd pulled from the dryer moments earlier on my lap.

"And you're not crashing anything," Ellie said.

I sighed with aggravation that was half-feigned and half-entirely-justified. "You're already spoiling me."

"As we damn well should. But if you insist, you can help me tidy up the kitchen after," Karina said, like that was some kind of concession instead of something I wouldn't be able to stop myself from doing whether she liked it or not. "For now, you girls relax. Please. Alright?"

"Isla, it's fine," Ellie said, and I looked at her, almost betrayed that she'd take her mom's side over mine. "Come on, let's watch a movie. It's not really Christmas until we watch *Die Hard* at least three times, and we've only watched it once so far this year."

"But—"

Ellie flashed a grin at me. "Trust me, Ella Two."

And I did. Reluctantly, and still fighting the urge to get up every five minutes and offer to help again, and groaning inwardly because I'd already watched *Die Hard* with Ellie and I didn't enjoy rewatching movies because I always got bored and fell asleep, but I trusted her.

Which nearly undid me.

"Isla, hon?"

I opened my eyes, blinking as the room came into focus around me. Karina's head was poking through the entryway, a soft smile on her face.

"Sorry to wake you," she said. "But Ellie's about done getting dinner ready."

I frowned, confused as I realized I'd fallen asleep during *Die Hard* just like I'd thought would happen, then by the fact that Ellie wasn't on the couch on me anymore, and finally by the fact that she'd said—

"Ellie made dinner?" I asked. "I would've helped. I wanted to help!"

"She wouldn't have let you." Karina's eyes were sparkling as I untangled myself from the throw blanket. "She wanted to make it a surprise."

I couldn't figure out what she was talking about until I followed Karina to the kitchen and froze at the sight in front of me.

"I know it's not Christmas Day," Ellie said the moment she saw me, wiping her hands on a towel. "But since we're going to the cabin, I thought we could do it tonight instead. Plus, this way my mom could help. Trust me, her cooking is *way* better than anything I can make."

It wasn't quite the same. Even if she hadn't said her mom made it, the flour scattered along the counter and floor made it clear the dough wasn't from the frozen section at Safeway. Sauce was in a simmering pot on the stove, not a pull-tab can with a spoon sticking out of it. There were three types of cheese waiting in clean white bowls, not a bag of pre-shredded mozzarella. Slightly smaller white bowls contained various toppings: mushrooms, peppers, red onions, and—controversially—pineapple. Beside that, a carefully arranged plate of various types of pepperoni, salami, and ham.

It had been three Christmases since I'd had homemade pizza.

It had been three Christmases since I'd felt like this.

"Isla?" Ellie asked. Her voice was nervous. "I didn't want to overstep. But you just sounded like you missed it and I wanted to do something special for you because even if your family doesn't do much for Christmas, I thought you deserved to, you know, do something. Because I know it's been a crazy few months for you and I mean, at the end of the day, everyone loves pizza, right, so I figured—"

"Ellie-Bellie, you're rambling," Karina said softly.

Ellie winced. "Sorry. I just wanted to, you know make sure that—like, is this okay, Isla? If not, I'm sor—*oof.*"

I threw my arms around her and buried my head against her shoulder, scrunching my eyes closed and letting the warm comfort of my best friend's hug help stifle the tears in my eyes until all that came out was a gentle sniffle.

"Thank you," I tried to whisper.

I don't know if the words actually came out, but Ellie seemed to hear them all the same.

Chapter Twenty
The Tradition

Ellie

In hindsight, I was not the brightest cookie in the tool shed when I invited Isla to my family's Christmas.

The only reason hanging up from my mother's call about spending Christmas at my grandparents' cabin and inviting Isla to said cabin didn't happen in the same breath was because I was too pretty to remember to breathe sometimes.

And clearly both of the brain cells I had left had checked out early for Christmas vacation instead of lifting the little red flag of bad ideas. So the train of thought between "Oh no, I'm spending Christmas in hell" and "I should invite Isla to Christmas" derailed and exploded into a shower of glittery soft snowflakes that blinded me to the realization that I was subjecting Isla to my grandmother until we turned into the driveway of the cabin.

And yes, there was plenty of time for me to warn Isla about what was to come after she parked. Or I could've warned her when she stopped to marvel at the view surrounding the cabin: tell-tale gangling pines that screamed "You're in the Rocky Mountains!" And towering mountains that very gently whispered "Dude, seriously, how could you not realize you're in the Rocky Mountains" as they jutted up above the treeline, their tips coated in the same kind of glittering white snow that my bad-idea-train-derailment had exploded into.

But she was so enamoured with the view that I couldn't bring myself to do it.

I could've warned her when we got inside and a handful of my cousins cornered us before we could even go to the guest room that had been not-so-lovingly prepared for us. Or when we were *in* said guest room instead of spiralling when I realized that this was not a bed, it was a futon, and yes it was a very cozy looking futon but my God, I had a hard enough time not responding to Isla's body next to mine when we were in a regular queen-size bed.

But she'd set her bag on the dresser and turned to me, her cheeks rounded by her adorable smile, and said, "Well, I guess it's a good thing we like spooning, right?" and my brain shorted out for a bit because those goddamn brain cells were *still* on vacation.

So it wasn't until we joined the rest of my vast amount of aunts and uncles and cousins and second cousins in the living room that I decided I should get over my kink for making horrible decisions without considering the consequences and warn Isla about The Tradition.

"Um, head's up," I whispered after we settled in the two folding chairs my aunt Melanie directed us to that, while expensive-looking, were still exactly as comfortable as folding chairs are. "My family does something kind of weird before dinner."

"Weird how?" Isla whispered back, frowning.

"Well, we all open a single present. The one from my grandma."

"Presents? On Christmas?" She raised her eyebrows. "What kind of sick fucks are you?"

I tried not to laugh at the same time that I tried to laugh, so all that happened was an awkward snorting sound and a weird face twitch. "Yeah, but before you get the present, she wants everyone to tell her the thing they're most—"

"Well now, if Ellie is ready, perhaps we can get started?"

Fuck.

I sat back in my chair, my eyes snapping to the figure standing in front of the roaring fireplace for the first time since we'd arrived.

The version of her that existed in my mind had hair that was pitch black, as were her eyes. But in person, the black was streaked with a large chunk of grey in the front and multiple strands scattered throughout, while her eyes were unmistakably blue.

"Sorry, Gran," I said. "I was explaining The Tradition to—"

"Ah, of course. I haven't had a chance to meet your... guest?" my grandma said.

Something that was like fear but that I wouldn't call fear lumped in my throat. "Sorry. We just got here. This is my friend, Isla."

"Nice to meet you," Isla said cheerfully.

"Isla," my grandma repeated. "What a lovely name. Did Ellie give you the rundown?"

"She sure did," Isla lied.

"Oh," my grandma said, sounding surprised I'd actually done something useful. "Well, then. As our guest, why don't you start us off?"

Fuck.

My stomach knotted. The last thing I needed was for Isla to get on my grandma's bad side, too. It was one thing for her to be shitty to me, but if she caught Isla lying—

"Mom, let Isla get a feel for the Tradition first," my mom said. "There's no need to put her on the spot like that."

Oh, thank God.

My grandma's mouth tightened, but she couldn't exactly disagree with what Mom had said, so she tilted her head in concession. "Fine. Paige, Matthew, it's your year to pass out gifts. Start with a few others before we get to Ellie's friend so she can listen and learn."

"Sorry," I whispered as my cousins got up to bring presents one-by-one to everyone in our family. "I should have warned you."

Isla smiled prettily. "Don't worry about it. What am I supposed to do?"

"You tell people your top accomplishment of the year," I whispered. "Your goal is to impress her. The person with the best one gets an extra gift."

"Oh, okay," she said, looking nonchalant. "That's easy. I thought the way you were all talking about it, I was going to have to recite Shakespeare from memory or solve a quadratic equation or something."

Both of those things were easier than impressing my grandmother, honestly. I'd never even come close to being considered for the extra gift.

Not when I came from a family of overachievers.

"I was promoted to senior sales manager and led a team that broke the record for yearly sales... in *June*," said Matt before opening his gift.

"My company secured a massive contract with an influential stakeholder under my leadership and returned record-breaking profits," said my uncle Donny, who was Matt's dad and also his boss.

"Game-winning goal in NHL western conference final," grunted Johan, in his heavy Swedish accent.

"You have a cousin in the NHL?!" Isla whispered, her eyes round.

"Technically he's my cousin's husband," I murmured back. "He's married to Paige."

"I ensured my hard-working husband came home to a spotless house, warm food on the table, and happy, healthy children," said Paige. "Oh, and I documented all that plus the entire process of growing and birthing our fourth little blessing on social media, which made me the third-highest followed wife-fluencer and earned me a publishing contract to share my mothering philosophy with the world."

"I turned eighty-three children from cancer patients to cancer survivors this year," said Tanner, who said the same thing every year save for the number of children he operated on being different.

I wasn't sure what Isla was going to say when it was her turn. The answers from my family varied so much that I wasn't sure she'd be able to pinpoint what my grandma would actually value. Like, yes, Bethany ran a successful re-election campaign for a provincial MLA and got engaged. And Aunt Melanie saved a bunch of orphans from Haiti or something with her church.

But Uncle Lucas had won a massive lawsuit for a pharmaceutical company... after they released a drug that caused multiple people to go blind. And Aunt Bella also considered it a success when she forced a bunch of people from their tribal lands so an oil company could build something.

I didn't know how Isla would react when she realized ethics weren't part of The Tradition's rating scale.

"I helped my friend with event planning and marketing at the bar they've been running and it was pretty successful," I said when it was my turn.

"How did you measure that success?" my grandma asked, even though none of the others had been asked follow-up questions about their accomplishments.

"Uh... they made good money that night?" I said.

"I see." She set her eyes on Isla. "And you?"

"I found my best friend," Isla said.

There was confused silence in the room.

"That's the best thing you did this year?" my grandma finally asked.

Isla blinked at her innocently. "Have you ever tried making friends as an adult? It's not easy. Especially after you break up with your boyfriend, run away from home, and move to a random town in Alberta where you don't know anyone. Yeah, I might be rebuilding my life from scratch, but I wouldn't be doing half as good as I am without a friend like Ellie."

I loved her.

As a friend, obviously. I loved her as a friend. She was just a friend.

Just a friend who'd slept in my arms two nights in a row.

Just a friend who'd snuggled in under my arm while we watched a movie, unaware that her head was resting against the side of my breast.

Just a friend with horrifically sexy legs and plump lips and soft curves.

Just a friend who I loved because you can love your friends. Of course you can love your friends. You're *supposed* to love your friends. That doesn't mean you're *in* love with her.

You're just friends.

"That's so sweet," my mom said, pressing a hand to her chest. "Aw, Isla. You're such a sweetheart."

"Yeah," said Bethany, smiling encouragingly. "What a nice accomplishment."

There was a round of murmured agreement. Almost none of it was genuine, but that was fine. It was enough to cover the actual genuine confusion on Isla's face when Paige handed her one of the packages wrapped in shiny white snowflake paper.

"Wait, she really got me a gift?" she asked quietly.

"Everyone gets a gift no matter what," I said.

She looked at my grandma. "Thank you. It was very thoughtful, especially since I was a last-minute addition."

My grandma smiled almost begrudgingly. "It was no problem, dear."

Which was true. Isla unwrapped one of those bath gift sets that, while expensive because my grandma would never allow herself to be seen as cheap, was pretty generic. But that didn't change the fact that its existence alone meant something, as much as I hated to admit it.

"Here's yours, Ellie-Bellie," Matt said, handing me a package wrapped in bright blue paper.

And in hindsight, I should've noticed the smirk and the overly innocent tone and the fact that my present was wrapped differently than the others.

But I didn't. I just took the package from Matt and tore it open to reveal a rolled-up T-shirt. I lifted it, letting it unfurl, and took one look at the front before slamming it down on my lap.

"What's wrong?" Isla asked, alarmed.

"Show us what you got, Ellie!" Tanner said loudly. He was fighting back a grin.

My heart thudded in my chest, too fast and too hard and too loudly for my liking.

"Yeah, what did Gran get you?" asked Paige.

"Must be something nice if you don't want to show it off," Uncle Brock said.

"Come on, show us," Matt said. He wasn't even bothering to try hiding his laughter.

"No, thanks," I said, crumpling the shirt in my hand.

"Aw, come on!" Bethany said.

The way she said it made my stomach sink even more, not because it sounded like she was in on it, but because she *didn't*.

Which made the other people who probably had nothing to do with it press for me to turn the shirt around.

I glanced at my grandma. She watched the scene in front of her with a practiced expression. Either she didn't want everyone to think she'd forgotten what she'd got me, or she didn't want them to know she was as confused as everyone else.

Because there was no *way* this was what she'd gotten me.

"Stop being a bad sport, Ellie," she said condescendingly. "Show off your gift."

And I still probably shouldn't have.

But she asked for it.

Holding her gaze, I raised the shirt again and flipped it around. There was a pause, then a swell of laughter as Gran's eyes flicked down and took in the words printed on the shirt:

Grandma's Favourite

"Well, that is most certainly not from tere," she said.

Some of the laughter turned to low *ooo*s. Some of them disappeared altogether. Isla's jaw dropped.

"*Mom!*" my mother said, the hurt loud in her gasp.

My grandma's shoulders flipped towards her, the sharpness of the turn cutting through the room.

"Because I don't *have* a favourite grandchild, Karina," she said, like anyone who thought otherwise was an idiot. "I love them all equally."

"Except Ellie," Matt whispered. Tanner snickered, but his wife, Angie, smacked him on the arm.

"I love my children, and I love their children," Gran repeated. "I love all of you the same, even if Ellie could stand to make more of an effort with her accomplishments."

"What's that supposed to mean?" Isla asked loudly.

The room went silent. Gran gave her a hard look. Isla didn't flinch.

"Simply that I want to see all my grandchildren flourish," Gran said.

"She *is* flourishing," Isla said.

"Not when you compare her career accomplishments to her peers."

"Work isn't everything."

"It is a large portion of things when you're thirty and single," Gran snapped. "What else does she have going for her?"

And maybe it was fate.

Maybe fate had decided that this year, I'd invite Isla to Christmas.

Maybe fate was why this was the year Paige and Matt had decided to arrange this prank.

Maybe it all happened so my grandma was unsettled. So the woman who was usually so in control cracked, just a bit. So she said something harsh and flippant in front of everyone instead of just me.

No one else was used to hearing things like that. Which made the room uncomfortably quiet. My mom stared at her own mother, her lips parted in shock. Even Matt looked embarrassed and uncomfortable.

"Well, that's rude," Isla said.

Her voice cracked the thin ice she'd been stepping on. It was loud, deafeningly loud, but only because the world around us was as silent as the winter day surrounding a deceivingly frozen lake.

"I'm sitting right here," she finished, and the ice shattered as her hand enveloped mine.

Chapter Twenty-One

Bacon

Isla

"I'm so sorry," I said as the door swung closed behind us. "I didn't even think... I mean, I *really* didn't think. At all. It just came out. I was so mad—"

"It's okay," Ellie said.

"It's not. None of that was okay." Cold air bit at the heat of anger and embarrassment on my cheeks, leaving an icy burn on my skin. "I'm sorry I mouthed off to your grandma—actually, no. I'm *not*. I *shouldn't* have mouthed off to your grandma, but I don't think I've ever been that mad. That tradition... that's *stupid*. Like it would be one thing you all talked about what you're proud of but the—it's just one-upping each other and bragging and trying to be impressive so you get, what, an extra fucking bubble bath basket? And the—the, that *prank*?! And what she said—"

"You're not wrong."

"I didn't even think. It's like it just spontaneously came out and—actually, is this what being spontaneous always feels like? Because I hate it."

Because it *had* been spontaneous. Truly spontaneous. The words were hanging in the air and Ellie's fingers were woven between mine before I even realized I'd opened my mouth.

But how could I not?

It was *Christmas*. I couldn't understand how something so thoughtlessly *mean* came from her own grandmother's mouth, just after her cousins made her the butt of a joke she didn't want to be part of. And yet despite all of us being in the same room, it seemed like no one else saw the hurt and discomfort on Ellie's face.

I couldn't stand it.

So I'd taken Ellie's hand and pretended to be her girlfriend.

For a brief second, the world froze, like the pause between the sound of ice breaking and the chaos of actually crashing through it. Ellie's grandma had set her burning eyes on me, her jaw clenched. I'd stared back as defiantly, like I was daring her to insult Ellie again, while secretly praying she not actually take the dare. I didn't know what to do next and I wasn't sure how much spontaneity one could take before combustion became a problem.

"I *knew* it!" Karina had shouted suddenly, and the tension broke as she clapped her hands together. "Just friends my *ass*, Ellie-Bellie!"

"Oh my God, *Ell-ieee*," said one of the cousins—Bethany, I think—as she'd leapt out of her chair. "Why didn't you tell us you have a girlfriend?!"

Which is when I'd realized I might have outed her. My stomach churned and sweat bloomed on my palms, so sudden and so intense that I thought my hand might slip from Ellie's.

But after a moment of sitting beside me in silence, she tightened her grip.

"We *were* friends," she'd said. "But we just... just started. Dating, I mean." Her lisp had been more pronounced than usual and she'd cleared her throat before continuing. "I didn't want Isla to be alone over Christmas but we didn't want to get into the whole 'Welcome to the family' thing since it's still early." She'd squeezed my hand again, turning to shoot a scolding but playful look at me. "But *someone* is awful at keeping secrets."

"Yeah, I dunno how you thought anyone was going to believe you're 'friends,'" Matt had said, making exaggerated air quotes beside his head. "Clearly you're into each other."

The sound of bustle and chatter started to return to the room, like Ellie's family wanted to layer voices on top of actions on top of laughter so they could pretend I hadn't called out their family matriarch. So they could push past the awkwardness and the tension of facing the reality of the asinine, horrific "tradition" they had. Paige made a joke about knowing who the *Grandma's Favourite* t-shirt would really go to, then brought the shirt to their grandfather, who I hadn't noticed snoozing in a recliner by the fireplace the entire time, before giving Ellie the actual gift they'd snagged from under the tree. Which was another bath set.

I'd thought she might let go of my hand, but Ellie's fingers had stayed woven between mine as we watched the rest of the presents being opened. Which was fine. It felt nice, actually. She didn't quite clutch me, but she held on tightly enough that I got the sense I was grounding her.

It was only when everyone finished opening presents that she finally let go of my hand.

"Remember that patio I told you about?" she'd said after her grandma said dinner would be served in half an hour. "The one I helped build?"

"Yeah, of course," I'd said, despite knowing she hadn't said a single word about building a patio here.

"Wanna go see it?"

I'd nodded and we'd gone to the front door, grabbing our jackets and boots.

Then, as soon as we were outside and blissfully alone, I'd let the apologies spill from me, barely able to stop long enough to let Ellie acknowledge I'd said anything.

"...and I didn't even know if you were out to your whole family," I said after declaring I hated how it felt to be spontaneous. I closed my eyes, trying to stop the stinging sensation in them. "I could've outed you."

"You didn't. They knew. It's not—"

"Yeah, but I could've. I didn't know. God, I didn't even think. It just *happened*." I grimaced. "I'm so sorry. I yelled at your grandma. Who does that? Who yells at someone's *grandma*?!"

"The best—"

"Like, what kind of monster—"

"Ella Two, I'm gonna need you to let me speak."

"I ruined it. I ruined your family's Christmas, didn't I? And after you—"

"Isla." She grabbed my hand again, jerking me back so I faced her. "Shut up."

My mouth still hung open, but the only thing that left it was my breath hanging in the cold air. The corners of Ellie's eyes crinkled with silent laughter as she waited to see if I could stay quiet for more than thirteen milliseconds.

"Listen," she said, her voice low. "I'm doing this partly because I'm pretty sure people are watching from the windows back there, partly because I need you to understand, and partly as payback for pulling that stunt in front of my fam—"

I slammed my eyes shut in a cringe before she even finished speaking. "I *know*, it was horrible of me. I'm *sor*—"

And then she kissed me.

And I...

I...

I mean, I kissed her back.

Obviously. It would've been rude not to.

Probably.

But I'd never kissed a girl before.

That in itself didn't matter. At all. I had nothing against kissing girls. If it turned out that I was into women, it wouldn't have been a big deal. I just wasn't.

But that... that was something.

It was something I couldn't explain. I'd obviously been *kissed* before. Like, I'd been with Nick for two years. We'd lived together. We'd done a lot more than kiss. And I'd liked it. The kissing and the a-lot-more. But that's all it had ever been. Just something I liked. It wasn't something I needed or craved or sought out the way people sometimes talked about.

It was like bacon.

Some people loved bacon. Some people would consider a life without bacon to be torture. And I liked bacon. It was good. I enjoyed it.

But if there was an extra charge to add bacon to something, I probably wouldn't bother. If all the bacon in the world suddenly disappeared, it would have no effect on my quality of life. I didn't *need* bacon.

Just like I didn't *need* kisses.

But that kiss was the kind that would make me consider paying to add bacon.

Or... whatever.

It was just good. It felt good. And I couldn't explain why it was so different from any of the other kisses I'd ever had. Like, yeah, her lips were a little softer. And her breath was sweet. And her nose fit neatly beside mine. And it was gentle but deep and she probably didn't *have* to put her tongue in my mouth but I was really glad she did because it just...

It felt *nice*.

It felt really, really nice.

When she pulled away, neither of us said anything for a moment. I blinked a few times, trying to resist the urge to poke out my tongue to see if my lips still tasted like hers.

They did.

"Well," I finally said. "I guess that'll really sell it, right?"

Ellie snorted on a laugh. She looped her arm through mine, leading me down a shovelled path. "Sorry. I figured since my first thought when you grabbed my hand was 'Oh my God, I could kiss her for doing this,' I might as well do it. But I probably should've asked."

"It's fine." I stifled a cough, trying clear my throat without making it obvious how much she'd flustered me. "It makes us even. Kinda. Right? And like, it was a good kiss. And we're fake-girlfriends now. So that's what we would... you know. *Do*."

"We're fake-girlfriends but real best friends," she said.

"Yeah, and if you can't kiss your best friend when you're pretending to be her girlfriend because her grandma is a horrible person, who *can* you kiss?"

I thought it would make her laugh, which it did. But it was a soft laugh that ended in a sigh and silence.

We walked without saying anything else until we reached a patio that out of sight from the house. It was clearly intended for summer use, the stone firepit looking lonely without chairs surrounding it, but a snow-covered bench ran along one side. I could see why they'd chosen to put a patio there; aside from a wooden railing, nothing stood between the patio and a steep drop that showed off a view of the mountains.

"Wow," I said as Ellie used the sleeve of her jacket to brush snow off the bench. "You built this?"

"Not all of it," she said. "Just the cobblestone. And the firepit. And I installed the bench. Basically anything that's stone, I did. Oh, and the railing. Which sucked because I hate carpentry."

"So... all of it," I said as she motioned for me to sit.

"I guess." She took a deep breath as she sank onto the bench beside me. "So. About that."

"Yes," I said. "I have a few questions."

"Yeah?"

"Mm-hmm. First: what the fuck?"

She laughed, almost in spite of herself. "To which part?"

"Yes."

"Fair." A cloud of haze filled the air between us as she let out another deep breath. "Well, I guess I should start by saying that woman isn't my grandma." She was expecting me to say something, which was evident because she didn't continue until she looked up to see me staring at her. "What?"

"I have another question," I said.

"Is it 'What the fuck?'"

"Close. It's actually 'Why is everyone calling her grandma then, and also, what the fuck?'"

Her thin lips twisted into a smirk, though the amusement of it didn't reach her eyes. "Because she's everyone else's grandma. Not mine."

"How—"

"I'm adopted."

Oh.

Ellie glanced at me. "Are you asking 'What the fuck?' again?"

"No," I said. "Well, yes, but not to that. But I haven't met anyone who's adopted before so I don't know if what I want to ask is offensive or something."

"You probably have without knowing it," she said. "It's not something that comes up naturally in conversation very often. But you can ask. I'm not that easily offended."

I nodded and swallowed hard. "Okay. So... so if you're saying your grandma isn't your grandma, does that mean your parents aren't...?"

She'd already started shaking her head before I trailed off, which was good because I really hadn't wanted to finish the question. "No, they are. That's my mom and that's my dad. Legally, emotionally, physically. It's just the DNA that's different."

"Okay," I said slowly. "So then why isn't—"

"By choice." She smiled wryly. "My parents chose to be my parents. And I chose to be their daughter, sort of. They've never hidden that I'm adopted and didn't stop me from asking questions. They helped me track down my birthparents when I was eighteen. And they didn't pressure me to keep in touch with them when I decided I didn't want them in my life. I chose that." She jerked her head in the general direction of the cabin. "Gran didn't choose me. In her mind, I'm not and have never been her grandchild."

My heart ached, both in response to her words and in dread of what she was going to say next. "Does your mom know she feels like that?"

"Yes and no." She shrugged. "When my parents decided to adopt, I know Gran pressured them not to. I'm sure you can tell that she's all about appearances. All the 'accomplishments this' and 'motivational that' and 'have you met my grandson the chief executive officer of the horseshit factory.' An outsider with ADHD and speech impediments didn't fit into her gaggle of picture-perfect grandkids."

"You know that's not true," I said.

"In my grandma's eyes, it is." She shrugged again. "She pretends she treats me the same, but she doesn't. Like, when all the grandkids turned sixteen, she'd let them spend the summer here at the cabin. As a gift."

I could see why that was. One of the first things I'd thought when we pulled into the so-called cabin earlier that day was that I couldn't imagine how fancy her grandparents' house was if *this* was their cabin. The building was huge—big enough to house the massive amount of people here fairly comfortably—and looked rustic in the way that you knew was a choice because even though the wood looked kind of weathered, it had a five-car garage in the front and a huge wrap-around porch with at least two hot tubs on it.

"But I didn't go until I was seventeen," Ellie continued. "Because she didn't offer it to me until my mom asked. It was this huge amount of drama and when I got out here, instead of getting to fuck around and enjoy myself all summer like everyone else, I got to build this." She motioned at the patio.

"Why?"

"Either because my mom had gotten upset with her for forgetting to invite me to the cabin or because she had to spend a summer with me. It doesn't really matter, I guess. She still told me to my face that she hadn't wanted me there and that unlike her 'real' grandchildren who got to fuck around doing whatever they wanted all summer, I'd be building a patio to 'earn my keep.' And when I was like 'Well, fuck that, I'm calling my mom to come take me home,' she told me to go ahead, but did I *really* want to tell my parents any of this when it was already hard enough for them to love a child that wasn't their own?"

There were no words.

No.

Fucking.

Words.

"And I probably should've told them anyway." She leaned back on the bench. "But every time I thought about doing it, I could just hear Gran telling me I was hard to love. And even though my parents have always been open and supportive about the adoption thing, there's this piece of me that thinks she might eventually convince them to stop loving me."

Somewhere in the trees around us, a bird chirped. Another responded. Gentle air swished the pine needles.

"It's not true," I finally said.

"I know," she replied.

"Your grandma is the worst."

She laughed a little. "I know that, too."

Part of me yearned to reach out and hold her hand again. The ferocity with which I wanted to touch her felt painful. "You're... you're everything, Ellie. You're amazing."

"I know." She shrugged. "Everyone else thinks so."

"And modest."

"The most modest." A smile spread on her lips. "My mom knows I don't like going to family events. She doesn't know the extent of it. And me coming to this stuff makes her happy. She still feels like she belongs with her family. I could tell her, but the risk of finding out if she'd take their side over mine..." She sighed, shaking her head. "It's easier to put up with being passive aggressively compared to all the other perfect, pretty, talented grandkids a couple of times a year."

"You're all those things, too."

The corners of her eyes crinkled as she looked up at me. "You think I'm pretty?"

I rolled my eyes. "Well, *obviously*. You're my fake girlfriend. You think I'd settle for anything less?"

"Whew." She faked fanning herself. "Coming on a little strong there, baby doll. I'll have you know I'm a respectable lady who isn't going to drop my pants just because her fake girlfriend is flattering her a little."

"We both know it takes a lot less than flattery," I said.

"Oh, absolutely." She grinned. "Ask me nicely and they're off."

"If I ask you meanly, will you flop back and spread 'em for me, too?"

"Isla!" Ellie's eyes went wide and she let out a shocked laugh, which made me laugh. "Since when do you make hilariously lewd jokes?"

"I dunno." I shrugged. "Since when do you question if you're pretty and talented? You know as well as I do that you are."

Her smile faded. "I mean, compared to my cousins, I'm objectively not as accomplished. I don't even know what I'm doing with my life."

"So? The way they live their lives works for them. Not you." I turned my knees so I was facing her. "I don't know what I'm doing with my life either. You don't have to know what you want to do with your life right this second. You don't have to know ever, really."

"Then what's the meaning of it?"

There was a plainness to her tone. A bluntness. An absence of anything to hide the vulnerability in her voice and her eyes.

"Forty-two," I said.

She frowned. "What?"

"The meaning of life is forty-two. According to Douglas Adams, anyway."

"That doesn't make sense."

"Because that's the answer. It's the question that's wrong."

She looked intrigued. "So what's the question?"

"They've been trying to figure that out for a few billion years," I said. "Or at least since 1979. There are a bunch of theories, but my favourite is that it's nonsense."

"The question or the answer?"

"Both. We ask what it all means, right? What's the meaning of life? And the answer is forty-two. So we say, well, what's the actual question? And I think the question is still 'What's the meaning of life?' The answer doesn't make sense because the *universe* doesn't make sense."

Ellie blinked at me. "I'm not following."

"The question itself is trying to apply our logic to something that doesn't have to follow it. Kind of like—" I stopped, then stood up in inspired excitement." It's like fried chicken for breakfast."

"What?" Ellie looked bewildered. "Where did the fried chicken come from?"

"The first day we met." I grinned at her. "You told me we get so caught up in rules that we don't realize we're still following the rules, even when we think we're rebelling. Remember?"

"Vaguely."

"Because you think you're breaking the rules by only eating the marshmallows from the Lucky Charms, but that doesn't even consider that you don't have to eat only breakfast foods at breakfast." I paced the patio, moving towards the railing and looking out at the trees and mountains and sky. "You don't have to know what the meaning of life is to live it. And you don't need the meaning of your life to fit in anyone else's box."

"Isla, I love the motivational-speaker vibe you've got going on right now because you're adorable when you get worked up like this," she said. "But what does this have to do with my cousins and everything?"

"Because them knowing what they're 'doing' with their life doesn't make them better than you. When someone asks what you're doing with the rest of your life, you could say that you want to eat fried chicken for breakfast every day. That's still a valid answer. Because the question shouldn't be what's the *meaning* of it all." Turning to face her, I spread my arms, then leaned against the railing. "The question is what—"

There was a loud crack, and then I was on the ground.

"...the fuck?" I finished. It came out muffled because in addition to being on the ground, I was on my belly, with my face buried in a pile of snow.

"Holy fuck," someone said beside me. "Holy *fuck*."

I pushed myself up, blinking snow off my eyelashes, and twisted to slowly take in the world around me as if that would tell me what the hell happened.

Which it did.

The railing had failed at its one fucking job, which was to not let people fall over the edge. But based on the trench of disturbed snow from the bench where Ellie had been sitting to where she was now sitting, which was on her ass in the snow beside me, she'd lurched forward and grabbed me with an impossible strength. Well, not impossible. But improbable, I think, given the fact that we'd ended up six feet away from the now-broken railing and I'd fully face-planted from the force of her yanking me.

She stared at me, her eyes wide and her face pale. I blinked a few times, then wiped some of the dripping water off my face.

"Or," I said. "Or, I'm completely wrong about everything and the universe wanted to make sure I knew it."

"Or maybe you were way too close to the truth and knowing both the question and the answer would make you far too powerful," she said.

"Yeah. Yeah, that's probably it."

"Totally."

She looked at me.

I looked at her.

And then we both started *howling* with laughter.

"Thanks for catching me," I said when I'd stopped laughing long enough to talk.

"I couldn't let you fall," she said. "Can you imagine your tombstone? 'Here lies Ella Two, who died falling off a cliff because of her fake girlfriend's shoddy teenage carpentry skills.' Wait." She frowned. "Is it still called a tombstone if it's not on a tomb? Or do I have to spring for an actual tomb instead of a hole in the ground?"

"They don't usually put the manner of death on whatever grave marker is most appropriate," I said.

"Well, regardless, it's my job as your bestie to make sure you don't die in a dumb way." She climbed to her feet and extended a hand to me. I took it, letting her help me to my feet, though she didn't let go once I was on them. "But now that we're not precariously close to a cliff, what were you saying before you almost died? About knowing the meaning of life?"

I felt a smile tug at my lips. "I was saying the question is wrong. It's not 'What's the meaning of life?' It should be 'What gives life meaning?'"

She contemplated silently for a moment. "And the answer... is fried chicken."

"For breakfast," I agreed solemnly.

And it was a good thing my hand was still in hers. Otherwise, we probably would've toppled to the ground again while we laughed, and with the railing being broken and all, there was no guarantee the universe wouldn't make another attempt to communicate via sudden death.

Chapter Twenty-Two

Full Steam Ahead

Ellie

"I can't believe he did that in front of your *grandma*, though," Isla said, pulling her shirt off as we got ready for bed later that night.

I busied myself looking through my backpack for the face wash I was ninety-eight percent sure I'd forgotten to pack, but it was better than trying not to stare as she put her pyjamas on. "Matt and Tanner can get away with almost anything."

She made a scoffing noise. "There were kids in the room. Neither of them thought 'Hey, maybe a gag gift of a pair of boxers with mistletoe over the crotch isn't the best thing to give in a room full of children'?"

"Probably not," I said.

Fabric shuffled behind me. I thought Isla had pulled back the covers on the futon, but when I turned around, she was pulling on the blue sleep shorts she'd packed. I swallowed hard and turned back to my bag to search for my face wash again.

"And you can tell Ashley's used to it. That was quick thinking, telling the kids the joke was about hanging underwear on the ceiling."

There was a gentle creak as Isla climbed onto the futon. Finally. I gave up looking for my definitely-still-at-my-parents'-place face wash and pulled on a sleep t-shirt.

"Although I'm pretty sure it's a Christmas miracle that no one lost an eye after they put the boxers on that lightsaber Hunter got so they could dangle it over everyone," she continued.

I glared at the short-shorts I'd stupidly brought to sleep in before undoing my pants so I could put them on. "Yeah. Lucky."

"And I'm pretty sure they were targeting us," she continued.

"Maybe," I said, even though I knew they definitely had been.

"Ah well." Isla giggled. "There's worse things than having to kiss your best friend under the mistletoe underwear, I guess."

I fiddled with my phone charger on the desk. "Yeah, I guess."

"Not the food, though. My God." She made a chef's-kiss noise. "I would marry that trifle, honestly."

"It was pretty good."

I finished plugging in my phone, then made my way to the futon. Isla had pulled back the covers on my side for me already.

"And the turkey," she said as I slipped between the blankets. "I don't have a turkey family. I mean, clearly, given the 'pizza for Christmas dinner' thing. But still. Best turkey I think I've ever had."

There was a pause, like Isla was expecting me to say something else.

"Well, thank you," she continued when I didn't. "For bringing me."

I swallowed hard. "Thanks for coming. And... everything else."

"Anytime."

It wasn't quite dark enough for the outline of Isla's head to disappear into the darkness, so I stared at the back of her head as silence stretched over the room again. I hoped she'd already falling asleep. Not because I was tired. I wasn't. And normally I would consider it sheer torture to lie in bed awake when I couldn't sleep. But it was better than the alternative.

"Are you okay?" Isla asked.

"Yeah. Are you?"

"Yeah." Another brief pause. "Do you want to talk about stuff?"

"What stuff?"

"Whatever's bothering you."

My heart thudded in my chest hard enough that I worried it might shake the futon. "Nothing's bothering me."

"Are you sure?"

"Yeah."

The mattress moved as she shifted, but she didn't roll over.

"Is it your grandma?" she asked after a bit.

"I'm fine, Isla," I said.

"Okay." Her voice was quiet. "So, did I... did I do something wrong?"

I blinked. "What? No. No, you're fine."

"You're not mad I pretended to be your girlfriend?"

I forced a soft chuckle. "You've asked me that eighty times already."

"I've asked, like, twice. *Maybe* three times."

"Even if it was eighty, I still wouldn't be mad about it."

"You promise?"

"Of course I promise."

"Okay, but—"

"You know that scientist?" I interrupted.

Her voice was as cautious as it was confused. "What scientist?"

"The one you mentioned earlier. Just before you tried to invent the new Olympic sport of dry land cliff diving. Who said the theory for life is forty-two or whatever."

"The... oh." A hint of laughter threaded its way into her response. "He wasn't a scientist. He's an author. It's from *The Hitchhiker's Guide to the Galaxy*."

Perfect. That was even better. "Can you tell me the story?"

"What?"

"What's the book about? I might want to read it someday."

Isla didn't respond right away. When she did, it wasn't what I'd hoped for.

"Seriously. What's wrong?" she asked.

"Nothing—"

"You're lying to me."

"I'm lying near you, actually," I said.

The futon creaked as she rolled over to face me. Between the far-too-small size of the mattress and the dim light filtering in from various cracks in the surrounding room—the window, the door to the hallway, the way-too-bright digital clock on the desk—Isla could clearly see I was indeed lying both to and near her.

"Ellie," she said. "You don't like reading. You've told me that every time I mention reading or going to Books or see my bookshelf."

Well... she had me there.

"Please tell me what I did wrong," she pleaded. "I don't like not knowing. Talk to me."

"Why do you think you did something wrong?" I asked.

"Because you're... you're not..." She paused, then sighed. "You're not spooning me."

Shit.

Of course that's what tipped her off.

Of course she'd thought we'd sleep the way we always slept. Technically we were supposed to take turns for who got to be little spoon, but nine times out of ten, I curled myself around her before she could even ask.

And I wanted to. I did. I wanted to pull myself closer to her and hold her in my arms. Especially knowing that not doing it was hurting her. I didn't want to hurt her. Isla was my best friend.

Which is why we couldn't do that tonight.

"And we always spoon," she continued. "This bed is smaller than mine, so I thought—and I mean, it's not impossible that you could've decided you are mad about me randomly pretending to be your girlfriend. And I don't think you know how much it means to me that we're friends so I don't want to risk that and if you aren't honest with me I can't do anything to fix it and I hate feeling like—"

"Isla," I said.

She stopped talking. Thankfully. The last time she'd rambled like that, I'd done something so fucking stupid to make her be quiet and that was *not* an option now.

"You didn't do anything wrong," I said, not quite looking at her. "I promise. I just don't... feel like it."

She waited for me to say more. I didn't. She let her head bounce in an unconvinced nod. "Okay. If... if that's all."

It wasn't. She knew it wasn't. And she'd just said—*agh*.

I hated this.

I *hated* this.

But it wasn't fair to not tell her.

"Don't hate me," I whispered, not sure if I was asking her or praying.

"I'd never hate you for not wanting to cuddle," Isla said. "That'd be silly."

I tried to laugh. Or not to laugh. I don't know. "No, not for that. Because of the reason."

"What's the reason?" she asked.

"I'm... bisexual," I said.

"Uh..." Isla replied. "I know? We're fake girlfriends, so—"

"No, I know. It's not—" I couldn't look at her. I couldn't look at anything. I slammed my eyes shut, my stomach churning. "We've been... touching. A lot."

"And you think that's bothering me?" she asked, genuinely confused. "We always touch a lot."

"Not with our mouths, we don't," I said.

"Well, yeah, but I don't mind that we are."

"Right, but—"

"Like, I wasn't complaining about the mistletoe boxers thing, if that's what this is—"

"Isla, I'm fucking horny."

Which wasn't what I meant to say.

I mean, it was. That was the problem I wanted to communicate.

But I didn't mean to blurt it out like that, abrupt and blunt and almost crude, the words shot point-blank in Isla's face.

I wanted to say it gently. To lead into it. To tell her it was killing me to sit here acting like a fucking cliche. That I didn't get turned on by every single person in the world just because I was bi. That I knew she'd never imply that but we lived in a bi-phobic world and those bullshit beliefs cut *deep* and I was terrified I'd lose her if I admitted it.

But I was exhausted.

Even just being physically present at the cabin was exhausting. I'd rather go to three of Anthony's Aquasize classes in a row than face the anxiety in the melancholy memories of this place. Add in my extended family over Christmas, the whole gift debacle, and the mask I had to wear around my grandma because she'd hate me even more if I didn't, and I could barely hold on.

And that was before Isla.

That was before she held my hand.

Before I'd caught her in the snow.

Before we'd gone back inside and she'd sat on the couch, tucking her legs beneath her and letting her curvy thigh press tight against mine.

Before a group of my cousins' kids came over because we were the only same-sex couple there, which made us a curiosity, and she'd rested her hand on my knee while she patiently answered the innocent questions most adults would be too embarrassed to ask.

Before those same stupid kids had taken the boxers with a sprig of mistletoe on them and hooked them onto a toy lightsaber, running around the room and dangling it over everyone's heads. And since Isla was nice to them and we were a novelty, they kept coming back over and over and over.

And I kissed her each time.

I shouldn't have. I *knew* I shouldn't have. I knew I shouldn't be enjoying the warmth that radiated through me each time I tasted something that reminded me of cupcakes on her lips. Or caught a hint of the scent of pears in her hair. Or when she put her arm around my waist and let her hand fall above my hip. Or when she rested her head on my shoulder or curled up beneath my arm.

I should've told her earlier.

I should've stopped it earlier.

Because yes, we were fake girlfriends.

But my body thought those kisses were real.

"I'm sorry," I said, my eyes still pinched closed after my admission hung in the air for way too long. "I know that's so... so weird. And not cool of me. I know you're straight. More importantly, you're my best friend and I don't want to wreck that. But you're hot." A weird laugh bubbled from my throat. "And you are way too good a kisser. Like, it's stupid how good you are at it. Too good. Because I'm—" Another weird laugh slipped out. "I'm so sorry. It's also been ages since I've been with anyone so it's like my body is getting confused and the stupid thing isn't listening to my brain when I'm like, 'Hey by the way, this is Isla and we're just friends so stop... stop that.' You know? And I can't think about anything else and it's killing me and that's why I can't spoon you."

"Oh," she said. "And here I thought I smelled or something."

I opened my eyes. Isla's cheeks were pink, but she didn't look mad. Amused, if anything, but with softness in her eyes.

"You do smell," I said. "Like pears."

"In a good way?" she asked.

"Too good a way, maybe."

She let out an awkward giggle. "Oh."

I cringed again. "I know. I'm sorry. I made this so fucking weird. But I didn't want you to think *you'd* done something wrong because I'd feel bad touching you when I, uh... feel like this. And I know I'm going to be restless because it's not like I can just go jerk it in the shower or something, so I didn't want you to fall asleep and then I'd end up waking you up because I couldn't sit still and—" I cut myself off with a sigh. "I'm sorry."

"Do you want me to go?" she asked.

"No! Of course not."

"I mean, temporarily," she said. "So you have some... space."

Oh my God.

Oh my *God*.

"I... no," I said. "I'm not kicking you out of bed so I can—and then you'd come back after knowing—" I shook my head. "I just need a little time to settle down. It's fine, okay? It's not your problem to solve."

"Well, it kind of is," she said. "I caused it."

"You did not. I mean, okay, you *did*," I said. "But it's still my problem. Not yours."

"But it's a problem I can solve," she argued.

"I don't want you to leave the room so I can flick the bean, Isla," I said.

"I'm not talking about me leaving."

I laughed. I couldn't help it. "Look, we're pretty close, but I don't think we're 'casually sharing a bed while I get myself off' kind of close."

"I'm not talking getting yourself off."

I stared at Isla. She stared back. My stomach knotted. Curled. Tensed and tightened and flipped, bumping into my heart as it started pounding harder.

"Isla," I said slowly. "Are you attracted to women?"

"No," she said. My stomach uncurled. "Not... no."

"Wait, are you saying 'not no' or skipping a word? Because those are different things and one of them technically means yes."

She laughed, half-shaking her head and half-shrugging. "I'm not. But I'm also kind of, um, aware that we did do a lot of kissing today. And touching. And that you, um, are also, you know. Very good at it. So I can relate, a little. I think. To what you're feeling. Even if that's not my typical, um... flavour. Of. Things. I might still like to... try it."

Oh.

Oh.

"Though, now that I say it out loud, it sounds horrible," she said, cringing slightly. "I don't want you to think I'd use you or something. But I also don't see myself... with... you know?"

"You don't want a relationship with a woman," I said. "But you'd be open to experimenting with some kind of mutually beneficial situation where neither of us have to leave this room but both of us could get off."

"Well, when you put it like that, it sounds exactly as horrible as it did when I said it my way," she said. "But... yeah."

"I don't think it sounds horrible."

"You don't? But I thought the whole 'experimenting' thing—"

"Yes and no. You're being upfront about it. And if you *were* going to experiment with anyone, I would hope you'd ask me."

Her eyebrows arched. "Really?"

Fuck. I shouldn't have said that.

"Well, yeah," I said. "I said you're hot. And you're my best friend, so I know I'd look out for you. But that's also a downside. It doesn't seem smart to risk making things weird with my best friend just because I'm kinda horny."

"What if you were really horny?"

I laughed. Maybe because it was funny or maybe I was in shock. "I mean..."

"What if we agreed to keep it totally platonic and not let it get weird?" she asked. "What if we agreed we're both really turned on because we're both good at kissing and in order to get a good night's sleep on this futon, we're going to need to spoon, and we'll feel better about spooning if we get some of these hormonal things out of the way?"

Right.

Because *that* was a thing that could happen and hadn't been disproved in eighty million movies and prime time dramas and reality TV shows. And probably books. I wouldn't know.

But a lot of things happened in movies that weren't real, right? And those situations were always between two people who had compatible sexualities. And who weren't us. Isla and I were different.

I couldn't quite explain *how* we were different.

But we were. We had to be. I mean, *obviously* it was different. I was the one sitting here overthinking the whole fucking thing while Isla had her bottom lip sandwiched between her teeth, not like she was nervous but like she was ready to go full steam ahead with this ridiculous plan despite the fact that *she* was the chronic overthinker and I was the impulsive chaos gremlin.

"Look, I'm just saying," she said. "If you can't help your best-friend-slash-fake-girlfriend platonically get off because you're both turned on from being really good at kissing and now you have to share an itty-bitty futon mattress, who *can* you help platonically get off?"

I laughed.

I had to.

Because oh, this was a bad idea.

And oh, I was already moving full steam ahead.

Chapter Twenty-Three
What Kisses Say

Isla

THE CONCEPT OF KISSING is strange.

Like, the mechanics alone are weird, but the real weirdness of kissing is how versatile it is.

It's intimate, but it's not.

It's romantic, but it's not.

It's meaningful, but it's not.

In a single day, a person could kiss their children, little pecks to communicate love and adoration. Moments later, that person could kiss their partner, deeper moments that share love again, but a totally different kind of love.

They could sit down to write a letter, signing x's and o's at the end to send the aura of kisses to the recipient. Leaving the house to mail their letter, they could run into a friend, kissing the air above each cheek to say hello. At the post office, a kiss no one would know was there could be pressed to the back of the envelope. And then when they left, they could cut off another car in traffic and blow a sarcastic kiss out the window before getting to work and going up to their boss's office, where they would metaphorically kiss ass to get ahead in life.

And maybe after work they go out to a bar. Maybe they see someone who isn't their partner, someone anonymous, someone beautiful. And maybe the clandestine kiss they aren't supposed to share communicates nothing except the need for a physical release.

Because kisses communicate to people who aren't being kissed, too. The kiss of two lovers caught mid-affair says betrayal. Someone pressing lips to the ring of another says respect, but if it's the knuckles, it might say seduction instead. A public kiss between two people says they're together, and a kiss pressed to a person's temple paired with an outward glower says "*Mine.*"

Every kiss I'd shared with Ellie that day was meant to say one thing, and one thing only. Whether we were sitting on her grandma's couch or standing around the kitchen or walking out to the patio, those kisses said "Look, we're a couple. An actual couple, who like each other and do couple things like share beds and go on dates and kiss publicly for everyone to see, because for some reason the family of one person in this couple considers it an accomplishment to be with someone you can kiss in public."

But then we lay down.

And suddenly every kiss that day had said *"More."*

I'd decided when she finished laughing at my comment that I'd tell her it was okay. Not that I was joking about what I'd suggested, but that I wasn't trying to pressure her or anything. I just wanted her to know that I was open to the idea and that it wouldn't make things weird. Like, the only way it would be weird would be if it was about more than just sex, and that wasn't an option.

I was straight, despite what those kisses might be whispering.

So as her laugh faded, I started to speak. To tell her I'd still be fine leaving the room for a while. Pretty much everyone was in bed, but this so-called "cabin" had about a thousand bathrooms. So I'd take my e-reader and go hang out in one of those for a while, and if anyone asked, I'd blame the turkey.

Before I could say anything, though, Ellie kissed me in a way that clearly said "*Yes.*"

And I kissed her back.

But to be really sure because, you know, consent and all, I only kissed her for a moment before double-checking.

"So that's a yes?" I whispered against her lips.

Her chuckle puffed against my mouth. "Yeah. I'd say against my better judgment, but we both know I don't have that. So let's do it."

"Oh, my," I said, adding an exaggerated giggle at the end. "'Do it?' I didn't know you had such a filthy mouth on you, Ella Prime."

"Then you haven't been paying attention, Ella Two," she said. "And how else was I supposed to say that? 'Let's get it on'?"

"Only if you sing it to me."

"Isla, I'm trying to fuck you," she said. "If I'm gonna make you scream, it's gonna be because you're clenching your pussy hard enough to break my fingers while you come, not because your ears are bleeding from my singing voice."

I laughed. And also blushed. And also couldn't look her straight in the eyes because, oh my God, I didn't expect *that* to come out of her mouth.

But I was so glad it did.

Because that's why this wouldn't be awkward or weird.

And maybe it should have been weirder. Playful flirting between friends was one thing. Playful flirting between friends who were making out in bed together was another. Especially when said friends were only doing it because they'd turned each other on by pretending to be girlfriends all day even though one friend was't even gay. Maybe it *should* have been awkward.

But it felt like us.

All of it felt like us. The laughter. The teasing. The mutual understanding, the way it felt natural to agree to help each other, the unquestioning acceptance of us not needing to make it more than it was.

It felt easy.

It felt right.

She leaned in while I was still laughing, a grin of her own closing into a smile as she pressed her lips to mine yet again. And again. And again. Until my laughter had faded into a smile of my own, and those smiles had faded into kisses, and those kisses deepened into a plea for more.

Ellie's hand rested on my waist. I didn't know when she'd put it there, or when I'd put my hand on her upper arm. But I noticed it when I felt her hand tighten, her fingers pressing into my side after she'd traced her tongue along my bottom lip.

"You okay?" I asked.

"Huh?" she breathed. "Yeah. Why?"

"You kind of... squeezed," I said. "I wanted to check in."

"Right." She half-laughed. "Yeah. I... your lips are really, uh... really soft. And that stuff... whatever you're wearing. It tastes good. Really good."

"Oh. Thanks. It's called Sprinkle Cake, I think. I got it from your mom's welcome basket."

She laughed, which made me laugh. "Are you?"

"Am I what?"

"Okay?"

"I think so," I said.

Her eyebrows arched up. "Uh..."

"I mean because I haven't done this before," I said quickly. "*I'm* okay. I just don't know if I'm doing it... right."

"Doing what right? Kissing?"

"Well, yeah. And... what comes next."

She looked at me suspiciously. "You told me you've had sex before."

"Not with a woman."

Her mouth twitched. "Right, but with guys?"

That made me blush, for some reason. "I mean, Nick and I, like, lived together."

"...and had sex, right?"

"Yes. Yeah. Of course." I shifted, suddenly feeling vulnerable. "He usually took the lead with things, though."

"And did you like it?"

"Well, yeah. I wouldn't 'do it' if I didn't."

"I meant him taking charge."

"Oh." I blushed deeper. "I mean, yes. Mostly. I don't like just lying there doing nothing while someone does whatever they want to me. Or being ordered around. Like, I want to be told what to do, but nicely."

The corners of her eyes crinkled. "Got it. You want instructions, not for me to go, 'Isla Athena Monroe, get on your back and stick out your tongue so I can ride your face' sort of thing?"

My mouth went dry. Probably because all the moisture in my body suddenly seemed to collect in my core, a dull ache beginning to radiate down to my pussy.

Which was kind of new. I'd been turned on before, but those words had *done* something. And it was especially surprising given I'd just told Ellie I didn't exactly like that, but now...

"Isla?" Ellie said, looking concerned.

"Maybe, um, a little of that is okay," I said.

A dangerous-looking smirk widened on her lips, but there was a softness in her eyes that didn't match it. "As fun as *that* little realization seemed, I think you and I should keep things simpler. Since we're just helping each other out, you know?"

"Right," I said. "Yeah. That makes sense. But also, what does that entail?"

"I think maybe we keep some clothes on," she said. "Keep things, um, on top of the fabric as much as possible, you know? Since we're kind of focusing on the 'getting off' part of things?"

"Sure," I said, not really knowing what she was getting at, but I also didn't need her to justify her boundaries. "Except then how do we...?"

"I'm gonna tell you what to do," she said. "But nicely."

I laughed again and she smiled, then proceeded to not tell me what to do at all.

But only because she was showing me.

She kissed me again. Her tongue slipped between my lips and I let mine meet it, not sure if I was tasting mint or just smelling it when she sighed against my mouth. After indulging herself for a moment, her hand started to move. It travelled to my hip, resting there for a moment as she used her knee to nudge my legs open. Once she'd slid one smooth, bare leg between mine, she brought the other over my outside hip so we were straddling each other's thighs as we lay facing each other.

And then she reached down, grabbed my ass, and pulled me tight against her body.

I let out a soft gasp; she absorbed the sound with her mouth, kissing me hard as her thigh pressed against my pussy. The hand on my ass tightened, squeezing with delightful pressure before letting go and pulling back from my mouth just enough to speak.

"Put your arm around me," she said. "And roll your hips."

I wrapped my arm around her waist obediently, using the leverage of holding her to push my hips forward like she'd said, then made a soft, knowing noise as the friction of her thigh gave a moment of relief to that needy ache in my core.

And then another soft, pleased noise when I repeated the action and it happened again.

And then a third when Ellie's fingers dug into my ass and she bowed her head, a quiet moan muffled in the small space between our bodies as she mirrored my actions. The fabric of her shorts was thin enough that I could feel the heat between her legs, thin enough that I could tell it was already damp, thin enough that I knew when she adjusted her position slightly and spread her legs a little more, it was so her clit was pressed directly against my thigh.

Which meant I was pretty sure she could tell I was just as hot and wet and in need of friction as she was.

We didn't find a rhythm. We didn't need to. The moment we began, we fell into sync. Our movements, our breaths, the noises escaping from between our kisses; it just happened like it was supposed to. She let go of my ass at some point and moved her arm up to my shoulder. At the same time, I tightened my arm around her waist. Our bodies pressed together even more, my shorts riding up my thigh as the spot she was grinding on shifted closer to my hip.

"Fuck, Isla," she murmured, a dizzying heaviness in her voice. "'I don't know what I'm doing,' my ass. You're a pro at this."

I wasn't sure if it was the way she said it or the words themselves, but something electric tingled through my body. "I don't know how, though. I've never done this before."

Her laugh was breathless. "You must just be a natural, then."

"Maybe." I squeezed my eyes closed, focusing on the sensations washing over me. "It does mix my two favourite parts."

"Which are?"

I laughed a bit. "Cuddling and kissing."

"Those are your favourite parts of sex?"

"Yeah. I like being held. Don't you?"

"I mean, I *like* it, but—" She paused, a shiver running through her. "I do like the way you're holding me. And how you're holding onto me."

"But it's not your favourite?"

"I mean, orgasms *are* a thing."

"Well, yeah. I wasn't counting those."

"Oh, well, if we're not counting orgasms..."

I laughed again. "What's your favourite, then?"

She looked like she was thinking. At first I wasn't sure if she actually was or if she was distracted by the sensations running through her body, but after a moment, she answered.

"It's a... a position, sort of," she said. "An action."

"Show me," I said.

She hesitated, then bit her lip and started shifting.

In hindsight, I wasn't sure why she seemed hesitant. At the time, I thought it might be because she was going to get me to do something that would require stretching first or something. But all Ellie did was lower her head, pressing kisses to my shoulder and upper arm before pulling back and using her body to roll us over. Our legs stayed entwined, her weight heavy on my leg and her thigh pressed tightly to my core.

And it was nice, yeah, but...

"This is your favourite?" I asked, trying not to sound judgmental.

"No."

In one fluid motion, she reached down, gripping my wrists in either hand, and moved them beside my shoulders. My breath hitched as she leaned forward, using her weight to pin me to the mattress.

"*This* is," she finished. "I like being able to do anything I want. And the view is just spectacular."

"Oh," was all I could say.

"Plus, it makes this a lot easier."

She dipped down to kiss me, her lips scorching hot.

Then she started riding my thigh.

And *fuck*.

I'd been trying to be quiet. Yeah, the cabin was big, but I had no idea how thick the walls were or who was sleeping in the rooms closest to us. But Ellie shifted back and forth, somehow chasing her own release against my leg while keeping hers in the perfect position to push me to my edge. Her pace was fast and noises I couldn't control slipped from my lips, though they were thankfully muffled by Ellie's mouth over mine. Less thankfully, they were drowned out by the creaking of the futon frame, which was probably far more noticeable than the gasps and sighs and moans Ellie was urging from me.

Luckily, I did not give one single flying fuck.

"Ellie," I panted far sooner than I'd expected. "You're gonna make me come."

"Damn fucking right I am," she said. "Do it, Ella Two. Come for me. Be so good and come all over my fucking thigh."

"I need—" I started, then moaned. "I need... I need—"

"What?"

I half-gasped, half-sobbed, my shoulders straining as I tried to move my arms. She knew what I needed instantly; barely a moment later, Ellie let go of my wrists, slipping her arms beneath me as she kissed me again.

And that was all it took.

I held onto her as I shattered, trying not to writhe too much as I shattered. She didn't stop moving, even though it must have been hard to keep her pace when she was tilted forward and wrapped tightly in my arms; whether it was or wasn't, though, it didn't matter. Ellie's lips were crushed against mine, so I felt her moan as she unravelled just after I did, her hips bucking as she finished. She held me just as closely, just as tightly, kissing me hard until the pleasure faded and all that was left were panting breaths and afterglow.

It had never been like that before.

I didn't know what that meant. Or how I felt about it, really.

After we caught our breaths, Ellie looked at me and I looked at her. We each let out laughs. Shaky ones at first, almost nervous ones, but it only took a few moments before we were giggling the way we always did.

And after cleaning up and getting settled again, Ellie curled up behind me like she always did, her arm slung over my body and her legs tucked beneath mine, her breath warm against the back of my neck as we faded into sleep.

Chapter Twenty-Four
Sham Pain

Isla

"Well, Isla almost died."

Jayce's eyebrows shot up. Between that, their slightly hooded eyelids, and the massive false lashes they'd let Anthony put on them, the glittery eyeshadow on their lids disappeared completely.

"I did not almost *die*," I corrected Ellie. "I just almost fell off a cliff."

"Today on *Answers I Wouldn't Expect To The Simple Question of 'How Was Your Christmas,'*" Jayce said flatly. "How in the fuck did you almost fall off a cliff?"

"Ellie's not too good at handling wood," I said.

Ellie let out a loud scoff. "I can handle wood perfectly well, thank you very much. Ask any of my exes who have wood-related appendages. I'm experienced at handling both the attached and strap-on variety of branches, sticks, twigs, logs—"

"Yes, yes, you know how to take a dick." Jayce began to collect themself, straightening their bow tie and pressing down the front of their tuxedo jacket like they'd jolted during their moment of shock, though they hadn't moved an inch. "And how, exactly, is that relevant to Isla falling off a cliff?"

"*Almost* falling off a cliff," I said.

"Because I built the railing," Ellie said.

"What railing?" Jayce asked, frowning.

"Around the patio. At the cabin."

"*Oh.*" Jayce gave Ellie a significant look. "*That* patio. That, uh, I only know about because... you... showed me pictures... one time."

"You're about as subtle as Lady of the Lake's sequin merkin," Ellie said flatly. "I told Isla about everything."

"Well, how was I supposed to know?" Jayce asked haughtily.

"If you'd let me finish the story—"

"If you could keep one thread of the story going for longer than ten seconds—"

I swear, bickering was their favourite hobby. I couldn't even tell what they were arguing about half the time, or why it mattered. Knowing they'd be at it for a while, I sat back and took another long sip of the Flat Tire's signature cocktail while watching Lady of the Lake host the worst wet t-shirt contest ever.

That wasn't me being judgy, either. It was what Lady had called it. Because not only was a mid-winter wet t-shirt contest a terrible idea, it exclusively featured men wearing water balloon boobs that were popped to provide the aforementioned wetness for the aforementioned t-shirts. Which is exactly what one would expect at The Worst New Year's Eve Party In Town.

That wasn't judgy, either. It was literally the theme. Jayce had picked it after getting a string of bad reviews in early December. The reviews themselves were obviously fake, but it wasn't like they could prove it. And even if they could, there was no telling whether they were from a rival bar owner or a snippy customer or one of Jayce's uncles trying to sabotage them.

Jayce had been devastated, but Ellie convinced them to embrace it.

"If *other* people call this the worst bar in town, it's bad," she'd said. "But if *you* say you're the worst, it's cheeky and defiant. Trust me."

So they'd reluctantly printed all the reviews and hung them around the bar in frames above little plaques engraved with "The Worst Bar In Town." Bruce and his crew had walked in after work the next day, then nearly pissed themselves laughing as they went around the bar reading each of the reviews.

"Jayce, bud, you gotta get t-shirts for us," Bruce had said. "'I'm A Regular At The Worst Bar In Town.'"

"No, man, no!" said one of the others. "Go with 'Proud Survivor of Aurora Flats' Worst Bar.'"

"'I Drank At The Worst Bar In Aurora Flats And All I Got Was This Lousy T-Shirt,'" said another.

"'—This Lousy T-Shirt And A Bitchin' Hangover,'" added a third.

So anyway, Jayce embraced the name, decided the New Year's Eve party theme was The Worst New Year's Eve Party In Town, and had to place a second order for t-shirts because the first order sold out before it even arrived.

Maybe that was why Jayce and Ellie hadn't seen each other since Ellie and I had got back from her parents'. Normally, she and Jayce had lunch a few times a week at least, but Jayce must have been working extra hours or something. They'd made a point of slipping into the booth Ellie and I were lingering in under the guise of taking a break during the party.

Which was fine until they'd asked how our trip was and Ellie let it slip that I'd, in her words, almost died.

And now they were arguing about—

"—the audacity to remind me I'm old enough to be talking about something that happened ten years ago!" Ellie was saying. "It was *one* bad haircut, Jayce!"

"I looked like a llama who got into a fight with a lawnmower!" Jayce shot back. "And I'm telling you, it wasn't ten years ago. It was almost fifteen years ago because I was crying about it to you at the same time you were crying about building that fucking railing!"

Oh, perfect. They'd circled back to the actual conversation.

"Well, there's your answer," I said, making them both look at me. "Ellie's perfectly capable of handling wood, but the stuff used to make that railing was just experiencing the timber equivalent of erectile dysfunction."

They both stared at me silently for a moment.

"Exactly," Ellie said, grabbing her half-finished cocktail. "I'm old, that railing was older, and Isla didn't die because of my super speedy yoinking reflexes that kicked in when she fell."

"I *did* almost suffocate in the snow you threw me face-first into," I said.

"Yeah, but you didn't fall off a cliff." She took a big swig of her drink.

"And thank whatever forces are out there for that," Jayce said, lifting their non-alcoholic version of the drink in a slight toast. "It's too bad a tall, handsome stranger wasn't conveniently passing by to catch you instead. That would've been perfect for your little meet cute experiment."

"True," I said. "But it might not've gone over so well with my girlfriend's family being there."

This time, Jayce's eyes didn't widen. Instead, emotion drained from their face before it froze in an even expression. "Your... what?"

"*Fake* girlfriend," Ellie said hurriedly. "Isla, uh, pretended we were dating. Because my grandma was being herself."

"It was the least I could do," I said. "She was *awful*."

Jayce had an odd expression on their face. Or maybe it was a mix of expressions. I was pretty sure at least part of the expression was sympathy, though.

"It was very much appreciated," Ellie said. "Although my parents are going to be devastated when I pretend we broke up."

I frowned. "Shit. I never thought of that."

She waved a hand at me. "It's a problem for future Ellie. And they'll get over it."

"Especially if we find our actual soulmates by then," I said. "I bet they're here tonight."

"Who is?" Jayce asked.

"Our soulmates. It's New Year's Eve. There's gotta be, like, extra-special fate vibes out tonight or something. You know, so you can do the whole midnight-kiss thing?" I grinned at Ellie. "Good thing I brought that Sprinkle Cake stuff, hey?"

"Sprinkle Cake?" Jayce repeated.

"This lip balm," I said. "Ellie said it tastes good and it makes my lips soft."

"Were those two different statements, or did Ellie say both?" The question was for me, but they were looking at Ellie.

"Well—"

"My mom got it for both of us," Ellie said before I could answer. "And you know, she's right. Tonight *is* the perfect night to meet a soulmate. I bet we can do the whole 'stumble into someone with a drink' scenario." She threw back the rest of her drink, then set the empty glass on the table. "I'm sure you have to get back to work, Jayce. Isla, let's go get refills."

And then, despite saying we were going to get a drink together, she slid out of the booth without waiting for me.

"Hmm," Jayce said.

"Did I say something wrong?" I asked.

They shook their head. "I don't think she liked what I was implying." They glanced at me. "Jokingly, of course."

I frowned. "What were you implying?"

Jayce didn't answer right away. They just looked at me. After a moment, the corners of their eyes crinkled, glitter flashing beneath the pseudo-club-lights of the bar, and they pressed their lips together.

"It's a good thing you and Ellie have found each other." They stood up and reached for me, taking a moment to straighten my black pork-pie hat. "You're both the same level of stupid."

With that, they turned and disappeared into the crowd. I stared after them, confused about what was going on and not entirely sure they'd meant what they said affectionately. Once they'd disappeared, I slipped out of the booth myself and went to join Ellie at the bar.

"Are you okay?" I shout-asked over the pounding music playing to celebrate the winner of the wet t-shirt contest, a chubby man with a thick beard who was currently posing like a pin-up girl while wearing his new "I Was The Winner of the Worst Wet T-Shirt Contest Ever and All I Got Was This Championship T-Shirt" tied in a knot to show off his hairy belly.

"Why wouldn't I be?" Ellie yelled as the bartender handed her two cocktails illuminated with the fancy LED ice cubes Jayce had insisted on using.

"Jayce thinks they said something you didn't like."

She rolled her eyes. "They're just being an asshole. Don't worry about it."

"But—"

"Hey, the band is here." She tilted her chin towards the other side of the bar. "You think he's cute? The blue-haired one? I think he's the lead singer."

I followed her gaze. Milling around the employees-only door was a group of men who were clearly a band. The singer in question was the kind of person my mom would have loved and my dad would have been, at the very least, perturbed by. He had pale white skin covered in tattoos, shown off by the torn denim vest he wore with no shirt underneath. A strake of blue slashed across his face, the only colour in his unnaturally straight, long, pitch-black chair. I was too far to see all the details of his face, but I imagined he probably had a lip ring or an eyebrow ring, too.

"Do you?" I asked.

She shrugged. "Doesn't matter. He might be my soulmate."

"What if he's my soulmate?"

She shot me a lopsided grin. "Too bad. I called dibs. Maybe he'll introduce you to the drummer." She lifted her glass to her lips and chugged her drink, the LED ice cubes clicking together once she set the empty glass on the bar. "Come on, let's go get in position."

"Position for *what*?" I asked.

"For fate to bring us together so I can become his muse, which is why I'll need this." Ellie reached over, snatching my pork-pie hat off my head and putting it on hers. "He'll write a hit song about me and we'll live happily ever after. Well, until he gets too involved in the drugs part of sex, drugs, and rock 'n roll, at which point I'll inform him it's me or the blow, and he'll clean his act up and go on to be the greatest rock star of all time. And in the meantime, you'll be busy getting your bongos banged by the drummer, so when they go on tour, you and I can tag along and party on their tour bus while they're raking in that sweet, sweet music money."

"Which one's the drummer?" I asked, frowning at the group.

"I dunno." She took back the cocktail she'd handed me. "I'll need this, too."

"Hey!" I protested, but she downed half the drink in one gulp before turning and starting across the bar, and suddenly it was like I had double vision.

I could see what Ellie was planning. The singer wasn't looking in her direction, so she could run into him and her half-full drink would slosh down his bare chest. After gasping with embarrassment, she'd insist on helping clean up since, oh no, he was *just* about to go onstage. He'd be enamored by her charm and hat, so invite her to party with him and his band for the rest of the night. At midnight, surrounded by crowds of drunken people and shouts of Happy new Year, he'd lean in and kiss her, and that was it; that was fate.

But I could also see what was actually happening.

And it wasn't that.

"And now, to lead us into the chaos of live lip syncs—that is, lip syncing to a real live in-person band—please give a warm Flat Tire welcome to the homegrown Aurora Flats talent that is The Arson Raccoons!" Lady said into the microphone.

I was too far behind Ellie to warn her that the singer turned and noticed her. All I could do was grimace as he stepped out of her path so she wouldn't run into him. And all I could do was cringe as Ellie missed her target and instead ran directly into the wall next to the employees only door.

The thud of her face hitting the wall was loud enough that the band members all winced. Ellie's drink sloshed out of the glass, soaking the front of her shirt as the LED ice cubes in the drink went flying. One clattered along the floor and disappeared under an occupied table.

The other ended up beneath Ellie's foot as she tried to correct her stumble.

She let out a surprised yelp as the ice cube shot out from beneath her and threw out an arm, desperately trying to keep her balance. Luckily, the lead singer had only taken a single step back, so he could've easily reached out to keep her from falling.

Unluckily, he was stupid, and took another step backward as he watched Ellie flail in front of him.

But luckily again, I'd caught up enough that when I lurched forward, I could grab Ellie's other arm, steadying her before she tumbled to the ground.

"Yikes," the lead singer said. "Better watch where you're going!"

He and the rest of Arson Raccoon chuckled as they made their way to the stage. Ellie watched them leave, then looked at me. Her cheeks were red, but her eyes were sparkling as she struggled not to laugh.

"You were supposed to let my soulmate catch me, Ella Two," she scolded.

"Your 'soulmate' was going to let you fall flat on your ass," I replied.

"Details, details." She wrinkled her nose as she looked down at her shirt, which was stained bright green from her spilled drink. "Think I can talk Jayce into hosting another wet t-shirt contest so I can get cleaned up?"

"Maybe if you promise to stop throwing their fancy light up ice cubes all over the bar."

She fake gasped. "But how will I find my midnight kiss, then?"

"We could try things that don't involve spilling drinks on people. Like joining the live lip sync contest."

"So the lead singer can tell everyone what just happened? No thank you."

I tried not to laugh. "Okay. What if we try to find our soulmates by talking to other people?" She wrinkled her nose. "Or dancing, maybe?"

"Dancing? How's that going to help us find a soulmate?"

"I dunno. It works for birds. Maybe they're onto something."

She shrugged. "That's as good a reason as any. Let's go interpretive dance our way into a midnight kiss."

But we didn't.

We danced, yes. After a quick stop in the bathroom to salvage Ellie's stained shirt, then a quick stop in the employees' only area so Ellie could steal one of the "I Drank At The Worst Bar In Aurora Flats and All I Got Was This Lousy T-Shirt (the rash was completely unrelated)" t-shirts that weren't selling as well as the others for some reason, we made our way to the dance floor near the stage, dancing and lip-syncing to the live band along with the people competing to win... something. Probably another t-shirt. But I was having too much fun with Ellie to pay any attention.

And maybe that's why our dancing-to-attract-a-mate strategy didn't work. Ellie and I were too busy dancing together, shimmying and jumping and doing stupid little waltzes. We laughed, and we bumped into people, and we ebbed and flowed into other groups of people who were dancing along with us, but it was always *us*.

Her. Me. Music and movement pushing us forward so smoothly that I barely noticed the passage of time until Jayce was tapping into a microphone on the stage and the music had cut out.

"Good evening, assholes," they said, which was their favourite non-gendered greeting. "I would like to inform you that we've entered the final minutes of this wretched year and we're currently sixty seconds or so away from the beginning of yet another wretched year."

A whooping cheer went up, led by Ellie. Around us, nearly every staff member who worked at the Flat Tire started milling through the crowd, passing out plastic cups of champagne.

"So I'd like to thank you all for being here now rather than later when you'll be too drunk to process the words," Jayce continued. "Thank you for spending the last moments of this year here at the worst bar in town. I don't believe in resolutions, but if I did, I'd resolve that by this time next year, this would be the worst bar in the province."

Ellie and I each grabbed a cup of champagne off one of the passing trays, taking a few sips as the crowd chuckled. On stage, Jayce lifted their glass.

"Here's to the new year. May the only pain you have this year be this champagne, and the only sham you have this year be this cheap-ass sparkling wine that I'm telling you is champagne."

Another swell of laughter filled the bar, leading into the countdown. I wrapped my arm around Ellie's waist, holding onto her as we started chanting the numbers along with Jayce.

Five.

Four.

Three.

Two.

One.

And then a pause, half a heartbeat longer than usual, before the world around us exploded into noise and laughter and music. Light swirled around the room like confetti, bouncing off the disco ball Jayce had hung on the ceiling at some point and showering fractured reflections over the celebrating crowd.

"Happy New Year, Isla!" Ellie shouted in my ear, giving me a side-hug. "Sorry we didn't get those midnight kisses."

I wasn't.

I'd been the one to bring it up. But now that I was standing at the precipice between an old year and a new one, I didn't want anyone else standing with me.

Just Ellie.

I couldn't say why. Maybe it was because of that date, the arbitrary change of calendar marking the end of a strange year. Not the strangest year of my life, not by far: that designation was reserved for the year I lost my dad.

This had been a year of loss, too. I'd lost my relationship. My sense of place. My understanding of who I was and what I wanted to be.

But it had also been a year of gain. I'd gained friends. Laughter. Moments with Ellie doing things I didn't usually do because truthfully, no one had ever urged me to do them before. I couldn't hold that against anyone. I was no one's responsibility and wouldn't place that expectation on a person, but it was yet another thing I had gained: a person who, for some reason, *wanted* that responsibility.

I couldn't quite believe that Ellie had only been in my life for a matter of months. It was already nearly impossible to imagine life without her.

So maybe that was why I did it. Maybe that was why it felt right. Maybe that was why I let impulse take control, why it seemed like I moved before I'd even thought of doing it, why I caught a glimpse of light dancing across her cheeks and nose like ethereal freckles before my eyes closed.

Maybe that was why I kissed her.

Maybe that was why I had to.

She tasted like champagne. The real kind. Like the cheap sparkling wine in our plastic cups had evolved just by being on her lips. And she kissed me back without hesitation, without pause, like she'd known it was coming.

When I pulled back, I smiled up at her.

"Happy New Year, Ellie," I said. "Here's to our first full year of being best friends."

Ellie smiled, too. She lifted her cup, tapping it to mine.

"To best friends," she said, her voice soft beneath the buzz and rumble of the surrounding crowd.

We drank. I finished my glass first. As I lowered it, I glanced towards the stage, where Jayce was still standing.

They caught my eye, a strange expression on their face; something between amusement and vexation. It startled me, but before I could even really be certain I saw it, they smiled and lifted their own glass of champagne towards me before turning and disappearing towards the bar.

Chapter Twenty-Five
Sprinkle Cake

Ellie

"So Sprinkle Cake, eh?"

"What?" I mumbled, my fingers rattling across the keyboard of my laptop.

"I said, 'Sprinkle Cake, eh?'" Jayce said, enunciating each word with a crisp sarcasm.

"I do not know what that means," I said.

"It's one of the many awkward segues I've considered trying since you've been avoiding me."

"I haven't been avoiding you."

"I haven't talked to you since last year."

I scoffed. "That was, like, three days ago."

"It was over a week ago, Ellie."

I didn't take my eyes off my screen. "Same difference."

They sighed. "Ellie."

"Jaycie."

They reached across the table, firmly pushing down the laptop screen full of gibberish I'd been typing to look busy so I had no choice but to yank my hands out of the way. "Answer me."

With nothing else to look at, I glared up at them. "You didn't ask me anything."

"Oh, you're playing stupid? Fine." They pulled their phone out. "Let's see, where's that note I've been keeping for the week full of potential ways to bring up this conversation neither of us want to have… ah! There we go." They cleared their throat. "So how about that Isla? Pretty kissable, wouldn't you say?"

"Who's Isla? Never heard of her."

Jayce tilted their head condescendingly. "You're not even trying to lie convincingly."

"Yeah, but the longer I stall, the less likely I am to have to talk about this," I said, glancing towards the entrance of the Flat Tire like Isla would magically reappear despite only having stepped outside to answer a call a minute earlier.

"What makes you think I'm going to stop asking once she's back?" Jayce asked.

"Common human decency."

"How dare you imply I'm common," they said. "Or decent. Or human."

Fuck.

My cheeks were trying to tug my lips into a smile. Because stupid Jayce knew what kind of stupid jokes would make me stupid laugh, even though I was trying very hard not to because that would make them think they were winning this stupid conversation even though it wasn't a competition.

Mashing my lips closed as I tried to prevent a laugh from bubbling out was as bad as if I'd just laughed, though. Jayce saw me doing it and a cat-like smirk spread on their lips.

"You know I saw you kiss her," they said.

I took a deep breath through my nose. "You're making shit up. You definitely didn't see that."

"I know what I saw."

"Clearly you don't."

"Don't gaslight me, Ellie."

"I'm not gaslighting you. You're remembering things wrong."

"Need I remind you that aside from that single glass of champagne I had in my hand when I saw you, I wasn't drinking at all on New Year's Eve? Because I was working? Here, at my bar, where I witnessed you kiss your best friend?"

"I didn't kiss her," I said.

The switch from patiently calling me out to aggravated annoyance was instant. Jayce's eyebrows pinched together and their eyes darkened. "Ellie, I swear to God—"

"*She* kissed *me*," I said.

The annoyance on their face didn't disappear, but the aggravation faded into disbelief. "She kissed you."

"Believe it or not, sometimes people want to kiss me. It was for a joke."

They didn't seem convinced. "A joke."

"Mm-hmm. Because of the whole midnight-kiss-soulmate thing. We didn't find anyone else to kiss, so Isla jokingly kissed me at midnight."

"On the mouth."

"On the mouth."

Their lips pressed together harder. "In public."

"In public."

"With tongue."

"There was no tongue that time," I said.

"*That* time?"

Fuck. "It was the only time."

"Mmm. And yet somehow you know she tastes like Sprinkle Cake and has soft lips."

"Because I got the same lip stuff from my mother, who treated us like ten-year-olds at a sleepover and made little welcome baskets for me and Isla at Christmas," I said. "That's it."

"See, I don't know about that," they said lightly. "I can't imagine why you'd avoid me for a week because your best friend 'jokingly' kissed you."

"I wasn't avoiding you. I was busy."

"Busy avoiding me."

"Busy with work."

They let out a loud, unexpected laugh. "Okay, now I *know* you're lying. You're *never* busy with work."

I glared at them, grabbing my laptop and flipping the screen open. "Busy with work for *you*, asshole. Because you asked me to make a bunch more designs for your Worst Bar In Town merch and edit a bunch of photos from the party for social media *and* come up with ideas for your Valentine's Day party. Which is what we're supposed to be doing right now, so let's—"

"Ellie, cut the shit," they said. "You can deny it all you want, but I know what I'm seeing. And what I'm seeing is someone who insisted she wasn't going to fall in love with her new bestie because—"

"I'm not *in love* with her!" I snapped.

"I know you don't want to end up with a broken heart again," they said. "But refusing to address what's going on between you isn't the way to avoid it."

"Why would I end up with a broken heart?" I asked, unlocking my laptop and aggressively clicking on the trackpad to open the note of ideas I'd brainstormed for their stupid party. "Nothing's going on except you being annoying. Yes, we kissed. It wasn't a big deal. Not every kiss has to mean something. Most of them *don't*. If I'd known you'd overreact about the whole fake girlfriend thing, I wouldn't have told you."

"You didn't tell me," they said. "Isla did, and you looked like you'd give anything to shove those words back in her mouth. And if it's something you were trying to keep from me, that means it's something you *know* I'm right about."

"I don't know shit," I said.

"Exactly."

My cheeks warmed. "Shut up. You know what I mean."

"I do, and I also know you're blurring the lines."

"I am not!"

"You invited her to Christmas with your grandmother. *I've* never been to that, and we've been friends since we were kids." They folded their arms. "You kissed her on New Year's Eve. You stare at her when you think no one's watching with the softest, stupidest, most love-drunk expression I've ever seen. I adore Isla, but I am saying this for your sake, not hers. If you're not going to tell her how you feel, you need to stop blurring those lines and setting yourself up for heartbreak."

"There's nothing to tell her. There's nothing there that isn't platonic in every way."

They sighed in aggravation, pinching the bridge of their nose. "For someone you haven't spoken to since he pistol-whipped me with a soda gun, you sure are giving Nico a lot of power over you."

"Fuck you."

Normally when I said something like that to Jayce, they'd spit the words back at me. This time, though, the words came out low and soft and even so there was no mistaking the anger in them. Even without looking directly at them, I saw their expression change.

Or maybe it was more that I saw their fingers shift ever so slightly, grazing the bald patch that cut through their left eyebrow, and I could feel their expression without needing to see it.

"I'm sor—"

"It's fine."

"No, it isn't," they said. "You say it's fine because it's easier for you to build a wall of 'I'm fines' and 'Don't worry about its' and 'I'm overreactings' to hold in anything that hurts you, but that wall doesn't allow for the fact that sometimes, it isn't fine, I should worry about it, and you are *not* overreacting." They sat back a bit. "Everything that happened with Nico was one of those times, as is this. I said something carelessly critical when I know your rejection sensitivity thing makes that all the more hurtful, and I'm sorry."

"My 'rejection sensitivity thing,' as you put it, was what caused the issue in the first place," I muttered.

"Nico caused the issue. I exacerbated it."

"And I started. Ergo, that's the cause, dumbass."

"He could have decided not to talk about you behind your back," they said. "He could have prioritized the person he'd been friends with for years over getting laid. It's not your fault he couldn't see what he'd be losing when he made the choices he did."

"He got fired, Jayce."

"Which was *my* fault. I'm the one who caused a scene. And need I remind you, I'm the one who got myself banned for life from that gay bar. Not you." They looked at their nails. "I regret nothing, despite having missed multiple high-profile drag shows over the past decade."

I stared at my computer in silence.

Jayce and I hadn't always been a couple of menaces. Once upon a time, we were a trio of menaces, and the third menace was Nico. We were inseparable as kids. Inseparable as teenagers. And we would have probably stayed inseparable as adults if I hadn't gone and ruined everything.

Nico had been out of the closet longer than I'd even known there *was* a closet. He'd moved to our small town from a far larger, far more progressive city, and had basically walked out of the womb and informed his parents he was gay. So it wasn't like I didn't know about his sexuality.

I fell for him anyway.

I expected nothing from him. I knew it would never happen. Not once did I think maybe I was that one girl he'd "go straight" for. I couldn't help the way my heart felt, but I could help how I reacted to it, and I would never disrespect someone's sexuality like that.

What I *did* expect was for him to understand when I asked him to stop being so touchy-feely with me. We'd always been affectionate friends, so he'd known something was wrong when I had to ask him to please stop hugging me and kissing my cheek and cuddling up to me on movie nights.

I thought we were friends, so I told him the truth.

I'd expected him to tease me a little. That's what friends do, especially in awkward moments like that. But it had been a good conversation. I'd told him how I felt, that I knew nothing would ever happen, that I just needed some space from that aspect of our friendship while I got over those feelings.

I thought he understood.

I hadn't expected him to laugh with me and say it was okay, that he got it, that we'd still be friends no matter what, then call up some guy he knew and tell a revised version of the story where I'd begged him to give women a try and sobbed when he'd tried to gently let me down. All so he could get a sympathy fuck.

I hadn't expected him to do that twice.

Or three times.

Or enough times that the next time Jayce and I stopped by the bar he worked at, the other bartenders and servers all referred to me as Closet Key or Fruit Fly Barbie or Ms. Wrong Team. And when I'd finally started crying and told Jayce what happened, the resulting confrontation between them and Nico resulted in Jayce being kicked out of the bar, Nico getting fired, and the bar owner having to replace two of the soda guns behind the bar.

Which wasn't fair. Yes, Jayce was the one who started it by going behind the bar and blasting Nico with diet cola from the soda gun, but Nico was the one who nearly took Jayce's eye out by hitting them with it.

Of all the aspects of my ADHD that made my life a living hell sometimes, the rejection sensitivity was the worst. It hurt the most. It was the hardest to explain, to have to admit the most innocuous of comments repeated and twisted and became thundering echoes in my head that overtook any reasonable logic I had.

Jayce understood more deeply than anyone I'd ever met, not because they experienced it but because they'd watched me fight it for my entire life. They'd watched me let people walk all over me to avoid criticism; they'd watch me struggle to try new things that came with a risk of failure; they'd watched me excuse inexcusable things because I couldn't tell when my reactions were reasonable and when they were a result of my brain working against me.

They tried to help me as much as they could. But they'd never understand how much it hurt. How I could feel it, physically *feel* the pain, of being rejected.

It was why I still went to family events with my mom even though I hated being around my grandmother. It was why I couldn't start a business myself. It was why, even though logically I knew Nico had been a jackass who betrayed my trust and ruined our friendship, I couldn't help blaming myself.

That summer, every time Jayce and I realized we couldn't go to whatever cool drag show our friends were going to because it was at that bar, my heart remembered the pain of it all.

Every time Jayce and I sat down to watch a movie, my heart remembered those nights would never be the same.

My heart remembered the good times, and even though my head remembered the bad ones, it didn't change how much it hurt to lose Nico's friendship.

My heart remembered that falling for your friends led to pain like nothing else, and my head and my heart agreed that we'd *never* go through that again.

"I'm going to say this one last time," I said to Jayce, keeping my voice low. "Isla. Is. Not. Interested. In. Women. You know that. I know that. We've been doing this whole meet cute thing to find her a boyfriend because she wants to meet her soulmate, who is obviously a man because she's *straight*, Jayce." I looked up at them. "She's my best friend. That's it. I'm not in love with her, I'm not interested in dating her, and I'm not going to continue arguing about this with you. So drop it."

For a moment, I thought I'd actually convinced them to drop it because they didn't say anything. But before I could marvel at the fact that I'd finally bullshitted Jayce into believing something, the chair beside mine moved and Isla sat down.

And she didn't say a word.

I felt sick. Completely fucking *sick*. If she'd heard what I'd said... but I only thought it for a moment before it became clear that even if Isla had been close enough to hear my low whispering to Jayce, she hadn't been paying any attention.

No, this was something else.

"Are you alright, Isla?" Jayce asked after a moment.

Isla nodded.

"Liar," I said.

"I am," she said.

"I know. That's why I called you one."

She laughed softly. "No, I am alright. I'm just... a little not okay."

"Which is very distinctly different," Jayce said. "What happened?"

Isla was wearing her pork-pie hat, so her eyes were hidden beneath a shadow unless she was looking at someone directly. But I didn't need to see her eyes to know they were sad.

"That was Venus," she said. "My sister. Calling about her engagement party."

"Oh," Jayce said. "That is... devastating?"

Isla laughed again. "Yes and no. She's marrying my ex's brother. And my ex is the best man. And Marcus—Venus's fiancé—told Venus his mom doesn't think it's a good idea for me to come to the party. Because Nick might be uncomfortable."

My mouth dropped open. "So are they not inviting you, or...?"

"No, they are," Isla said quickly. "Venus insisted. She was literally calling to make sure I'd still be there because she was so annoyed with Marcus for bringing it up. Except I don't think she thought about how uncomfortable it's going to be for me to show up at a party I'm clearly not wanted at. So I told her I appreciated it but I didn't want to make things weird or awkward for anyone and I could sit this one out and she *lost* it."

"Like she was yelling at you?" I asked.

"Ye—no," Isla said. "It was more the uncontrollable sobbing that got me. She was just like, disproportionately upset. It's only an engagement party. She and I aren't exactly close. The last time she mentioned it, she even said she'd understand if I couldn't go because of travel and time off work and stuff. But now..." She shook her head almost disbelievingly. "When she calmed down enough to talk again, she said she's pissed I might not come because one person might be upset about it. I told her it's more than that because I know Nick. He's not the grudge-holding type. So if he's still upset with me to the point that his mom is telling people he wouldn't be able to be in the same room as me, it's *bad*."

"In fairness, though, it's not a party for Nick," Jayce said. "It's your sister's engagement."

Isla's mouth twisted wryly. "The two of you would get along disturbingly well. She said the same thing."

"So Venus wants you there?" I asked.

She nodded. "And what Venus wants, Venus gets. She always has. So I'm... I'm going. It's the week before Valentine's Day. And she said if I wanted to, I could bring a plus one."

Fuck.

Isla's head tilted up, the shadow on her face disappearing so there was no doubt that her bright blue eyes were locked on mine.

Fuck.

"Will you come?" she asked.

Fuck.

Jayce's eyes were on me. My mouth was dry.

"Are you sure you want me to?" I asked.

Isla glanced down, her cheeks going pink. "I know it's a lot to ask. I'm sorry. I just don't want to go alone. I don't know if I can *do* it on my own."

Fuck. Fucking fuck fuckity fuck.

"Then I'll be there," I said. "I wouldn't miss it for anything."

Isla let out a relieved sigh. "Oh, thank God. I'll book our flights."

Shit shitting fuckity fuckballs—

"We're flying?" I asked.

"It was a long drive when I did it in September. Mid-winter would suck," she said. "But it's okay. I'll buy your plane ticket." She pulled out her phone, then laughed. "Actually, this is perfect timing."

"How so?" Jayce asked.

"Because our bet ends on Valentine's Day." She tapped her phone screen a few times. "But fate loves saving things until the last moment, right? So we might meet our soulmates there. Or on the plane or something. It's almost *too* easy for fate to get a soulmate to us, you know?"

Jayce was still staring at me. I knew they were. Their eyes were lasers burning my skin.

"I hope mine's a pilot," I said. "Something about those uniforms, you know?"

"So don't pick a discount airline is what you're saying?" she replied. "That's fine by me, it looks like they only fly out at like six a.m."

"Well, sounds like the Ellas have an excellent opportunity for mile-high meet cutes," Jayce said. "However, should this not deposit a soulmate directly into your lap during a random bout of turbulence, I have a backup plan for you."

I shot a look across the table. Not a glare, since Isla looked up from booking plane tickets at the same time and I didn't want her to ask why I was glaring. But they obviously knew what it meant.

"What do you mean?" Isla asked.

Jayce didn't so much as glance at me. "An idea. For the Valentine's Day party we're supposed to be planning at the moment."

"Oh, shit," Isla said. "Sorry, Jayce. We've done almost nothing to help."

"So you think, but actually, it's thanks to the two of you I thought of it," Jayce said. "See, if I go with a 'Fuck Valentine's Day' party, I'm missing out on that sweet, sweet date night money. But if I go with an ultimate date night, I'll miss that sweet, sweet 'single with disposable income' money. *But*"—they tapped the end of their pen on the notebook in front of them—"we could let fate decide."

"On which party to do?" I asked.

"No. That would be stupid." They tapped their pen on the notebook again. "A date night. But in addition to couples, we sell a bunch of solo tickets. And whoever you end up seated with that night is your date."

"Leave It To Fate Night," Isla said, her eyes going round with excitement.

"That's an excellent name suggestion, Isla," Jayce said far too sweetly. "So you think it's a good idea?"

Isla grinned. "I'm already sold. I want the first ticket."

And not that Jayce was right about anything they'd suggested while Isla was outside on the phone. But if they had been, Isla's response told me everything I didn't need to be told.

"Sign me up," I said. "I'll make sure I have my Sprinkle Cake lip balm ready to go."

Chapter Twenty-Six
Flying High

Isla

"My soulmate better be on this goddamn flight," I muttered.

"Pardon me, miss?" asked the gate agent.

"I... uh... my... soul will be made better," I said. "On this flight. You know. Because... clouds. Silver linings. That sort of thing."

He blinked at me skeptically, then seemingly ignored whatever nonsense I'd spewed and handed me the boarding pass. "Right. Well, hopefully your soul doesn't need a reclining seat because the last row doesn't recline. You can contact customer service about refunding the seat selection fee. But unfortunately, the other passenger who booked that seat has already checked in and the flight is sold out, so we can't move either of you."

"Fuck," Ellie said as we walked away from the agent. "What are the chances of that?"

"Probably pretty low," I said. "Which actually makes this perfect."

She chuckled dryly. "Tell me you're sick of spending time with me without telling me you're sick of spending time with me."

I shook my head. "Don't you see?"

"See what?"

"Fate *could* have let us sit next to each other," I said. "But it didn't. It separated us, put us in very specific spots on this very specific flight that we were only on because of very specific, arguably strange circumstances."

She nodded slowly. "You think we're going to get on that plane and fate is going to put our soulmate in the seats next to us."

"Of course. And we can't sit together because otherwise we'd be fighting over one soulmate."

She glanced down at her boarding pass. "Maybe I'll get two soulmates. I'm in the middle seat."

Once the idea was in my mind, I couldn't let it go. Wouldn't that be perfect? To find my soulmate on a flight I didn't want to be on? To have something good happen after I'd spent almost a month fretting about this party, wondering why it all felt so *wrong*? Maybe this would be a reward of sorts, an offering from the universe to me after handling the things I'd handled. That in returning to my hometown, in not avoiding things that felt hard and keeping the peace with Nick and showing my happiness for my sister and the future she was facing, I would find the thing I'd left to search for.

As Ellie and I sat at the gate, scarfing down mediocre airport fast food and an even-more-overpriced-than-usual honey oat latte with whip, I looked around, wondering if he was there. If, of all these people milling about, he was in the same boat as me: moments away from meeting someone who would change his life forever. If he was the man around my age with the hood of his hoodie up and his headphones on, his head tilted to the left as he snoozed away the wait. Or if he wasn't there yet, if he was sitting at one of the restaurants and I'd only see him after we boarded the plane. Or maybe he was one of the flight attendants, or the pilot, or...

He could have been anyone.

I hoped, whoever he was, that he was from Edmonton. Or somewhere nearby.

Because somehow, I'd gotten to a point where I didn't want to leave Aurora Flats.

I liked my life there. I liked my friends. Ellie, of course, but Jayce too, and their collective group of friends. Anthony-slash-Lady-of-the-Lake. My other coworkers. Betty and the other ladies at Aquasize. Even the guy who lived upstairs and sometimes peed off his balcony, whose name I'd finally learned was

Keith. He'd seen me and Ellie traipsing down the stairs with our suitcases before we left for the airport and insisted on taking them for us.

"Because that's what gentlemen do, ladies," he'd said as I reluctantly relinquished my carry-on.

"It's very nice, Keith, but I hope you know I'm not going to sleep with you," Ellie had said.

Keith had nearly fallen down the stairs. "What? Was that an option? Oh God. Did I ask you to sleep with me?"

"No," she'd said. "I'm just telling you."

He'd breathed a sigh of relief. "Thank God. I thought maybe I'd done shrooms and forgotten or something. The only time I've ever thought I was straight was on shrooms and let me tell you, I had some serious regrets the next day."

"You're not straight?" Ellie had asked.

Keith had snorted. "I've been gay longer than you've been alive."

"That would make sense, seeing as you're older than me," she'd said. "But also, I *was* joking."

He'd sighed heavily. "Ellie, I *just* said I'm gay. It doesn't matter if you're joking."

"No, I meant—you know what, never mind." She'd given Keith a side hug after he put her suitcase in the trunk of my car. "Thanks for carrying our bags. You're a real gentleman."

"Yeah I am," he'd said, then he'd farted and walked away.

But even though that's the kind of person Keith was, I liked knowing him. He was thoughtful in his way and hadn't peed off his balcony at all since I'd told him it bothered me. I'd miss being his neighbour if my soulmate lived somewhere else and I had to move.

And Ellie...

Just the *thought* made my stomach turn.

No, I decided as Ellie and I sipped our lattes. Fate wouldn't do that to me. Fate wouldn't bring me Ellie and then make me leave her behind. Fate would find me a soulmate who'd make sure the Ellas could stay together. And who'd be okay with her coming over to spoon occasionally, maybe.

By the time we boarded the plane, I was convinced this was it.

I was convinced he would be here.

"See you on the other side," Ellie said when we reached her row. The seats were still empty, so she wiggled her eyebrows suggestively as she tucked her backpack beneath the seat.

I'd been lucky enough to end up in the window seat, even if it was in the very last row of the plane. Like Ellie, my row was also empty. I tried not to let a thrill rush through me as I took my book out of my backpack and watched as people made their way down the aisle, wondering who it would be and how I would open the conversation.

Or maybe I wouldn't have to. Maybe he'd spot my book and comment on it, or maybe he'd make a joke about us being flight neighbours. Maybe he'd be talkative and charming and ask where I was going, and I'd feel so comfortable with him that I'd tell him everything about Nick and Venus and Marcus and leaving home.

And he'd be sympathetic and sweet and as the plane descended into Vancouver—because yes, we were going to Burnaby, but we had to fly into Vancouver—he'd cautiously reach over and take my hand in his. He'd ask—no, offer, he'd offer to be my date, if I'd allow him to, because he didn't want me to be alone at a party where I felt like I wasn't wanted.

"I can't imagine why someone wouldn't want you there," he'd say softly. "But there's nowhere else in the world I'd rather be."

"But what about your initial reason for flying to Vancouver, which I haven't bothered to invent over the course of this particular daydream?" I'd ask.

He'd brush it off, shaking his head as if it was nothing.

"You're worth it, Isla," he'd say, and I wouldn't be able to stop myself from kissing him as the plane began rushing towards the tarmac.

The daydream faded from my mind as boarding continued. The man in the hoodie approached and I looked down at my book, but when I looked up a few moments later, he was in the window seat two rows ahead of me on the opposite side of the plane.

Then came a young family, a mom and a dad and a baby who looked maybe six months old. They slid into the row across from mine, the mom shooting an apologetic glance in my direction when she saw me watching. I smiled at her, trying to show her I wouldn't be mad if her baby cried because that's what babies do and I wasn't an asshole.

A few more people filled the rows around us, but the seat beside me remained empty, as did the seat beside that. A few minutes later, a slightly muffled announcement played over the intercom and two of the flight attendants—both women—walked past me to the small section at the very back.

Another minute went by, and then another, and a few more after that, the plane began to taxi towards the runway.

And if there ever was a sign that fate was a cynical bitch, that was it.

Because really. It couldn't have been a sign that fate didn't exist. No, if fate didn't exist, the seats beside me would have filled up with someone. A married couple, maybe, or someone and their kid, or an absolute asshole who would yell at the baby for crying on a flight and who would therefore not be soulmate material. If fate didn't exist, the sold-out flight would have been just that; a sold-out flight, a short stretch of time spent sitting next to someone that I would mean nothing to in the grand scheme of their life.

But for those seats to be empty when I knew the flight was sold out? Those *specific* seats to end up empty?

Fate was laughing.

The plane stopped for a moment, then rushed forward down the runway. From the row beside me, the baby began to wail.

"Same, buddy," I muttered, then looked down at the book in my lap as my hair covered the side of my face, shielding the world from the ridiculous tears in my eyes.

It was stupid. It had been a stupid daydream. I shouldn't have been so upset.

But I couldn't help but think maybe fate had put my soulmate in those seats after all, and the fact that they were empty said something.

By the time we were in the air and the baby had stopped crying, I'd regulated my emotions enough to tuck my hair behind my ear. My book was still on my lap, open to the same page it had been when we'd been on the ground in Edmonton. I couldn't focus on it. I couldn't even bring myself to ask the flight attendant if Ellie could move back once they turned the seatbelt sign off. The thought of admitting to her that fate had decided I didn't *have* a soulmate made my nose sting and my chest hurt all over again. Plus, just because I was destined to be soulmate-less didn't mean she was. I didn't want to take away her chance at a happily ever after.

It didn't end up mattering, though. The seatbelt sign was off for about thirteen seconds when Ellie barrelled down the aisle.

She didn't even glance in my direction before disappearing behind the curtain to the back section of the plane, but she didn't have to for me to see the chalky greyness of her skin. Seconds later, I heard the telltale bang of the bathroom door opening.

I winced, fairly certain Ellie was in the process of losing her overpriced latte in the questionably clean bathroom of the airplane. That was confirmed a few minutes later when she reappeared, her face still chalky but with a slight redness to her cheeks and a sheen of clammy sweat on her forehead.

"Are you okay?" I asked as she braced herself unsteadily on the backs of the aisle seats in the final row.

"Uh-huh," she grunted. "Just my usual air sickness."

"Air sickness?" I repeated.

"Oh, yeah." She pressed a hand to her lips, then shook her head. "I hate flying."

"Ellie!" I closed my book. "Why didn't you tell me? I never would've made you come on a plane!"

"Exactly. And then you would've been doing this alone and I didn't want that." She swallowed hard, then took a deep breath. "Okay, I gotta sit down before standing makes me feel sick again." Carefully, she started forward again, then stopped. "Wait. Why are you by yourself?"

I tried to laugh. "I guess I don't have a soulmate."

She stared at the empty row, then up at me. "Well, you know what that means."

"What?"

She collapsed into the aisle seat with a groan, leaning against the backrest before lolling her head to the side to look at me. "It means fate realized I was gonna need a seat near the bathroom. Sorry I cost you a potential meet cute, but in fairness, you probably wouldn't be able to hear each other over the sound of me puking in the bathroom."

A raspy laugh accompanied it and I almost laughed with her, but she hiccupped and a hand flew up to her mouth as her eyes went wide. She sat up and I grabbed the paper bag out of the pocket on the back of the seat in front of me, barely managing to get it open before Ellie ripped it from my hands and hurled into it.

The flight attendant kindly brought Ellie's carry-on from her previous spot and gave us a complimentary ginger ale, though she couldn't bring herself to drink more than a few sips. Aside from one more trip to the bathroom for her to puke up those few sips of ginger ale, I spent the rest of the flight with Ellie's head on my shoulder, thinking that maybe fate wasn't such a cynical bitch after all.

Maybe fate was telling me my soulmate wouldn't take me away from the kind of friend who would put herself through this kind of torture just to make sure I was okay.

Chapter Twenty-Seven

Two Different Kinds Of Crazy

Ellie

"Oh no," Isla mumbled as the Uber dropped us off in front of a dated-looking townhouse in a yard that dripped with eccentric personality. "Why didn't she tell me they'd be here?"

"Who?" I asked.

She motioned to a Volkswagen Beetle parked on the street, the cherry red paint broken up by a collection of colourful bumper stickers. "My mom's parents. I didn't think Gam and Pops would come up for this. Let alone *drive* it."

"Where do they live?" I asked.

"Depends. In the summer, kind of near Yellowknife. But winter in the Northwest Territories isn't exactly conducive to their totally-not-nudists lifestyle, so they spend winter in Arizona at what all of us pretend isn't a nudist resort."

"Your grandparents are nudists?"

"Gam'll use half the dictionary to talk around the fact that they are, but yeah."

"And they... walk around naked?" I asked.

She laughed. "Not around us."

"Then what's the problem?"

She motioned at a practical black SUV parallel parked a few spots away, both bumpers meticulously equidistant from the cars in front of and behind it. "My dad's parents. Who I also didn't think would drive all the way from Lethbridge for this."

"Maybe it's not their car."

"No one else in the world has that angel ornament hanging from the rear-view mirror," she said. "Seeing as I was eight when I made it and I only ever made one of them."

I twisted my mouth to the side. "And let me guess, they don't get along with your mom's parents?"

"They don't get along with my *mom*, let alone her parents." She sighed, adjusting the backpack she'd slung over her shoulder. "Gam and Pops are flakier than an overcooked croissant and just, like, a *lot*. But they're fine. Grandma and Grandpa Monroe... well, their views don't lean so far to the right that they'd have to lie down to see straight, but they'd have to tilt their heads."

"Oh." I ran my tongue along my teeth. "Is me being here going to be a problem?"

She shot me a look that was part offended, part calling me stupid. "Never."

"I'm queer, Isla. I'm not gonna hide that."

"I'd never ask you to. If they don't like it, they can leave. My mom'll say the same thing and Dad made it very clear it was *her* house before he—"

She stopped talking. I tried not to reach out to take her hand because I seriously had to stop touching Isla that way, but my arm ached almost as much as my heart and a moment later, I compromised by putting a hand on her shoulder.

"It's fine," she said. "Just, apologies in advance for the crazy that's about to happen."

"It can't be any worse than the crazy I threw you into at Christmas," I said as I followed her up the sidewalk.

And technically, I was right. But so was Isla.

They were just two different kinds of crazy.

"*Isla*!!!" screeched a loud voice as soon as Isla had opened the front door. "Oh good golly, it's about time!"

"Is that Isla?" said two male voices in unison.

"Oh Lord in Heaven." I stepped into the house behind Isla as an older woman with short brown hair, round glasses, and freckled white skin raised herself from a couch in the living room directly beside the entryway and waddled towards the door. "You had to show up when I just sat down after that long car ride, did you?"

"Sorry, Grandma," Isla said, putting her backpack on the ground beside her suitcase.

"Pah!" Her grandma flapped a hand at her, then used it to aggressively wave Isla forward. "You couldn't control it, dear. Come here, hug me before your mother gets back from her blatant excuse to avoid me and hogs you to herself." An arm wrapped around Isla's neck, jerking her forward into a hug. "It's been so long since I've seen my oldest grandbaby. You know you don't even have to dial phones these days? You can say 'Steery, call Grandma Monroe' and it'll connect you right to me."

"For the thousandth time, it's *Siri*," muttered a tall, thin older man who'd joined us in the progressively more crowded entryway.

"*Excuse* me for not knowing the name of your pretend assistant," Isla's grandma snapped.

Isla winced as the arm around her neck tightened.

"That must be the problem," she joked, carefully extracting herself from her grandma's grip. "I've been pronouncing it wrong."

"Hmmph." Her grandma half-stepped to the side like she was getting out of the way so Isla could hug her grandpa, but it accomplished exactly nothing because there were too many of us. She seemed to realize it at the same time she seemed to realize there was a fourth person standing there.

That is, me.

"And who's this, then?" she asked, raising an eyebrow.

"I'm Ellie," I said. "Isla's friend."

The other eyebrow joined the first one. "Her friend? Or her... *friend*?"

"Grandma—" Isla started.

"It's fine, dear," her grandma huffed. "But I would've at least liked a text message about this development!"

"We're friends," Isla said, her cheeks flushing red.

"Best friends, actually," I said. "Practically sisters. So I guess that means you're my grandma too." I stuck out my hand. "Nice to meet you, Grandma. I expect a crisp hundred-dollar bill in my next Christmas card."

Isla's grandma stared at my hand silently, her lips in a tight purse that made wrinkles radiate along the bottom of her face.

Then she laughed.

Isla's eyes went wide. So did her grandpa's.

"Is Cynthia *laughing*?" someone said in the living room. "I didn't even know she knew how to do that!"

Isla's grandma—Cynthia—didn't seem to hear the quip. She grabbed my hand, her bony fingers squeezing tight enough that it hurt, but I didn't flinch even as she yanked me forward to hug me, too.

"Well, forgive an old lady, but you have to know what it looks like, dear," she said. "Now, you've got some catching up to do to earn that hundred. Help me back over to the couch, would you?"

I slipped past the older man so he could lean over and give Isla an awkward hug, but Cynthia and I didn't even make it to the coffee table before a whirlwind of frizzy hair and colourful chiffon wrapped in the faint yet skunky scent of weed soared past us.

"My turn!" the woman hollered. "Get over here, my sweet little mermaid."

"Hi, Gam—*oof*," Isla said from behind me. The ball of chiffon bowled into Isla, stubby arms wrapping around her as she finally stopped moving long enough for me to make out a chubby older woman with tanned white skin and the same hair as Isla, if Isla chose to style her hair by brushing out her curls before sticking a fork into a toaster.

"Oh, *you*!" the woman squealed. "Oh, Isla dear. You must be so *excited*!"

"Huh?" came Isla's breathless response as the air was squeezed out of her.

"Where's that rascal who's making you his queen?" she demanded. "I need to have a talk with him to make sure he's treating my girl like the goddess she is, even if that silly son-in-law of mine—rest his soul, of course, you know David would never mind me saying this—refused to give her a proper goddess name."

Cynthia sighed. "Freya, that's Venus."

Freya blew out a raspberry-like sound. "Have you had your eyes checked recently, Cynthia? This is *Isla*. Eye-lah. Not Venus."

"I know that!" Cynthia snapped, her hand tightening on my arm.

"She just means I'm—" Isla gasped.

"—getting *marr*-ied!" Freya said in a trilling, sing-song voice.

"No!" Isla managed to pull back and wheeze in a deep breath. "I'm not getting married."

Freya gasped, pressing a hand to her mouth. "Oh no. What *happened*? What did he do?"

"Nothing," Isla said. "I'm just not the one who's engaged. Venus is."

Freya looked confused. "Venus?"

"That's what we've been trying to say," Cynthina muttered, finally letting go of me and sitting on the couch.

"Oh dear." Freya's voice was full of genuine bewilderment and embarrassment. "Oh, I am so sorry, Isla."

"It's okay," Isla said, chuckling.

Freya shook her head, then pulled Isla in for another bone-crushing hug. "There's too much happening in this old brain. It's getting confused." She let go, but kept a hand on Isla's upper arm. "I thought it was *Isla* and Nick, not *Venus* and Nick."

Isla cringed. "Oh. No. I mean, you were right about that. But Nick and I broke up a while ago."

"Oh," Freya said, her voice high-pitched as the friendly chaos on her face morphed into something scary. "And now Nick is with Venus?"

"No!" Isla said quickly. "She's marrying Marcus."

"Who's Marcus?"

"Nick's brother."

"Okay." Freya frowned. "So you're... getting married."

"No—" Isla said.

"You're not getting married," she corrected. "But you're dating Nick's brother?"

Isla drew in a deep breath. "No, I—I'm not seeing Nick anymore. We broke up. After we broke up, *Venus* started dating *Marcus*, who's Nick's brother."

Freya nodded slowly and I thought it was all sorted out.

But then she turned and caught sight of me.

"Wait," she said. "Then who's this?"

"I'm Ellie," I said.

"She's my friend," Isla said.

"*Oh*!" Freya said, drawing the word out. "That makes sense. Sorry, dear. I didn't know you were gay."

"No, we—"

"They're *friends*, Freya!" Cynthia said.

"Exactly," Isla said. "Ellie's here to come to the party with me."

Freya looked from Isla to me and back at Isla. "What? But if you're just friends, why aren't you marrying Nick? You know you don't have to do that anymore, right? You can marry whoever you want, my sweet mermaid."

"Oh sweet Jesus on the Cross, Freya!" Cynthia exclaimed. "Venus is getting married. Isla is not. Marcus is the groom, Nick is out of the picture, Ellie is Isla's friend, and no one here is gay!"

I didn't say anything. Isla looked at me and, after a moment, raised her eyebrows in a question.

Was she asking...

I mean, I told her I wasn't going to pretend I wasn't queer. But she'd been right about the level of crazy we'd walked into. So I didn't think... I mean, for her sake—

But she wasn't asking me not to say anything.

I couldn't explain why. There was just something in her eyes that made it clear she was asking me if I *wanted* to say something.

That her silence was an invitation to say something.

That she'd never ask me to hide that part of me, not to her family and not to anyone.

So I didn't.

"Well, that's rude," I said. "I'm not no one."

Cynthia's mouth dropped open. Isla's lips pressed together to hold back a laugh.

"But I guess *technically* I'm not gay," I continued. "I usually go with bisexual, so like... half gay. On my birthdad's side, probably. I'm adopted so I don't know for sure."

"Oh. Oh my," Cynthia stammered. "That's—Obviously, I didn't *know*—and I didn't mean—"

"Wait just one second." The fourth person in the room, an older man who'd been mostly silent up to that point as he sat in an overstuffed recliner near the window. "Why are we here if Ellie is marrying Marcus?"

And Cynthia Monroe nearly burst into tears.

Chapter Twenty-Eight

Spreadsheets and the Mona Lisa

Ellie

"Well, at least *that's* out of the way," Athena Monroe said after closing the door behind Cynthia later that night. "I thought they'd never leave."

"Your door is not soundproof, Athena," came a muffled voice from outside.

"Take it as a hint for next time, Cynthia," Athena said, flipping the deadbolt before turning to me and Isla. "Now, who wants a nightcap?"

After meeting her mom, I was certain Isla's dad must have been the prototype for a stereotypical nerd, right down to the pocket protector and the thick glasses and the too-short khaki dress pants.

It was the only way Isla made sense as a concept. For Isla to be a delightfully unusual mix of a type-A personality wrapped in ethereal whimsy, her dad *must* have been the nerdiest nerd to ever nerd his way about life, following every rule and ensuring the plaid bow tie industry never went out of business.

Because Athena Monroe was anarchy personified.

When she returned from wherever she'd been when Isla and I first arrived, Isla and I were in the kitchen, letting Cynthia calm down from her encounter with us in the living room. Athena walked in carrying a carton of eggs and a pint of ice cream, took one look at Isla, and dropped the eggs.

Not accidentally. She just stopped holding them and let them fall to the floor.

Without a word, she set the ice cream on the counter, stepping over the broken eggs and pulling Isla in for a hug. She said nothing; not a hello, not a "How was your flight?", not an "I missed you more than anything."

She just hugged Isla so tightly that she didn't need words for it.

They were hugging for so long that I thought they might not ever let go. But eventually Athena pressed a kiss to the side of her head, then turned to me and threw open her arms.

"Ellie!" she exclaimed, like I was an old friend and not a stranger standing in her kitchen. Like the room hadn't just been silent. Like she'd walked in the door with excitement and energy and had shouted in glee instead of clinging to her daughter.

"Mrs. Monroe!" I replied just as exuberantly, stepping forward to hug her.

She had the same colour blonde hair as Isla and Freya, but where Freya's hair had stuck out everywhere and Isla kept her curls neatly styled, Athena's hair fell in waves around her head. Her eyes sparkled in a way that was all-too-familiar, bright and brown and lively, and she had the same full lips that curled into a calming smile. Where Isla was all curves and softness, Athena was gracefully toned, not chubby but not thin, either.

"Call me Athena, would you?" She squeezed me as tightly as she could before letting go. "I'm so thrilled to finally meet you."

"Me too," I said. "I can't wait to hear all the embarrassing stories you have about Isla."

Athena's familiar lips curled into a mischievous smirk. "Oh, I have *plenty*. And I very much want to know about all the trouble you've been getting my girl into over in Aurora Flats."

"I've unfortunately failed at that, I'm afraid," I said, sighing heavily. "I haven't even gotten her arrested yet."

"A shame. I'm so tired of being the only one in this family with a record," said Athena.

I laughed, because it seemed like a joke.

And then I laughed a little more, because I glanced at Isla, who was shaking her head in a way that made it clear it was absolutely not a joke.

We'd spent the rest of the evening bouncing between the chaos of Isla's grandparents and the chaos of everyone trying to grill Isla at once about what, exactly, had happened: why she'd left and where she'd gone and no, really, *why* did you up and leave like that, it simply *couldn't* have been that you just wanted a change and we're simply not taking a hint that you don't want to get into the real reason. Isla handled it the way Isla handled everything: well on the outside, spiralling into anxiety and despair on the inside until Athena had finally got all four grandparents out the front door.

"A nightcap sounds good," Isla said in response to her mother. "But I need a shower."

"Yeah, you stink," I said. "I do too, but you can go first."

She stuck her tongue out at me, but took me up on it and went up the stairs, leaving me and Athena in the living room.

"Well, let's get started on that nightcap," she said. "Would you like a hot buttered rum?"

"Why is that even a question?" I said. "Who wouldn't?"

Athena pointed finger guns at me. "That's my kinda response. But also, my husband despises hot buttered rum, the damn heathen."

I frowned as I followed her mom into the kitchen, confused. "Your... current husband?"

"Yes," Athena said. "Isla's dad."

I frowned. "I thought he, um, passed."

"He did," she said.

"But you said despises, not—"

"I refuse to believe that whatever iteration of David may or may not be floating around the universe in whatever capacity he might be would suddenly decide he was a fan of the stuff," Athena said, opening a cupboard and pulling out three mugs. "Not after that one time in Lunenberg. I think he pissed rum for three days afterwards and never touched it again."

"That's a lot of rum," I said.

"He drank the distillery out that night. But to answer the question you wanted to ask but didn't because social norms make it uncomfortable to ask why someone would refer to her dead husband both in the present tense and as her current husband," Athena continued as she filled the kettle. "David knew when he married me that one, he wouldn't be getting out of it so easily with the whole 'death' thing, because two, I had no desire to marry anyone at all but made an exception for him because he was the other half of my soul. So he is both my past, future, and current husband, whether he likes it or not, for all of eternity."

"That's beautiful," I said.

"Yes, well, I said it intending to scare him off back in the day," she said. "That whole 'for eternity' thing should've been overwhelming. But David was one of those practical atheists who didn't believe there was anything after this." She laughed, shaking her head as she pulled ingredients out of a cupboard. "He said to me, 'Well, Athena, either I'm right and it doesn't matter what I agree to because nothing will happen, or you're right and it doesn't matter because I can't think of a better way to spend an eternity.'"

"Wow. No wonder Isla is so dead-set on the whole soulmate thing."

"The what?" she asked, placing a mug full of rum and spices and a scoop of ice cream in front of me.

"Soulmates," I said vaguely, avoiding saying anything about the meet-cute bet. "You know. Destiny and stuff."

Athena nodded slowly, a hint of pain on her face. "I know that's part of what made her dad's death so hard on her. It's difficult to lose someone who doesn't believe in an afterlife, especially when they choose to go. Even if that going is inevitable either way."

Sadness prickled in my chest. It was obvious Isla tried to view her dad's death from a standpoint of logic and compassion and wanting the best for the people you loved, but there were so many more layers to it than that. "I'm sorry for your loss."

"Our loss, the universe's gain." She smiled. "David's out there somewhere plugging numbers into spreadsheets and reviewing the process of predetermining destinies so he can prepare a report on their efficacy. Or whatever."

"He sounds a lot like Isla," I said.

"Oh, absolutely," Athena said, laughing. "Isla is so much like her father that I see him every single time I look at her, even though she's practically my clone. I knew it from when Isla was just a little girl and David caught her playing on his computer."

"Oh, is it time for the first embarrassing story?" I asked excitedly.

"Eh, it's not exactly *embarrassing*," she said. "But it's funny. It was one of the few times Isla was a little anarchist. The girls knew they weren't allowed to use David's computer. But when David went over, he found her sitting there with a spreadsheet open, and Isla told him she *knew* she wasn't supposed to use the computer but she really needed a way to keep track of all her doll clothes. She wanted to know how many outfits she had for them, since she thought she couldn't ask for a new doll for her birthday if she didn't have enough clothes for all of them.

"And David looked at the computer, then sat on the floor beside her and said she should add a column for colour, and one for where each item was stored, and that she could use formulas to add everything up instead of trying to add it herself. Because it was one thing for her to disobey the no-touching-Dad's-computer rule, but quite another to not even make a *proper* spreadsheet while she was doing it."

"Oh my God," I said, laughing.

Athena grinned. "It gets better. Three hours later, I go into the living room and find David sitting at the coffee table, perfecting a spreadsheet that could calculate which outfits went with which shoes and which dolls considered that their favourite outfit. Meanwhile, Isla's upstairs playing in her room because she got bored waiting and decided to count all the doll clothes manually."

I started laughing as the kettle whistled. Athena stood, bringing it over to the table.

"That was just David, though. He was so smart, but so stupid." She shook her head, smiling fondly as she poured steaming water into our mugs. "He loved those rows and columns and boxes. He said you could always find an answer with a spreadsheet. But I think that day with Isla and her dolls reminded him that spreadsheets don't actually *give* you an answer. That the answers are outside the box, and it's just using the details you give it to point them out."

I wasn't sure if that was really how spreadsheets worked, but it sounded pretty profound, so I didn't question her on it. "That makes sense."

"Maybe it does. Maybe it doesn't." She sighed, stirring her drink until the butter and ice cream both melted. "I wish Isla would discover that, too."

"What do you mean?"

Athena waved a dismissive hand. "Nothing. And I think that's enough talk about spreadsheets and things we won't know more about until we die. I don't think I said thank you, Ellie."

"For what?" I asked.

"Joining us for Venus's engagement party. And supporting Isla through it. Being a good friend to her. Especially since I know you had to take time off of work."

"It wasn't a problem at all," I said. "Anything I can do to get out of that hell hole, I will."

Athena tilted her head, lazily stirring her hot buttered rum. "Why do you go back to it, then?"

"I mean, money." I chuckled. "And Isla's there, of course, so I guess it's only hell-adjacent now."

"You could make money other ways, though," Athena said.

I half-shrugged. "Maybe."

There were a few moments of silence as I sipped my drink.

"I didn't mean to upset you," Athena said when I set the mug back down.

"I'm not upset," I said.

"You just don't seem like the kind of girl that thrives in the machine."

"Oh, I'm definitely not," I said. "But that's mainly because I don't thrive anywhere."

"I find that hard to believe."

"Well, no where I've discovered so far, then."

"What about photography? Or marketing?"

The words pulled my eyes up to her. Athena was studying me from across the table.

"How—" I started.

"Isla talks about you all the time," she said. "She mentioned you're a talented photographer. And I have to agree."

"You've never seen my work," I said, laughing.

"I certainly have," she replied, tilting to dig her phone out of her pocket. "She sent me links to that bar you like to show me some of the things she's getting up to these days and mentioned you help the owner with their marketing and such."

"Well, they're a friend of mine," I said as she tapped her phone screen, then slid it across the table.

She'd screenshotted a post from the Flat Tire's social media page. Jayce had asked me to take some candids on one of our typical Friday nights, so I'd brought my camera along. The photo in question was of Isla, of course—why else would Athena have screenshotted it?—sitting at the bar. She was wearing the plaid skirt I loved, one leg crossed over the other and a heel dangling off her foot. Her head was thrown back in a laugh, the pork-pie hat on her head slightly askew, and she was holding a glass of wine.

God, she looked good.

"Okay, but I had an excellent model for that," I said. "It's not hard to take an amazing picture of Isla."

"You have skill, Ellie," Athena said. "There's no denying it."

"That doesn't mean it's a viable way of making money."

"Why not?"

"Because there's a difference between taking pictures of what I like and what I'd be paid for." I motioned at the phone. "Taking pictures of Isla is fun. It's easy to make her look good. I spend all my time with her, so I know her mannerisms and her expressions and how to catch them. And I *want* to take good photos of her because I like when they make her feel good."

Athena didn't say anything, just nodded as she looked at me with a tilted head.

"And even if I deal with taking pictures for profit instead of fun, that still doesn't mean I'd succeed," I continued. "The idea of taxes and invoices and, I don't know, accounting stuff makes my brain shut down. I flunked out of college because of it. There's no way I could support myself running my own business solely because I couldn't handle the actual business side of it."

"I'd do it for you."

I startled. Athena didn't, casually sipping her mug of hot buttered rum as I turned to see a freshly showered Isla walking into the kitchen.

"What?" I said.

"I'd do that stuff for you," she repeated, grabbing the kettle off the stove and bringing it to the table to pour into the third mug Athena had prepared. "Like, help with your paperwork and accounting tand stuff. I can't do art worth shit, but I can make a spreadsheet look like the Mona Lisa."

Athena pressed her lips together, not parting them until she lifted her mug to her lips to sip from it.

"I couldn't afford to pay you for that, though," I said. "Not at first, at least."

Isla rolled her eyes. "Does Jayce pay you for doing stuff for them?"

"No, but—"

"So whatever. You can buy me a drink at the Flat Tire once in a while." She sipped her drink. "That's what friends do, Ella Prime. So when are we starting this?"

A lump started to swell in the base of my throat.

"I, uh, don't know," I said. "I haven't thought about it that seriously. I might not even want to, still."

"Where's your heart leading you?" Athena asked. "Follow it, and you'll find the answer."

It was one of those profound statements meant to make someone think of things at a deeper level. It wasn't something anyone would expect to have an immediate answer for.

But I didn't even have to consult my heart before it screamed the answer at me.

Worse, it was the right answer, even if it was the wrong question.

The answer I got was Isla.

And the question should have been what my heart wanted.

Because of course it was. Of fucking *course* it was. I didn't know who the fuck I thought I was kidding when Jayce had confronted me weeks earlier, but of *course* I wanted her.

I wanted to hold her hand because I wanted to hold all of her. Just like I had since the day I'd met her. I wanted to hold her hand to pull her closer to me and touch her cheek as I kissed her and gently cup both her breasts because even after literally fucking her that one time, I hadn't got to touch her like that and it was awful of me to even think that because it didn't matter.

Isla.

Was.

Straight.

She'd held my hand for a favour. She'd kiss me for a ruse. She'd fucked me for relief. A relief for me moreso than her, I think, though her cheeks had been flushed and a sheen of sweat made her glow post-orgasm.

Athena Monroe asked where my heart was leading me because she thought it would inspire me to change my career. But my heart didn't give two fucks about spreadsheets. It wanted Isla.

And that would *never* be the answer.

Chapter Twenty-Nine
Home

Isla

"I like her."

I looked up from my hot buttered rum. "Ellie?"

Mom nodded, lazily circling her spoon around her mug. "She's the type of person I hoped you would meet when you ran off to Edmonton."

"Aurora Flats," I corrected.

"Right, yes." She set her spoon on the table. "You need an influence like her in your life."

My mouth twitched, not quite with laughter. Of course my mom would say that. "Because she's spontaneous and chaotic?"

"Because she's genuine. With a big heart that loves easily and vulnerably."

I frowned a bit, not looking at her. "Are you saying I don't have a big heart? Or that I'm not genuine?"

Mom gave me a dusty look, which was her version of a dirty look. "Of course not. Having influences in your life that amplify your good qualities is as important as influences who push you out of your comfort zone." She tilted her head. "Though, the loving easily part is one to note."

"What's that supposed to mean?"

She gave me a small smile. "Just that it's okay to open your heart, hon."

"My heart is open," I said.

"Is it open to everything?" she asked.

"What's that supposed to mean?"

"Having an open heart—a fully open, free, and untethered heart—sometimes means letting go of things we don't know we're holding onto," she said.

I loved my mom. But the speaking in ethereal riddles thing got really old, really fast. "How can you let go of something you don't know you're holding?"

"By remembering to check outside the box," she said simply.

I sighed. "Mom—"

"Oh, I know. I'm driving you crazy." She lifted her mug, but didn't sip it, instead shooting me a cheeky smile. "Don't concern yourself with my rambling. All you need to know is that I'm happy you and Ellie found each other."

"Thanks," I said. "I am, too."

"It's obvious," she said. "You look beautiful."

Warmth filled my chest. She was my mom and she had to say that, but it was still nice to hear.

"Everything about you is softer," she continued. "Softer, but more settled. You look the way I wish your sister looked right now."

I opened my mouth to thank her again, but paused. "Wait, what's that supposed to mean?"

Mom sat in silence for a moment, staring at nothing in particular. It was unusual for her; Mom was a "think as you speak" person, not a "think before you open your mouth" one. So for her to collect her thoughts and organize them into something before speaking was a big deal.

"Love can open your eyes to an entire life you never considered," she finally said. "One day, you're running from the cops because you shit on the roof of a truck restricting bathroom access to a group of peaceful protesters, and the next you're telling some accountant that you'll move to the city and officially finish your high school diploma because you want to be his wife and have his babies. Even though you were *certain* there wasn't a man alive who could make you consider that."

"So love makes you want to change?" I asked, trying not to sound as skeptical as I felt.

"Love makes you change what you want." She leaned back from the table, lifting her feet to rest them on the empty chair beside her. "Or it can, at least. It doesn't force you to. But it makes you want to."

"...so love makes you want to change," I repeated.

"It makes you want to *want* to change." She chuckled, shaking her head. "Love makes you want to grow. To open yourself to new things. It makes your world brighter. Something with that kind of power affects how a person carries themself." She gave me a pointed look that I didn't understand. "How they think of themself. How they interact with people. All things that change the way they're interpreted outwardly." She tapped her hands on the table. "I don't see that in Venus."

I swallowed hard. That was kind of a huge thing to spill when we were literally here for Venus's engagement party.

"You don't think she loves Marcus?" I asked.

"I think she thinks she loves Marcus," Mom said.

I gave her a pointed look of my own. "So... no?"

She shrugged. "Maybe I'm crazy. She just seems different."

I didn't bother calling her out for evading the question. It would get me nowhere. "But you just said that love can make you different."

She sighed. "I know. But something doesn't quite sit right. And I can't get Venus to tell me about whatever's giving these vibrations that are so *off*."

Clearly, I was out of practice talking to my mom. It took far too long for me to realize where she was leading me.

"You want me to talk to her," I said.

"If it's related to what I think it is, Venus just may appreciate knowing there's someone in her life who understands what she's dealing with," Mom said. "And sometimes, people need to see a reminder of what things like this are supposed to look like. What they should feel like."

"I mean, I guess I can deal with half of that," I said. "But you'll have to find someone else to show her the other part. I haven't even been on a date since Nick and I broke up. And not for lack of trying."

Mom pressed her lips together, then nodded. "Well, maybe Venus will see you as a reminder of David. Or maybe I'm wrong altogether. Who knows." She lifted her arms in an exaggerated shrug. "Not me!"

I tried to get her to tell me what she was talking about, but my mom was as stubborn as she was flighty, so it was hopeless. Once I finished my hot buttered rum, I excused myself and went upstairs to get ready for bed. Ellie was in the guest room, her clothes in a heap on the bed. The nightstand lamp was on, illuminating the room with gold-splashed shadows as she brushed out her wet hair.

"You alright?" she asked as I closed the door behind me.

"Yeah, of course," I said. "Just tired. You can go hang out with my mom if you want, though. She's probably going to be up for a while still."

Ellie gave me a derisive look, like I was crazy to suggest she hang out with my mom instead of go to sleep. I shrugged and took off the sweatpants I'd pulled over my pyjama shorts, folding them neatly and tucking them into my suitcase before folding the clothes Ellie left on the bed and tucking them in hers.

Once I was done, I grabbed my book and crawled beneath the covers, curling up on my side. Ellie grabbed her hair dryer from her suitcase and looked at the walls, then turned to me.

"Where's the best outlet for this?" she asked, holding up the cord.

"Uh..." I twisted my mouth to the side. Venus's old room had become the guest room, since my mom had turned my old bedroom into an art studio almost immediately after I'd moved out. "Well, there's one by the door. Or this one might be closer to the mirror."

"I think it is." She shrugged. "Guess you get a front-row seat while I dry my hair."

"Lucky me," I said.

She smirked. "I'll try not to get water on your book."

"Don't worry about it. Unless I drop it into the ocean or something, Books will still probably take it back to resell."

But honestly, I could've just put my book away. Because despite the pages being open in front of me, I couldn't focus on the words.

It wasn't because Ellie was standing right there. Not totally, anyway. My mind kept wandering back to what my mom had said. To her claim that love could make someone look different.

I didn't think she was wrong, exactly. But I didn't see how she could be right when I hadn't even found someone I might want to take out for a coffee date, let alone spend the rest of my life with.

Unless she believed me and Ellie were dating and lying about it for some reason.

But we obviously weren't. My parents had always made it very clear we were a family of love and acceptance. From the time Venus and I were little, it was ingrained in our minds. When Grandma Monroe would joke about us growing up and having big fairytale weddings to our future husbands, Dad always added a perky "or wives!" to the end of the sentence. If Ellie and I were dating, I wouldn't have even thought to keep it a secret. There was no reason to.

I'd just never looked at a woman and thought, "Oh yes, I sure would like to have sex with her."

Granted, I'd never said it about a man, either. But only because I liked to get to know guys before deciding if I wanted to be with them like that. That's how it had worked for me and Nick; we'd dated for quite a while before I felt ready to be intimate with him.

And not "intimate" as in a euphemism for sex. Intimate in general. We held hands and he'd put his arm around me at the movies and stuff, but it was a few months before we'd kissed. Venus had gaped at me when I admitted that, like I was crazy for being able to keep my hands off Nick for any stretch of time, but I just... I'd needed to be closer with him first.

He'd been patient. Understanding. He hadn't pressured me. It was why I'd insisted to Ellie, back when I'd told her about our breakup, that Nick was a good boyfriend. Because he *was.* He was respectful and sweet and never made me feel like I had to do anything I didn't want to. So when I was ready, it felt right. It felt good.

And yes, Elie and I had kissed. We'd done more than kiss. We'd been intimate in every sense of the word. But that hadn't been because I wanted to have sex with *her.* I'd wanted to have *sex* with her.

That sounded awful. Like I'd only wanted her for a physical release. But it wasn't just that. Yes, it had felt good for me—obviously, because she'd made me come *hard*—but I'd wanted to do it for her. Because she was my friend. My best friend, not just now, but ever. Everything else aside, I knew I needed to keep Ellie in my life. I needed to keep her with a desperation I couldn't quite explain, something I couldn't compare to any other friend I'd ever had. I couldn't even compare it to any boyfriend I'd ever had.

But that wasn't the same as being attracted to her.

Still, I couldn't deny that Ellie had quickly become one of the most important people in my life. And maybe that was what my mom was picking up on. Maybe she was wrong, but also right.

Maybe she was sensing the love I had for Ellie as a friend. For my new life in general.

Maybe that kind of love, that strong, all-encompassing, life-changing kind of love wasn't just meant for couples. Maybe I could platonically "date" my best friend. Maybe I could just platonically spoon her sometimes. Maybe we acted like a couple because you didn't need to be a *couple* to love someone like that. And maybe I was spending all this time searching for a soulmate when the real soulmate was the friends I'd fucked along the way.

I bit back a laugh, which Ellie thankfully didn't notice. Not that she would've thought I was laughing at her, but I didn't want to admit what I'd been thinking of.

But she wasn't paying attention to me. She was bent forward, half facing away from me with her hair flipped over her head to dangle in front of her. The hair dryer was pointed at her scalp as she worked her fingers through the roots, scrunching and releasing like she wanted to shake the water out to make it go faster.

It was interesting, honestly. Yes, I'd seen her dry her hair before—multiple times, since we'd been going to Lady of the Lake's Aquasize class regularly—but I didn't think I'd ever get tired of watching her do it. Because it was so different from dealing with drying my own hair, which was an entire production.

That was obviously why I couldn't stop watching.

And a little because it was mesmerizing. Watching the tiny drops of water that fell from the strands, leaving marks on the stretched blue hockey t-shirt she wore. The way her fingers moved through it, gliding back and forth. The way it rippled when she caught it with the stream of air a certain way.

God, her hair was pretty.

"Enjoying the show?"

I blinked out of my transfixation to see Ellie grinning at me as she unplugged the hair dryer.

"Of course," I said. "I like looking at you."

She let out a surprised laugh. "Damn. Give a girl a head's up before you flatter her like that."

I should've said something in response to that, but I didn't. "Want me to braid it?"

Ellie tilted her head. "What?"

"Your hair." I closed my book. "I can braid it, if you want. So it doesn't tangle while you sleep."

She stared at me for a moment, her face unreadable.

Then she shrugged and held her brush out to me. "Sure."

I pushed the blankets back and sat up. "Pass me a couple of elastics and sit here."

We were mostly quiet as I brushed her hair out before parting it down the middle so I could braid it into two thick Dutch braids. After I finished, Ellie took her brush back and put it on the dresser. When she turned back around, I'd already snuggled back under the covers.

"You wanna be big spoon or little spoon tonight?" I asked as she crawled into bed beside me.

She didn't answer, just scooted in closer and reached over me to turn off the lamp, then kept herself tucked around me, her chest pressing into my back and her arm around my waist.

"Night, Ella Two," she said softly.

And somehow, even though we'd spent the evening in the house I'd been raised in, it was only then that I felt like I was home.

Chapter Thirty
Look At Her

Isla

THE DRESS I'D BOUGHT for the engagement party was almost perfect.

It was dark blue and fitted to my waist before flaring out into a skirt with a glittery lining beneath the chiffon-like fabric, so it sparkled in addition to swishing beautifully when I spun, which was the second-most important feature on a dress.

The first being pockets, which it unfortunately didn't have, and thus it wasn't completely perfect.

But it was close, and since I was waiting in the guest room for Ellie and my mom to finish getting ready, I decided to amuse myself by twirling.

And then, after making myself dizzy because I'd spun so many times, by shimmying my hips back and forth so I could watch the skirt swish and sparkle around my legs, which is what I was doing when the door flew open and Ellie's boobs stumbled in.

I mean, Ellie came too, but... I mean, her boobs were right there.

The dark purple fabric shimmered, clinging to her slim frame in a way that turned her usual gangliness into something model-esque. She'd twisted her hair into a simple updo that showed off her shoulders and the halter-style neck.

And then there was just so, so much boob.

Like, I'd seen Ellie change multiple times, and I was still pretty sure I'd never seen that much of her boobs. The damn things were defying gravity and I had no idea how. I couldn't see a bra, even though the dress was cut low in the back, yet somehow, her breasts were sitting high and perky and—

"Um, excuse me, hi," Ellie said, waving her hand in front of her chest.

Alarmed, I snapped out of it and looked up to see an amused expression on her face. "Huh?"

She raised an eyebrow. "My eyes are up here, Ella Two."

"Sorry." My face burned as she giggled. "I'm sorry, I didn't mean to stare. That dress is... You look..."

"Look amazing?" she finished, striking a pose. "I know your ex is off-limits and all, but who knows? We might run into my soulmate tonight."

"And you're making sure they can see just how big your *soul* is, huh?"

Ellie stuck her tongue out at me, adjusting the front of the dress to make sure it sat properly. "You're sure it's okay?"

"Yeah. It looks great." I said it with every ounce of earnestness I had, which was a lot because I was being completely earnest. "You look gorgeous, Ellie. Fate would be ridiculous not to put your soulmate in your path tonight."

"You look great too, Ella Two." She studied me for a moment, then frowned. "But something's missing."

I looked down, panicked. "What? What's missing?"

"One sec."

She turned, digging into her bag for a moment. A second later, she turned back to me with a grin.

"My hat?" I asked, raising my eyebrows. "I didn't even pack this."

"I know. I did. Because I saw you'd forgotten to pack it. You're welcome."

"I didn't forget. I didn't bring it."

She frowned. "Why not?"

"Because... it's a fancy party," I said.

"And this is a fancy hat." She placed it carefully on top of my head.

"Yeah, but it stands out too much," I said, though I let her adjust my curls beneath the brim.

"You can't blame that on the hat, Isla," Ellie said. "*You* stand out wherever you go."

I didn't know if that was true regularly, but I definitely stood out when we got to Venus and Marcus's engagement party. Though Ellie was right; it wasn't because of the hat.

No, the quick glances from Nick's mom and some of the other older women in the Cooke family were because of who I was.

Because of what I'd done to Nick.

Because I'd left without a word. I'd ghosted him. And I'd never told him why.

I didn't see him when Ellie and I first followed my mom into the hotel ballroom Mrs. Cooke had rented for the party. There were too many people milling around, too many men in suits and women in cocktail dresses for this unreasonably formal engagement party. For a moment, I thought that might be a blessing. Why track him down and torture myself with an uncomfortable situation longer than I had to?

But my mom excused herself to say hello to Gam and Pops, stepped out of the way, and I saw him instantly.

He stood at the bar, looking uncomfortable in a navy blue suit with a tie around his neck. I gave it an hour, tops, before that suit jacket would end up discarded on a nearby chair, much to Mrs. Cooke's chagrin. The tie would be gone long before that; I couldn't believe he had it on in the first place. The bartender slid two glasses towards him and he nodded in appreciation, then turned around. Before I could even pretend like I wasn't staring, Nick's eyes met mine.

Surprise flitted across his face, replaced immediately by a composed expression that was eerily reminiscent of the one his mother had on her face when Ellie and I first walked into the room. He held my gaze and I couldn't bring myself to do anything: to look away, to swallow back my fear, to press my lips together nervously as I tried to figure out what, exactly, that silent expression meant.

"Is that him?"

I jumped at the sound of Ellie's lowered voice and tore my gaze away from Nick, my cheeks burning. "Mm-hmm."

"Wow." She sounded impressed. "I mean, really, *wow*. He's hot as *hell*."

I must have looked stunned because Ellie laughed and nudged me.

"You know damn well I wouldn't. I'm just saying you have good taste in guys. You pull in some seriously fine ass, Ella Two."

It wasn't quite enough to make me laugh, but my mouth twitched as I looked at Nick again. He was still looking at me, surprisingly enough, and I saw his eyes flit to Ellie and back to me. A heartbeat passed before his cool expression melted into a smile that I didn't understand.

And then he started walking towards me.

Which I understood even less. If Mrs. Cooke had told Marcus to tell Venus to tell *me* that Nick might be uncomfortable with me attending the party, that had to mean Nick was more upset than I'd ever seen him when we were together. I'd been gearing myself up for that awkward moment, worrying about what he would say and how I should respond and if it would cause drama at my sister's party.

But that look, that expression as Nick walked towards me...he looked almost... Happy wasn't the right word.

He looked relieved.

I drew in a breath as he walked across the hall, steeling myself for our first conversation since he'd begged me to give it time before we called our relationship over.

"You can do this," Ellie said.

But, as it turned out, I could not do this.

"There you are, Isla," said a bored-sounding voice.

I turned, my attention suddenly captured by my sister, who I also hadn't seen in months. Venus was wearing a one-shoulder dress in a gauzy pink fabric that flowed over her curves, the hem hovering just above the floor. Deep pink lipstick made her lips look full and pouty, and her eyelashes were so long I could've seen them from halfway across the room. Her golden-blonde, impeccably highlighted hair was crowned with seasonally inappropriate flowers.

She should have looked gorgeous.

But I immediately saw *exactly* what my mom was talking about.

"Venus," I said, trying not to stare at the bags under her eyes or the way her lips were more downturned than usual. "Hi."

"Hi," she said. "Thanks for coming."

"Thanks for inviting me."

There was an awkward beat where I shifted from one foot to the other. Then Venus put out her arms and I stepped forward, hugging her tightly.

"*Thank you*," she whispered. "Seriously."

"For what?" I whispered back.

"Being here."

I frowned as we let go of each other. "Is everything okay? You seem—"

"Well, if it isn't Isla," interrupted a man's voice.

Venus's shoulders sagged. Not in disappointment; her expression read more like resigned annoyance.

"Hi, Marcus," I said to my sister's fiancé as he walked up beside her. "Congratulations on getting engaged."

His smile was tight. "Thanks."

I swallowed nervously. "This is my best friend. Ellie."

"Ellie," Marcus repeated, nodding stiffly. "What a pleasure."

Ellie smiled brightly. "Thanks for inviting me."

He looked like he wanted to remind Ellie that he *hadn't* invited her, because if he'd had it his way, I wouldn't be there either. But social politeness dictated otherwise. "Well, we'll be doing a welcome toast shortly, but in the meantime, there are drinks and food over there"—he motioned to the back wall—"and my dad insisted on an open bar even though Venus and I are doing a dry February, so feel free to—"

He kept talking, filler words that spilled from his mouth and accomplished nothing except not allowing me a moment to talk to my sister before their attention was redirected to some other Cooke family member. When I glanced back towards the bar, Nick was gone, because of course he was; he wasn't going to stand there awkwardly while Venus and Marcus greeted us.

Which was fine. There would be plenty of opportunities for awkward interactions with Nick over the course of the night. Like when Ellie and I were refilling our drinks after Mrs. Cooke gave her welcome speech.

"Hey, Isla."

My mouth went dry but sipping the beer I'd just gotten from the bartender seemed rude, so I didn't. "H-Hi. Hi, Nick."

He was leaning on the bar and smiled, for some reason. "Love the hat. Did you—"

"There you are, Nick!"

Penny, a friend of Venus's from high school who was probably one of her bridesmaids, given the large button pinned to the strap of her slinky black dress that read *Bridesmaid* in sparkly gold letters, nearly knocked the beer out of my hand as she inserted herself between me and Nick.

"Marcus needs you to handle something for him." With a simperingly fake smile, she turned to me. "Sorry to interrupt. Best man duties call!"

Before Nick or I could say anything else, she tugged him away from the bar towards the exit.

Which was fine. Because there were at least four or five people who'd inched a little closer when Nick had said hello, clearly hoping for the inevitably entertaining drama of the bride's sister and the groom's brother interacting for the first time since they'd broken up.

It wasn't the first time that night. Each time I looked up, someone was just turning their head away. I thought I was imagining it until Ellie and I found a quiet table to sit at near the wall of large windows along one side of the room.

The windows looked out on a patio, but given that it was winter, said patio was empty except for the reflections of the partygoers in the room behind us.

And at least a few of those reflections were staring at me and Ellie, leaning into each other and whispering as they giggled.

So between the stress of catching people watching me and that same stress making me susceptible to the belief that alcohol would settle my nerves, it wasn't long before I'd drank enough to turn the event from my personal version of hell to that same version of hell, but where I was drunk enough to be having a fucking blast while I was there.

"You have to dance with me!" Ellie shouted when the DJ started playing music after making an announcement for everyone to refill their drinks because there'd be a speech or something happening soon.

"What?" I asked.

She gestured wildly. "The song! It's Freddie Mercury's Law that you have to dance with your best friend to '*You're My Best Friend*.'"

"What if I don't want to dance at all?" I asked, glancing around the room as I let her lead me onto the dance floor.

"Everyone's already seen you," she replied patiently. "And you know what, Isla? Fuck 'em. Fuck 'em if they want to judge you for having fun at this party."

"Do I have to fuck all of 'em or can I pick and choose?"

A few pairs of judgmental eyes turned towards us as Ellie lost it, but I was too busy grinning at the sound of her laughter and the way her eyes crinkled as she giggled to pay attention to anyone else.

The dance floor wasn't particularly crowded, but it wasn't empty, either. I recognized a few of Venus's friends swaying to the beat, and Gam and Pops were out there doing a strange kind of waltz that they insisted on teaching me and Ellie.

It went horribly. Both Ellie and I were reasonably okay dancers, but we were laughing too hard to follow any of the steps my grandparents were doing.

"I'm just gonna twirl you," Ellie finally said after we tripped each other for the fifth time.

"What?" I asked.

"Twirl," she demanded, and then I was.

My skirt flared out. I knew it didn't go high enough to show off anything I didn't want seen; I'd practiced twirling in this dress enough to know that. But it went out enough to show off the glittery lining beneath my skirt, enough to swish air and fabric around my legs when I twirled back in the other direction, enough that Gam started clapping on the other side of the dance floor, and I caught a few smiles on the faces that spun past me.

Enough that I didn't notice him until he was there.

"That looked like fun."

Delight was still coursing through my body when he spoke, so when I turned towards Nick, I was smiling. He, surprisingly, smiled back.

"It was," I said, mostly because I had no idea what else to say.

He looked at Ellie, warmth in his eyes, and extended his hand. "We haven't met. I'm Nick."

"Ellie," she replied, letting go of me so she could shake his hand.

"D'you mind if I cut in for a dance with Isla?"

Ellie glanced at me. I looked back at her, giving the biggest nod I could manage, which was barely a shift of my chin.

But it was a nod.

"Not even a little bit," Ellie said to Nick. "My feet need a break from her stepping on my toes." She smirked at me. "I'll hit up the bar and get us drinks for that speech or whatever."

I watched as she strode across the dance floor towards the bar by herself. Coincidentally, a small rush of what seemed to be Marcus's friends and perhaps a few single male cousins who also suddenly needed a drink followed, which I was sure had nothing to do with the low neckline on Ellie's dress.

"Dance?" Nick asked again.

I tore my gaze away from Ellie to see him holding his hand out towards me.

"Yeah, of course," I said, taking his hand.

He placed his other hand on my waist as I rested mine on his shoulder. I felt like I was in junior high all over again and half expected my eighth-grade teacher to appear with a wooden ruler to make sure we'd left, as she put it, room for Jesus when we were boy-girl dancing.

"I like this song," he said.

I listened for a moment. "*Can't Fight This Feeling*?"

Tilting his head towards the DJ, he smirked. "REO Speedwagon. I have no idea where Mom found this guy, but he doesn't seem to have anything from later than 1986."

We both chuckled, but didn't say anything else. As we moved to the music and awkwardness threatened to fall between us, I cleared my throat.

"So," I said nervously.

Then, like a complete fucking dork, I went silent.

Nick laughed and squeezed my hand. "I'm not gonna bite, Isla. How have you been?"

I couldn't bring myself to look at him. "Will it be an insult or something if I say I've been... you know. Not horrible?"

"No. I've been pretty not-horrible too."

That got me to look up into his eyes. I needed to; I needed to know if he meant it, if he really was doing... well, not-horrible might not mean "good," specifically, but it didn't mean bad, and suddenly I realized just how badly I'd wanted to know if Nick was okay.

And he was.

He really was.

"I am really glad to hear that," I said.

"Good." He said it firmly. Decisively. "So we're okay? We can get within ten feet of each other without recreating a scene from *Beverly Hills Cat Fights* like my mother seems to think we will?"

My laughter surprised me. "Yeah. Yeah, of course. I'm cool if you are."

"Absolutely."

But despite agreeing that we were both cool, another awkward silence filled the gap between us. The song wasn't anywhere near over yet, so I cleared my throat and took a breath. "So, uh... what have you been up to?"

"Same old," he replied. "Work's been steady. Not great, but when has it ever been? How are things with you?"

"Good," I said. "I'm good. Aurora Flats is a lot different than Burnaby."

"Aurora Flats? Where's that?"

"Oh." I pressed my lips together. "Um, kind of near Edmonton. About an hour from there."

"So, uh... small town vibes?"

This was awful.

I had so many things I wanted to ask him. So much I wanted to say. But anxious thoughts were mixing with panicked whispers in my brain, voices that screamed and murmured about what I should and shouldn't bring up.

I didn't want to stand here and make small talk.

And, I reminded myself as we moved in a slow circle, I knew Nick well enough to know he probably didn't, either.

"Is it weird for me to ask if you're seeing anyone?" I asked bluntly.

He looked surprised, then shrugged. "Maybe, but I don't mind."

I waited for a beat, then laughed when he didn't say anything. "So are you seeing anyone?"

He grinned. "Yes and no. I've been dating a little. Swiping right and all that. But nothing serious."

"Is that a good or bad thing?"

"Good thing." His fingers flexed against my waist. "Is it weird for me to admit that it's kinda nice to not be serious with anyone?"

"I have no idea, but I don't mind, either."

"Good."

I waited, thinking he was going to ask me the same question, but he didn't say anything. That was fair, I thought. There had to be a limit to the things that Nick felt were not-horrible and not-weird and didn't-mind.

But this time, the silence that settled wasn't awkward.

My eyes wandered as we spun in a slow circle. Past Nick's arm I could see two of the black-dress-clad bridesmaids, who were at the edge of the room with Marcus. My mom was sitting at a table near the windows, laughing with Gam in a way that made me suspect they'd taken an edible before coming to the party. At the bar, a group of people had gathered to watch the man who'd made the mistake of trying to outdrink Ellie.

A laugh almost bubbled out of me as she waved the bartender down and held up two fingers, making the people surrounding her cheer excitedly as who I thought might be one of Marcus's groomsmen slapped his hand on the bar. She turned her head towards him and said something; I couldn't hear the words, of course, but the glimmer in her eye made it clear she'd called his bluff on something.

"How did you meet her?" Nick asked suddenly.

I glanced up. He was looking at the bar, too.

"Ellie?" I asked.

"Yeah."

"Technically we ran into each other at Starbucks, I guess, but we work together."

He nodded. Though the smile didn't exactly fade from his face, something sad bloomed in his eyes as he turned them back to me. "You could've told me, you know."

"What?"

"I mean, I get it," he said. "I understand why you didn't and why you might've been worried or whatever. But I wouldn't have been mad or... I just wish I knew why you'd think I wasn't the type of person who would be supportive of that kind of thing."

I stared at him, doing nothing to hide my confusion. "What kind of thing?"

Nick looked at the bar, then back to me. "You being... you know."

Oh.

Oh, shit.

"Nick, I—"

"It's okay, Isla," he said. "It makes sense."

"No, it doesn't," I said, stopping in place as I looked up at him. "I'm sorry if I'm, I don't know, ruining some kind of closure you got by thinking she and I are... but we're not. She's my best friend."

"Your grandma has spent half the night telling everyone that your 'new friend' likes women."

Fucking Grandma Monroe.

"She's bi," I said. "But I'm not. We're just friends." My chest ached as the words came out. "I'm sorry for how I ended things. But it wasn't because... I told you the truth."

He raised his eyebrows. "Did you?"

"Yes." My voice shook. "Mostly. I mean, I did. I didn't lie."

"Isla—"

"Nick, I'm *sorry.*" I swallowed hard. "I'm sorry for how I left. I'm sorry for what I did to you. You didn't deserve that, even if I thought I was doing the right thing. I wasn't trying to hurt you. But it wasn't because of that."

He stared at me, his face unreadable, before he slowly shook his head. "The truth could be slapping you in the face and screaming in your ears and you'd still ignore it, wouldn't you?"

There was nothing unkind about his tone. If anything, it was sympathetic and far more understanding than I'd ever deserved. But I recoiled all the same.

"What's that supposed to mean?"

"It means okay, fine. Maybe you think you're not... something. But do you know how much you've changed in the last five months?" he asked. "You look happier than I've ever seen you. You look happier than you did the *entire* two years we were together. Fine, maybe that's not *why* you ended things or maybe you don't want to admit it because you think it'll hurt my feelings if you admit you weren't attracted to me."

The words winded me. It wasn't intentional. Nick didn't know I was hearing echoes of him telling Marcus he wanted me to be more like Venus. Nick didn't know I'd been there that day. He didn't know I'd heard him say he felt like furniture, like he was resenting sex with me because he felt like I didn't want him.

"Whatever it was, it doesn't matter right now," he continued. "Because you can't tell me there's nothing between you and her."

"There is nothing between me and her," I said. "I'm not attracted to women."

"Look at her."

"Nick, I—"

"*Look* at her," he repeated, his face hard. "Then say that to me again."

I don't know why I looked, but I did.

Her neck was tilted back as she chugged a beer, and even though her boobs were still on full display, hardly any of the men were staring at them; instead, they were cheering her on as the groomsman tried to chug his beer faster. Unfortunately for him, he was a total amateur. He pulled his mouth away before he'd finished, gasping for breath as foam sprayed over his mouth and chin. Ellie's other hand went up in the air, a cheer erupted from the people around her as she kept chugging, and I felt a strange surge of pride.

Even from a distance, I could tell her eyes were sparkling. Even from a distance, I could feel the excitement rolling off her, the unbridled passion and exhilaration that existed in Ellie's presence.

"You never looked at me the way you look at her," Nick said softly.

She finished her beer, slamming the bottle on the counter with a final dramatic swallow. With a raised eyebrow, she nudged the groomsman who was still mopping spilled beer off his face and shirt, saying something to him that made the people around her roar with laughter.

"I never made you smile the way she makes you smile," he continued.

She turned her head. From across the room, my eyes met my best friend's. She lifted her hand in an excited wave, then grinned that shining, dazzling, slightly crooked grin I'd seen almost every day since I'd moved to Edmonton.

Only this time, it was different.

"So tell me, right now, that you're not completely in love with her, Isla," came Nick's sympathetic voice.

Oh.

Shit.

Oh *shit*.

Chapter Thirty-One
The Guest Bed, Right?

Ellie

Fuck.

I shouldn't have left her with him.

All the excitement of proving to fuckin' Brad that I could drink his ass under the table evaporated as Isla and I made eye contact, a stricken expression on her face as that goddamn ex-boyfriend of hers said… well, *something*. His eyebrows pinched together, a pitying expression on his smug-ass face—ugh, how could I have thought he was *hot* when I first saw him?—as he looked at her.

I'd let her down.

She'd brought me here to prevent this, and what did I do? I'd gone off to drink at the bar because some guy with pretty eyes—less pretty now, because he was clearly a dickhead who was making her cry—seemed like he wasn't as bad as she thought he'd be.

Nick said something to her. It must have been something awful because it tore Isla's eyes away from mine, her lips parted as she stared up at him from beneath the brim of her hat with round eyes. He tilted his head to the side and said something else.

Isla dropped his hand, turning so quickly that her glittery skirt swished around her legs. Nick stepped towards her, but she'd already started speed-walking towards the exit.

Fuck.

"Come on, Ellie," said one of the random guys who'd followed me to the bar. "Let's do a shot."

"No," I said. "I gotta go."

"Aw, come on. Let's—"

"Fuck off." I pushed past him, the collective of people at the bar letting out a surge of low chuckles.

"The fuck's her problem?" someone muttered.

"Think someone's dancing with her girlfriend."

"She's not my girlfriend," I muttered, pushing between the two people who had spoken without taking my eyes off Isla's back.

At least, until she disappeared through the doors far faster than was reasonable.

Like, seriously. Isla was not typically a fast person. Not that she wasn't capable of it; when we went to Aquasize or danced at the Flat Tire or raced up the stairs to her apartment for no particular reason other than it was fun, she was fast. But she was also so damn *careful* about things. I'd teased her more than once about shuffling along the sidewalk with her arms out for balance because she wasn't used to ice and snow in the winter. She'd never race me *down* the stairs at her apartment because it was too likely she'd trip. And while she was reasonably steady in heels, she'd also tugged on my arm and asked me to slow down after we'd gotten out of the Uber earlier, since her short legs couldn't keep up with my long ones.

In hindsight, that might have been because she was dreading walking into this godforsaken room, but still.

Isla was walking *way* faster than she'd usually risk in heels. Fast enough that even Nick, who'd had a head start on me, didn't catch up before she'd left.

Unfortunately, he did catch up before me.

They weren't in the hotel hallway when I left the room. I stopped, looking left, then right, frowning as I tried to figure out where they'd disappeared to. There were bathrooms across the hall, but they were gendered, and I couldn't imagine Nick would follow Isla into the women's bathroom.

Then again, I hadn't imagined Nick would make her look like that after dancing for half a song.

But a quick shove of the door revealed they weren't in there. I bit my lip, my heart racing as it froze in indecision, until I heard a door snapping closed somewhere to my right. I followed it and a moment later, rounded the corner and found the outdoor patio attached to the ballroom.

Winter in Vancouver wasn't anywhere near as cold as in Alberta, but it wasn't patio weather. So even though I assumed the ballroom rental came with access, it was abandoned except for a curvy figure in a shimmering dark blue dress facing the railing and a taller figure in dress pants and a shirt pleading with her.

"—to go," I heard her say as I pushed the door open again. "I can't—"

"Am I right?" he pressed. "Because if I am, Isla—"

"Leave her alone," I snapped.

Both of them turned as I spoke. Nick's face flushed red and he held up his hands defensively.

"Hey," he said. "We were just—"

"What did he say to you?" I demanded, ignoring him.

"Ellie, I'm fine," Isla said. Her voice cracked.

"You don't *look* fine," I said, glaring at Nick. "I wouldn't have left you with him if I knew he was going to be a dick."

"I wasn't a dick," Nick said, returning my glare.

"Says who? Because you sure look like a dick to me."

"I didn't *do*—"

"It isn't what it looks like," Isla interrupted, looking at me almost sheepishly.

"What do you think it looks like?" I asked.

She bit her lip. "I... don't know. But it's not that."

"Are you sure about that?"

The three of us jumped at the sound of an unexpected voice. Even as I turned to see who it was, I took a step towards Isla, like I had to be closer in case someone else was trying to hurt her.

"Because to me, it looks like you're causing a scene," Marcus said, letting the door he'd caught when I pushed my way through it fall closed behind him. "Whether it's because you're mad at my brother or because you can't let your sister have a drama-free wedding—"

"I'm not causing a scene," Isla said, sounding hurt. "I came outside to get *away* from the party."

"And you picked the worst possible time to do it," he said. "I don't know what Venus said to you before all this, but I'm going to say it to you now: get over yourself, Isla."

Isla stared at Marcus, her eyes round. Nick gaped at his brother.

"This is happening," Marcus continued plainly. "Venus and I are together. We're happy. We're getting married. If you can't figure out how to act around him, then you need to stay the hell away from my brother. And if you can't do *that*, you need to leave."

"Marcus, what the fuck?" Nick finally said. "Where is this coming from?"

"I'm protecting my future wife," Marcus replied, shooting him an annoyed look. "That's what I'm signing up for. She's too nice to tell Isla how she really feels, so I'm doing it for her."

Isla stared at him in confusion. "No she's not."

"Excuse me? Are you saying my wife isn't *nice*?" Marcus asked.

"I've known Venus her whole life," Isla said. "She's never been too nice to do anything."

"Maybe you don't know her as well as you think you do," Marcus said. "It doesn't matter. I'm still doing what Venus can't to make sure *you* don't."

"Man, you need to back off," Nick said. "This isn't—"

"What's your problem?" Marcus snapped at his brother. "You've been pissed at her the whole time, but now that she's trying to ruin the most important day of her sister's life, you're over it?"

"Since when is an engagement party the most important day of someone's life?" I asked, frowning.

"Since it's not an engagement party." Isla's voice was soft with realization.

"What?" Nick asked, looking as confused as I felt.

Marcus finally fell silent, staring at Isla. His face was vulnerable; hers was unreadable.

"That's why you didn't want me here," Isla said. "You didn't know if I'd be upset and you didn't want to risk it. And maybe that's why she was so mad when you said I shouldn't come. That's why she's stressed, isn't it?"

"She's not stressed," Marcus said, his voice gruff.

"I *do* know my sister," Isla said. "She's not happy. That's why she cried when I said I wouldn't come so there was no tension or whatever, isn't it? Because this is the wedding."

"What do you mean, *this* is the wedding?" Nick repeated.

"You didn't want me at my sister's wedding," Isla said. "I'm right, aren't I?"

There was a long, tense beat of silence. Nick looked up at his brother, shocked. Defiance was etched on Isla's face, even though the corners of her lips tugged down. Marcus's throat flexed.

"Yes," he finally said. "Venus and I are getting married tonight."

Isla's defiance turned to hurt. Nick's shock turned to... well, even more shock, I guess. And my heart was racing in my chest, thumping like it was trying to escape so it could drag me closer to Isla and stand in front of her protectively. No one said a word.

"Like hell we are."

The voice that broke through the night was haughty and crisp. The four of us turned at once to see Venus standing in the door to the patio, her arms crossed over her chest and the long, gauzy fabric of her skirt fluttering in the breeze.

Because of course she was. Of *course* she was standing there, listening to her fiancé admit he'd tried to keep her sister from attending their wedding. Of course Isla was right and now she was going to feel awful because her sister was about to call off the wedding minutes before it was going to happen. I hadn't dedicated my life to watching every dramatic reality TV show in existence to *not* see this coming.

"Venus—" Marcus started.

"Is this why you were mad I wore pink?" she asked, her voice flat. "You decided we were just gonna get it over with and do it tonight?"

"Wait, *Venus* didn't know this was a wedding?" Nick asked, his eyes wide. "She's the bride, dude."

"It's not 'getting it over with,'" Marcus said, ignoring his brother. "I don't want to wait anymore. I don't want—"

"—your mother to lose her shit when she finds out you knocked me up," Venus said.

There was another heavy pause before we all realized that I had not, in fact, seen this coming.

"Venus," Marcus muttered, shaking his head.

"You're pregnant?" Isla asked.

Venus swallowed and nodded.

"Congratulations," I said. "I... think."

She glanced at me, the corners of her mouth flicking up. "Thanks."

"So that's why you're doing this so fast?" Nick asked skeptically.

"It's not that fast," Marcus said. "We've been together—"

"—for three months," Venus interrupted, turning towards Marcus again. She took a step forward, then another one, hugging her arms closer to her. "We've been together since I called up Marcus and said, 'Hey, by the way, remember when we hooked up that one time when I was getting all my sister's stuff out of your brother's apartment? Yeah, I'm pregnant, and I'm planning to keep it, and I don't care if you're involved or not but I thought you should know,' and you somehow talked me into pretending we'd been together way longer so your mom didn't yell at you."

Marcus glanced around, embarrassment in his eyes. "Can we talk about this privately?"

"No." She shook her head emphatically. "No, because when we talk privately, I forget how to be a big girl and stand up for myself. When we talk privately, I let you convince me into getting engaged because now the whole lie about us being together for ages isn't good enough. I don't know if it's the hormones or what, but if we talk privately, I'll end up agreeing to have this surprise wedding, and I don't *want* that, Marcus. I don't want to get married. Not ever."

I felt almost bad for Marcus. Almost. The crestfallen expression on his face made him look smaller, somehow, like he'd slumped in on himself and shrunk right before our eyes.

"Venus, please—" he whispered.

"Do you love me?" she asked.

"Ye—"

"Do you love *me*?" she said. "Not the idea of a wife. Not having sex with me. Not because I'm having a baby. Do you love *me*?"

"I—" He stopped, sighing. "I will."

"Yeah, I don't love you either," she said bluntly. "I'm sorry your mom is gonna be mad at you, but also, you're a grown-ass man. Deal with it." She turned to her sister. "I miss you. I hate you a little for leaving. Which isn't your fault. The only reason I hate you is because I had no one to talk to about the fact that I fucked up, and all because I was angry the day I had to pack your shit up at Nick's and there was a bed right there and I don't have your impulse control."

"The... the guest bed, right?" Nick asked, glancing at his brother.

Marcus stared at the ground.

"The *guest bed*," Nick repeated. "Right, Marcus?"

"We fucked on your bed, Nick," Venus said, sounding almost bored. "Sorry. I washed your sheets after. Also, you should probably keep some condoms in the nightstand or something."

"Jesus Christ," Nick muttered, grimacing.

Venus turned back to her sister. "I need your help."

"With what?" Isla asked.

"Figuring out what to do."

Isla nodded. "Okay. What do we need to figure out?"

"I don't want to get married," Venus said.

"Then don't get married," Isla said.

"And I want to keep my baby."

"Then keep your baby."

"How am I gonna be a single mom?"

Isla shrugged. "I'll help. Just because you're single doesn't mean you'll be alone."

Venus nodded, then burst into tears.

"*What* is going on out here?"

Yet another voice pierced through the cold air. Marcus's face turned an ashy shade of grey as everyone turned to see Nick and Marcus's mother standing there, patches of red on her cheeks and her eyes wide and glazed with anger.

"*What baby are you talking about*?!" she half-screeched.

"I don't want to be here for this," Venus sobbed.

"Then don't be here for this," Isla said.

"Venus, no," Marcus said. "You can't—"

"You convinced her to lie to everyone she knows and tried to force her to marry you to cover your ass," Isla snapped, her voice suddenly vicious. "You can deal with this your damn self. I'm taking her out of here."

"Good plan," Nick said. "I'm also gonna find a reason to not be around for this."

"Thanks," Marcus said flatly. "I appreciate it."

"You knocked my ex-girlfriend's sister up on my bed," Nick said, patting his brother on the shoulder. "And *she* was the one who washed the sheets after."

"Yeah, but—" Marcus sighed, looking resigned. "Fair enough."

And then, as carefully as we could given the simmering human bomb stomping towards her son, the rest of us fled inside.

Chapter Thirty-Two
Needs

Isla

"You're back," Ellie mumbled.

"Yeah," I whispered, which was kind of stupid because she was clearly awake. "Sorry. I didn't want to wake you up."

"I wanted you to." She yawned, stretching out beneath the covers. "Figured the night didn't end with an 'And we all lived happily ever after,' so wanted to make sure you were okay."

I swallowed hard as I crawled in beside her, pulling the blankets up to my chin. "I'm fine."

"No you're not."

"I'm mostly fine."

"Isla." My back stiffened as her body moved in close to mine, but I hid it under the guise of shifting closer to her. Which was also a mistake. "You're lying."

"So are you. That's what you do in a bed."

Her laugh puffed against my neck. "Talk to me, Ella Two. I know you want to."

She was wrong about that. There were a lot of things I wanted from Ellie right now, but disturbingly, talking was not on that list. Talking was the opposite of what I wanted because the idea of saying some of the things in my head made my stomach threaten to crawl up my throat.

But *not* talking would only make it more obvious that I wasn't mostly fine.

"Isla?" Ellie whispered.

"Sorry." I swallowed hard. "Where do I even start?"

She chuckled. I felt that one, too. "Well, is your sister okay?"

"She... will be."

"What'd you two talk about after I left?"

God, what *hadn't* we talked about?

After escaping the patio, we'd had about thirty seconds to help Venus stop crying before the rest of the shit hit the fan. Because of *course* everyone had seen us talking outside through the enormous windows that looked over the patio. Of *course* that's why Mrs. Cooke had scurried outside to do damage control on whatever was going on. Of *course* it was all my fault because in my desperate need for air after Nick had made me realize—

After he'd told—

After Nick had pointed out what he thought was happening, it was like gravity had doubled and my lungs compressed into tight bundles. Like a thousand industrial strength rubber bands had appeared around my chest at once. Like there wasn't enough oxygen in the room or the building or the whole fucking world to take away the sudden light-headedness that descended over me.

So it was my fault that we'd gone out there. It was my fault everyone had seen us. It was my fault that one of Nick and Marcus's nosy aunts had followed Mrs. Cooke and heard her tearing into Marcus for getting Venus pregnant, then returned to the ballroom and hiss that news to everyone.

Including my mom.

She'd been surprisingly ecstatic. At first, anyway. Which only made the devastation we'd expected worse, because she couldn't understand why Venus hadn't told her earlier.

So even though Mom was trying to be supportive and protective and all those things she was supposed to do, she was hurt, and it had been tense. Given that I'd ended up being right about her having an edible before the party, there was a zero-percent chance she and Venus could have a productive conversation about any of this. Not when they were both in big emotional states. So I'd stepped in and said we should all talk about it in the morning. Over brunch. When we'd had some sleep and could have waffles to keep us full and happy while we talked.

They'd agreed, thankfully, but Venus had latched onto my arm and looked up at me with uncharacteristic tears in her eyes again.

"Please don't leave yet," she'd whispered. "I need you."

And I couldn't say no to that. But I also couldn't let Mom go back to her house alone, knowing she was upset and had a tendency to be impulsive when she was high. So I'd asked Ellie if she'd go with her.

She'd agreed, of course, because that's what best friends do. And it worked out well because it meant I didn't have the distraction of her in my mind while I tried to help Venus.

It was also a disaster because it meant there was nothing stopping Nick from continuing the conversation we'd had earlier.

He'd offered to drive Venus and I back to her place. We could've gotten an Uber, of course, but Mrs. Cooke had started lamenting loudly at the bar and he clearly wanted to escape. And that was fine, since I trusted he wouldn't bring anything up while Venus was in the car. And since Venus wanted me to come up to her apartment so we could talk, I told him I'd Uber back to my mom's place later.

So Venus and I had gone upstairs. We'd sat down at her kitchen table. And we'd talked about *everything*.

How upset she was when I left, not because she wanted me to stay, but because she felt alone. How much we both missed our dad. How she felt like our family had fallen apart when he died and she didn't know how to put it back together. How I felt the same, and how much it hurt when we both realized we'd pulled away from the other over it.

I told her how much I admired her. How much I wanted to capture the spontaneity she had. She told me how much she looked up to me, and how much she wished she had the qualities I thought she'd always dismissed as unnecessary.

It was the kind of conversation that opened old scars and created new ones before clumsily stitching them back up. And yes, those stitches were delicate, but they'd been made lovingly.

And of course, she told me how all this happened. How a quick fling to burn off anger and energy with Marcus had snowballed into an almost-wedding, how she'd almost gotten stuck in the cycle of appearances maintained by lies and hypocrisy that Nick and Marcus's parents were part of.

"I don't think he intended to be manipulative," she'd said about Marcus. "I don't think he was trying to be hurtful, either. I think *he* thought he was trying to do the right thing."

"So you're not mad at him?" I'd asked skeptically, not adding the rest of what I wanted to say, which was that his intentions didn't matter when the result was nearly trapping my sister in a toxic situation at her most vulnerable.

She'd snorted. "No, of course I am." Then she'd paused. "Well, actually, no. Not as mad as I should be, anyway." She'd let out a sigh, tapping her hands on the table. "I feel bad for him. It's honestly amazing Nick turned out as normal as he did because that family is *so* messed up. Marcus is under a lot of pressure from his parents, and I think he took the brunt of it so Nick never had to. But I'm not ready to forgive him for, you know"—she'd gestured vaguely—"all of this. Which probably doesn't make any sense at all."

"It does," I'd said. "It's complicated, so your feelings are rightfully complicated, too."

"True." She'd rolled her eyes, but in a loving way. "See, before you left, I never had to do the logical thinking myself. Now I'm a pro at it. So thanks for that."

When we finished talking, I got her into bed, making her laugh as I tucked her in the way I did sometimes when we were kids. Then I'd quietly left, pulling out my phone to order an Uber.

But I hadn't even been connected to a driver when I got to the front of the building and realized Nick was still there, his car parked in the drop off spot right in front of the door so I couldn't even pretend I hadn't seen him.

"Do we have to do this?" I'd asked as I reluctantly got into his car.

"No," he'd said. "I just want to make sure you get back safe to your mom's. We don't have to talk about anything right now. I'd like to eventually, though."

I'd nodded as he pulled out of the parking spot. Neither of us had said a thing the entire drive back to my mom's house. He parked and I'd taken off my seatbelt, opening my mouth to thank him for driving me home.

Instead, I ended up telling him everything.

It sucked. The conversation with Venus was hard, but I couldn't even bring myself to look at Nick when I admitted I'd heard him tell Marcus how boring I was that day that felt so long ago now. He'd been staring at the steering wheel, but I could see the way his head was tilting down, the flush on his cheeks, the way his lips were pressing together as I told him I knew he wished I was more like Venus and that he felt like he was settling for me.

"Isla, I'm so fucking sorry," he'd finally said, his voice choked with sincerity. "I'm sorry you heard that and I'm more sorry that I said it."

"You can't help how you feel," I'd said.

"Maybe not, but that... I didn't mean it." He'd shaken his head. "I mean, I did, but not... not like that. Not the way I said it. That was flippant and exaggerated and there are ways to say all this without hurting someone you care for, you know?" He'd finally looked up, a sorrowful look on his face. "I never wanted to hurt you. I swear. I just..."

"You weren't happy." I forced a smile. "Despite trying to convince me not to leave you right after that."

He'd sighed. "Yeah. I know. I was caught off-guard. I was trying to convince myself you were wrong. But we weren't meant to be together. Not like that, anyway."

I'd frowned. "What do you mean?"

A faint smile had spread on his lips. "Well, we had some pretty good times, right?"

I couldn't deny that. "Yeah, of course."

"We had fun." His smile widened. "Laughed a lot. Had a ton of inside jokes. Enjoyed being around each other. At least, I did."

A smile of my own started. "I did, too."

"So… let's be friends." He'd shrugged, looking hopeful. "I like having you in my life. A relationship doesn't need to be romantic to be worth having, right?"

I couldn't help it. I'd grinned. "Yeah. I'd like that."

"Awesome." Nick had grinned back. "And speaking of romantic things…"

The grin disappeared. "Let's not."

"Isla—"

"No. I—no. You're wrong." I'd shaken my head, like that would prove something.

"You're telling me you don't feel *anything* for her?"

"I feel like she's my best friend."

"You're not attracted to her at all," he'd said. "Not even a little."

"No," I'd said.

"Are you attracted to anyone?"

My mouth had dropped open. "What's that supposed to mean?"

He'd shrugged.

"I was in a relationship *with you*," I'd said. "We've had sex, Nick."

"You don't need to be attracted to someone to have sex with them."

I'd opened my mouth to snap back something about him making it personal. Like he thought I'd never wanted him. Like he was upset because I'd heard him say I made him feel like furniture because I'd never initiated sex or something.

But nothing had come out.

Because I'd heard those words before. Ellie had said something like that when I'd told her about breaking up with Nick. And I'd *felt* those words, not phrased quite like that but close enough, when…

When I'd had sex with Ellie.

When I'd thought to myself it had never been like that before.

But that hadn't meant anything. I'd never had sex with a woman before, so of course I hadn't felt like that before. Like yes, it had felt good, and yes, I'd enjoyed myself, but the things I'd liked the most were the things that weren't all that sexual.

I liked cuddling her.

Holding her.

Kissing her.

Listening to her.

Being pinned under her.

Which was a little sexual, I guess. But those are the parts I liked best with men, too. So it wasn't that I liked it *because* Ellie was a woman. I liked it because it was *Ellie*.

Which...

Which was...

Wait.

I hadn't said much more to Nick. I'd just told him I couldn't think about this anymore and I needed sleep. He'd agreed and asked if we could talk again soon.

I couldn't remember if I'd said yes or no.

I barely remembered going inside. Barely remembered going up the stairs. Barely remembered anything until I slipped into the guest room and heard Ellie's gentle breathing, steady and soft in sleep.

And now I was lying next to her. Now she had her arms around me because I'd woken her up, even though I was praying she'd stay asleep.

Now her body was touching mine and I was thinking about that night at her grandparents' cabin. Now something in the core of my body was starting to ache. Now I was trying to picture Nick in her place, trying to convince myself it was only physical, trying to tell myself I was confused.

And of course, it wasn't working.

"Isla?" Ellie said. "Did you hear me?"

Fuck.

I hadn't answered her yet.

"Yeah," I said, swallowing hard. "I just... we talked about a lot. Me and Venus, I mean. And Nick... Nick and I talked, too. He drove me home."

"Oh, God." She half-chuckled. "How'd that go?"

"Fine."

"Really?"

"Mm-hmm. We agreed we want to be friends."

"What did he say to you?"

"Um... that he wanted to be friends?"

She laughed again. "No, I mean when you were dancing. What'd he say to make you leave? Because I don't care if he's your friend now, I'm still ready to fight him for upsetting you."

"Nothing."

"You're lying again."

"I know. I just don't want to talk about it right now."

"Okay." She tightened her arms like she was hugging me. "I want you to know I'm here for you if you need anything at all, okay?"

I almost laughed. What I needed most right then were some answers, but that was hopeless. All these thoughts about Ellie and sex and attraction were swirling around my head, a bunch of variables that led to nothing concrete. What I really needed was—

My mouth went dry.

"Isla?" she said again, her head raising up with concern.

I had what I needed to find the answers. Maybe not in the most ethical way, but I...

I could find out.

"Um," I said.

Smooth. Really fucking smooth.

"Actually." I tried to stop my voice from shaking. "There is... something."

"Name it, bestie. It's yours."

Fuck.

Fuck.

"This might sound weird. Or... or bad. Actually—"

"Nuh-uh. Don't you dare say never mind," she said. "Tell me what you need."

"Okay." I coughed slightly. "So, you... you know how... I mean, you—" I stopped to take a deep breath and blow it out. "You remember how we had sex that one time?"

I *felt* Ellie react. It was subtle, but it was there. A breath catching. An arm shifting a millimeter. Her hips tilting back.

"Yep, I do remember that," she said, sounding far more casual than I expected.

I grimaced, squeezing my eyes shut like it would make the situation disappear. But the room had already been dark, so it did a whole lot of fucking nothing to help.

"Was there a follow up to that question?" she asked.

I shoved the blankets against my face. "Nope. That was it."

Ellie's body softened, somehow. Like she'd only tensed after I asked that stupid, stupid question so she could melt forward again.

"Isla," she murmured, her voice next to my ear. "Do you need me to make you come?"

Half of me wanted to laugh, convinced she was saying it as a joke. Half of me wanted to disappear into the void, embarrassment overriding everything else.

But every nerve in my body caught fire. Every cell. Every bone.

"It's stupid," I whispered. "We're just friends. And I know we weren't, like, kissing or touching or anything, but I... I don't know why. You don't have to. Actually, we shouldn't. We—"

"Isla."

I grimaced. "What?"

Her lips met my shoulder. "Shh."

"But—"

"Do you want me to make you come?"

My heart fluttered so fast, it made me dizzy.

"Yes," I whispered, so soft I wasn't even sure I'd *thought* it. "But—"

"Then *shhhh*," she said again, and her hand moved to my breast.

She hadn't done that the first time. All we'd done the first time was cuddle and kiss and grind. So yes, she'd felt my breasts pushed against her, but not like that. Not with her hand cupping it through my shirt. Not with my nipple pressing into her palm beneath the thin fabric. Not in a way that sent a shiver of desire through me.

The first time, she'd touched my body with hers, her leg between my thighs, her hips and belly and ribs rubbing mine through the layers of our pyjamas.

This time, her hands moved over my curves.

This time, her chest pressed to my back.

This time, she lifted the hem of my shirt, pulling it over my belly and breasts until it was tucked under my arms. This time, her palm skimmed along bare skin, leaving scorching trails of electricity in their wake, tickling along my sides and ribcage until she held a breast in each hand, my nipples pinched between her thumb and forefinger as I squirmed reflexively.

The first time, she'd kissed me.

This time, she kissed me more.

Not on my lips. She couldn't reach them from behind me, and she didn't seem particularly inclined to move. But I'd pulled my hair up in its typical bun for sleeping and her mouth quickly discovered the spot between my neck and shoulder was an excellent place to kiss if she wanted me to gasp for breath.

It hovered there as she explored me, one hand moving to my side and my hip while the pad of her thumb ran over my nipple. I shivered, my head tilting back of its own accord.

"Need something?" she asked, the words muffled by my skin.

"Ellie, please," I breathed.

"You need Ellie?" she teased, snickering as I let out an annoyed huff. "Don't worry, I've got that right here for you."

"Right whe—*oh*." The sound came out from deep in my throat, a low groan as she slipped her hand into my pyjama shorts.

The first time, she'd touched me there. But only through our clothes, and only with her leg.

This time, I think she thought I would be wearing panties beneath my shorts. But I wasn't, so I felt the heat of her palm against the heat of my skin as she cupped my mound.

"Holy hell, Ella Two," she mumbled, her fingers dipping deeper between my thighs. "Crazy family drama really gets you going, hey?"

"Shut up," I muttered. "Please just... just help me."

A wordless mumble slipped out of her lips, something that said she'd liked what I'd said. As her finger worked between my folds and brushed over my clit, I closed my eyes, took a deep breath, and tried to picture someone else.

I tried to picture Nick. I tried to picture the guy from the rugby team all my friends had a crush on in university. I tried to picture actors and models and that one guy who played hockey for the Edmonton Snowhawks that Ellie always said she wanted to peg, for some reason.

All I could see behind my eyelids was Ellie.

I couldn't even force myself to think of someone else touching me. And when I finally gave up and let myself think of her, heat rushed over me so intensely that I couldn't stop myself from writhing in her arms.

And I knew.

Long before it hit, I knew my orgasm would be big, and explosive, and just what I fucking *needed* even though I wasn't supposed to need any of this at all.

But I did.

I needed her fingers.

I needed her lips on my neck.

I needed her body pressed up to mine.

Her breath in my ear.

Her smile.

Her laughter.

Her eyes, sparkling and joyful and mischievous all at once, sparking electricity as they caught mine across a crowded room filled with people who didn't matter.

Because they weren't her.

I needed *her*.

Everything had crashed around me when I looked at Ellie across the room; now her hand was between my legs and she telling me to fucking come, come for *her*, and I was crashing again. I was falling again. I was coming, my back arching and my eyes closed and a hand over my mouth because I didn't trust myself not to moan and the last thing I needed was my mother to hear us from her room.

When I could finally breathe enough to open my eyes again, Ellie's fingers were still stroking my clit. I swallowed hard as she lazily finished playing with me before taking her hand back.

"What are you doing?" she asked as I started to turn over.

"Uh... reciprocating?" I said, though it came out uncertain. "If you want... I mean, it's only fair."

She laughed softly. "Honestly, I don't need it."

Which was...

Disappointing?

"I might've taken care of myself while I was waiting for you to get back," she admitted, then giggled. "A couple times, actually."

I pictured her. I couldn't help it.

Because Nick was right.

Chapter Thirty-Three

Platonic Overcompensation

Ellie

"AND THEN THE SECURITY agent goes, 'Well not *only* do all the liquids have to fit into a one-liter bag, they *do* need to be contained in their own container,'" I said. "And then points out I have waffle batter inside my jacket."

"*How* did it get in your jacket?" Jayce asked, bewildered.

I shrugged, snagging a fry off Isla's plate. "One of life's great mysteries. So yeah, then we got on the plane and came home. And the ginger vitamin thing Isla's mom gave me worked great. I didn't puke at all on the flight back."

"Hmm. And that's it?" they asked, glancing at Isla.

"What do you mean, that's *it*?" I replied. "Isla just told you about her sister's secret pregnancy and the crazy mother-in-law she narrowly avoided getting for herself, and you're asking if there's more?"

"I guess you could tell them about meeting my grandparents," Isla said. "Although Grandma Monroe didn't even try accidentally leaving Gam and Pops on a deserted highway somewhere this time."

Her voice didn't shine as much as it usually did, but that was unfortunately nothing new. Isla hadn't quite sounded like herself since we'd gotten back from Burnaby.

Which Jayce knew, because they'd commented on it *multiple* times.

"You can't blame me for thinking there may be something else," they said nonchalantly. "You seem out of sorts compared to your usual bubbly self."

"Nope," Isla said. "I'm fine. Nothing else happened while we were gone."

"Too bad," they said. "Here I had high hopes for another hysterical misadventure from your soulmate mission. Which of you lost the bet, then?"

"Neither of us," I said. "We have until midnight tomorrow."

"Ah, of course. That's still plenty of time to find some romantic schmuck who'll put up with you for the rest of your life."

I rolled my eyes. "Aww, you're just saying that so you don't have to pity-marry me when we're forty."

"That's not the only reason. I *do* want both of you to find the happy, loving relationships you want."

It was quiet, but that got Isla to laugh. "I knew there was a big softie in there somewhere."

Jayce gave her a tight, knowing smile. "So there were really no potential soulmates to meet cute while you were away?"

"I mean, there were a couple of sexy options at the engagement party," I said.

Isla's eyes shot up, round with surprise. "There were?"

I smirked. "Yeah. You and me."

I'd hoped that would get another laugh from her, but Isla just blinked a couple of times before looking down at the table. "I wasn't aware we were options."

"Oh, I was—"

"Now *there's* an idea," Jayce said, their voice a low hum. "Why don't the two of you get together? You've already gotten your first kiss out of the way."

That fucking traitor.

I glared at them, but despite doing my best to prove that looks could kill, Jayce sat across from us in the booth with an innocent and yet somehow smug expression on their face.

They had to be talking about the New Year's Eve kiss, obviously. I hadn't told them about the ones before that, and Isla and I hadn't kissed at all since then.

Not really.

I mean, we'd done other things.

I'd made her come undone in my arms. I'd teased her nipples and felt her body shudder. I'd felt guilt wash over me as I surreptitiously slipped a finger in my mouth so I could fucking *taste* her after making her come all over my hand.

But we hadn't kissed.

And I'd told myself it was fine. It was *fine*. It didn't matter what I did or didn't feel for Isla, it was fine because she needed my help. She needed it badly enough that she'd asked for it and I knew that had been hard for her. She needed it because someone in her life had spun a story that snowballed right up until it crashed down, shattering into a cloud around her.

I wanted to help her. And I figured as long as I made it about *her*, it would be okay. It didn't matter if I was so attracted to Isla it was starting to hurt; if I didn't let her touch me, kiss me, reciprocate the way she'd immediately thought she should, we wouldn't make it weird.

Unfortunately, despite the soundness of my logic, it didn't change the fact that things had been weird between me and Isla ever since.

Which Jayce, asshole that they were, had clocked as soon as Isla and I got to the Flat Tire for our lunch break, promising us food in exchange for helping them with the finishing touches for the Leave It To Fate Valentine's Day party they were hosting the next day. And instead of being a decent fucking human, they were pushing, and pushing, and now Isla's cheeks were turning pink and she wasn't looking at them. She wasn't looking at me either. She was clearly uncomfortable with the conversation.

But I couldn't snap at Jayce and tell them to knock it off. It would look like it was getting to me, and if they knew it was getting to me, they'd know something was up, and I couldn't let that happen. But I had to do something.

So I laughed.

I laughed *loudly*.

"God, can you *imagine*?" I asked, then elbowed Isla. "We could never be together."

Jayce's eyes flicked to Isla and then back to me. The semi-contemptuous amusement faded off their face.

"It'd be a disaster," I continued, ignoring them. "We're great as friends, but that's it. Like, both of us might be absolute goddesses, but I'm definitely not Isla's type. And she's not mine, either."

"How do you know what Isla's type is?" Jayce asked.

"Uh, I met her ex-boyfriend, remember?" I rolled my eyes. "Funnily enough, you two have almost the exact same type. Seriously, Jayce, you would've *melted* over Nick. He's gorgeous. Like, model-level gorgeous."

"Sounds like Isla has good taste," they said. "Aren't you of the opinion that you're the type of person that people with good taste are into?"

"When they swing the same way, which we *don't*," I said. "You can't push someone to change their sexuality, Jayce. That's shitty of you."

"I'm not," they said evenly. "I simply think—"

"And even if Isla and I swung the same way, we'd drive each other crazy." I laughed. "Isla would *hate* putting up with me impulsively doing shit all the time and I would probably lose my mind staying at home reading five nights a week."

"Ellie," Jayce said, their voice soft with warning.

"What? No offense. Isla knows what—"

And then I finally looked at her.

She wasn't looking at me. She wasn't looking at Jayce. She was staring down at the table, her lips pressed together into the thinnest line I'd ever seen.

Fuck.

"—what I mean," I finished, though there was no steam left in it. "Right?"

"Of course." She let out a laugh that sounded nothing like hers. "Who would want to be with someone that boring?"

Oh, fuck.

I'd said—and that was what Nick—

Fuck.

"That's not what I—" I started.

"And just because we've kissed a few times doesn't mean we'd be good together, like, romantically. Kissing doesn't have to be romantic," she said.

Shit.

"Wait, a few times?" Jayce repeated, flicking their eyebrows up. "How many times have you two kissed?"

"Oh, I have no idea," Isla said. "I wasn't counting. But we've fooled around twice."

I'd never seen Jayce's eyes so wide. Technically, I still hadn't, since I was doing everything I could not to look at them and cringe under the intensity of their stare.

"Fooled around?" they finally said. "You two have had sex?"

Isla looked at them, then turned to me. "Was... was it supposed to be a secret?"

"No," I said quickly. "Of course not. Well... I mean, *yes*, but only because I didn't know if you'd want people to know. Like, I didn't want anyone to be embarrassed or something."

Which was true. It wasn't the whole truth, but it wasn't a lie.

"Right," Isla said. "Of course. I thought you told Jayce everything, but I guess... I mean, I guess I can see why you'd be embarrassed."

"Not me!" I said. "Isla, I meant *you*. Because you haven't... we never talked about it and I—"

"It's fine," she said.

"This is coming out wrong," I said. "I'm sorry."

"I said it's fine, Ellie," she repeated. "You didn't want people to know we slept together. It's *fine*."

"Oh, it's the *opposite* of fine. It's a big fucking problem, actually."

It was a shocking thing to say, which is why I turned to Jayce with shock on my face. But what was more shocking was the fact that I thought the hoarse, raspy voice that had said those words belonged to Jayce when it sounded nothing like them, and was also coming from the booth behind ours instead of from across the table.

At least, until a moment later, when our boss slid out of that booth and stood beside me.

"Paulette?" Isla said. "What are you doing here?"

"Having lunch," Paulette said, crossing her arms. "And apparently learning that two of my employees who were *very* clearly told that we have a zero-tolerance fraternization policy have fraternized. Twice, apparently. Which means one of you is out for good."

Isla's cheeks were still red, but the rest of her face had whitened.

"It's my fault," I said immediately. "I'm responsible for all this."

Isla looked at me like she'd been betrayed.

But what else was I going to do? It was the truth. I'd kissed Isla first. I'd told Isla I was turned on and couldn't sleep. I'd given in and slept with her. I'd done it again even though I knew it was a terrible idea.

It was my fault.

And honestly, wasn't it about time? After all the times Paulette had fired me only to not mean it, maybe this was fate's way of kicking my ass in gear and making me leave Air-U-Need. Maybe this was the push I needed to finally make something of myself. Isla had said she'd help me, and Jayce would too, and—

"I don't give a shit whose fault it is," Paulette said. "Isla, you're fired."

Every molecule of air was sucked out of the bar.

"No she isn't," I said.

"You have no say in this," Paulette replied.

"You can't fire her." Without thinking, I stood up. Paulette stumbled back a step. "I have seniority over her. Which means I should be the one fired."

"You're not her superior," Paulette said. "You're both the heads of your respective teams. And as much as I dislike you, Ellie, I can replace a customer service agent in a day. You, unfortunately, cannot be replaced so easily." She tilted her head, looking past me at Isla. "You're done, effectively immediately. Your girlfriend can grab your things this afternoon."

"She's not my girlfriend!" I half-shouted. "We're not together. We're never going to get together because neither of us want that."

"Mouth off to me one more time and you're fired, too," Paulette said.

"Good!" I shot back. "If you can fire me for that, you can fire me instead of Isla."

Paulette clearly hadn't thought of that. But it didn't matter. She scoffed and rolled her eyes.

"I'll see you at the office," she said to me. "And you—" She looked at Isla, shaking her head in disappointment. "I really thought you had what it takes to go all the way in the world of discount air conditioning and HVAC."

And then she left.

Chapter Thirty-Four
More Than A Heartbeat

Isla

"I'LL BE FINE," I said for what felt like the eightieth time.

"We'll fight it," Ellie said, patches of red anger on her cheeks. "We'll talk to the labour board. It's discrimination. Or... or something. She can't—right, Jayce? You have a business. She can't do that."

"She can," Jayce said reluctantly. "I'm sorry."

"It's fine," I said. "I'll figure something out."

Ellie bit her lip. "I mean, you'll have lots of time to help me start a photography business, right?"

I knew she was joking. Trying to make me feel better. I *knew* that. But that was about the last thing I wanted to do right then. I pushed myself out of the booth, suddenly completely uninterested in the food in front of me. "I think I'm gonna go. I'll pay for my lunch, Jayce. Since I didn't do much to help you for the party tomorrow."

"Like hell you will," they said. "It's on the house. Don't worry about the party."

"Okay. Thanks."

"I'll walk you back to your car," Ellie said.

I shook my head. "You need to stay and help Jayce."

"Like hell she does," Jayce said.

"And you have to go back to work."

"I need to be there for my bestie," Ellie said. "Come on, I'll—"

"Please don't."

I did everything I could to keep my voice from shaking, which meant the words came out flat and blunt and impersonal. Ellie looked stunned and I swallowed hard.

"I'd like some time alone," I said. "And I... I'd like my stuff back from work. There's a book on my desk. And the sweater on my chair. And that mug, the blue one? I brought that one from home."

She hesitated, then nodded. "If that's what you want."

"It is," I said, despite it being the exact opposite of what I wanted.

But I couldn't tell her that.

Not when I'd found out that Ellie didn't want me the way I wanted her.

It had been weighing on me since the day after my sister's engagement party. Since I'd realized I wasn't only in love with my best friend, but that I wasn't straight at all.

The latter had been the easier thing to accept. There was no self-loathing or worry that people in my life wouldn't love me after I came out. I knew that made me lucky. More than anything, it was embarrassing realizing how absolutely certain I'd been that I was straight when there was so much evidence against it. Embarrassing, and leading me to question every bit of my life to this point.

Like, *how* had I missed that? This huge part of me, this thing that everyone in the world seemed to define as part of what defined a person, was something I didn't recognize it at all. This thing that I'd thought was a universal experience, a truth that linked me to other people like me, wasn't true.

Existentially, it was a disaster. I didn't like not knowing things. I didn't like knowing there wasn't a word for me, at least not that I'd discovered. That despite reading hundreds of books over the course of my lifetime, I'd never properly defined what sexuality and attraction and romance were. What they meant, specifically to me. Because none of the labels seemed to fit. I didn't feel bisexual. Or pansexual. Or lesbian or... or anything. Nothing felt *right*.

But I'd been able to accept it. Labels would come with time. After I had time to think and consider and teach myself. Realizing I was in love with Ellie, though...

That was terrifying.

I'd never felt like this before. And paired with all those other questions, all those uncertainties because I'd spent twenty-four years believing one thing about myself only to find out it wasn't true, I was shaken.

What else didn't I know?

When I looked in the mirror, who was that girl?

What about her was real?

And would Ellie love that girl back?

Because that was the real fear. This was my best friend, and the first woman I'd been with, and someone I couldn't picture my life without.

What if I told her and it changed everything?

What if those changes were bad?

And what was I going to do about work? Because no, I *hadn't* forgotten about Paulette's fraternization policy. It was a little hard to forget something when you found out the person you'd been hired to replace was fired for that exact reason. So something would have to change; I'd have to leave, or she would, or neither of us would, and I'd spend every day in an adjacent cubicle, so close and so far from what I wanted.

And what if she didn't want me?

That had kept me up the most. That had been the thing lingering in my head and stomach and heart, tying my tongue every time I tried to figure out how to handle this.

What if Ellie didn't want me back?

I hadn't thought I could handle the answer. But lucky me, it was the first answer I'd found.

She didn't want me.

I wasn't her type.

She never had and never would want me the way I wanted her.

And lucky me, just as I found out that it would totally not be worth breaking the fraternization policy over this, I got caught breaking the fraternization policy.

"I can bring you in for some shifts here, if you want," Jayce said as I pulled my puffy winter coat on. The usual flat cynicism in their voice was gone. "And I can talk to Anthony. He works at—well, everywhere." They half-laughed. "I'm sure at least one of his jobs is looking for someone. He'll be here for the party tomorrow night, if you want to chat with him yourself."

"I, um... I'm gonna sit this one out," I said. "I don't think fate's really on my side right now."

Ellie looked crestfallen. "Seriously? But..."

"But what?" I asked.

"Our bet," she said softly. "There's still time to meet your soulmate."

My throat closed for a moment, a stab of pain stealing my breath.

"It's just a stupid bet, Ellie," I finally said. "It's not real."

"You're just upset—" she started.

"I'm *not*." The sharpness of my words shocked me almost as much as they seemed to shock Ellie and Jayce, but that didn't stop the rest of them from slicing past my lips. "I'm not 'just upset,' Ellie. I got to sit here and listen to you talk about how undesirable and unlovable and *boring* I am, realize how embarrassed you are about what we did, and then get fired because apparently I've caught a case of zero impulse control from you." My voice cracked. "If that's how someone who—how you—how... If that's what my best friend thinks of me, why would fate even bother?"

She stared at me, her lips parted with a silent answer.

It wouldn't, she didn't say. Fate wouldn't bother.

Because if fate had been at *all* involved in this whole shit show, when Jayce made the totally-out-of-left-field comment that maybe Ellie and I should get together, it would've made Ellie say something like, "Oh, I would in a heartbeat, but unfortunately Isla is straight."

Then I would've looked up from my plate, my heart racing as I turned to look into those sparkling eyes beside me. And she would think I was going to laugh along with her, but I wouldn't.

"Well, actually," I might've said. "I don't think I am."

And she'd freeze. She'd stare at me. Her face would be unreadable and I'd be terrified, but then her eyes would flick down to my lips before returning to mine.

Then, if I was really brave—which I was, since the whole thing was a fabricated fantasy that would never happen—I'd say something smooth, like, "It's been more than a heartbeat, Ellie."

And then she'd kiss me. Because in my daydreams, Ellie wanted me.

In reality, she was standing in front of me, her eyes full of shame and her cheeks red.

In reality, Ellie and I had made a stupid bet to find our soulmates, and it proved that either fate wasn't real, or it was cruel.

In reality, fate had put Ellie in my life, and then made it clear I couldn't have her.

Chapter Thirty-Five
So You Fucked Your Best Friend

Ellie

"Have you heard from her yet?" Jayce asked, their head materializing out of nowhere.

I jumped, my phone clattering to the floor, then let out a yelp as my head hit the table above me. "Ouch!"

"Careful. You don't have enough brain cells left to sacrifice them like that," they said.

"Ha, ha." I grabbed my phone, rubbing the top of my head. "What do you want?"

"An answer to the question I asked," they said. "But I'll settle for you telling me what, exactly, you're doing hiding under one of my booth tables."

"You already answered that," I muttered.

They frowned. "Huh?"

"I'm hiding, dumbass."

"From what?"

"No one, now."

They smirked. "So since I've found you, does that mean you'll come out and enjoy the party?"

"No," I said.

They let out a heavy sigh. "Fine." With a groan, they crouched before getting to their knees.

"What are you doing?!"

"Crawling around the dirty floor of the worst bar in town and ignoring my paying patrons as they file in so I can join you." They pushed their way under the table. "Move. I don't have enough room."

"That should be a hint."

"Oh God, is this a fried pickle?" They made a retching sound. "I took those off the menu six months ago. Maybe this really *is* the worst bar in town."

Rolling my eyes as they pulled themselves forward in a way that managed to be both dainty and clumsy, I scooted back, hunching so I didn't hit my head on the table again. Once Jayce had situated themself beside me, they wiped their hands on the thigh of their bright red pants and shuddered a final time before taking a deep breath.

"So you fucked your best friend," they said. "Despite knowing she was into men, despite insisting you weren't going to fall for her, despite knowing it was against the policy of the company you both worked for, you decided to have sex with her. Twice. And hide it from your other best friend—"

"You're not my best friend," I muttered. "You're a menace."

"—hide it from your favourite menace before implying you find her unlovable and boring in an attempt to overcompensate for your insistence that things are purely platonic."

"That's not what I meant," I said.

"What's that saying about intentions?" they asked lightly. "An intention in the hand is worth two other fish in the sea?"

"Did you crawl on a sticky floor and discover a mummified fried pickle just to tell me I'm not feeling bad enough about this?"

"No," they said. "I did it because people are starting to arrive for Leave It To Fate Night and this booth is supposed to be table twenty-one. And even if that was your chosen table—which it's not—you don't have enough brain cells to sacrifice them by getting kicked in the head by the people sitting here."

"I don't want a table," I muttered. "I'm only here because you said I had to come."

"For good reason." They sighed. "Elle, Isla's the forgiving type."

My nose stung as I stared at my phone. "She hasn't texted me back, Jayce."

"You know as well as I do that this is your rejection sensitivity stuff flaring up—"

"That's maybe forty percent of it," I interrupted. "The rest is valid guilt for being a total fuck up."

"You being a fuck up is maybe fifteen percent," they said calmly. "And you *have* heard from her since yesterday."

I gritted my teeth. They weren't wrong, technically. I'd stopped by her apartment with her stuff after work the previous day—well, I'd stopped by mid-afternoon, when I'd finished gathering her things and stormed out of the office without saying anything. I figured there was no point in staying the whole day; clearly Paulette wasn't serious about firing me and there was a zero-percent chance I'd get anything done while I was freaking out about Isla.

But when I got to her building, she didn't answer.

I tried calling. I rang the buzzer. I *emailed* her.

Nothing.

I'd ended up buzzing Keith's apartment, since he lived above her. Frustratingly, he refused to buzz me with the aggravatingly reasonable, entirely justified, and shockingly protective explanation that *he* didn't know if Isla was purposely avoiding me and didn't want to put her in an uncomfortable or dangerous situation. But he agreed to come downstairs and take the bag of Isla's things for me so she could grab them from him when she was ready.

"Can you please ask her to let me know if she's okay?" I'd asked when he took the bag from me.

"Yeah, of course," he'd said. "And if she's dead or something, I'll let you know too."

"Thanks," I'd said. "Hadn't considered that possibility, but now I'm not going to stop freaking out about it until I hear from her."

"You're welcome," he'd replied. "Don't worry, I'm pretty sure she's fine. What are the chances of the last two occupants of that apartment *both* dying in it?"

"Wait, what?!" I'd asked, but Keith had already shut the front door and started towards the stairs.

Thankfully, shortly after I got home, Isla had messaged to say that Keith had pounded on her door until she'd answered and thanked me for bringing her stuff back. I'd immediately texted her back apologizing again.

The checkmarks appeared showing she'd read it, but she didn't reply.

"That doesn't count," I said to Jayce. "She was letting me know she wasn't dead. She's still mad at me, and I still fucked everything up and still lost another friend because I can't control my stupid feelings for people and now I'm never going to see her again."

"Ellie, her message literally said she needed some space and she'd talk to you another time," they said. "That doesn't sound like someone you're never going to see again."

"I hurt her so bad she stopped believing in fate," I said.

"She was upset. She said things she probably didn't mean," they replied. "You know as well as I do the bet and the meet cute thing and the soulmates-fate-whatever was just for fun. And you also know—or at least, you should know—that it's going to take a hell of a lot more than this to ruin a friendship between you two."

"Why would I know that?" I asked.

"Common sense," they said. "Do you really think your relationship with Isla isn't strong enough to overcome a miscommunication trope? It's the most nonsensical of the romance tropes, Ellie. People misspeak all the time. If every relationship ended when someone said one thing and another person interpreted it another way, we'd all die alone."

"Instead, I'll be the only one who dies alone. I'm alone in my aloneness."

"Stop with the dramatics.

"Why can't you let me wallow in peace?" I grumbled.

"Again, because I need this table for the event," Jayce said. "And I need you to go to your chosen table. If you don't, it means there's an odd number of Fate tickets left and I promised a full refund to anyone who didn't get matched."

"And it's all about you, of course."

"Main character energy, remember?" They nudged me with their elbow. "Look, Isla *said* she'd talk to you again. You may only have been friends for a few months, but there's no way in hell you two are going to be victims of the weakest of the tropes. She stood up for you to your grandmother. She pretended to be your girlfriend. When she was faced with family drama, you were the person she turned to for help."

"It's not the weakest of the tropes," I said.

"If that's the only thing you have to say right now, it means you know I'm right."

I sighed, staring at my blank phone screen. I wouldn't say they were right, but that was only because I didn't want to admit it.

Because admitting it meant I had to face a much bigger, much more painful question.

"Ellie, it's gonna take a hell of a lot more than this for you to ruin your friendship with Isla," Jayce continued. "And besides, it would be an outright crime for you to stay hidden all night in that dress. Seriously, no wonder Isla couldn't keep her hands off you after her sister's party. I don't even swing your way, and I can appreciate how phenomenal you look in it. So even if you don't find a soulmate tonight, I imagine you'd still find someone who'd bend you over and—"

"What if I wanted it to be more than a friendship?" I whispered.

"Do you think that's what Isla wants?"

I swallowed hard, then shook my head.

"Then you have to ask yourself if you'd be satisfied with that," Jayce said. "Could you be her friend, knowing you'd have to watch her find someone else and fall in love? Could you move on and do the same?"

"But what if I'm wrong?" I swallowed hard. "What if she does?"

"Are you willing to ask her how she feels?"

My nose stung. A moment later, the slice of the world I could see from beneath my table blurred.

It was the wrong question.

It didn't matter if I was willing or not. There was nothing, not a single inkling or hint or realistic *hope* that Isla would answer in a way that didn't hurt. Rejection sensitivity or not, Isla was straight. And I knew, all too well, how that story would go. I knew what her answer would be. I knew it had been years since Nico did what he did, but I knew history always repeated itself.

Which meant the question wasn't "Was I willing to ask Isla how she feels?"

It was "Was I willing to *risk* her to find out?"

And there was only one answer to that.

Blinking away the tears blurring my eyes, I took a deep breath, then let it out slowly.

"What table am I supposed to meet my date at?" I asked.

Jayce patted my thigh. "Not this one."

Chapter Thirty-Six
Omen

Isla

FEBRUARY IN ALBERTA WAS fucking cold.

For the rest of the year, people always joked that if you didn't like the weather in Alberta, you just had to wait five minutes.

But in February, if you didn't like the weather, you toughed it out or you left, and either way you questioned why anyone even lived here in the first place.

Or, more importantly, you questioned why you decided it would be a good idea to try cheering yourself up with a trip to the bookstore when you already had a bunch of books at home. And access to an e-reader, so you could get digital copies of almost every book in existence. And going to the bookstore meant you'd have to change out of your flannel pyjamas and put on real pants. And socks. And a godforsaken bra. And you'd have to find your hat, which you'd apparently left at the job you'd just gotten fired from, so now it smelled like weed because it was the in the tote bag of stuff your best friend had left at Keith's because you couldn't handle talking to her right now even though that made you feel like absolute *garbage* because you weren't mad at her, not really, since it wasn't *her* fault she didn't love you the way you wanted her to.

And then also, your car wouldn't start.

Like, at all.

I stared at the dashboard stupidly, my key still twisted in the ignition as literally nothing happened. The dashboard lights didn't turn on. The engine didn't start chugging. There was a single click, and then nothing.

I tried again, and again: nothing.

A third attempt resulted in... nothing.

Fourth, nothing.

Fifth, paired with stepping on the gas like that might do something, led to nothing.

Maybe it was a sign.

Didn't I keep asking for those? Signs from something saying I was on the right path. A sign that said I was in the right place. That I was doing the right thing. That it was the right time, and soon all the things I was looking for would find me.

But maybe I was looking for the wrong signs.

Maybe the signs were telling me I was on the wrong path. I mean, it made sense. Signs didn't always point out good things. They weren't always neon, flashing lights that told you exactly where you wanted to be. Signs didn't stay "No Road Construction Ahead" or "U-Turns Allowed Here" or "Here's a nice picture of a deer because we think it'll brighten your day."

Maybe getting fired was a sign I shouldn't have fallen in love with my best friend.

And maybe finding out she would never, ever see me like that was a sign I shouldn't be here at all.

What was keeping me here, really? I'd left Burnaby because Nick thought I was boring, but I was boring here, too. I'd come to Aurora Flats because I found an apartment I could afford. I'd stayed because I found a job. And friends. I'd found Ellie.

But I'd lost the job. I was on the brink of losing Ellie. I didn't want all my neighbours to lose their homes if the unluckiness of me being here eventually caused the apartment to burn down, too.

I called a towing company after trying to start my car a sixth time.

"You're in luck," the operator said. "Cold snaps like these are always crazy busy, but we can get someone out to you right away."

"Oh, awesome," I said. "About how long do you think they'll take?"

I heard faint typing sounds in the background. "Based on the number of stops... he'll be there in about four hours."

"Four... hours," I repeated. "That's right away?"

"Last time we had a cold snap, towing wait times were about thirty-two hours," the operator said. "We stop taking new requests once we hit forty-eight, though."

So there went my bookstore trip.

Which was fine. I had other things I could do. Like look for another job. And research what rent was like back home for a one-bedroom apartment. And wonder if I could stand living with my mom for a while I got back on my feet because I couldn't afford a one-bedroom on my own unless I found an actual job doing stuff with my actual degree, which looked as unlikely as it did every other time I'd job hunted.

And it meant I could put my pyjamas back on, so you know. Silver linings.

Six hours later, I finally got a call from the tow truck driver, who ended up being a grumpy-looking heavy-set man in his thirties.

"You're supposed to be waiting with the car," he grumbled when I came out of the building, still in my pyjamas because I hadn't bothered changing that time.

"I was inside," I said. "And it's been six hours."

"Not my problem." He jerked his head towards the parking lot. "All these other cars here and no one else could boost you?"

"What do you mean, boost?" I asked.

"Your car's frozen. It needs a boost to start up."

"I didn't know that," I said.

He sighed heavily. "God, you'd think they'd teach shit like this in driving school. Yeah, you just need jumper cables and another car. Easy peasy. Coulda been out of here hours ago. Or you coulda waited until it warmed up. It's the last day of the cold snap. Actually, it's warmer now than it was this morning." He motioned at my car. "Go, try starting it. I bet you it starts. Then you can call my wife and explain why I had to work late on goddamn Valentine's Day before she loses her shit on me again."

Glaring at him, I opened the car door and got in the driver's seat. Holding his gaze, I put my foot on the brake and turned the key in the ignition.

The car didn't start.

The tow driver rolled his eyes. "Whatever. Pop the hood, would you? If this goes fast enough, I can make it back before my wife—*what the FUCK!?!*"

He'd barely lifted my hood when he dropped it, leaping backwards from my vehicle like it was about to bite him. I scampered out of the driver's seat, panicked.

"What's wrong?!" I asked.

The driver's eyes were wide and his face was pale white. "There's a fucking cougar in there."

I stared at him. "A... what?"

"A cougar!" He looked terrified. "There is a big fucking cougar in your car."

"No there isn't," I said.

"Lady, I swear to God—"

"Cougars are huge!" I said. "There's an entire engine in there. There's no way a cougar could fit in the hood of my car."

"Then it's a fucking... I dunno, a bobcat or something." He gestured at the car. "I can't deal with that. That's outta my pay grade."

"If you don't want to jump it for me, fine," I said. "I'll call someone else. You don't have to make things up just because your wife's gonna be mad at you."

"Make shit up?" he repeated with a dry laugh. "You don't believe me, take a look. But I'm not gonna jump in and save you when that cougar starts eating your goddamn face."

I looked at my car, then back at the driver, then reached for the hood of my car.

I couldn't hear anything but the sound of the tow truck driver's footsteps crunching the snow as he backed away. No growls or snarls, which one would expect if there was a wild animal magically living in the hood of their car. Still, I slipped my fingers into the gap to grab the latch cautiously, pausing for a moment to listen again before raising the hood an inch, then two, then—

"Oh!" I gasped as a large orange paw shot out from the gap.

"I fucking told you!" the driver half-screamed.

"It's not a cougar." I raised the hood slowly, careful not to move too suddenly or jarringly. "It's a cat."

"A cat," he said in disbelief. "That's not a fucking—"

I got the hood up enough to prop it open with the stick thingie, then stepped out of the way.

"A cat," I repeated.

In fairness to the driver, it was a *huge* cat. I had no idea how the thing got under my hood in the first place, but it was definitely not a two-hundred-pound cougar. It wasn't even a bobcat. But I figured it had to be at least part Maine Coon or something, even though I couldn't see all of it. Most of its body was sandwiched into a gap, but it was clear the cat was chonky as hell. And probably fluffy when it wasn't cold and covered in dirt and car grease.

"Well, cats are just as bad," the driver said. "That thing tried to claw my eyes out!"

"It's probably scared," I said.

The cat, who had taken its paw back and was now looking up at me with big green eyes, let out a confused "*Mrow?*"

"Scared or not, it's lucky it's not guts on the pavement like it would've been if your car had started," the driver grumbled. "Here, move. Let's get the damn thing out so we can jump your car."

"Hey!" I said as he reached into the hood and grabbed the cat by its scruff. "Be careful!"

The cat let out a yowl. The driver cursed and tried yanking it out again, but the cat hissed and batted a paw at him again as it shrunk back.

"Stop!" I said. "You're hurting it."

"I'm not waiting around while you call a vet or whatever to come get the thing out," he said.

"Then let me try."

The driver huffed and rolled his eyes. I ignored him.

"Hey, bud," I said softly. "Is it okay if I help you out of there?"

The cat didn't respond because cats don't talk, but it did look a little calmer now that the driver had stepped back.

"You probably went in there 'cause it was warm, huh?" I said, putting my palm flat and keeping it in front of me as I reached for the cat. "But it's probably not warm now. If you let me help you, I bet we can find somewhere much, much warmer for you to hang out, okay?"

I was close enough to pet it. The cat let me put my hand on its head, barely reacting until I started scratching it gently. The big green eyes closed and opened in a slow blink, and I couldn't be sure, but I thought it might have purred.

"You seem pretty cool," I said. "I'm gonna try lifting you out now."

The cat blinked again, holding still as I put my other hand under it. But I'd barely touched it when it let out another "*Mrow*" and stood, pulling itself out of the gap it was sitting in and walking directly into my arms.

"Oh," I said. "Okay. That was easy. Thank you."

"Mrow," said the cat, then bumped its head against my chest.

"That cat is fucking massive," the driver muttered.

"Just jump my car, please," I said, lifting the cat and hoping I was holding it tight enough that it wouldn't get loose and run away before I could check its collar.

Except it didn't have a collar.

"Where did you come from, hey?" I asked the cat. "Maybe you have a chip or something? Are there any vets open this late, or—"

"Hey! You found Omen!"

I jumped, startled by the voice coming from above us. I looked up to see Keith on his balcony, a thick winter coat over his typical bathrobe and a huge joint in his left hand.

"I found who?" I asked.

"Mildred's cat." Keith leaned on his balcony. "The poor old biddie who lived in the apartment before you. Hey, beautiful boy."

The cat hissed.

Keith laughed. "Always a joker, that one. Glad he's still around. I thought they'd carted him off to a rescue or maybe a coyote got him."

"She didn't take him when she moved?" I asked, frowning.

"Nah," he said. "I don't think they let you do that anymore. Pretty sure the whole 'buried with your pets' thing was more for people who had pyramids or crypts or whatever."

Oh.

Oh, *God*.

"So... he doesn't have a home anymore?" I asked.

"Only if you don't let him live with you," Keith said.

"Our building isn't pet friendly."

"Right, but I mean, he's lived in that apartment longer than you have," Keith said. "And Mildred was in there for like, two weeks before anyone found her, so I don't think they're that concerned about it."

"Two weeks?" I said. "She *died* in my apartment?!"

"No, of course not," he said. "It was her apartment at the time."

I looked at the cat, horrified. He looked back up at me and let out another soft *mrow*, then snuggled into my chest.

"What do I do with him, though?" I asked.

"You keep him," the tow truck driver grunted. "It's the goddamn system. Damn good thing you found it and not me because I'd be sending it right back to wherever it came from."

"What system?"

The tow truck driver gave me a skeptical look. "You never heard of the cat distribution system?"

I stared at him for a moment, then looked down at Omen.

I knew about the cat distribution system. Jayce and Ellie had told me about it ages ago. After we'd run into Corbin for the third time.

I'd said it was stupid and they'd said the more I denied it, the more I was tempting fate.

I'd questioned the existence of fate itself, and what had fate done?

It had given me Omen.

Chapter Thirty-Seven
Truth (Glitter) Bombs

Isla

IF I'D CALLED ELLIE, she probably would've materialized at my apartment door eighteen milliseconds later.

We had gone nowhere near this long without talking to each other since we'd met. I knew she was worried; hopefully, that worry hadn't morphed into anger. I'd tried to make it clear I just needed space without getting into the why of it all. I wasn't sure if I'd succeeded.

I hoped she'd forgive me if I hadn't.

I hoped she wouldn't make me explain why.

My heart was still stinging, rubbed raw but ready to heal. Even still, I didn't call Ellie to tell her I'd changed my mind about going to the Flat Tire. Part of me felt like if I did, I was giving up the hope of her before I had to, even though I already knew it was hopeless.

And even if I talked myself into giving up that hope, I was going to Leave It To Fate. It didn't feel right to have her there while I got ready to do that.

So I got ready alone. Mostly. Omen was there, of course, but he didn't help me pick an outfit or keep my glass full of cheap wine the way Ellie usually did. No, as soon as I'd gotten him upstairs, he'd curled up on the couch in a divot I'd never been able to explain and taken a nap while I took my now-running car to the grocery store to pick up cat supplies. A litter box and toys and a bag of treats and two types of food because I had no idea if he'd been a wet food cat or a kibble cat.

Considering his size, I hoped he was a kibble cat. Wet food was going to add up *real* fast.

Once I was back and determined that Omen was a "wet food or kibble doesn't matter just give me more of it" cat, I picked out my outfit. I ended up going with the plaid skirt Ellie had chosen for me to wear the first time she'd taken me to the Flat Tire—though I paired it with thick black stockings and leather boots because of the weather—and a cropped sweater instead of the bra thing she had picked.

And my hat, of course. Since it was the last time I'd get to wear it.

Because a bet was a bet, even if I'd told Ellie it was stupid in that moment of pain and anger after I'd gotten fired. I didn't meet my soulmate, so Ellie got to take my hat. And Ellie didn't meet hers, so I got to be Ella Prime.

I didn't really want to be Ella Prime, but Ellie would probably insist on it. Or she'd try to give me my hat back if I refused, which I didn't want either.

She'd won it, fair and square.

There was a short lineup outside the Flat Tire when I got there, which was surprising. I'd never seen people lined up before. Whoever was at the door was letting people in four at a time, though, so it seemed to move quickly. I tucked my hands into my pockets and tried not to shiver as I joined it.

It was almost my turn to go in when someone got in line behind me, but I only noticed because she let out a distressed sort of scoff.

"Seriously? A *lineup*?"

I looked over my shoulder to see a woman who wasn't wearing pants. She probably had a dress or a skirt underneath her winter coat, but whatever she was wearing, it was short; her coat hit just above her knees, and pink light from the buzzing neon sign above the Flat Tire splashed across smooth, bare legs. Next to her, a man who was clearly her date sighed.

"Babe, I told you it was cold out," he said. "You could've worn something else."

"I wanted to wear *this* dress," she said, her voice trembling. "I feel good in it."

"It'll only be a minute," the man said.

She shivered and pulled her coat around her tighter, like that would do anything to help given that she was bare-legged in February.

"Next?" said the staff member at the door.

The couple in front of me went in. I started forward, then paused and turned around.

"Go ahead of me," I said.

The woman turned in surprise. "What?"

"Go ahead," I said. "No one should have to freeze because they wanted to wear a cute dress. I'm sure it's beautiful." I jerked my head towards the door. "Quick, before they let all the hot air out."

"You are an angel," she said. "Thank you so, so much."

It wasn't that big a deal. I was only outside for another couple of minutes before the staff member called me forward. It was a woman I recognized vaguely as one of the bartenders, though she didn't seem to know who I was even though I came in on a weekly basis. I showed her my ticket and she marked it down on the tablet in front of her.

"Coat check is over there," she said, motioning to the rack in front of the community bulletin board. "Your ticket includes a welcome glass of champagne, they'll bring it to the table once you're seated. And your fate-chosen table is..." She dragged the word out as she tapped the tablet screen. "Table twenty-one. It's a booth near the front."

"Thanks," I said, stepping out of the way so the people behind me could check in.

I glanced around the Flat Tire as I waited to hang my jacket on the rack. All of the tables had tablecloths, except for the booths that lined the outside of the bar. The small stage they usually had for events was set up, though the dance floor was much smaller than usual since they'd put even more tables there. Some of the tables were still empty; many had couples sitting at them; a few had a solo person who was clearly waiting for another Fate ticket holder to arrive. All of them had flickering fake candles and single roses in a vase.

I didn't see Jayce. Normally they wandered around before an event, chatting with people or dealing with those unexpected little things that came up. I didn't see Ellie, either. Not at any of the tables, or lined up at the bar, or wandering around with her camera like Jayce sometimes asked her to.

Which was fine. Totally fine. She might not have been there yet. Or maybe she was helping Jayce with something. Or maybe she'd decided to sit this one out, too, and I'd made a horrible mistake by showing up without telling her.

Or maybe she was at my table.

The booths at the Flat Tire had high backs, so each one felt like a private area for whoever was sitting there. It was why we hadn't seen Paulette when she'd overheard me tell Jayce that Ellie and I had slept together. And the booth that had been designated table twenty-one was right by the stage, which was angled in a way that made it almost impossible to see into.

My heart thumped in my chest.

What if she was sitting there?

It would be fate, I decided. Maybe not the soulmate type of fate, but fate regardless. It would be fate telling me to hold onto her, to let this idea of being in love with her go, to value her for the friend she was.

I was so convinced that my tall, gangly, dark-haired best friend would be sitting there that when I got to the table, I was momentarily convinced that I'd just forgotten what she looked like. After all, the person sitting there was also tall and dark-haired.

But they definitely weren't gangly.

"Oh, thank our lord and saviour Cher," Lady of the Lake breathed when I stopped in front of the table, stunned by the sight of her. "I got you."

Lady was wearing a dark brown wig styled into a beehive, along with a bright red retro-style dress that had a sweetheart neckline. She'd tucked herself all the way back in the booth, pressing against the wall and scrunching herself down so even the people waiting at the bar would've been hard-pressed to see her there.

"Uh… hi," I said, staring at her. "What… what?!"

"Come on, sit down, honey," Lady said, waving me in. "I was worried whoever they sent over would spoil it, but fate's doing a good job with those tickets tonight and sent me someone I know."

"Spoiled what?" I asked.

Her painted red lips curled up into a smile. "My big entrance, of course. Isn't it brilliant? No one knows I'm here. They think it's just another table. So it'll be a total shock when I burst out, right?"

"Yeah," I said, trying not to sound disappointed as I slid into the booth. "Right. Of course."

Lady frowned. "Let's try that again with a bit more enthusiasm." She cleared her throat. "It'll be the most outrageously talented and amazing thing you've ever seen in your entire life when I burst out, right?"

I smiled in spite of myself. "Hey, give me a break. I just found out fate's not giving me a date tonight."

"Why would you think that?" she asked.

"I mean, you're working," I said. "I'll be on my own here."

"Oh, Isla." Lady rolled her eyes. "It's a good thing you're pretty. And so very smart. On an unrelated note, that was a really stupid thing you just said."

"What?!" I said, laughing in surprise. "Why was it stupid?"

"Like Jayce would risk upsetting a customer by not giving them what they paid for." She scoffed. "No, of *course* you'll end up with a date. This is only for the first part. Jayce's going to introduce the evening as if they're the MC and I'm going to interrupt by causing a scene and demanding a new date so we can lead into the second chance draw."

"What's that?"

She grinned. "A last-minute idea I had. It's a small town. What if you showed up here and I was your ex-boyfriend? Or you got seated with that girl who bullied you in high school? Or two of those cishet guys who are totally cool with gay people but just, like, it's not for me, *brah* ended up together?"

"So you give fate a second chance," I said slowly.

"Exactly. Anyone who's not happy with their date can draw again. Plus, if somehow the math didn't math properly, we can sneak in a ringer if there's an odd number so no one actually ends up dateless."

"Smart," I said. "But what if I don't like the person I get if I don't have a second chance?"

"Then you can take your adorable hat and be my tip collector for the night again," she said. "And I'll buy you a shot once you're done working. Or I'm sure whoever Ellie ends up with would be happy to have you join them."

My stomach flipped at the sound of her name. "Ellie is here, then?"

"Of course. Didn't you..." Lady trailed off, looking concerned. "Are you two fighting?"

"No," I said quickly. "Not... not really."

"Mmm." She sat up a bit. "I don't like the sound of that. What happened?"

"It's nothing."

"Isla." She leaned forward, being careful to keep her head tucked down so no one could see her. "Not to play into stereotypes, but have you ever met a drag queen who couldn't give you some good, hard, salt-of-the-earth type wisdom?"

"Yes," I said. "I definitely have met some drag queens who give the kind of advice that should come with a gift receipt."

She burst out laughing. "See, that's the type of read that makes me think I should put *you* in drag one of these days. But for real, Isla. If not as a drag queen, talk to me as your friend."

I looked up at her. "We're friends?"

She scoffed. "'Course we're friends. And I'm the kind of friend who's gonna tell it to you like it is. Being a drag queen just means I add a little glitter to my truth bombs."

I laughed again. It was hard not to. It was also hard to figure out how, exactly, to tell her what was going on.

"Can I ask you a question that might be inappropriate? Or maybe even offensive?" I finally asked.

"God, I hope so," she said. "Spill it, girl."

I swallowed hard and looked down at my hands. "How did you, um... how did you know you were gay?"

"Mmm," Lady said. "Two for two on the stupid questions tonight, my beautiful friend."

I grimaced. "Sorry. I just—"

"For one, I'm not gay," she said.

My face *burned*. "Oh. God. I'm sorry. I didn't... You talked about having a boyfriend one time and—"

"Oh, I do date men," she said patiently. "But I identify as bisexual. My attraction does skew a bit more to the masculine, but not exclusively. Like a lot of things, it's a spectrum."

"Oh," I said.

She smiled. "And for two, let me ask you a question in return. How did you know you were straight?"

"I... don't," I said quietly.

"Oh. *Ohhhhh*." Lady sat back a bit. "Okay, well, now I'm the one saying stupid things. Let me try again." She took a deep breath and let it out. "Once upon a time, I was a young boy with friends who did stupid young boy things like steal their dads' porno magazines that they sometimes still have, especially in small towns like these where technology takes a little time to catch up. And I looked at some of those pictures and thought, 'Well, that sure is nice.' But then when I was a stupid young man, I saw some other dudes' dicks and thought 'Ah yes, I would also like to put those in my mouth.' And something clicked, so I did."

I tried not to laugh. "So you just knew, sort of?"

"Kind of." She tilted her head. "And the reason you're asking is because you felt that click and you don't know what to do about it."

"Yes," I said softly. "But also... no."

"Mmm. I'm intrigued. What does that mean?"

"I, um... I felt the 'click,' I think," I said. "But I didn't know that I hadn't felt the click before and also it's, like, one person. And even when I try to think of other people who might be like that one person, there isn't a click, and maybe my clicker is broken or something but—"

"Oh, honey," Lady interrupted, chuckling softly. "You know gay and straight aren't the only options, right?"

"Of course," I said. "I could bi or pan or—"

"Or asexual," she said.

My leg bounced under the table. "I like sex, though. And I want... I want to be with someone."

"So do plenty of ace people. You can be asexual and not aromantic or sex adverse." I must have still looked confused because Lady smiled patiently. "What's your favourite food?"

That clarified nothing. "Um... fried chicken."

"Okay. And what's your least favourite food?"

"Probably applesauce." I wrinkled my nose. "I can't stand the texture."

"Perfect. So, think of a rating scale that's a spectrum. On one end is fried chicken. On the other is applesauce. If the way you feel about sex is the same as how you feel about fried chicken, it means you enjoy it. You seek it out."

"And sex aversion would be applesauce," I said.

She nodded. "Something you won't seek out. You wouldn't eat it unless you really had to. And anyone who made you eat it when you hate it that much would be an honest-to-god asshole. So if there's a food that you like, maybe not to the point that you seek it out but if it's there, you'll enjoy it—"

"Oh my God," I said. "It's bacon. Sex is bacon on my scale."

"Bacon? You monster," she said. "But okay. Let's talk about the person you had a 'click' for. Where on the scale would you put having sex with them?"

My throat felt dry and my chin trembled. "She's the only person I've ever felt fried chicken about."

"So maybe you're demisexual," Lady said. "Or maybe you're asexual but not aromantic. You don't have to know right now."

I stared at the table. "So... what do I do if she doesn't feel the same way?"

Lady paused long enough that I looked up. When I did, she reached out and put her hand on mine.

"The same thing anyone does when feelings aren't reciprocated," she said gently.

"Respect it and move on," I said sadly.

"Oh, that too," she said. "I was going to say drink an entire bottle of prosecco and hit Add To Cart on the highest-end, fanciest vibrator you can afford, but—"

She stopped when I started laughing, squeezing my hand just as the crackle of a microphone rang through the bar.

"Well, hello," came Jayce's voice. "Welcome to the Leave It To Fate Valentine's Day party. We'd like to get started, so has everyone found their Fate Date?"

"You've got this," Lady whispered, squeezing my hand before sliding as gracefully as she could across the booth.

"Great," Jayce said. "Now that everyone's got their dates and fates—"

"Absolutely the fuck *not*!" Lady said in a loud, indignant voice, standing up. "I refuse to spend my evening at a table with someone who is so much more attractive and hilarious than I am. It's simply intolerable. Let someone else handle this gorgeous creature. I demand a redo!"

Chapter Thirty-Eight
Table Twenty-One

Ellie

THERE WERE AN ODD number of dates.

It made sense. Isla wasn't coming. But Jayce said Lady of the Lake had a brilliant idea for her grand entrance and they'd decided that I'd get sent into the fray during the Second Chance round.

Which was fine by me. I could down a lot of cheap beer before the evening officially started and I had to go make small talk with someone who wasn't the person I wanted to be with all night.

From my spot at the back of the bar, I watched people file in and find their seats. A few people had ended up with people they knew and were chatting cheerfully; a few others were people who had never met before, some of whom were making awkward small talk and others who'd clicked almost instantly. Near the center of the bar, two men in their early twenties sat awkwardly at a table, neither of them looking at each other as they nursed bottles of domestic beer. The Date Night tables, which had been sold in pairs for people who didn't want to Leave It To Fate, were all filled up with couples who were mostly people watching the way I was.

God, this would have been so much fun with Isla here.

It hurt to think about her, so I was doing it as much as possible. Each pining moment was one step closer to living in a world where I could move on, hopefully, and find the person I was truly meant to be with.

Not tonight, though. Despite agreeing to be someone's Fate Date, I wasn't quite ready for that yet.

Still, I put on the happiest face I could after Lady burst out of the booth closest to the stage, screaming that whoever was in her booth was just too attractive for her and that they needed to do a second chance round. I couldn't help but laugh; Lady was super hot both in and out of drag, so I couldn't imagine how gorgeous that person must be. She took the microphone from Jayce, who half-heartedly acted like they were protesting before side-stepping off the stage to let Lady take over.

"—so if you want to let fate take another crack at it, stand up now," Lady said.

There was an awkward silence in the bar. After a moment, the sound of a chair scraping the floor echoed through the room, followed by laughter as the two guys at the center of the room stood up in unison.

"Of course," Lady said. "Two bros sitting five feet away from each other in the hot tub, right?"

I snorted into my drink.

"No, no, not both of you. Just... you." Lady pointed at one of the men. "You come up here, and you stay at the table. What table number is—fourteen? Perfect." She grabbed a piece of paper and wrote on it, then frowned. "I need a—hey, here. Yes, you know what. Just for a minute." She went back to the booth she'd just escaped from and grabbed a hat. "Okay, anyone else?"

After all was said and done, there were eight people standing on the stage. I hovered near the back, half-hoping they'd forget about me until Jayce appeared and took the almost-empty beer out of my hand, replaced it with a full one, and shoved me forward.

"And one more back here!" they shouted.

"Excellent. *Excellent*." Lady grinned as I made my way up to the stage. "Are we ready for our second chance at romance, friends?"

I was not, but everyone else was, so we started anyway.

A pretty woman with red hair was sent to table fourteen. The man originally from fourteen went to table five. I got distracted looking around the room as some of the others were drawn, but tuned back in when me and one other person were left at the front.

"Alright, Mr. Cowboy Boots," Lady said to a man who was indeed wearing cowboy boots. "Let me draw for you here..." She clicked her tongue as she reached into the hat. "Table eleven! Which is perfect because that means you"—she held the hat out to me—"can bring that back to table twenty-one, where your date awaits."

"Am I getting paid extra to carry things around for you?" I asked, taking the hat.

The audience chuckled and Lady grinned.

"I think you'll like what fate has in store for you," she said.

I didn't think much of it. Just like I didn't think much of the hat. It wasn't until I got to table twenty-one and saw my date sitting there, all curly hair and blue eyes and nerves biting at her bottom lip, that I looked back down and realized I was holding a black pork-pie hat.

"Hey," Isla said softly.

Nerves stole the moisture from my mouth and my heart skipped a beat or five.

"You're here," I said.

"Sorry." She grimaced. "I was gonna tell you, but then I figured I'd see you here. Except then I didn't see you at all but I guess even if fate isn't giving us soulmates it wanted to make sure we could talk tonight, like if you want to. But if it's awkward I can go because I know you're probably mad I didn't text you back and—"

"Isla," I said. "This is literally the best possible thing that could have happened."

She let out a breath as I slid into the booth across from her, pushing her hat across the table. "You're not mad at me?"

"Of course not," I said. "Are you, um—"

"No," she said.

"Can I apologize?"

"Can I?"

"For what?" I said. "You don't need to."

She wasn't quite looking at me. "I do a little. I'm sorry."

"Please don't be." I tapped my hands on the table. "I made you feel awful. I didn't mean to, but there's that whole saying about intentions and sea bushes or whatever—"

She looked up, bewildered. "Sea bushes?"

"Because my brain wasn't on the same wavelength as my mouth or something." I shrugged. "I don't know. But you must know I think you're amazing, okay? *Anyone* would be lucky to have you as a soulmate. I only wanted to say that you and I—"

"Ellie," she said. "You don't have to try again."

"Fair." I half-grimaced, half-laughed. "And then you got fired because of me."

"It wasn't your fault."

"I slept with you, didn't I?"

She pressed her lips together. "Yeah, but that means it's my fault, too."

"No, I—" I tilted my head to the side. "Well, actually, that's not a bad argument. But it's wrong."

"Because you're the only one allowed to feel bad about this?"

"Exactly. Now you're getting it." I grinned as she rolled her eyes. "Look, I get why you needed space. I'm sorry I did something that made you need it. And I really, really hope we can be friends again—"

"Were we ever not?" she asked, looking panicked.

And every ounce of stress and fear and regret from the past day floated out on my next breath.

Because it was going to be okay.

We were going to be okay.

"I'm so glad you're—" I started.

"—and if everyone is ready to *listen*," Lady said in a sing-song voice, her hand suddenly clapping down on the booth table and making Isla and I jump. "I'll be going over the schedule of structured fun for the evening. So if you want a chance at the prizes—"

"What prizes?" Isla said, perking up.

"The ones I'm about to tell you about if you *both* stopped clicking so hard the entire universe could see it," Lady said, giving a meaningful look to Isla, who blinked and then turned red for some reason.

"Yes, ma'am," Isla said in a high-pitched voice.

"Ooo, *ma'am*." Lady fanned herself, then winked at me. "I might've made a mistake by giving up on this one so soon. Don't follow in my footsteps, sweet pea."

I laughed, but Isla sank back in her seat a bit. Lady had barely sauntered away to heckle someone else when Isla reached across the table and took my beer, lifting it and taking a long slug.

"Where's your drink?" I asked when she finally set it back down.

She shrugged. "No one came around. Probably because Lady was hiding here."

I'd been hiding at this table earlier, too. And that came in handy because instead of passing my beer back and forth across the table so I could share it with Isla, I knew for sure that I could crawl under it without much trouble.

Well, without much physical trouble. I didn't account for the fact that Isla would be wearing that fucking *skirt* of hers.

"Your outfit is cute," I whispered when I popped up beside her, hoping she'd assume my flushed cheeks were because I'd hit my head and not because I'd caught a flash of thigh that meant she was wearing thigh-high stockings, which was the *reason* I'd hit my head.

"What are you *doing*?!" she half-whispered, half-cackled.

"Making it easier to share drinks." I grabbed my beer and pulled it towards us. "And easier to talk to my hot date."

She stifled a giggle behind her hand, but happily took another swig of my beer.

We split the rest of the bottle between us, quietly passing it back and forth as Lady went over the different activities Jayce had planned for the night in between jokes, then did her first lip sync set of the night. Isla cheered loudly and when Lady came around to our table, offered her hat to collect tips, but Lady brushed it away with a manicured hand. I took the hat and set it back on Isla's head, though I didn't take a moment to fluff her curls up like I usually did.

I couldn't do that anymore. Not to her, and not to myself.

"Thank you all!" she said once her number was done. "I'll be back with you all in a few minutes for the first game, and in the meantime, someone get a bottle of bubbles to twenty-one, stat. These poor fate-found lovers are splitting a single beer between the two of them, which is *not* what we intended when we said you'd be swapping spit by the end of the night."

It worked out well, since she said it while Isla was taking a sip of beer, and it sprayed all over the table as she started laughing.

"Anything new and exciting happen in the last day?" I asked as a server came over with a bottle of cheap champagne, a couple of flutes, and some napkins. "I feel like it's been forever."

"Not really," Isla said, mopping up the beer she'd spit on the table. "My car froze in the cold and I had to call a tow truck. Oh, and I got a cat."

"You... what?"

"An orange one. His name's Omen and he belonged to the lady who died in my apartment." She lifted her glass. "RIP Mildred. Thanks for the sign."

"You got a cat," I repeated. "An *orange* cat. From a dead woman?"

"No, from my car," she said. "I found him in my engine. I think he's a Maine Coon."

"A Maine Coon."

"Like, he's massive." She put her hands out. "Just a big ol' chonk. And so fluffy. I gave him a bath when we got inside."

"Right. And you understand that I'm still stuck on the part where *you* got a cat?" I said. "I thought you hated cats."

"I don't hate them. I just didn't like them. But that's the cat distribution system for you." She grabbed her purse. "Wanna see a picture?"

"Of course I want to see a picture," I grumbled, then appropriately *aww*ed at the photo Isla had taken of an absolutely gigantic cat snoozing on her couch.

I couldn't have said what the first game they played was. Or the second. Lady got our attention long enough for us to cheer her on for her second set, but for the most part, Isla and I lived like nothing existed outside the high walls of our booth, talking like we hadn't seen each other in weeks instead of a single day.

It wasn't all about cats. She asked if anyone at work had said anything about her getting fired and I told her I didn't know because I'd left early. And that I'd spent the rest of the day trying to figure out what I actually needed to do to start my own business.

"But you still have a job," she said.

"Yeah, but you're not there," I replied. "If I can get my shit sorted out, maybe we can keep working together." Suddenly self-conscious, I looked down at hands, hoping she didn't notice my face turning red. "If you want."

Isla didn't say anything immediately. She didn't actually say anything at all. She just paused and then a moment later, her head was resting on my shoulder, like she wanted to hug me but couldn't because we were tucked into a cozy booth, watching our friend lip sync to some random cover of *"L-O-V-E"* by Nat King Cole.

"Wanna enter the dance contest?" she asked when it was done.

"I thought you didn't like dancing that much," I said.

"Yeah, but Lady said the prize is another bottle of champagne and ours is empty. And your dress'll either give us an unfair advantage or it won't matter because someone'll buy your boobs a drink."

I laughed. "We're at a date night event, Ella Two."

"Half these people met tonight," she said. "And there's, like, a fifty percent chance your boobs could break up an established couple. Those are pretty good odds for champagne. And we technically have until midnight."

I frowned. "For what?"

"For the bet." She sat up, not quite looking at me. "Not everyone here is in a relationship. Plus there's the band."

"Because we've had such good luck with bands in the past," I said.

She twisted her mouth to the side. "True."

Something in my chest felt tight, but not necessarily in a bad way. It wasn't guilt or sadness or loss. It was like... inevitability.

So I bumped Isla with my elbow, urging her out of the booth.

"Let's go enter the dance contest and find our soulmates," I said. "Tonight's the night. I can just feel it."

Chapter Thirty-Nine
Snow Filled Night

Isla

"I STILL SAY IT was rigged," Ellie grumbled.

"It wasn't rigged," I said, finding her coat on the coat rack and passing it to her. "It's what happens when you're up against people who are secretly figure skaters."

"Yeah, but this is *my* bar."

"It's Jayce's bar."

"Yes, but *figuratively*—"

I giggled as Ellie gestured, catching her arm before she swatted someone else in the line of people trying to get their coats. "Figuratively nothing. If you won just 'cause you know the owner, *that* would be rigged. And we still won This or That."

"Yeah," she said thoughtfully, then dissolved into laughter again. "That poor dude's gonna be sleeping on the couch tonight."

I tried not to laugh. Lady asked us to fill out the roster for This or That, which was exactly what it sounded like. The host—Lady, of course—asked a series of this or that questions and one member of each couple had to scribble down what they thought the other person would choose, while that person wrote down what their answer actually was.

Ellie and I had nailed all but two, as had one other couple, so it had gone to a tiebreaker where Lady asked one final question that wasn't a this-or-that question. Instead, they'd told us to split our whiteboards in half and write our answer on the left and our guess of our partner's answer on the right. This was especially hilarious when the question turned out to be "What is your partner's go-to comfort food," since Ellie and I ended up with four whiteboard halves that all read "Fried Chicken."

The wife of the other couple had gotten her husband's comfort food correct. Her husband, on the other hand, guessed that her comfort food was strawberry ice cream.

"I'm allergic to strawberries, you dumbass!" she'd screeched, and his face started to resemble a scoop of strawberry ice cream as Lady had declared Ellie and I the winners and instructed us to ask the bartender for our bottle of champagne. We'd ignored those instructions in favour of finding Jayce and making them go behind the bar to get us our prize, then convinced them to sit with us at table twenty-one and have a glass before we left for the night.

"Which means I should pee before we go," Ellie had declared loudly, setting her glass down and disappearing, leaving me alone with Jayce.

Which was a little awkward, since I hadn't talked to them since they'd seen me get fired at their bar the previous day, but I smiled at them anyway.

"So this was pretty successful," I'd said, smiling as I turned to them.

"Uh-huh, disgusting and capitalist as Valentine's is, the lights will stay on here for a few more months, at least," they'd replied. "Now, about yesterday..."

I'd grimaced, looking at my hands. "I'm sorry."

"Why are you apologizing to me?"

"Because you were there," I'd said. "And it was probably awkward and weird and, like, disturbing the peace at your place of business or whatever. And I've already apologized to Ellie."

They hadn't said anything right away. When I looked up, they were frowning.

"She apologized to you as well, right?" they'd finally asked.

I'd nodded. "We're good. We... things are fine."

The frown faded from Jayce's face, replaced by a solemn expression that lacked their usual snark.

"She was distraught," they'd said. "I haven't seen Ellie that upset in ages."

My face had gone red. "I know. I'm sorry."

"It's perfectly understandable," they'd said. "I'm only telling you because I think you need to know she really, truly cares about you. And I wanted to make sure you understand how much your friendship means to her."

I'd smiled, pushing down that brief and breathless moment of pain from the reminder that was all Ellie and I would ever be, and nodded at them.

"Hmm," they'd said after a moment. "You didn't like that word, did you?"

"What word?" I'd asked.

They'd cocked an eyebrow. "Friendship."

Even though my heart was pounding so hard I was sure Jayce could see it pulsing through my skin, I'd feigned confusion. "What's wrong with 'friendship'?"

A slow smile began to spread across their face. "I knew it."

"Knew *what*?" I'd pressed, but before they could respond, Ellie bounded up to us.

"Alright, I've cleared the cheap champagne from my kidneys," she'd said, and Jayce had gotten up, patting her on the shoulder and telling her to stumble home safely before floating away. I'd stood, my heart lodged in my throat, and followed Ellie to the coat rack. We'd bumped into the people who won the dancing contest, who'd congratulated us again, and who Ellie had congratulated back before grumbling as they walked away.

Once we had our coats on, we waved goodbye to Lady, who was dancing with a couple of people from the fate tables who'd decided they were better off as singles, and braced ourselves to step out into the cold night air.

Except it wasn't cold.

Well, it wasn't *that* cold.

"Wow, it warmed up a lot," Ellie said as the music and chatter from the bar was cut off by the closing of the door.

"And it snowed," I said, surveying the layer of fluffy white tinged pink as the neon sign above the door flickered and buzzed.

"Yeah." She wrinkled her nose. "I was going to walk home, but I guess I could call a cab."

It took me a moment to realize what she said. Once I did, I looked up at her, trying not to look as hurt as I felt. "You're going home?"

Clearly, I'd done a horrible job of hiding the fact that my heart had fallen. Ellie stepped forward, grabbing my arm.

"I just didn't want to assume," she said. "My car's not parked at your place like it usually is. And if you didn't want me there—"

"I do," I said. Because even though I was as terrified as I was comforted by the thought of sharing a bed with her—wrapping my arms around her or having hers wrapped around me—the thought of things being awkward between us terrified me even more. "And besides, don't you want to meet Omen?"

And of course she did.

It took longer than usual for us to get back to my apartment given that the snow made the sidewalk more slippery than it looked, but that was okay; it just meant our tipsiness wore off faster than usual. White light from the streetlamps guided us as the occasional car drove by, but mostly, it was quiet, neither of us feeling the need to say much of anything.

It wasn't until we were walking past the gas station down the street from my building that Ellie said anything, and that was only because the lights in the parking lot and building suddenly went out all at once.

"What was that?" she asked.

"Looks like they're closing. It must be midnight," I said, then realized what that meant. "So, congratulations."

"Huh?" she asked, then realization dawned on her as I reached up to take my hat off. "Oh, I can't. Isla, I can't actually take it."

"Are you kidding?" I asked, trying to laugh. "A bet's a bet. I'm sure as hell cashing in on being Ella Prime."

She took the hat from me reluctantly. "I feel bad taking your hat, though."

"Is it because you're now forever known as Ella Two?"

"A little bit," she said, then we both laughed as she put the hat on. "What do you think?"

"You're beautiful," I said honestly.

"Thanks, Ella Prime," she said, then frowned as we started down the sidewalk that led to the entrance of my building, passing by my second-floor balcony. "Wait a sec. There's something in your hair."

"Anyway, it wasn't the worst bet ever," I said as I turned, intending to let her grab whatever was stuck in my hair. "We might not have found our soulmates, but think of all the ridiculous memories we—*oh*!"

The heel of my boot shot forward and I threw my arms out. Skidding, I tried to catch myself, but I could only move my legs so far since my skirt was tight around my thighs. That meant my other foot ended up on the same patch of ice hidden beneath the snow, completely useless as I began to topple.

Moments before I fell on my ass, a hand wrapped around my forearm and yanked me forward, but said hand was attached to a woman with gangly legs, heels, and all the grace of a newborn giraffe. She stumbled and I reached for her, as though I could balance both of us, then the next thing I knew, I was flat on my back in the snow piled next to the sidewalk.

I landed with a soft "*Oomph*," then gasped as icy coldness immediately soaked into the thick black stockings on my legs and made its way up to my bare thighs. Then, because Ellie was still clutching me, I let out a repulsive sounding grunt as she landed on top of me, the weight of her forcing the air out of my lungs and directly into her face.

"Ungh," she groaned, then lifted her head and looked at me. A heartbeat passed, and then she pressed her lips together, stifling a laugh.

I laughed too. At least, I thought it was going to come out as laughter. But what actually came out was a crackling cough-like sound, and to my horror, my eyes began to sting. I slammed them shut, because what the fuck *else* could I do to stop her from seeing me cry when her face was so close to mine, but it was too late.

"Isla?" Ellie said, concern soft in her voice.

"Wow," I said, trying to force myself to laugh, even though nothing about it was convincing. "Fate really wants *us* to have this fucking meet cute, doesn't it?"

She didn't say anything. Not at first. Not until I finally couldn't stand the silence and pried my eyes open, looking up to see my best friend staring down at me.

There was an odd look in her eye and she was close. Too close. Close enough that she could see my thoughts. So close that I could have picked out my tears in the reflection of myself in her eyes.

"Isla," she said again, and her voice was even softer than before. "Are we in love?"

She knew.

Everything crashed around me.

She knew. She knew and this was it and she would laugh and tell me there was no way she'd ever—

My heart thundered in my ears, then faded as I processed her words again.

She hadn't said "Are you in love with me?"

She'd said...

"Yes," I whispered.

A soft breath warmed my lips for half a second before her mouth was on mine and I was surprised to see—well, feel, I guess—that she was trembling as much as I was. Snow and silence surrounded us, and above me, it was only Ellie and her lips and the stars.

It wasn't our first kiss. It wasn't the first kiss that mattered. It wasn't even our first real kiss; looking back, I couldn't stop myself from seeing that every kiss we'd shared, from the one she'd surprised me with on her grandparents' patio to the countless ones under mistletoe to the impulsive one on New Year's Eve had been *real*.

But it was everything.

It was perfect.

Her lips were soft and eager, tasting like crisp champagne and fruit and something else, something that I couldn't name and that I would always and forever identify as just being the taste of Ellie. My senses filled with her; her taste, her scent, the feel of her body pressed against mine and the sound of her breath. I lifted my arm, letting it rest on her waist and feeling the muted sensation of her ribs rising and falling beneath her winter jacket. As I touched her, she pulled back, and I panicked for a moment thinking she'd suddenly realized what we were doing, but the look on her face and the brightness in her eyes calmed me.

"Isla," she whispered again, and this time my name was nestled in joy and excitement and relief.

"Ellie," I whispered back, hoping she could hear the same bliss in mine.

She smiled and I felt my heart flutter at the sight of it.

"This feels right, doesn't it?" she asked.

"I think it does."

"Good. Me too."

I couldn't hold back a smile of my own. "Well, I'm glad you agree. But, um, maybe we could sit up so I don't freeze to death in the snow?"

"Or at least roll over so I can watch the action," came a voice from above that made us both jump, and Ellie nearly did roll off of me as she started laughing.

"Shut up, Keith, you perv," she called up to the third-floor balcony.

"What? It's not my fault you're out here. Go get a room."

Ellie's eyes sparkled, then she pressed her lips to mine again. "Wanna go upstairs and spoon?"

"Eventually," I said. "First, I want everything else."

Chapter Forty

Snow Angel

Isla

THE FIRST THING I had to do was show Ellie my pussy.

"Oh my God, *look* at you," she cried when we got into my apartment and heard a loud *thud* as Omen jumped off the couch and came to the door to greet us. She crouched, not even bothering to take her shoes off before showering him with baby talk and scritches. He purred, bumping his head against her hands and rubbing up on her legs.

"Good thing he likes you," I said. "Isn't that one of those red flag things? If your cat doesn't like someone?"

"You'd take his opinion over mine already?" she asked, looking up at me from the floor. "You've known him for, like, half a day."

"Not even," I said, shrugging. "But I mean, maybe. Cats just know, right?"

She snorted on a laugh, giving Omen a final scritch under his chin. "How did you ever convince yourself that you aren't a cat person?"

"Probably the same way I convinced myself I was straight," I muttered.

It was loud enough that Ellie heard it, which made sense. I hadn't been trying to hide it. But it made an awkward electricity flicker between us as she stood up, a solemn look on her face.

For a moment, we were both quiet. We needed to be. We needed that discomfort, of not knowing what to do next. We needed it because this was *us*.

She was my best friend, and I was hers, and that meant something.

"I think I'm supposed to tell you we should talk about this first," Ellie finally said.

347

"Supposed to?" I repeated.

A smirk played across her lips. "Yeah. I'm pretty sure it's, like, part of the official syllabus for Handling A Bisexual Awakening 101."

I choked on a laugh, glancing down as I felt my face turn red. "Um... I don't think I'm bi, actually."

She grimaced. "Oh. Sorry. You don't need to label it or anything. I meant—"

"I think I'm asexual," I said.

Something about saying it out loud to her made my stomach flutter. Nerves, maybe, or a fear of what she'd say, but when Ellie stepped forward and took my hand, I looked up and found a strange comfort in my vulnerability.

"I don't think I've ever been, like, attracted to anyone," I whispered. "I like it. Sex, I mean. And I want... *you*. I want to be with you. I don't know if that... I haven't... This is kind of all new and I don't think I know yet."

"That's okay." Her voice was low, husky and sweet and reassuring. "Whatever that label ends up being, I'm still gonna love you, Isla."

"You won't be, like, bothered?" I asked quietly. "Because I do feel differently about you than I've felt before, but I don't know if that's, like... sexual or whatever and if that would bother you and Lady and I just talked about this a few hours ago so I haven't had time to overthink it yet, okay?"

She laughed, shaking her head.

"Isla, you love me," she said. "That's what matters most overall. And the thing that matters most right *now* is that you're sure about doing this."

"I am," I said. No hesitation. No doubt. No questioning.

"I mean really sure." She looked nervous, like she was certain I was about to change my mind. "I want you in my life. If that means I can't be with you the way I've been wanting you, that's okay. I'd much rather be with you however I can. I don't want to hurt you. I don't want to *lose* you."

Her words spun in my mind, dancing with the emotions I didn't know we'd shared. "How long have you—I mean..." I swallowed hard. "You said I wasn't your type. Yesterday."

"Remember when I was late for work the very first day we met?" she said.

"Uh... yeah."

"We saw each other at Starbucks," she said. "You were wearing"—her hands went to my hips like magnets—"this skirt. This fucking skirt, Isla."

"Okay," I said. "But—"

"I couldn't focus," she said. "I went to get breakfast to cool off because I couldn't stop thinking about your thighs."

My face burned. "Oh."

"Everything about you is my type," she said. "Everything about your body. Everything about your heart. Everything about your mind. You are so my type that I was doing anything and everything I could to convince myself you weren't because I didn't think this could ever happen. I kept telling myself it was like having a crush on a hockey player or a rock star. You know, completely unattainable and unrequitable because *someone* was straight."

I burst out laughing. "I thought I was."

She grinned, playing idly with my fingers. "And what about you?"

"What about me what?"

"How long have you been carrying a torch for my sweet, sweet ass?"

I laughed again and shook my head. "Longer than I thought, but I kept telling myself it was... not like that."

"How'd you realize it was like that, then?"

"Um... Nick kinda pointed it out."

Ellie's eyebrows were as high on her forehead as they could go. "Wait, at the party?"

I nodded.

"... your ex-boyfriend figured out you were madly in love with your sexy best friend before you did?"

Her eyes sparkled as if it was meant to be a joke, but I couldn't laugh when it was very much the truth. Instead, I nodded again, and Ellie's expression changed.

"You know I'm kidding, right? I mean, not about being sexy, but I'm teasing about the 'being madly in love with me' stuff."

"I'm not."

I said it before I thought it; I meant it, long before I'd realized I felt it. And I stood in front of Ellie, heart open and legs trembling, still meaning it with everything in me and hoping that she believed me. More importantly, I hoped to whatever might be out there that she didn't think I was clingy or naïve or fickle or insane for being completely in love with her when I'd found out she had feelings for me moments earlier.

For a harrowing moment, I thought she might run, but she smiled again and tugged me forward.

"Good," she said simply, and then she kissed me.

For as many times as Ellie had thrown her arms around me, I'd never melted in them the way I did then. And melting was an apt way of describing it; my tights were still soaked with melted snow and her touch made me realize my skin was still freezing.

"What's wrong?" Ellie murmured against my mouth as I shivered.

I chuckled breathlessly. "I'm kinda wet."

Her eyes went comically wide.

"From falling in the snow!" I said, but it was too late; Ellie had to let go of me because she was cackling so hard.

Which was fine, because I loved how she laughed.

"Well, should we get you out of these wet clothes?" she asked teasingly once she was able to breathe again. "Or are we moving too fast?"

I looked at her, then instead of saying we weren't moving too fast and I was fine and I wanted her more than anyone I'd wanted in my entire life, I brought my hand up to her face. Pulling her towards me, I captured her lips again, and Ellie made a sound that sent electricity roaring through me.

The only light in the apartment was the golden glow from the fixture next to the door. It spread through the space, illuminating it enough to guide us after

Ellie pulled my body against hers and started using her hips to urge me towards the bedroom. We only almost tripped over Omen twice, and he only yowled for a few minutes after I shut him out of the bedroom.

"Shit," Ellie said after the door closed. "That thing is still stuck in your hair."

"What thing?" I asked, my hand flying up and patting my curls.

She nudged my hand out of the way, carefully pulling out whatever it was. She glanced down and paused for a moment before a smirk spread on her lips.

"What is it?"

"Nothing." She set a scrap of paper with the number eleven on it on my dresser. "Come here and kiss me again."

Our clothes came off fast. Too fast, maybe, but also not fast enough. Ellie was topless but still in a thong when she pinned me to my bed; I'd gotten my sweater and skirt off, but the soaked thigh highs were clinging to my legs, and I still had my bra and panties on. They didn't *stay* on for very long, but Ellie put it off so she could run her hands down my body, from the flushed skin on my chest to the smooth front of my bra to the softness of my stomach and the definitely-not-wet-from-just-snow-anymore fabric of my panties.

"This feels like a fucking dream," she murmured as she leaned in to press a kiss against my belly. "You're irresistible..." The sentence faded away unfinished, and she chuckled.

"What?" I asked.

"Are you a 'babe' girl?" she asked.

"A what now?"

"You know. A pet name," she said. "I know you're technically Ella Prime now, but that feels kind of weird to—"

"Wait," I said. "You don't think we're soulmates? Because I only got to be Ella Prime if we didn't find our soulmates, but—"

"By Valentine's Day." Her mouth twitched as she looked up at me. "At midnight. Which was before you made that unintended snow angel. Wait!" Her eyes went wide. "I could call you 'snow angel.'"

I groaned and protested and laughed, of course, and she kissed a spot a little lower on my belly with a smile on her face.

"Too late, snow angel," she teased, and started to tug my panties down. "I'm not giving up my new hat, and it feels weird calling you Ella Prime, and you didn't tell me if you're a 'babe' or 'baby' or 'honey' or 'darling' type of girl, so now you're Snow Angel."

"But then I might melt," I said, which was a real concern because the way she teased my panties down my hips made heat rise through my entire body.

"Nah." She kissed a spot right at the base of my belly, just above my mound as she stripped my panties off completely. "There's that whole song about how hats keep snowmen alive with magic or whatever, and you have a magic hat, so—"

"So I *do* get to keep my hat?"

"Wait. No. I... hmm." She thought for a moment, then looked up at me, a devious smile on her face. "How about another bet?"

I raised my eyebrow. "For the hat?"

"And the title of Ella Prime. Winner takes both."

I licked my lips. "How?"

Her smirk widened. "First one to come loses."

And see, I shouldn't have taken that bet.

In my mind, we were going to do what we did the first time. Or something like it. Ellie would ride my thigh again, or we'd lie beside each other and touch each other until one of us lost, or maybe she'd get on top of me and I'd have to learn incredibly quickly how to use my mouth on another woman.

But I clearly wasn't thinking properly. Because no sooner than when I took the bet did I realize she *hadn't* said we were going to work together.

And she had me on my back.

I lost. Hard. Hard, and fast, and gladly. She peppered kisses and small bites on each of my thighs as she peeled my stockings off, my skin damp and chilled but warming quickly beneath the scorching heat of her lips. Once they were off, she parted my legs, kissing up my inner thigh.

"You don't play fair," I whispered.

"You're not going to have any complaints about that," she whispered back, and then proved it.

I was fairly sure half the building heard me come. I didn't care. Ellie stayed where she was, her mouth still working magic between my legs until they fell open to release her. I sighed, trying to catch my breath as she crawled up to lie next to me.

"I guess that means I'm Ella—" she started, then let out a shocked laugh as I lunged forward to kiss her.

"So it was okay, then?" she asked me between kisses.

"I want to lick your pussy," I said.

"Tell me how you really feel."

"Like it's going to suck because it's my first time."

Her chuckle puffed against my mouth and she rolled onto her back, pulling me with her. "It's not going to suck. If you're bad at it, I'll grab your head and ride your tongue, so we'll get there either way."

I laughed and she nipped at my bottom lip.

"Besides," she continued. "I'll tell you what to do."

"You will?"

"Mm-hmm." She kissed me one last time, then wiggled as she spread her legs further before reaching up to touch my face. "Step one: you're kissing the wrong lips right now."

She did end up grabbing my head, but not because I was particularly bad at it. It was more that she was really, really close to coming and couldn't stop herself from winding her fingers through my curls and pushing her hips up. Before that, she seemed more than happy with the way I licked her, exploring her pussy with my lips and tongue and fingers. It was enthralling, figuring out what I could do to make her gasp and what would make her moan and how to make her legs quiver uncontrollably around my head.

When she came, it was like nothing I'd ever felt before.

Ellie's entire body tensed, her legs tightening around my ears as she cradled my head to her core and ground her clit against my tongue. Her breath came in quick bursts, getting faster and louder until she let out a musical cry that was muffled by her thighs.

I looked up as best I could so I could watch her body writhe as her pussy tightened around my fingers, drinking in the sight of her as much as I was the taste of her. My eyes stayed on her until she sighed and relaxed, her legs dropping away from my head. It was another moment before she realized she still had an intense grip on my hair, but I didn't mind; I was still lapping at her lightly, enjoying the occasional tremor that ran through her.

When she let go of my hair, I ran the back of my hand over my mouth, moving up to join her on my pillow. Her eyes were closed, her head tilted back, pink bliss tinting the skin on her cheeks and chest, but she put an arm out so I could curl up against her side.

"How in the hell was your first time doing that *that* fucking good?" she mumbled.

"I dunno. I just did what I like when I'm getting it," I said.

She laughed softly. "Of course. And since we're soulmates, we obviously like the same things."

I smiled, closing my eyes.

"Congratulations on being Ella Prime," I said. "Enjoy your hat."

"Oh, you can keep the hat," she said. "I just wanted the title. Besides"—she kissed the top of my head, then held me closer—"what do I need a magic hat for? I have everything I ever wanted right here."

Chapter Forty-One

The First Week Of The Rest Of Our Lives

Isla

"Really?" I asked skeptically. "You want to move *here*?"

"Yeah," Venus said. "I'm gonna be a single mom. I need to be around people I can trust and rely on."

"What about Mom?" I asked.

"I said rely on, Isla."

I tilted my head to the side in concession, even though I knew my sister couldn't see me over the phone. "Fair."

"You'll help me, won't you?" she asked, her voice barely betraying the vulnerability of the question. "I don't mean, like, let me live with you or support me or anything, but—"

"Even if you did mean it like that, the answer's yes, Venus."

"Really?"

"Of course."

She burst into tears, then cursed at me for making her cry, then admitted pretty much everything was making her cry right now so it wasn't my fault and cried harder because she felt bad for blaming me. I told her it was fine and not to worry, I'd start looking for apartments she could rent around Aurora Flats so she was close by, and that way she didn't have to take the first apartment she found if the guy who lived above her peed off the balcony sometimes.

"She could sublet my place," Ellie said when I hung up.

"And where would you live, then?" I asked. She raised her eyebrows at me. I stared until I figured out what she meant. "*Oh*. Really? You don't think it's too soon?"

"Omen's gonna make us come up with an official custody arrangement if I have to keep going back to my place," she said. "And of course not. We've been in love for ages."

"It's been a week, Ellie," I said.

"We've been *together* for a week," she said. "We've been in love for longer than that. And anyway, it makes more sense for me to move in with you than for you to move in with me. For one, if you ever did get tired of me, I can stay with Jayce—"

"That's not happening," I said.

"—and two, my place isn't pet friendly."

"Neither is this one, technically."

"Yeah, but you rented it fully furnished. He's basically a cushion, so really, he came with the apartment." She scratched Omen beneath the chin and leaned in, putting on her baby talk voice. "He's the kind of cushion we hope the landlord won't notice if we steal him when we move out one day, isn't he? Yes he is. Such a good little cushion."

Omen, idiot orange cat that he was, purred until he fell asleep on her lap.

Despite her insistence that Omen threw a fit every time she left, he barely noticed Ellie move him to his usual spot on the couch half an hour later, when the episode of *Secret Rednecks* Ellie had forced me to sit through during her lunch break was over.

"Don't worry. If you don't want to move in together yet, I get it." She bent over to kiss me. "I'll see you after work. Or sooner if I get bored."

"You can't keep leaving work every time you get bored," I said.

"What's Paulette gonna do? Fire me?" She scoffed. "Biggest mistake of her life was letting me find out she needs me more than I need her. She should've fired me when she had the chance. Half the reason I go in at all anymore is so I can use the printer for these business forms you keep sending me."

I rolled my eyes, but secretly, I didn't care that Ellie was printing stuff for her own business at Air-U-Need. Yes, she and I had technically broken the fraternization policy, but that didn't mean I wasn't annoyed about getting fired. Especially since I hadn't been there long enough to qualify for employment insurance, so until I found another job, I'd be living off the meager savings I'd built up.

Which made Ellie moving in with me even more enticing. Not that I needed to be enticed. But she'd only been my girlfriend for literally a week.

But it had been a good week. And I already knew in my heart it was just the first week of the rest of our lives.

I'd spent most of my time job hunting and doing what I could to help Ellie start a photography business. Based on everything I'd put together, there was no chance of turning into her full-time income for a good while, but that was okay. We'd work towards it.

The job hunt was a little less hopeful. There weren't many positions open in Aurora Flats, at least not that I qualified for. Eventually, I was sure some company or another would have a finance position open when someone retired or left, but in the meantime, not even the grocery store was looking for help. I'd started searching for jobs in nearby towns and even into Edmonton, but hadn't found anything that would justify the long commute.

After Ellie left to go back to work, I tried to do a few more things for her, but I was stuck until she printed the forms she needed to fill out and sign. I went through the job listing sites again, but nothing new had been posted. Sighing, I put my laptop away, then sat on the couch, tapping my hands on my thighs and trying to figure out how to amuse myself for a few hours.

I could read. Or watch TV. Or go upstairs and visit Keith.

"Or I could go to the bookstore," I said to Omen, who was still asleep, then sighed. "No, you're right. I don't have spare money lying around to spend on books." I tapped my hands again. "That is a good point, though. Used books *are* less expensive. And if I bring a couple to trade in, they'll be half price. Which is basically like saving money, right?"

Omen snored at me.

"Okay. You're right. I'll go to Books."

I mean, who was I to not listen to my cat when he made such great suggestions?

Books wasn't busy because it was the middle of the day and everyone was at work, but there was a customer at the till when I walked in, so I waved at the woman who owned the store and started wandering the aisles. It looked nearly the same as it had the last time I was there, since the last time I'd been there was the day before, but I still examined each of the shelves.

And a lot of things happened for that moment to exist.

Some of them were obvious. Some of them weren't. Some of them were big, and some were heartbeats of a moment that never seemed important until I looked back.

And those were just the ones I knew about. There were more, countless more, *infinitely* more moments that had to happen to other people for things to align like that.

Every moment leads somewhere. And maybe something is out there that urges those moments along. Maybe there isn't. Maybe things are meant to happen, or maybe they just do.

No one knows for sure. No one ever would know for sure, at least not while they were this iteration of themselves. No one knows if there are other iterations, if the world we lived in now is the only one or if there's something waiting for us after we're done.

No one knows if things happen for a reason, or if we just assign reason to things that happen.

But sometimes, it's really, *really* hard not to believe there's something out there.

Because yes, for a moment, I could've believed it was coincidence. A moment of luck.

For a moment, I stared at the cover of my favourite book, almost in disbelief that it was there.

My hands shook as I reached for it, much faster this time, even though there was no one around me. I wasn't going to risk losing it again, not when it was right there and it had the right cover and everything.

And for a moment, I smiled. I ran my fingers along the spine that had a million cracks in it, flicked the curled corners of the pages beneath my thumb. I laughed, almost, and asked myself what were the chances that I'd come across this exact version of *The Hitchhiker's Guide to the Galaxy*, even though I'd been actively searching for it.

But that laugh died when I opened it.

Because how could I not wonder?

How could I not believe?

How could fucking *anyone* tell me that there wasn't something out there when I opened that book in my hands and, a thousand kilometers from the last place I'd seen it in a bookstore I hadn't discovered until after I knew I'd lost it, stared at my dad's name written in his meticulously tidy handwriting?

They couldn't.

They *couldn't*.

I stood in that aisle for a few minutes, my head bowed so my hair hid my face from both sides, making it look like I was flipping through the book instead of doing everything I could not to sob. Once I'd collected myself, I took a shaky breath, then brought the book up to the till.

"Oh, good, you're still here," the woman who owned the store said. "I saw you come in, but I was dealing with that other person and I need to talk to you."

"You do?" I asked.

"Yep." She held her hand out and I passed her my dad's book. "Remember when you came in here asking if we were hiring?"

"Yes," I said.

She scanned the book and set it on the counter, where it flopped open to the page I'd taped together after accidentally ripping it. "Well, my one cashier decided to up and quit on me. Dumped her boyfriend, broke her lease, and moved to God knows where. You're in here all the time, so I figured I'd see if you were still looking."

"Absolutely," I said. "I'd... yes, of course. I'll get you a resume right away."

"No need. Take the weekend off and come by Monday around ten. We'll get you started." She looked down at my dad's book, then handed it to me. "And here. You can just take this for free. I didn't realize it was so badly damaged."

When I got back to my car, I set the book on the passenger seat and took a breath.

Then, I grabbed my phone and sent two messages: the first to my sister, telling her I had found her a good place to live, and the second to my girlfriend.

When are you moving in?

Epilogue: Forty-Two

Ellie

It was a beautiful day for a wedding.

Every day is a beautiful day for a wedding, I guess, but an outdoor wedding in Alberta tempts fate in the worst way. When the weather changes every five minutes and the winter months can stretch from October through the end of April, planning any sort of outdoor event is a risk.

But despite Isla's certainty that it would rain, or snow, or a tornado was going to rip through unexpectedly, it didn't.

If it had, it wouldn't have been the worst thing. There was a large hall on the property that we could use in case of shitty weather, though it meant all the decorations we'd obsessed over for weeks and weeks would be useless and likely destroyed. In the case of good weather, though, we'd planned to use it to hide the wedding party and family before the ceremony started, which is why I was standing in the loft, watching people make their way to the semi-circle of chairs surrounding an arch that looked like a vibrant, multi-coloured rose bush had puked all over it.

Despite knowing exactly how many people had been invited, it felt like there were more than I'd anticipated. Co-workers, friends, family: people who had no good reason to associate with each other besides this specific event, were mingling, trying to figure out what the signs at the ends of the aisle meant.

Isla had insisted no one but us would get the reference, but I didn't care. I wanted them like that.

"Anything interesting out there?"

I jumped, whirling around at the sound of Jayce's voice. They held up their hands as if to calm me.

"Whoa, tiger," they said. "Put the nerves away."

"What nerves?" I asked, turning to look out the window again.

"You're not nervous?" they asked.

"Why would I be? I've never been more certain about anything in my life."

They joined me at the window, looking out at the people waiting. "Did she show up?"

They didn't need to say more than that for me to know exactly who they were talking about. Probably because there'd only been one source of drama over the entire course of our wedding planning, and it was the tantrum my grandmother threw when she found out she wasn't invited.

I'd waffled back and forth on it from the moment Isla and I had gotten engaged. Or, well, close to. The moment we'd gotten engaged, I was too busy being fucking ecstatic about the fact that she was *marrying* me to worry about my grandmother. And when we'd gotten home, I'd been too busy fucking my ecstatic fiancée to think of anything else.

Because I'd initially held her to the terms of the bet that I'd won fair and square, Isla had always insisted that *technically*, our official anniversary was the day after Valentine's Day. So I'd proposed to her on our second official Valentine's Day together, which was our one year and three-hundred-and-sixty-four days anniversary. I'd planned it for weeks—well, years, technically, because I knew exactly how I was going to do it when I woke up the morning after our first night together, just like I knew I was going to marry her one day. But I'd been *logistically* planning it for weeks.

That's how I knew it had truly been *my* idea and not, as some suspected after, something Jayce had planted in my head after I'd asked for their help. They were as crafty as they were our biggest supporter, but it wasn't *their* plan.

It wasn't especially creative. It didn't need to be. What it needed to be was me and Isla on Valentine's Day at the Flat Tire, her in that fucking skirt I couldn't wait to tear off her later and me in my purple dress that I knew she'd be tearing off later, too. I asked Jayce to put the ring in the free glass of champagne, but when the server brought them over and placed a glass with a sparkling ring at the bottom in front of me, I'd panicked.

"Oh, fuck," I'd said.

Isla had looked up. "What?"

As quickly as I could, I grabbed the bottom of the glass so she wouldn't see the ring.

"Uh... nothing," I'd said. "Just, um, they... I think this one's yours."

She frowned until I slid the glass across the table. For a moment, she stared at it.

"Right," she'd said slowly. "This one must be yours, then."

And then she'd passed her glass to me.

Which also had a ring sparkling away at the bottom.

I'd screeched with laughter so loud that the server rushed back over to make sure everything was okay. Isla said it was because I sounded like I'd started choking, but I liked to think it was the excitement in my voice.

"It's fine," I'd said, coughing as I tried to take big sips of champagne between laughs so I could see what my ring looked like. "We're fine. We're getting married!"

"Technically you didn't say yes," Isla had said.

"We *both* proposed, snow angel," I'd said. "I'm pretty sure that's the biggest fucking 'yes' I could give you."

I'd texted my mom to tell her Isla said yes, and Isla texted her mom to tell her we got engaged, and then we'd celebrated. We'd celebrated hard. We'd gone back to our apartment and listened to Omen yowl away as we continued celebrating until Isla barely had the strength to walk across the bedroom and let our beautiful fat boy into the room so he could see that neither of us had suffocated whilst taking our turns sitting on each other's faces.

And the next day, first thing in the morning, I saw a message from my grandmother.

We hadn't spoken since the Christmas Isla came to. It had taken a lot of convincing, but I'd finally sat down with my mom and told her the truth about my grandma. How she'd treated me. How she'd acted. The things she'd said to make it clear I wasn't part of her family.

It had gone a little better than expected. My mom had cried, of course. She'd apologized. She told me she hadn't known, she didn't realize, she didn't intend. She'd tried to explain, or maybe to justify, why she couldn't just cut my grandmother out.

"I'm not asking you to," I'd said. "But I need you to understand I'm not interested in being around her anymore."

She'd respected that, hard as I knew it was. And people had noticed, of course, that I'd stopped showing up at family events. But it wasn't until I got engaged that my grandma even realized she'd been cut out of my life.

Congratulations on your engagement, Ellie, my grandma's message had said. *I look forward to celebrating at your wedding.*

Part of me wanted to make my mom tell Gran she wasn't invited to the wedding, since my mom was the one who'd clearly told her in the first place.

The rest of me was controlled by impulse, and that impulse sent an immediate response informing her she wasn't invited, then blocked her.

That had snowballed, of course. Gran had flipped out, my mom had to explain that I was distancing myself because of her, half of my family said I should invite her to keep the peace, and the other half was popping popcorn watching everything unfold. Two weeks before the wedding, Gran had found out where our venue was and told my mother she'd be in attendance whether I liked it or not, and I'd asked Isla in a panic if we could move the wedding.

"If that's what you want to do, we'll make it happen," she'd said. "Alternatively, we ask Anthony how much it would cost for him to come dressed as Lady of the Lake and toss your grandma *into* the lake if she shows up."

As it turned out, Anthony was willing to do it for free if he could record himself throwing Gran in the lake for marketing purposes. I told him we couldn't guarantee she'd actually show up and he said that was fine, it just meant he'd be officiating our ceremony while in drag.

I don't think he realized we would've paid extra for that.

Which was good because we were trying to save money anywhere we could. I'd only recently been able to quit Air-U-Need to start working full-time as a photographer, and that was only because Isla had finally and reluctantly quit working at Books because she'd gotten a job working remotely for a publishing company doing some kind of money-related thing that turned my brain to static anytime she talked about it. Not that I'd ever tell her that. I liked listening to her talk whenever I could. But the point was, any money we could save on the wedding, we did.

"Ellie!" my soon-to-be-sister-in-law hollered from the lower level of the building. "If you don't get your ass down here right *now*, we're starting without you."

"That's your cue," Jayce said, smirking. "Are you ready?"

I nodded. "This is it."

"This is it," they repeated, then put their arms around me in a weird but entirely welcome hug. "See you on the other side."

Then they were gone, and I was alone, ready to walk down the aisle. I waited for the music to start, shifting nervously from side to side until I realized if I peeked around the corner of the building, I could see the aisle and the door in the middle that everyone else would be entering through.

Well, almost everyone else.

The music started and time stopped. I watched, blinking back tears as Isla's mom walked to her seat wearing a blue dress with a gold shawl. When my dad stopped to twirl my mom as they walked, making her pink skirt flare out, I had to stare up at the sky so I didn't ruin my makeup.

Then Jayce, looking as solemn and smug as they always did, escorted by Nick, who'd chosen to be called the "dude of honour." And Venus, running after the rambunctious toddler sprinting towards "Am-To-Mee," better known as Lady of the Lake in a Judge Judy-inspired getup.

And then the music changed.

Isla had one song she'd wanted us to use. At first, she'd said it should be our exit song after the ceremony.

"Why don't you walk down the aisle to it?" I'd asked, which is how I'd found out she wasn't intending to be walked down the aisle.

"I know my mom would do it if I asked. Or Venus. Or Nick. Or Pops. But they're not my dad," she'd said, trying not to let me see the tears in her eyes. "I don't want someone else to do it just because he's not here."

"Then we'll walk down together," I'd said.

"Ellie, *no*." She'd looked up and one of the tears had spilled out. "You should get to walk down the aisle with your dad. I'm not taking that away from you. I'll meet you up there. Grooms do that sometimes at weddings."

"You're not the groom," I'd said. "You're my bride, and you deserve to walk down the aisle to the song you want."

She'd fought me on it, but considering the opening notes of *"Can't Fight This Feeling"* were blaring through the speakers on either side of the seating area, it was clear I'd won.

My breath hitched as her head poked out from the other side of the hall. I hadn't seen my fiancée since the previous day because we'd stupidly decided we didn't want to see each other until we met to walk down the aisle.

But there she was.

I didn't remember choosing to move forward. It was instinct, more need than anything, because the woman I loved was walking towards me and I had to see her. I had to witness that white dress up close, though I could already tell it was the most beautiful thing I'd ever seen in my life, mostly because it was on her. It fit her perfectly, flaring out from her waist and showing off her curves, the hem swishing around her calves and showing off the sneakers that matched the ones I wore.

And, of course, the finishing touch.

"Hey, Ella Prime," she said when we reached each other.

"Hey, Ella Two," I replied, then grinned as I flicked my eyes up. "Nice hat."

She extended her hand to me. I took it, entwining my fingers in hers, and we turned to walk down the aisle between the crowd of our friends and family seated on Ella's Side and Ella's Side.

The Story Continues...

Looking for just a little more?
Strap on—er, strap in for the bonus epilogue to Fate & Fried Chicken as Ellie and
Isla steal away for a "quiet" moment together during their wedding reception here:
geni.us/ffcbonus

Acknowledgments

Another book, another afternoon of staring awkwardly at my computer trying to figure out how to properly express my gratitude to the countless people involved in making my books what they are and panicking that I'll forget someone because every time I say to myself "I'm gonna start writing this down," I do not, in fact, do that.

But in any case, there are many wonderful people I have to thank for their help with this book. I had some exceptional people who allowed me to pick their brains or beta/sensitivity read this book for me. Huge amounts of thanks go to Nora Fares, Charlie, Kristi, Kaitlyn, Nathan, Becca, and River Kai for your input and education. Thank you to Nazarea Andreas from Inkslinger PR for all your help and keeping me sane!

Thank you to my incredible supporters on Patreon for your continued enthusiasm for my books: PM, KJ, MidNyt, R, Carrie, VS, Natalia, M Johnson, S, GW, Michael, WA, Lee Mc, and Vicki Weber, as well as all my Meet Cute & Friends With Benefits subscribers! To all my readers: thank you for enjoying the journey with me.

I am so grateful to have amazing friends and family in my life who uplift and encourage me. Thank you to each and every one of you.

And as always, my husband, the soulmate I thankfully did not have to fall down a flight of stairs or trip on a curb or wear a funny hat to find: thank you. I love you.

Xoxo, Cheryl

Also By Cheryl Terra

Also By Cheryl Terra

Find all of Cheryl's books at cherylterra.com/stories

Aurora Flats Series

Fate and Fried Chicken

If You Can Series

The Boy Next Door
Kiss Me If You Can
Hold Me If You Can
Keep Me If You Can
Sleigh Me If You Can

Unicorn Confessions Series

The Unicorn Confessions
Unicorn For Sale
Death of a Unicorn

Love Across Canada Series

Get Over It
The Devil Made Me
Runaway
Finding Home

Standalones

When It Rains
Hearts at Play: Special Edition
One Little Question
What Happens In Vegas
Selfish Love
Another Last Call

About The Author

Cheryl Terra writes romantic and adult fiction with drama, sass, and a whole lot of... spice. Emotional and humorous, her books focus on contemporary relationships, inclusive characters, and happily ever afters. Living with her husband in northern Alberta, Canada, Cheryl relies on the heat between her quirky and memorable characters to help keep the gas bill down in the winter.

When she's not writing, Cheryl can be found listening to the same song(s) on repeat for hours at a time, spoiling her pets, keeping way too many house plants alive, and knitting or crocheting.

For more information and to get free books, visit Cheryl's website at **cherylterra.com**